The GIN O'CLOCK CLUB

Rosie Blake

sphere

SPHERE

First published in Great Britain in 2020 by Sphere

1 3 5 7 9 10 8 6 4 2

A CIP catalogue record for this book is available from the British Library.

ISBN 978-0-7515-7590-3

Typeset in Caslon by M Rules
Printed and bound in Great Britain by
Clays Ltd, Elcograf S.p.A.

Papers used by Sphere are from well-managed forests and other responsible sources.

Sphere
An imprint of
Little, Brown Book Group
Carmelite House
50 Victoria Embankment
London EC4Y 0DZ

An Hachette UK Company
www.hachette.co.uk

www.littlebrown.co.uk

Rosie Blake is a writer, recovering TV presenter and [illegible] of many children. She has written for *Cosmopolitan*, [illegible] *Lady*, *Best* and *Reveal* magazines. She has appeared on ITV, Channel 4 and Sky. She enjoys hosting writing panels and running creative writing workshops. She has written comic women's fiction for Atlantic Books and Sphere Fiction.

She continues to attempt to become Julia Roberts' best friend but is starting to worry it might never happen despite 'liking' all her Instagram posts.

Do follow Rosie on Twitter, Facebook or Instagram – she has twins so she is always keen to chat.

ALSO BY ROSIE BLAKE

The Hygge Holiday

Teddy Dowmunt, Dziadek, such an inspiration to me growing up. A man full of joy and fun, even in the face of pain. We all still think of you and love you.

Come now, don't make such a funeral face.
It isn't dying that's sad;
it's living when you're not happy

OCTAVE MIRBEAU

Darling Cora,

I'm sitting in the kitchen downstairs and you are upstairs propped up in our bed surrounded by pillows, our ancient bedspread pulled up tight: a wedding present from a friend we haven't seen in more than forty years.

For a second I stare at the mug I am about to carry up.

You'll give me a shadow of that former smile as you watch me place it on the bedside table next to you. I'll wait, offer to lift it to your lips, you'll tell me you're fine, grand: the words a whisper. It will grow cold, a thin film forming on the surface. I'll read you the daily news, trying to skip the depressing stories until all I am left with is the sport that bores you and the horoscopes you don't believe in.

The mug will sit there, your eyes will open and close, you want to stay with me, to listen: not quite able. Your lids will finally flutter shut and your chest underneath your thin cotton nightie will lift and fall as I quietly remove the mug to repeat the whole process again.

As I walk back down the stairs I'll feel the familiar lump build in my throat.

Don't leave me, I'll think as I swill the contents

down the plughole. As I turn on the tap, hold the kettle underneath, click it down once more.

Don't leave me.

I'll reach for the teabags in the tin, labelled in your steady hand a lifetime ago now.

Don't leave me: please.

What would I do without you?

Teddy

Chapter 1

Love is knowing someone's faults
but loving them anyway

GERALD, 87

My hand slipped on the pole as the Tube juddered. Shirt sticking to my back I shifted, awkwardly pulling out my mobile, arms squashed at strange angles, to check I was definitely late. The carriage jolted and my phone flew from my grasp.

'Oh, for . . .'

Going to crouch I slithered down the pole, past a yellow print dress and a man's navy T-shirt, focusing on not planting my face in his denim crotch as I felt around for my mobile. I touched flesh as I grabbed the foot of the girl in the print dress. Sweat pooled under my arms, beaded at my hairline.

'Sorry.'

Locating my phone I re-emerged, hair plastered to my forehead. Pressing at the screen again I groaned. A new crack had sliced across one corner.

'Bollocks.'

A man opposite looked up from his newspaper, eyes sliding over to me, a frown already on his face.

I didn't have the energy to apologise or smile. I looked back down to examine the new crack, just next to the last crack, currently covered with a strip of Sellotape. Jabbing at the screen I could see the phone still worked and I was still late. Carefully I put it back in my jacket pocket.

Why was I even wearing a jacket? Did I have a death wish? I didn't have the room to shrug out of it, bodies pressed up against me at every angle. The girl in the print dress looked away as my hand closed over hers on the pole.

'Oh, sorry. Sorry. Again.'

Her eyes rounded in fright; it was the second assault on her body in as many minutes, so her reaction was fair. In the early years of being in London I might have made a joke, struck up a conversation with her. Now though I didn't even blink, just wanting to get out of this oppressive heat, away from these sweaty strangers and on to the platform and away.

It had been the longest day: three trains, a walk through Reading town centre to the courthouse, a sobbing client, a judge who seemed to think a female barrister was still an exotic creature, and a delayed return journey. I shifted my weight, briefcase heavy in one hand, my wig stuffed somewhere inside, a thick wad of paper, a brief for a case the next day. I was going to have to work into the night to prepare for it. Closing my eyes I breathed out slowly: one stop left.

People pushed past to get on and off. A young guy appeared next to me clutching a crisp packet, the smell of Cheesy Wotsits immediately filling the confined space. Staring at him with narrowed eyes I cursed him in my usual silent custom: hoping next time he went to his wardrobe he found a small but deadly infestation of clothes moths: all his T-shirts just a tiny bit chewed.

Why had I agreed to go tonight? It seemed like such a good idea when Luke mentioned it the previous week, on a day when I had some energy left. The graphic design company he worked for always threw great parties. I'd been to loads of them, and liked his colleagues. He'd been with them since leaving university over ten years ago, worked from home when it suited him and had a fancy title I always forgot when people (my mum) asked. This was their Midsummer Party, an excuse to get everyone out on to their roof terrace in Pimlico with some canapés and cold beers.

I pictured a perspiring bottle of beer. What I wouldn't do to be dressed in white cotton, fresh-deodorant spritzed, an ice-cold drink raised to my lips. The girl in the print dress looked across at me in alarm as I licked my lips. The Tube juddered again and my hand slipped once more.

Oh God, why was I here? I didn't want to be on this packed Tube at 8.30 p.m. on a weekday night. I thought of the journey home I'd need to take in a couple of hours, the work I was going to have to do back in our flat. Someone nudged me and I felt a flutter of fresh anxiety.

When I finally shoved my way out on to the platform, a wave of warm air lifted my hair as the train trundled away through the tunnel. Placing my things down I was finally able to remove my jacket, and breathe out. Pulling my shirt out of the waistband of my skirt, trying to feel less sticky and uncomfortable, I wished I'd packed a clean top. I would have a beer, cool down, see Luke and then head home.

Examining my reflection briefly in the rounded mirror designed to let people know who was about to appear around a corner, I grimaced at my flustered, red face. Clipping my brown hair back, swiping my fringe aside, I grabbed at my things and strode on out, just wanting to get into the evening air. I knew Luke wouldn't care, or notice, what I looked like. He'd seen a lot worse over the years – after Phil and Jenny's engagement drinks (I still swear it was food poisoning), fresh back from my spinning class, and the time he'd walked in on me removing the moustache I'd convinced myself was real with hair removal cream – but I wanted to look nice. As a group, graphic designers were quite cutting-edge and I didn't want to stick out. I used to enjoy shopping for clothes – finding vintage pieces on Portobello Road, designer steals in charity shops – but now my wardrobe was pretty functional: a lot of blacks and greys, clothes suitable for a barrister that could double up at events like this too.

It was heaving, the roof terrace filled with people milling about as I pushed my way through, secreting my briefcase under a table of drinks. Peering round the crowd for a glimpse of Luke, his dark brown hair, his Romanesque profile (my grandmother always told me Luke had a good, strong jaw; I'd never really been sure how to respond so had often opted for 'all the better for chewing things with'), I reached for a beer bottle nestled in a bowl of melting ice cubes.

Just as my fingertips brushed the ice-cold glass I heard a noise, then someone stumbled into me, a stiletto heel sinking into my foot, cold liquid tipped down my shirt.

'Argh.' Tears stung my eyes from the sudden pain as sticky alcohol trickled down my chest.

'Oh God, oops, these shoes are the *actual* worst.'

Someone was clutching my arm and I looked down to see a tipsy Little Mermaid, all big caramel eyes and long red hair, swaying slightly in front of me. 'I told Mike not to pour me that third one.' She giggled, a high noise that made a few men nearby look round at us both. 'Fourth one,' she corrected herself. 'Fourth one. Naughty.'

I think she was talking to herself. She'd stopped clutching my arm at least.

'Let's get you a drink,' she said, eyes lighting on the table and selecting two champagne glasses from it. 'Here,' she said, handing one to me. 'I'm Storm, by the way. I don't think we've met. Are you one of the freelancers?'

I dabbed pointlessly at my shirt with one hand before accepting the fluted glass. 'I'm Lo—'

The mermaid didn't seem to register I was speaking. '... but then I'm new and everyone has been soooo welcoming. My last company was full of a load of bitches so it's been schamazing to be in a place where everyone is so nice, you know . . . '

I was suddenly desperate to get out of there. I shouldn't have come and now I was sticky with sweat and Prosecco and I just wanted a cool shower and to be back in my own flat, alone, dry, cool, in a place where schamazing was not a word.

The drunk mermaid was still yabbering at me though, her coral lipstick smudged. Suddenly her eyes swivelled over my shoulder. 'Oooh, squeeeee, Hot Guy alert. Three o'clock,' she said in a pantomime-whisper behind one hand, then she clapped her hand over her mouth. 'Oh my God that is sooooo inapprope at a work thing, but he's a dreeeeamboat, don't you think?'

Dreamboat? Is that a thing? I hadn't dated for almost a decade. Was this the kind of lingo kids were using nowadays?

'Who?' I followed her gaze, seeing Mike, Luke's boss, his stubbled head slightly sunburnt, who raised a glass at me. I nodded and then, as I did, I saw Luke just behind him, searching the crowd. His face lit up as his eyes came to rest on me.

'Oh my God he is totally looking over now,' Storm half whispered, sloshing Prosecco on the wooden boards between us. 'Have I got anything in my teeth?' A hand gripped my shoulder as she flashed me two rows of gummy teeth, right up close.

Cringing, I stepped backwards. 'You're all good.'

Luke was stuck in the melee, crushed between a girl

obliviously tapping on her phone and a guy telling a story that involved a lot of big hand gestures. He raised both eyebrows at me, pursing his lips.

'God, isn't he dreamy?' Storm sighed, her hand still on my shoulder, fingers digging into me, her nails painted scarlet. 'And *such* a genius. He was showing us his animatic for the Fruitshootz campaign and he's included some incredible images ... ' I felt a flicker of annoyance for this shapely Storm. What kind of name was Storm anyway? Bad weather, that was what. I shook off her hand.

'And he has been so nice to me since I've joined, so attentive. Oh, oh God, he's coming this way, play it cool ... ' She nudged me and I got the crazy urge to laugh out loud. Then I looked at her again, this uniquely named Mermaid: noticed the bronzed eyelids, the smooth skin, the toned figure, and repeated her words. *So attentive.* Oh, really? I couldn't help looking down at my own damp, frumpy work clothes. My mouth settled into a thin line as Luke appeared in front of us.

'Ladies,' Luke said, his left eye slightly out of focus, a sure sign he was pissed.

Storm giggled again and batted his arm. Luke leant in to kiss me, missed my lips, left a wet mark on my cheek.

'Luke,' I said, pointedly wiping my face, 'I've just met Storm.'

Was it nerves that made his eyes flick to her and back to me again?

'That's great, yeah, Storm arrived a few weeks ago as one of our junior designers. Glad you've hit it off.' He grinned and waved his bottle of beer around. He was not picking up on my icy tone.

Storm, however, was frozen to her spot, Prosecco tilted dangerously at a 45-degree angle, mouth half open. Her eyes flicking back to Luke, to me, to Luke, to me, as if she was trying to solve an extremely complicated crossword clue.

'You're . . . '

I stuck out my hand theatrically. 'I'm Lottie, Luke's girlfriend.'

Storm sucked in her breath. 'Girlf . . . soooo lush to meet you.' She didn't take my hand but instead nudged Luke with her hip, who spilt some of his beer. 'Luke, you dark horse, I didn't know you had a girlfriend.'

Luke, you fucking dead horse. I stared at him as he pretended to act oblivious. Why hadn't he told her he had a girlfriend?

'Yup. Lottie is.' He attempted to pull me towards him with one arm over my shoulders but my body remained stiff as a board and I just tilted like a skittle about to fall before returning to my original position.

Luke, of course, didn't notice.

'And what do you do?' Storm asked, focusing her caramel eyes on me.

'I'm a barrister.'

She whistled. 'What, like in *House of Cards*?'

I frowned. 'Um . . . no.'

'So you catch criminals.' She giggled as she lifted one hand to make the shape of a gun.

'That's more the police.'

Did this girl not know what a barrister was? Was she about to ask whether I made coffee?

'You know what I mean,' she tinkled, and Luke laughed.

I didn't have the energy, just wanted to turn around and go home. Everyone had obviously started hours before and I was feeling grouchy and like I didn't belong.

I also really didn't like Storm. I always tried not to send out negative vibes into the universe, knowing that is bad karma, but I couldn't help sometimes wishing for bad things to happen to people who piss me off. Not major things, like a fire or anything involving a missing limb, but, for instance, now I was staring at Storm and wishing that every time she went to roll out her Sellotape she would never find the end.

'Well,' Storm said, nudging Luke for about the fourth time and me out of my evil Sellotape fantasy, 'you guys are sooooo super cute together.'

'We're sho cute,' Luke slurred, nodding and drinking his beer. 'On our anniversary I sung her Ed Sheeran on my guitar.'

'Luke.' I felt my face grow hot. 'Shut up.'

He was laughing. Normally I would see the funny side but something about him was making me bristle. The evening sun had sunk but the day was still impossibly hot. I felt smelly and shapeless, wanting my bed. Storm was still gazing up at Luke, all winged eyeliner, tightly fitted dress, sunglasses popped on the top of her head, bobbing at his every word.

I hoped next time she got into her car on a hot day the windscreen got smeared, and when she went to use the wipers she found the water had run out, forcing her to pull over, stop the car, get out and clean the windscreen by hand.

'... hellooooo ... Lottie ...'

Luke was waving in my face.

'Sorry.' I tried to pull myself together. 'I was just thinking about ... stuff.'

I rarely wished bad things to happen to him. Rarely. So, so rarely.

'Hey, Storm likes Childish Gambino too, isn't that amazing? I've finally found someone who appreciates great music.'

I looked at Luke, hoping that next time he went on an aeroplane he had to sit in the middle of a row of three between a large man eating Monster Munch and a toddler with a penchant for making friends.

Chapter 2

Love is . . . what got me into this mess in the first place

BOBBY, 75

'Why are you giving me the cold shoulder?'

We had been back in the flat for all of three minutes. I ignored his question.

'You're being ridiculous,' he said, stumbling slightly over the long word.

'Don't patronise me.'

'I'm not patronising you.'

I had spent the rest of the party avoiding him, drank way too much Prosecco in a very short period of time and when I had gone to leave (no one else was looking close to departing) Luke had insisted on accompanying me. Storm gave him an enthusiastic wave goodbye which Luke had, of course, returned.

'You were being weird all the way back with your shifty eyes and your muttering I couldn't quite make out but was loud enough for me to know it was happening,' he said, following me into our bedroom. 'I knew something was up.'

I spun round. 'I don't have shitty eyes!'

'I didn't say shitty – *shifty*, shiiifffttyyy,' he said, still slurring the words. 'Is this about Storm?' He looked up at me and put one hand over his heart. 'I haven't done anything.'

'Apparently you have been *really attentive*.' I made sure to do the quotation marks with my fingers.

'What? So I'm not allowed to talk to women any more?'

'I wouldn't mind if it was just talking but it sounds like you are swanning round the office flirting with the new, young graphic designers the moment they arrive.'

'What? I don't do that . . . You're being irrational.'

'Oh, typical. Deflect attention back on to me being delusional. Crrrraaaaazy Lottie,' I said in a pretty crazy voice. 'She must be imagining things, it must be all in her head.' I jabbed at the side of my head with my forefinger.

Luke stared at me, dumbfounded.

'Gaslighter,' I muttered, knowing I was being rather extreme. I was past the point of taking anything back, though. I was at that stage of the argument where you just have to crack on. I had *committed* to this argument.

'I'm not a—'

'You didn't tell her you had a girlfriend,' I interrupted, triumphantly.

'What am I meant to do? Start every conversation with this information? We've only spoken about twice. And we were talking work: it would have been weird.'

'You still could have told her,' I repeated, determined to try and stay on track. 'How do you think it made me feel?'

'Oh, well, I'm sorry I wasn't wearing my *Luke luvs Lottie* sandwich board that day.' He threw up both arms to the ceiling.

'No need to be sarcastic.'

'There's no need for you to be so mad but it isn't stopping you.'

He started getting undressed and I held up a hand. 'Woah, woah, woah.'

He paused, one leg out of his jeans.

'What are you doing? I'm not sharing a bed with you tonight, we're not OK,' I said, indicating the space between us with rapid hand movements.

'Are you' – he stumbled, one hand out on the bed to right himself as he stepped out of his jeans and underwear – 'what the . . . you can't be serious. I haven't *done* anything, Lottie.' His voice was louder now and for the first time he seemed to have sobered up.

He sat stubbornly on the side of the bed, arms folded. 'I'm not sleeping on the sofa when I haven't done anything wrong.' He would have looked more serious if he wasn't wearing one sock and no pants.

'Well, I'm not sleeping on the sofa.' I moved across to the bed too.

He started mimicking my voice and that was all it took to make my blood boil again.

'Stop it, Luke.'

'Schtop it, Luke.'

'Seriously.'

'Seriously.'

'Oh my God, put some pants on. I can't fight with you if I can see your penis.'

He stood up abruptly, waggling said penis at me, and I squealed and threw a scatter cushion towards it. 'I'm being serious, Luke.'

He stopped then, voice low. 'Lottie, I'm being serious now. Please can we just go to bed? I don't want to argue with you about who I've been hitting on in or out of the office.' He was trying not to slur his words and had now, at least, put one hand over his offending appendage.

I tried to unscramble what he'd just said, the evening's bad mood still making a whooshing sound in my head. 'So you *are* admitting to hitting on Storm?'

Luke's mouth opened as he swiped his other hand through his hair. 'No, God, woman, no.'

'So someone *out* of the office.' I couldn't seem to stop myself.

'What? You're not even listening.' The other hand flew up so both hands were clutching his head, his voice growing increasingly exasperated. 'I am not hitting on anyone. I hit on you. When I get to see you. Now will you please just get in our bed and stop being a mad person.'

'I'm not being mad,' I said, wondering why I was continuing this, why my blood was still boiling, why I didn't just get in the cold shower I had envisaged earlier and then get under my crisp sheets? 'I've got the brief to do, I have to work. *Some* of us have jobs that—'

He cut me off with a hand. 'No, we're not doing this tonight.'

'Are you trying to say my job isn't stressful?'

Luke breathed deeply once in and out, his voice, when it came, slow and precise. 'I am going to bed now. In our bed. You do what you need to do and I will see you in the morning.'

'Me and my shitty eyes.'

He didn't respond.

'Fine.' I seized my pyjamas and marched out down the corridor and into the living room. Realising I had left my briefcase, I retraced my steps, sullenly walking back into our bedroom, catching his look of relieved surprise before scowling and picking up the forgotten item.

His shoulders drooped. 'Night, Lottie.'

'Yeah,' I muttered, closing the door on him.

Tear-stained, feeling stupid and stubborn and unsure how I even got into this row, I sat on the sofa, opened my briefcase and started pulling out folders, feeling even more miserable as I took in all the work. I couldn't concentrate, still running through how it had all escalated. It wasn't the first argument I'd had like that with him this month. Sometimes I felt like I came home with all this energy and just needed to lash out and Luke was there and I couldn't seem to stop myself.

I shook my head. Although this time obviously I was right. I was right to be cross. Storm had said it. He had been 'attentive' and how could any man fail to be attracted to her? She was so young and sexy and her crush on him was so obvious. How could he resist those doe eyes? Those adoring compliments? Oh fuck, was I being mad? I paused, swiping yellow highlighter over some typed notes. Concentrate, Lottie, I needed to remember some of this stuff for court tomorrow. Now wasn't the time to think about my relationship, or lack of.

My eyes fluttered closed, the lever arch folder resting on top of me. Hours later, the folder slithered off me and on to the floor with a *thunk*. I woke, mouth dry, cushion damp from dribble, not knowing life was about to get a whole lot more complicated.

Chapter 3

Love is like finding a part of you that
you didn't know was missing

ELVA, 91

I hadn't closed the curtains of the living room so I was awake at dawn, sunlight making rectangular patterns on the carpet. I groaned. My neck ached, my body stiff from the position I had adopted on our sofa.

Struggling into a sitting position, I wearily noticed the scattered papers from the folder that had slipped off my lap in the night, automatically stretching to scoop up the nearest one. I might as well keep working until I needed to get up.

I went to check the time, reaching for my phone, frowning as I noticed I had five missed calls. The time was 6.01 a.m. but I was distracted by the name that flashed up: Grandad.

Five missed calls. All from Grandad. All from this morning: 05.43, 05.47, 05.51, 05.56, 05.59.

I felt my palms dampen in an instant, a swirling in my stomach. I clicked on the '1 Voicemail' message and listened. I must have made some kind of noise because moments later Luke appeared in the doorway, hair sticking up at every angle, dark stubble, one eyebrow raised in a question.

There must have been something on my face because I saw my own fear reflected back in his as he rushed across the room and crouched down next to the sofa. Tears had already started spilling out of my eyes as I listened to my Grandad's choked sign-off.

Luke didn't say anything as I lowered the phone, as I whispered, 'Grandma.' He knelt on the carpet and folded me into a hug, his whole body reeking of beer, cigarette smoke and Luke. He was reassuringly warm from our bed, his arms clamped around me tightly, his thumb rubbing my lower back. My body was shaking in his arms, his T-shirt already damp from my tears.

'Hey,' he whispered. 'Hey, it's going to be all right. I love you. It's going to be all right.'

My eyes were squeezed shut, his words mixed up between all the thoughts and memories in my head, the shifting world, the things I had to do that day, my grandad. For a crazy second I wondered if I was dreaming. I heard the crunch of paper as I realised Luke was kneeling on the notes I had been working on.

I pulled back suddenly. 'I better get up; I need to finish this.'

Luke's face was slow to comprehend as he noticed the papers I was rescuing. He shifted his position on the carpet.

'You're crushing them.' My voice sounded different: higher.

He pulled one of the pieces of paper out from under his knee and smoothed it down, then started stacking the stray papers.

'Don't, you'll get them mixed up. I'll do it,' I said, dropping to join him on the carpet.

'Here.' He handed me his pile and stood up. 'Do you want me to get you a cup of coffee? Do you want to talk about it?'

'I . . .' I was still kneeling on the carpet, my head awash with emotion. I could barely make out what he was saying. I had to get going, get up. I bit my lip, absentmindedly shuffling papers.

'I need to ring Grandad . . .'

'OK, I'll make you coffee.'

I caught sight of a note I had highlighted on the top sheet of paper. 'I should get ready for work . . .'

Luke paused on the way to the kitchen.

'I'll ring Grandad, then I need to work.' I was talking to myself, my brain going nineteen to the dozen. 'I can't believe . . .' I tailed away, the thought of Grandma's face making my eyes swim.

Luke turned back around. 'You shouldn't have to work, Lottie.'

I didn't register his words, still lost somewhere else. 'I'll ring Grandad, no, I'll have a shower. Oh God, I was meant to be seeing Amy tonight, bridesmaid stuff, she wanted me to—'

Luke came back over to me, gently removing the papers from my hand. I looked up at him then, my eyes still watery so that his face was blurred.

'Hey,' he said. 'You take a shower. I'll make the coffee and I'll message Amy to postpone. She'll understand and then you can call your grandad back.'

I nodded at him slowly, relieved he was taking control. I could feel my heartbeat slow a fraction as I stared at his stubbled chin, his lips moving with the words.

Standing under the shower, letting the water pound at my skull, I closed my eyes, not sure if it was tears or water running down my face. My lovely grandma. What would Grandad do now? We had known this day wasn't far away but it was a shock that it had happened, that she was no longer here. I swallowed, reaching for the shampoo and squeezing it into my hand. What had I said to her last? I had been round there last week. I had sat and read to her from her book. Only Chapter Six.

I didn't want to think about that now. I couldn't. I had to get through the day. I started to run through all the things I had to do, rubbing furiously at my hair.

I needed to finish reading the court documents, remind myself of the details of the trial, get to the courthouse in time to meet with my client before we went into court.

After showering I moved through to our bedroom, needing work clothes, frowning as I tried to recall why it was I had spent the night on the sofa. It really didn't seem to matter any more. Luke had left my coffee on the chest of drawers, a banana next to it. I pulled out my clothes for the day.

I knew I needed to call Grandad back.

Luke came in and sat on the edge of the bed, two hands wrapped around his own mug. Coffee, no milk. He was watching me as I clipped my bra, bent down to pull on my tights.

'Don't go to work, Lottie. Can't you call someone in chambers, they co—'

'I need to go, it's too last-minute to call off and my client needs me.' I cut him off, tugging my tights up high and reaching for my shirt.

'But surely if you told them w—'

The words came out hard and quickly. 'You know I *can't*, Luke.'

I could see Luke straining not to raise his voice, keep a level expression on his face. 'Your grandad will be—'

'I know I need to call him,' I said, my voice getting louder, snapping at him as if spoiling for another fight. I was so quick to lose my temper these days, the shock of the news and the lack of sleep only making me feel more out-of-body.

I felt anxious, panicked, nothing made any sense. I just needed to get dressed, get out of the flat, look over my work, get to court, represent my client. I just needed to get through the day. Then I could think. I couldn't cope with anything else at the moment.

'OK. Look, make sure you call me, OK? Let me know how you're doi—'

I had already left the flat before he had time to finish the sentence.

Four hours later I was standing in court attempting to focus on what the man in the dock was telling me. He was a massive man, barely contained in the witness box, and he was swearing passionately that he had not hit my client with a chair leg. I was about to bring on a witness who was adamant he had, but that witness was also the sister-in-law of the man in the dock's ex-girlfriend, and he had already claimed she was lying. My head was spinning to keep up.

The phone call to my grandad had been short and desperately sad, made moments before I met with my client outside the courthouse, the facts of the case blurring in my mind. I had arranged to see Grandad that evening, blocking out the disappointment in his voice as he asked where I was.

'The funeral director's already here, they're taking her body away . . . '

I could barely focus on the case, the other barrister's latest objection, the judge's lined face glaring down at me as I stumbled to respond in any sort of decent time. 'Do you need a moment, Miss Campbell?'

The relief as we were released for the day was enormous. I barely remembered walking out of the courthouse with my client, shaking his hand, agreeing the details of the next day.

My parents had called from Singapore and I attempted the world's most disconnected Skype chat while nursing a coffee in Starbucks. They had lived out there since I was seventeen, when Dad got a big promotion for the trading company he worked for. I had refused to move with them, wanting to finish my A-levels. I went to live with my grandparents instead and somehow I had never moved out there.

I mainly spoke to Mum, who seemed to be peering over the lip of her laptop, the angle distorting her face. 'Your dad is dreadfully sad, obviously.'

Grandma and he had been close when growing up and Grandad had always hinted that Dad's emigrating had broken her heart a little. Dad moved into the screen over Mum's shoulder, tired eyes and mouth turned down. The distance between us seemed greater than ever. Coupled with the bad reception and delay, the conversation was stilted and sad.

Staring desolately out of the window at people passing, the day muggy and still, I felt an urge to hear Luke's voice, to apologise for flying off the handle the night before, to tell him I loved him. Today had been tiring and lonely and I kept thinking back to the way I'd felt when he'd wrapped his arms around me on the sofa that morning. Luke, who barely had any family of his own – both his parents had died when he was in his late teens and early twenties – knew loss: he had loved Grandma too.

Head pounding, the edges of a migraine beginning, I squeezed my eyes closed and listened to the ringing. Someone picked up Luke's work phone, the tail end of a throaty laughter choked down as a female voice said, 'Blaze Designs, how can I help you?'

'Oh, I . . . ' My eyes flew open. The only female voice I'd been expecting was Sandra, the receptionist who came on the line if it went unanswered. In her early fifties with a mouse-like voice, she would always promise to tell Luke I'd called, and then she'd update me on the latest developments in the lives of any member of One Direction. She had a massive crush on Harry Styles, which she knew was unusual. This had come out unexpectedly at one of their Christmas parties and had really tickled me. We had got on ever since.

'Is Luke there?' I asked the stranger, wishing he had answered. His work landline was normally a reliable way to catch him.

'Luke?'

'Yes – Luke Winters.'

'Oh, *that* Luke,' the vaguely familiar voice tinkled with a small laugh. 'And who shall I say is calling?'

'It's Lottie,' I snapped, already losing patience. I just wanted him on the phone.

There was a long pause on the end of the line and I scraped the toe of my shoe along the bottom of the window, wiping a mark in the steam.

'He left the office earlier, I'm afraid.' I still couldn't place the voice but then a picture floated into my head: long red hair, caramel eyes, smooth skin. In all the drama of the day I hadn't thought about Storm. My hand clenched tighter on the phone, knuckles whitening. Why was she answering Luke's work phone? Warming his desk while he was away from it?

'Shall I get him to call you back when he's around?'

'Don't trouble yourself,' I said, hanging up with a stab of one finger. I flung the phone back in my handbag, not caring if I made the cracks any worse. I stayed brooding in the window of Starbucks, glaring at anyone who looked vaguely happy. One woman was holding a bag containing a new shoebox, a big smile splitting her pretty face. I hoped she got home, lost the left one, and when she found it had already bought a new pair and worn them.

Chapter 4

Love is something we don't even know we are searching for

CLIVE, 82

'I've got up to make her tea three times today, got down her mug, you know the one she likes, with the strange sheep that wears a tutu. I only remember after I've put the milk in. It just sits there. Such a waste,' he said, wiping at one eye. He wasn't really talking about tea.

We were at the kitchen table, Grandad in his usual wooden chair with the armrests, me opposite in the chair I always sat in when I came over. My eyes had darted to Grandma's chair with the worn red cushion, indents on its surface.

'I know I've had some time to get used to the idea but it's still a shock, although you know your grandmother, organised to the end. She's left me a list.'

I laughed in spite of myself, glad to see his mouth twitch into an almost-smile too.

Grandma had loved a list. She told me she used to write them out on the chalkboard for when Grandad would get home on a weekend, after he'd been working all week. 'Paint front door, fix chest of drawers, take out bins.' One time the list had been so long Grandad had simply added, 'Build the Pyramids', turned and left for the pub.

I realised I'd never been alone in the house with Grandad before. They had been such a duo, a pair. I stared round the kitchen, the tick of the clock on the wall louder, the buzz of the oven's overhead fan, the gurgle of the boiler as the hot water kicked in. It seemed so much emptier. How could one missing person make this enormous difference?

I'd come over as soon as they'd let me out of court, still dressed in my sweaty work clothes, my briefcase jam-packed with the brief for the next day and my head crammed with everything I needed to do next. My best friend Amy had sent me a lovely message after Luke had called her postponing the wedding plans we'd had that night. I was shaping up to be the world's worst bridesmaid. The moment I saw Grandad, though, I forgot about everything else, knew the whole day had been putting off this moment. His face was rumpled, eyes deadened, eyebrows drawn together in a permanent frown.

I reached a hand out and leant towards him. He smelt of ginger and coffee.

'I'm sorry I couldn't be here earlier. I hate that you had to do all this on your own.'

He picked up my hand and patted it. 'I wasn't on my own,' Grandad said. 'Luke was extremely helpful, and very kind.'

So that's where Luke had been. He'd probably never gone into the office. He would have known I didn't want Grandad to be alone. I felt a surge of love for my warm-hearted boyfriend.

'And my golfing gang, Arjun, Geoffrey and Howard, were here, and Auntie Sue would have stayed longer if I'd asked her but the poor woman is as crushed as I am and it wouldn't have been good for either of us.'

Typical of Grandad to be thinking of others.

He got up and flicked on the kettle. 'Was it an interesting case?'

'Grandad, I'm not going to tell you about some guy who smashed someone so hard in the thigh with a chair leg he fractured his femur – allegedly. No court talk at all. I'm going to order us a Chinese takeaway. We're going to eat it and we're going to talk about Grandma.'

He nodded then and I was grateful to see the hint of relief cross his face. He seemed to have aged ten years in as many hours: his shoulders sagging, his feet shuffling as if he didn't have the energy to lift them off the floor any more.

The Chinese arrived and I pretended not to notice Grandad picking around the food. Every now and again a sound from the house next door would make us both look up, as if we were expecting Grandma to emerge in the doorway, to cross the room and sit in her chair. She'd offer us cocoa that we'd both politely refuse (Grandma could burn most things) and things would just be ... normal.

She didn't appear, of course, and it still seemed a shock. She'd been seriously ill for a long while now, Grandad insisting on nursing her in the last few months. But even though she'd grown frailer, with longer pauses as she sought to catch her breath, grimacing at the rattle in her chest, she still had the same spirit and the same mind. She could still smash us both in a cryptic crossword or a game of backgammon. It seemed impossible that she wasn't here. I felt a shiver run through me as I realised Grandad was now living on his own. For the first time in forty-four years, it was just him.

We talked about her then, Grandad telling me stories I'd heard before made all the more poignant because she wasn't here now. The time she'd been pulled over by the police after singing opera in her car at a set of traffic lights (they believed she was screaming from some kind of abdominal pain); the time she'd insisted on making jam and had ended up in the hospital with third-degree burns on her hand; the time she toppled over the fence into next door's garden after spying up a ladder because she thought her friend's husband was having an affair (it was a female plumber fixing the sink in their en suite).

Our laughter filled the room. At one point I was clutching my side, both of us on the edge of hysteria, before tears leaked down my cheeks, my sobs stoppered by a handkerchief proffered by grandad. Grandad and Grandma's house had been my home since I was seventeen. We still had Sunday lunches there, Luke and Grandad sneaking off to watch football as Grandma and I cleared up in the kitchen, listening to musical theatre soundtracks. Grandma loved to sing and whatever she lacked in pitch she more than made up for in enthusiasm.

I felt an ache in my stomach then for the woman I loved so much. She had held my hand when I didn't get the pupillage I'd so desperately wanted; when I'd heard Luke had injured himself skiing in Verbier and wasn't sure what was happening, how bad it was; when I missed my mum after failing my A-level English mock and needed a hug and realised she was 12,000 miles away. She had taught me how to laugh at myself, how to embrace show tunes, how to grow a herb box and how to be the woman I aspired to be.

And now what?

Looking at Grandad, his plate of uneaten food, which he'd barely noticed, I worried about the future. It wasn't that Grandad couldn't look after himself – he'd been doing that and more these last few months – it was the fact that overnight he had lost his best friend in the world.

How would he manage? And what could I do to help?

I thought then of the last few months in my job, which seemed to have become increasingly pressured the more work I was sent: the scurrying on to trains, off trains, into courthouses; the late nights staring at briefs, watching CCTV footage, wanting to impress the other barristers in my chambers. Trying to squeeze in friends, spend time with Luke, keep up with current affairs, Skype my parents, help round the flat, keep myself looking professional and groomed. Even thinking about the long list of things I tried to juggle took my breath away a little, and it was then that I would have turned to Grandma, who always made me feel a lot calmer and more capable.

My eyes flicked towards the clock next to the dresser and I moved to throw away the plastic containers and wipe down the table. I knew I would have to stay up late to ensure I was prepared for court tomorrow. There was so much more to say, though, and practical things to discuss too: we hadn't even talked about the arrangements. I wavered, palms flat on the surface of the table as Grandad told me to leave it.

'You'll need to get off now,' he said, false cheer in his voice.

I closed my eyes, feeling my body almost physically split in two. I wanted to send one half of me home, to stay up late, read the documents I needed to read and collapse into bed next to a sleeping Luke. The other half would stay here, help Grandad, ensure he was all right.

I removed his plate, landing a kiss on his forehead. 'Not quite yet.'

I did leave, Grandad practically shooing me out of the door. I took an almost empty overland train back to Clapham, trying to concentrate on the court document in my hand but unable to focus, just picturing Grandad brushing his teeth alone in the bathroom. Why hadn't I thought of removing Grandma's toothbrush? I bit my lip and rested my head back, the train shuddering beneath me, the smell of brake fluid in the air.

Luke was waiting up for me, enfolding me in the most enormous bear hug as I pushed through the door of our flat. It was almost a shock to feel his solid body pressed against me, his arms firm around me, the taste of peppermint as he kissed me. I felt some of the tension I'd been carrying back from the station drain away as I looked up into his face, his eyebrows drawn together in a worried line.

'How was your grandad? How are you?'

Perhaps sensing my overwhelming tiredness he ushered me through to our bedroom, steering me to the side of the bed. 'Sorry, sorry, stupid questions. You're shit, your grandad is shit and the whole thing is just shit.' He raked a hand through his hair and looked down at me perched on the edge of our mattress. 'Shall I make you a decaf coffee? Do you want a glass of water?'

His eager attentiveness lifted my mouth and I realised all I really wanted was to lie down in the bed I was sitting on and get him to lie with me, hold me close and tell me it would all be OK. I also knew I should thank him for going over to Grandad's.

I didn't do any of that, though. I felt the weight of the briefcase I was still clutching and looked up at Luke. 'I need to read some things for tomorrow. I've got to set the alarm a little earlier, too – the trains to Aylesbury aren't great.'

Luke didn't conceal his surprise. 'Do you really have to work tomorrow? Can a colleague not take over?'

I was shaking my head before his questions had even finished, bristling already at the look on his face. 'You know I can't, Luke. I've told you before it doesn't work like that, and the client needs me.'

'Your grandad needs you too. I'm sure if you rang chambers and explained—'

I didn't let him finish. All the emotion of the day, the train journey back, images of my grandad flashing into my mind as the wheels turned, made my next words come out cold and sharp. 'Do you think I don't know that? Do you think I want to leave him on his own now? God, Luke, you can be so insensitive. You just don't understand. You don't have a job like mine.'

On any other day this would be enough to provoke a fully fledged row. It was a line I often levelled at him when I wanted him to rise. It was stupid: I did respect his job, I did understand what I had signed up for and I did understand that he worked hard too. In this moment, however, I didn't care. I just wanted to lash out, could feel my veins bubbling with it, every muscle tense.

His face closed down. He looked at his feet and breathed out slowly. 'I'm sorry, Lottie. That's not what I meant, or rather, look'– he met my eyes again – 'it's not a good day to start this. I hated seeing your Grandad so sad earlier and I know how hideous today must have been for you.' He lifted me to my feet and held me again. I could feel the tears threatening, a sob catching in my throat.

I pushed him away, two hands on his chest. 'I better work.'

He opened his mouth to reply, then closed it again. He

nodded at me. 'You sleep in here tonight, you can work on the bed. I know you like to spread out.' He nudged me once, his eyes teasing.

'I . . . ' He was giving me exactly what I had asked for. Space, time to work. Why was I now wanting him to realise I needed him to stay? 'Thanks.'

He picked up the cashmere throw from the bottom of our bed and gave me a last kiss. 'Don't stay up too late,' he said, injecting a little brightness in his voice.

'I won't,' I whispered, watching him move across the room, gently closing the door behind him.

I sat down on the edge of the bed again and felt tears dripping from my face into my lap. I felt utterly sad and alone, with only myself to blame.

Darling Cora,

How can I be making plans for your funeral?

You've left a list, of course you've left a list, and your list cracked my heart open a little wider.

The day after you died was a blur of activity, then stretches of silence, punctuated with tea-making, whispers, the door opening and closing.

The list had been in an envelope wallet, along with the funeral director's details, your will and other relevant documents. It had been on your bedside table, your fountain pen resting nearby. When had you finished it? The thought made my eyes blink rapidly, stemming the tears that had yet to fall.

Lottie came with me to the funeral parlour. It was good of her. We weren't used to spending time on our own, I realised as she drove me there, apologising for the sudden boom of Radio 1, fumbling with coins for the parking meter when we stopped at a red light. I wasn't any use. All the words I should have been saying to reassure her stuck as ever somewhere inside. You had always been the one to settle things, to make things right. I felt awkward and bumbling as I tried to give her the 50p she was looking for.

'How long do you think we'll be in there? I'll put in two hours' worth. I can always pop back out,' she said, glancing in the rear view, biting her lip.

'Yes, good idea.'

'God, I hate driving in London . . . '

'Yes.'

'Is it that one?' She pointed to a building across the street, a dove grey facade, signage all in italic scroll.

'Yes.'

We walked into the funeral parlour in silence, discreet lights encased in brackets on the wall, soft pink curtains pulled back to reveal a door behind the counter. On one side of the room a choice of urns in different shapes and colours on pedestals, framed quotes on the walls, a picture of footprints in the sand, low classical music piped from somewhere. A man with a too-flamboyant moustache emerged from the back room.

'Mr Campbell.' He walked towards us, his hand outstretched.

I took it.

'Good to see you again,' I said, remembering that first morning, the men who had arrived to remove your body. I hadn't wanted to see any of them again, didn't want to think about that moment, then realised your body was here somewhere being prepared, that you were in this building. The thought made my head spin and I tried to focus on the present. 'This is Lottie, my granddaughter.'

Lottie was staring at the urns and it took a moment before the sound of her name sank in. She started a fraction before moving to shake the man's hand. In this soft light she looked less wan, less thin.

I pulled the pieces of paper from the envelope wallet I'd been clutching as we were directed to two soft leather chairs at a side table.

'Shall we? Can I get either of you a tea or a coffee?'

We both refused in low voices, a sombre mood settling over us. Simon should be here with me, not Lottie; it was such a lot to ask of her, she was only young.

Your list was thorough, decisions taken out of our hands. Short readings selected, brief, eloquent: you.

We were both grateful for your direction. The list meant you were in control, removing the need for us to second-guess, to worry it was something you wouldn't want. I realised Lottie was as lost as I was and I wanted to reach out and hold her hand, reassure her, thank her for being there with me. My hands stayed frozen on my thighs.

A coffee ring had almost obscured your last song choice but the funeral director had been able to decipher it.

'What do you think?' I'd asked Lottie, pushing the sheet across to her.

'It's what she wanted, at least.'

The funeral director had bowed his head.

She dropped me back at the house, didn't come inside, said she had work to do but that she'd call. I knew she was on the verge of tears and I wavered, wondering if I needed to force her out of the car, frog-march her into the house. My own energy levels were depleted, though, and I wouldn't know what to say or do. I thanked her for the lift, tapped on her window as she left. She wound it down and I told her a brake light was out. Nodding thanks, she drove away.

The night before the funeral I couldn't sleep. The house has been strange without you in it. I slept on my side of the bed, scrunched up far too close to the edge as if you were still starfished by my side. I miss the feel of your foot nudging me inch by inch, causing me to grumble, reminding me you were there. I haven't slept well since you've died, and yet I'm dreading a night when I do.

Did I regret saying I'd meet people there? The house was empty and silent that morning as I stared at myself in your full-length mirror, at the ill-fitting suit that had been dusted down for too many weddings and funerals. Why hadn't I bought something new for today?

I'd wanted to stay in the car park of the crematorium.

You would have been in the passenger seat, pressing your lips together as you fussed in the small rectangular mirror overhead, chiding me, reminding me who so-and-so was married to, and remember X had divorced Y a while ago so I mustn't put my foot in it. I glanced across at the empty seat, still unused to the silence, the space, the fact you were simply no longer there. And now I was about to get up and walk inside without you.

The funeral hearse was parked outside and I couldn't help but drag my eyes across to it, the oak polished and bright, the wreath we had selected woven with the flowers you so loved. You were in that box, in this car park. I froze in the seat, hand on the lock, watching people drift inside. I saw Geoffrey fussing over Arjun's tie before they disappeared inside, a woman I couldn't place following in their wake.

Moving quickly across the tarmac, skirting puddles, my shoes tight, I managed to make it inside and up the aisle, eyes down, not yet ready to talk. I shuffled into the front pew, Lottie and Luke already there at the other end, Luke's hand on Lottie's lower back making small circular motions. Your sister Sue stepped across the aisle to say hello, her eyes, the same shade of blue as yours, red-rimmed.

Clasping my arm, she asked, 'All ready?'

I nodded, not trusting myself to speak.

'She would have liked the arrangements,' Sue added, her head motioning to the enormous standing

spray Lottie and I had picked out, the smell hitting me suddenly, the sweet fragrance winding round me in the front row.

One of the pieces you had chosen was playing, Haydn, and there was a gentle hum of talk, low voices, people reaching across to squeeze hands or kiss cheeks. I had been to services like this before, rifled through the Order of Service or stared round at the congregation. Now it was your funeral, your plans and it all seemed incredibly important. I wanted everyone to be still, to be quiet, to listen, to wonder at why you'd chosen this piece.

The coffin was wheeled up the aisle and there was a general hush as it was manoeuvred close to the curtains ready for the committal.

The service began. The female officiant had tight ginger curls and a thickening waist. She welcomed us and introduced the service. Sue delivered the first reading, her voice faltering at the start and then growing in strength as she looked round at us all. I tried to raise an encouraging smile, couldn't hear the words, too aware of the coffin only metres away, the eulogy I was about to deliver. My palms dampened at the thought. I knew there wasn't long, stared at the small stand set up on the left as the officiant moved the service along.

'And now Cora's husband Teddy would like to say a few words.'

Cora's husband doesn't. He doesn't want to say

anything. He just wants you here, healthy, sitting next to him. He wants this to be someone else's funeral.

I felt my knees tremble as I walked past your coffin, couldn't stop my eyes travelling its length, a breath catching in my throat, before I turned my attention to the rows in front of me, all eyes watching. Hastily I stared down at the small square of paper I was gripping, unfolded it, smoothed it. A lone cough, someone rustled. The words on the page couldn't possibly be a sum of your parts. I read them softly, quickly.

Your sister gave me a watery smile as I passed her, dabbing fruitlessly at her face as the tears fell. Lottie was staring at the coffin. My heart ached for her, a small surge of anger at our son for not being the one standing next to her, and me. He should have got on a flight, he should be here. You'd never asked him for much; why wasn't he here at your funeral? How could he miss this?

Another reading. I could barely concentrate on what Geoffrey was saying, too aware of the moment the coffin with you inside would disappear behind the curtain. It finally did. I stared at the space, the curtains remaining stubbornly closed as the service ended and we were being dismissed. People lingered in the doorway opening umbrellas to protect themselves against the dribbling rain, not enough to really get drenched. Lacklustre weather. Cars moved on out, windscreen wipers going. We had hired the hall back at Maplelands club for drinks and canapés, normally a place I loved spending time.

How I longed to get in my car and drive in the opposite direction.

The hall was two-thirds full and I could hear the burble of chatter as I pushed through the double doors of the small vestibule. Luke and Lottie were together, Luke's arm around her shoulders, pulling her close: protective.

Howard, Arjun and Geoffrey stood in a tight circle together in one corner, picking at sausage rolls on napkins. Arjun had a mark on his lapel, had done something funny to his hair with gel or water or I wasn't sure what. How I wished we were all four on the golf course, walking in companionable silence between holes, only commenting on the awkward green or Howard's ridiculously showy swing or Arjun's ability to lose his new balls in the long grass. That was where I was comfortable, not here in a suit I hadn't worn in years that smelt of mothballs and damp, panicking internally at the amount of familiar faces whose names I couldn't recall.

I felt awkward and exposed, unable to deal with the tears of other people. I stuck out a hand to shake: old friends of yours, work colleagues ignoring the hand, pressing their powdered cheeks to my face, dabbing at their eyes. They wanted to tell me stories about you, they wanted to ask how you had been in those final days and weeks. I answered their questions in monosyllables, not able to give them the answers they wanted to hear.

You would have held their hands, produced tissues from a miniature packet in your handbag, asked the right questions, said the right things. You would have been so much better able to deal with this day.

Why aren't you here to help me any more? What am I going to do without you now?

I love you, my darling. I miss you. God, I miss you.

Teddy x

Chapter 5

Love is the space where nothing used to be

ISABELLE, 79

A few weeks have passed since the funeral and I've been dividing my time between Grandad's and our flat. I feel like I'm living my life on trains and tubes, often turning up to court dishevelled and trying to fix my make-up and clothes in the ladies'. I barely see Luke, who often drops in on Grandad when he knows I'm busy. I love him for that; I know he's doing it to ease my mind even though he has always got on well with Grandad. Still, somehow, by the time I've returned to sink into bed beside him, I never seem to get the energy up to say anything to him.

I miss Grandma. I miss my grandad's easy smiles, a little harder to summon these days. I miss the easy laughs, the endless tea, the Sunday roasts: the times when we weren't all noticing what, or rather who, was missing. My grief is a weight that drags my whole body down, keeps me in bed in the mornings, not wanting to get up.

I wasn't sleeping well, at times disorientated over where I was, and struggling to concentrate on my work. I would straighten my wig, take a breath and step into the court, trying to put on an invisible mask, Lottie the Professional, to ensure no one knew that inside I was all squiggles and confusion. I needed to look strong, to be strong for Grandad, and sometimes it felt as if the effort of that drained me in every other area of my life.

I had finished court early today, defending a man who had been charged with being drunk and disorderly on a plane when heading home from his eldest son's graduation day. He had been discharged after a not-guilty verdict, mostly because he was so charming and apologetic in the witness box. At the end of the trial he had clutched both my hands promising that his family would be lighting a candle for me that night at home in Romania. The image had made me a little tearful and I was reminded it was these moments – helping clients, being their mouthpiece – when I really loved my job.

I was out of court by two o'clock, the whole afternoon stretching ahead. I longed to return home, crawl under a duvet on the sofa and devour a mindless boxset, but I had a sudden image of Grandad alone in the house and knew how much he'd appreciate seeing me.

I let myself in with my key and called down the empty

corridor. Noticing Grandma's furry hat on a hook, the one Grandad always said made her look like she was wearing roadkill, I felt my mouth lift, was glad I had come.

'Grandad?'

The living room was empty: two glasses of water on the coffee table, an abandoned newspaper, but no people.

'Hello?'

I wondered if he was out playing golf. He seemed to play in any weather but I had noticed his clubs hadn't moved from the spot in the corridor for weeks now. It had worried me: golf and the club where he played had always been his passion. That, and Grandma.

'We're up here,' a voice called from upstairs.

I frowned and looked up, transported back to a moment when Grandma had been alive, then shook my head. Silly.

I climbed the stairs, finding Arjun and Grandad in the bedroom, looking like they were about to drown in a sea of black bin liners, carrier bags, shoe boxes and hangers.

'What are you doing?' I asked them both, standing in the doorway.

Arjun looked up, his black hair barely flecked with grey, glossy under the overhead light, his wiry frame practically buried under women's clothes.

'We thought we'd make a start sorting through some of your grandmother's things,' Arjun said, in a voice that suggested he was already regretting it.

I looked round at the room at the piles of clothes, shoes, belts, hats and more. My grandma had loved to dress and had never really changed shape so nothing was ever thrown away.

Grandad was sitting on the bed clutching a thin black leather belt, pulled from a pile of other belts by his side.

'Is that one particularly special?' I said in my most sensitive voice, moving towards him, ready to give him comfort.

'No,' he said, his fingers inching along the leather. 'I just can't believe how much stuff there is. She could have dressed every woman in Maplelands club ... for a year.' He sounded dazed. I couldn't help but giggle.

Grandad looked at me properly then, still dressed in my suit and heels. 'Lottie, did you come from work? You must be busy. We are more than happy to do this – you get off and do something fun for the day.'

'Don't be silly, I can help,' I said, not wanting to leave now, overwhelmed by the enormous number of things strewn on the bed, furniture and floor. 'You're going to need it,' I added, putting my briefcase down and folding my coat on top of it.

'I wouldn't leave that there,' Arjun said, clutching a roll of bin liners. 'You might find it heading to Oxfam.'

'Good point,' I agreed, picking my things up again and placing them in the corridor. 'I'll make more tea,' I called, heading back down the stairs.

'Just hot water for me,' Arjun called after me. Arjun had always tried to get Grandad and Grandma into various health kicks: he treated blueberries like they were the food of the Gods, played endless rounds of golf and had introduced them both to aqua aerobics (Grandad had only attended the first session, claiming the pop music they played was not to his taste).

The bedroom was stuffy and we worked in silence, heaping clothes into separate piles. Standing in front of the wardrobe I was overwhelmed by the scent of Grandma, a mix of mint and the outdoors, my hand shooting out for balance as if the smell would send me physically back through time. I could see her now at my cousin Nikki's wedding in a lemon yellow linen dress; leaving for bridge in a pale blue fitted shirt, her hair shining; sitting up in her bed in a white, high-collared cotton nightdress, still beautiful and dignified even that last time.

Once we had emptied the wardrobe I stepped into the fitted closet, reaching up and pulling things from the hanging space. Some of them I didn't recognise at all: they must have been in there for years.

'There are some extraordinary dresses from the 1980s back here,' I called, emerging, hair askew, with a collection of coat hangers. I held one up. 'Grandma loved a shoulder pad, it seemed.'

'Oh, she was smitten over that one,' called Grandad from across the room as I drew out a mustard yellow tea dress, pale pink roses printed on the fabric.

'I can see why: it's so pretty.'

The label was almost entirely faded. The dress must have been at least forty years old and yet it was still pressed and ready to wear.

Being among Grandma's clothes made me feel closer to her than I had in these last few weeks since she'd gone. Remembering how sociable she had been, dragging Grandad off to various events when he'd happily have stayed in and watched reruns of *Deal or No Deal* (Noel Edmonds really tickled him). I remembered occasions when she'd worn some of these dresses, how even as a teenager I had conceded that my grandma had amazing style.

Grandad had gone downstairs with another full bin liner and I was standing back in the closet, running a hand through the folds, feeling the different fabrics before pulling out a floor-length gown in dusky rose pink, tiny beads sewn into the bodice, a delicate chiffon skirt. I sucked in my breath as I removed it from the rail.

'How did I never see her in this? It's gorgeous.' I held it up against me and stepped back into the room in search of a mirror. 'Oh.' The bedroom was empty.

Arjun was in the corridor just outside, leaning against the wall, engrossed in a burgundy-leather-bound photo album. When he looked up at me, the dress still in my hands, he had tears in his eyes. 'I got to know her so well these last few years. She was always so good to me,' he said, sniffing and pulling out a tissue from inside the sleeve of his jumper. 'She was a beauty,' he added, indicating the photographs.

'She was,' I said quietly, picturing Grandma now at her dressing table, smoothing down her silvery-grey hair with the silver-backed brush.

At that moment Grandad reappeared at the top of the stairs, taking us both in. I was still holding the dress against me and he smiled.

'We got engaged when she was wearing that dress,' he said, his voice low as he inclined his head towards me. 'I took her to the opera, and then for dinner afterwards. I don't remember the show, I couldn't eat, and when it came to it I couldn't get the words out I was so bloody nervous.'

We were all crying now.

'You should take it,' he said. 'You and she are about the same size. She would have wanted you to have anything you liked.'

We locked eyes then and it was my turn to nod and swallow down the emotion. Grandma had always been generous to a fault, shielding me from bad weather with her own jacket while she got soaked, carrying me back from the bus stop aged eight when I'd twisted my ankle pirouetting around the pole, offering me food from her plate if I finished first. I smiled sadly as I fingered the shimmering material, pictured my own utilitarian wardrobe of blacks and greys: my uniform.

'I can't think of an occasion I'd wear it.'

Grandad's face fell immediately, the lines more marked as he turned away from me, his shoulders dropping a fraction. Arjun coughed and looked away. I regretted saying it the moment the words left my mouth.

What was wrong with me? I felt my insides swirl in confusion. Suddenly I felt the familiar bubble of anger, always so near the surface, and bit the inside of my cheek. I should have fixed things but instead I wiped at my face, turned and moved back into the bedroom, replacing the dress where I had found it, and continued to clear the piles around me.

Chapter 6

Love is like falling into a large hole
with no idea how to get back out

PETER, 75

I was running late for Amy, which Amy hated. It wasn't just the teacher in her, she'd always been like that. Even at school when we were little she would roll her eyes, cross her arms and look disapproving. She was right, of course. I knew it was selfish but somehow, even with the best of intentions, I still managed to be late. I started preparing a lie as I half jogged along the pavement. I had blamed the Tube last time. This time I might go big and invent a foiled handbag-snatching attempt. Too much time in court maybe – and anyway Amy was trained to see through extravagant tales.

I was still trying to divide my time between our flat and the odd evenings at Grandad's house and felt torn and stretched thin, living on buses and tubes and buying underwear when out because my stuff was scattered around the place. I wanted to help Grandad, make him less alone, but sometimes wondered if I was creating more work for him. I had heard him sigh as he turned off the smoke alarm and washed up the mess I had created in the kitchen after starting a meal for us before becoming distracted by a work document. Grandad had snapped at me to leave the scorched pan and I had stepped back, stung. We both missed Grandma. She had always been the calming influence, capable and relaxed as Grandad and I circled each other, both perhaps a little highly strung.

I'd apologised in a gruff voice, not meeting his eye, wanting to shout that I had just been trying to help, then wanting to be back in my own flat with Luke making me dinner. Then the crashing guilt after that thought.

Luke was often with Grandad when I wasn't, knew it was important to me that he had company. We could have spent this Saturday together – until I remembered I'd promised Amy I'd go wedding-dress shopping with her.

'It's important,' I'd barked, shrugging off Luke's hand inching around my waist in bed that morning.

His sigh had instantly made me bristle, feel cross. I was still tired, I wanted to stay in our freshly laundered bed with him too. I hadn't said that, had simply stamped off to the shower, muttering underneath the jet of water before racing around the flat as the clock ticked, Luke watching his iPad in bed.

'Are you just going to lounge around here then?'

'It's the weekend, Lottie. And you're abandoning me.'

'I told you' – I looked up at him – 'it's Amy, I can't not go.'

'Hey.' Luke raised both hands. 'I know, I know, there's no need to lose it on me.'

'I'm not losing it on you,' I said, my voice rising: there was nothing more likely to make me lose it than Luke accusing me of losing it already.

'No, you're chillaxed as ever,' he muttered at the screen.

'I heard that.'

'You were meant to,' Luke said, smiling sweetly up at me.

Huffing, I finished pulling on my clothes, wincing as I hit my shin on the corner of the drawer I had just pulled out.

'Fuck.'

'You OK?'

'Not that you care.'

Luke didn't respond, just went back to his iPad. I picked up my handbag. 'I'm late,' I said crossly, as if it was Luke's fault.

'Amy will understand. Come here.'

'She'll be angry,' I said, petulantly.

Luke put down his iPad, letting his breath out slowly.

'Well, you're late anyway so come here.'

I grudgingly stepped round to his side of the bed and he reached out an arm and pulled me down into a hug.

I let him hold me, my cheek on the cotton of his T-shirt, feeling strangely tearful all of a sudden. Blinking furiously, I wondered for the millionth time in the last couple of months just what had come over me.

'I've got to go,' I said, this time in a softer voice, gently pushing myself off him.

'I love you, Lottie Campbell,' Luke said, sincerity edging his eyes.

'I love you too,' I said, swallowing, my throat feeling full. I was gratified to see the edge of Luke's mouth lift, how adorable with his tousled hair and early-morning stubble. 'Sorry for being such a bitch recently.'

He shrugged, wariness edging into his eyes. 'You've got a lot going on, Lottie, you don't need to apologise.'

The lump in my throat made it hard to speak and anyhow I didn't want to respond, didn't want to ruin this tentative peace, so I stood up, picking up my bag again and walking out of the bedroom, Luke singing, 'Ain't no sunshine when she's gone' behind me, a giggle escaping as I slammed our flat door.

Amy was already there when I puffed my way into the shop. Surrounded by racks of ivory tulle, sequins and satin, she had one hand on a dress with a full skirt and was smoothing at the fabric as I arrived in front of her.

'Hey,' I said weakly, raising a hand.

She arched an eyebrow my way and in that tiny movement I got a taste of what all her students must feel when they were summoned to the deputy headteacher's office. I wasn't going to go for the foiled handbag snatch/witness to a murder story.

'I'm sorry, I'm sorry, I'm sorry,' I said, sinking dramatically on to a rust-coloured velvet chaise longue. 'Forgive me, forgive me—'

Amy, who hated scenes, was darting a look over her shoulder to see if the dress-shop owner was there. 'Oh my God, get up, ssh, you are an embarrassment.'

I looked up at her. 'I really am sorry,' I said, my voice serious.

Amy rolled her eyes, holding out a hand, 'I know. Now come and tell me if I should go for a tulle skirt in blush pink or a satin bodice with a lace bolero.'

'What on hell's earth is a bolero?'

Amy nudged me with a giggle as a woman with the sleekest, shiniest blonde hair and the most perfect eyebrows stepped across to talk to us.

'Ladies, welcome to Diamonds and Dreams,' she said, her smooth forehead frozen in place. 'And who is the lucky bride?' she tinkled.

'We both are,' Amy said brightly, and it was my turn to look at her. 'Lottie here's getting her ring re-sized, aren't you,' she said quickly, noticing Sleek Blonde was staring at my bare left hand. 'Aren't you, Lottie?'

'Oh!' I jerked to attention. 'Oh yes, it was too big. Kept slipping off into ... into stuff,' I said, the sentence tailing away into a whisper.

Sleek Blonde flicked her sleek blonde mane.

'Well, do have a look at our range and let us know when you want to try on your first dress. A magical day for you both,' she said, her voice still sparkling as if she was auditioning for Lead Princess in Disney movie.

'A magical day indeed,' I said aloud, both my arms thrust

out, palms raised. I had gone too big. Sleek Blonde raised another eyebrow and walked away. I turned back to Amy, who was holding up a bodice in champagne satin that made her black skin even richer. 'That looks—' I was about to compliment her when I remembered. 'Hey, I can't try on dresses, Amy. Isn't that bad luck or something?'

Amy laughed and turned back to the rail in front of her. 'Not unless Luke appears in the doorway and sees you in the dress you have selected for your imaginary wedding with him.' She placed the bodice back on the rail and spun round. 'Oh come on, Lottie, don't pretend you're not seriously tempted. You love dressing up. Any excuse. Remember Casual Clothes Days at school? There was nothing casual about your selections.'

Feeling the stirrings of excitement in my stomach for the first time in days, I suddenly didn't feel so tired. My workload was fading in my mind, Luke wasn't angry with me, even Grandad's worries were minimised in the face of the incredible mountain of fabric. 'Helloooo, Lottie, are you ready?' Amy was waving in my face.

I preened and pouted and encouraged Amy to get Sleek Blonde to pull on ribbons, fetch us more dresses, top up our glasses. We tried on fishtail dresses, meringues and bias-cut, sweetheart necklines and delicate lace.

I was dressed in full veil, tiara and feathered skirt when my phone rang and I hopped down off the box I was admiring myself on and padded over to my handbag.

'What are you doing?' Luke asked.

'I'm trying on a wedding dress!' I announced brightly.

There was a long pause and I pulled the phone away from my face to frown at the screen. Bringing it to my ear again I whispered, 'Luke? Luke, are you still there?'

'That is . . . well, that is . . . '

It was only then I realised I should probably add, ' . . . for Amy. I'm wedding dress shopping with Amy, remember?'

Did he have to sigh so loudly? 'Oh . . . oh well, I knew that. Great. Send Amy love.'

'Will do. Did you call for anything in particular?'

'No, I just wondered when you were getting back. I wasn't sure how long these things take, we haven't really seen each other.'

'I saw you this morning,' I pointed out, pulling the phone back so I could look at the screen. 'Less than three hours ago, in fact,' I confirmed.

'Ha, ha,' Luke said, deadpan. 'I meant seen each other as in hang out, talk about something, do something together rather than just inhabit the same space?'

I turned my back on Amy who was wearing an expectant look on her face. 'Oh, yes, I see.' Why didn't I laugh at this obvious tease? Why did I feel my shoulders tense, the grip on the phone grow tighter?

'Look, I can't be everywhere at once, Luke. I told you this was important. Amy hasn't seen me in ages, she had to rearrange this appointment for me and I can't just—' All the old panic was stirring within me as I warmed to my theme.

'Lottie.' Luke tried to interrupt me but I was in full flow. 'Lottie—'

'And Grandad, what am I meant to be doing about Grandad?'

'Actually I went round there after you left. He'd made these insane flapja—'

'Yes, but I said *I'd* drop in there later,' I cut him off. 'He'll be alone for the rest of the day and I ca—'

'Lottie, I didn't call to have an argument with you,' Luke said in a weary voice. 'And Arjun and him are playing golf.'

Amy had moved to stand next to me, her hand out for my phone. I shook my head at her but she didn't move. I could feel her looking at me, standing in a netted skirt and white satin corset, pissed off. I felt the physical pull of Luke on the end of the phone and of Amy standing in the room.

'Look, Luke, I've really got to go. I'll be back in a bit and we can make a plan then,' I said, my voice firm.

I could hear a sigh but then I was too busy jabbing at the buttons to turn the phone off. Amy's face was unimpressed.

'I thought you had all day,' Amy said. 'I haven't seen you in forever, Lottie. I want to catch up with you.'

Amy was never like this. I knew I must have really hurt her. We used to see each other all the time. We'd been flatmates up until a year ago when I'd moved in with Luke and she'd moved in with Will.

'I'm sorry,' I started to say, the words tripping off my tongue, used so often these last few weeks – months, if I was being really honest. 'Everything is so busy at the moment.'

Reminded of the time, of the things I had to do that weekend, I started to surreptitiously check my phone as I oohed over Amy's outfits, refusing to try on more myself. She could tell I was distracted, my foot tapping as I stared out of the window at the Saturday shoppers moving by.

'Hey,' Amy said, centred in the changing-room curtain as if on a miniature stage, 'it's OK, Lottie, do what you need to do. Go, OK?'

I had been looking at my phone again, crossing and uncrossing my legs on the rust velvet chaise longue.

'Really? Because I don't want to let you down,' I started, knowing I had barely been present for the last hour.

'Go,' she sighed, not quite meeting my eye.

I pushed myself off the sofa. 'Thanks. I'll make it up to you, I promise.'

Amy lifted a hand, swatted the air in front of her as if batting away my words. She didn't say anything in reply.

I scooped up my coat and bag and turned to her, trying to ignore the slump of her shoulders, the saddest bride in town. 'I'll call you,' I said, my cheek clashing against hers.

She nodded, a ghost of a smile on her face.

I paused. Something in her expression frightened me, a resigned look, one I had grown used to in recent months. She didn't believe me. And I wasn't sure she should.

Darling Cora,

Lottie is staying in the house for a trial and I'm making her bed in the spare room while she is out.

You teased me for ironing your sheets but in those last weeks, when I didn't know what else to do or say, it seemed important. I could make your bed up as nicely as you always made it, smoothing at the pillows, leaving the tiny sprigs of lavender in your top drawers, dragging the hoover around the room, wiping at the windows. You didn't grumble about being stuck in there, eating soup from a tray and playing endless games of Scrabble with me.

You always looked after me and then it became my turn, bent over tea-stained cookery books, measuring out ingredients. The day-to-day tasks allowed me to keep marching on, busy, busy, not thinking too much about you upstairs, a book abandoned in your lap, too tired to finish your chapter, your head lolling to the side. Sometimes I would appear in the doorway and see you there, so still, and I would think it had happened, would approach feeling nausea swirl in my stomach, until I could make out the gentle rise and fall of your chest. Another day with you. The relief would take my breath away.

Luke has been dropping in lately. He seems to know what to do when he's here. We sit in companionable silence in the kitchen or front room, my hands wrapped around your dancing sheep mug as he stands at the counter, both of us watching the television in the corner, occasionally looking up to swap useless sports trivia before returning to the screen. He doesn't force me to talk or supply me with an endless stream of inspirational quotes: he's just there. It has been good to see more of him. You always adored him, and I see him glancing across at the photograph of you on the mantelpiece with a small, sad smile and remember he has lost people in his life too.

He came last week. Lottie was out somewhere with Amy doing something for the wedding and he appeared with a bag of pains au chocolat.

'It will be nice to have Lottie here next week,' I said to him, pleased to see he was enjoying the flapjacks I had made the day before, a recipe I found in your handwriting in the pages of an old Filofax. You'd always had a sweet tooth.

Luke swallowed and nodded. 'Yes, less running around for her too. She is manic at the moment.'

He opened his mouth as if he was going to say something more but then bit into his flapjack.

There was a pause as he chewed and I waited, sensing he wanted to get something off his chest.

'I think this last case has been difficult, I mean a lot of them are, it's hard . . .'

Something about the way he trailed away made me bite my lip.

'She's, well, it is stressful, isn't it? I mean, I don't really know what it's like, people's lives in your hands and all that. But I don't really see her enough, not properly . . .'

I went to open my mouth to reply but, not wanting to overstep the mark, shut it again.

'I might call her when I leave here, actually, see where

she's at . . . pin the woman down.' His accompanying laugh sounded a little hollow.

'Good idea.'

You would have asked him directly if anything was bothering him but I didn't want to delve. I might be wrong. There was just something in his voice, a sadness. I didn't want to upset things, though, it was so nice to have him pop by. I knew when he left I would be wandering around the house again, straightening ornaments, opening the fridge, staring into it, forgetting why I was there.

'Did you see the Liverpool game at the weekend?'

Luke took another flapjack from the plate, nodding, enthusiasm restored. 'Amazing goal, they're having a great season.'

'Aren't they!'

Lottie arrived less than 48 hours ago and I understood a little more. It hasn't been what I imagined at all. I was a little nervous greeting her on the Sunday evening, had pre-prepared some topics of conversation – hoped she had seen the Sunday-night period drama last week. She hadn't stayed the night since she'd lived with us all those years ago and of course it was so different now without you and her, heads bent together in conversation.

I wasn't exactly sure what to expect but she seems jittery with energy, just as I feel I don't have enough to face the day. We seem to be out of synch with each other. She was tapping at the table on that first evening, her eyes scanning a document in front of her and her other hand shovelling food into her mouth. Her phone bleeped and pinged and she looked stressed as she glanced at it.

'It's Amy,' she said, after the third call she's ignored.

'Aren't you going to answer it?'

'I should,' she said, biting her lip. 'It will be something to do with her wedding. I'm bridesmaid. I just don't have time to get into it with her, whatever it is, or she'll want to meet and I know I should, I really should, but I can't. And I did see her on Saturday,' she said, as if she was trying to persuade me of something.

I nodded, pushed a half-finished potato across my plate, making a pattern in the gravy.

She pushed her own plate away. 'Do you think I'm being a cow?' She tugged on the sleeves of her jumper, pulling the fabric down over her hands.

Just listening to her had made me anxious. What would you say at this juncture? That Amy would understand? That she should answer her phone? I wasn't used to Lottie asking me for advice.

'I, I'm . . . you're not a cow.'

'No, but do you think I could be a better friend? She wanted me to organise the hen do a couple of months ago and I was so useless she's had to ask her sister instead. That's bad, isn't it?'

'Well, it's, I mean, I don't . . . hen dos aren't really my area of—'

The phone vibrated again and I glanced at it, relieved

it had cut off my feeble attempts to help. I got up to clear our plates, wipe the table down.

She ignored the phone again. 'I can do that, Grandad: you cooked.'

'It's fine, fine,' I said, moving across to the sink, running the hot tap and reaching for the washing-up liquid.

'So do you think it will be OK? That I'm not helping much? I mean, she should get it, shouldn't she? She knows I work long hours.'

'I'm not sure, maybe,' I said, circling a plate uselessly. Why couldn't I do this stuff? You always made it seem so natural, Cora. It was why Lottie always asked you for advice. I tried to think about it. Lottie had known Amy for years and Amy had always been a great friend to her. She should be there for her now. By the time I had constructed an answer, something along the lines of helping Amy's sister with the hen do, I noticed Lottie wearily picking up the various pages and folders in front of her, piling them into her arms. 'Perhaps you could—' I started to say.

My words were cut off. 'I think I'll take these up, work on them in bed.'

'Oh right, great, good idea.'

'Thanks for a lovely dinner, Grandad.'

We met awkwardly around the files, her lips just skimming my cheek.

'Sleep well,' she said.

I glanced at the clock. The period drama would still be playing, I could start watching it on catch-up. I felt a small bubble of relief as I listened to her retreating footsteps heading up the stairs, the pad as she crossed to the spare room. Knowing I hadn't done a great job of making her feel any better, I hoped she liked the lavender sprig I had left on her pillow that morning.

Teddy x

Chapter 7

Love is full of promise

ALISON, 80

It's been more than two months since Grandma died and for the last week I've been working on a case in Guildford Crown Court and staying with Grandad.

Tonight the 'golfing lads', as Grandma had called them, are coming over to drink gin and play gin rummy.

'We take turn hosting and someone is in charge of bringing a new gin to try,' Grandad explained as he opened up the drinks cupboard and produced four crystal tumblers. 'Your Grandma called it the Gin o'Clock Club.' He chuckled softly.

Feeling the same bittersweet sensation I felt whenever Grandma's name was mentioned, I got up to clear the table of court documents, errant biros and scribbled notes. 'I'll get out of the way.'

Grandad had moved through to the kitchen and was chopping limes, cucumber and orange. 'I never quite know what will work best,' he called out, already sounding happier and more relaxed than he had done all week.

I hadn't seen Grandad's friends all together since her funeral: all three dressed in dark suits, their heads bowed, their expressions sombre, so unlike the loud, guffawing group I knew. Geoffrey, his hands trembling so that the paper shook a little, had read beautifully from *Captain Corelli's Mandolin*, Grandma's favourite book. He had passed a handkerchief over his bald head when it was finished and had stumbled in the aisle back to his seat, the others nodding sadly at him.

The bell went and I ventured into the corridor to answer the door. Howard was first in, barrelling into the narrow space wielding two packs of playing cards still in their wrappers, bringing with him the smell of pipe smoke. 'Get ready, old man. It's gin o'clock and the fight is on,' he announced, full beard quivering. 'Lottie,' he said, drawing up short. 'Didn't know you'd be here.' He called over my shoulder, 'Running scared, eh, old man? Sending in the youth?'

'Never.' I could just make out Grandad's response from the kitchen and a low chuckle.

Geoffrey followed Howard inside, shaking his head as he removed his hat and giving me a one-armed hug, his face lighting up. 'Lottie, how lovely. You are so good. Teddy's been telling us how nice it has been to see so much of you.'

I felt a warmth fill my chest, glad that Grandad liked

having me round more. I had been worried recently that my temper would spill into his house and had tried to stay as calm as I could. But some days, after sleep had eluded me, work had piled up and Luke's short phone calls asking if I'd be home had been one too many, I'd been tipped over the edge.

Arjun arrived last, his lined face the picture of health, back from another of his foreign golf tours. 'Lottie!' He gave me a hug and I was reminded of how thin he was under all his layers. 'Excellent to see you.'

'Come in, come in,' I said, ushering them inside. 'Grandad's in the living room setting up the table.'

'Are you joining us, Lottie?' Geoffrey asked.

'I can't, I'm afraid, I've got work to do.'

'That's a shame,' he said, no malice in his reply. He lifted a bag he was holding, 'I'm in charge of the drinks and tonight it's gin flavoured with camomile flowers.'

'Sounds exotic!' I laughed, wishing then that I was about to sit round the living-room table with them, settle into the high-back chairs with a large glass of ice-cold gin and listen to their high spirits, teasing, seeing Grandad's face crease in amusement. Instead I dragged my feet into the kitchen where I had dumped the teetering pile of my work things.

They'd been playing a while and I was attempting to focus on the closing statement I was due to make the next day. I was trying to be as succinct as possible, drawing lines through some of the more flowery sentences to keep the spotlight on the facts of the case. Every now and again I would tune into the conversation leaking out of next door. Persimmon shares had gone up so Arjun was going to sell; someone from his yoga class had caught norovirus on a recent cruise and had stayed in his cabin and missed seeing the Northern Lights, and Geoffrey's handicap was now 20.

Then I heard a chair scraping back and Howard's booming voice. 'I've met a woman!' he announced. 'She's fantastic.'

The whole table groaned. I snuck a look at the door through to the hallway and smiled.

'She's one of a kind.'

'Didn't you say that about the last three?'

'Was that why you cancelled the lunch on Sunday?'

'Is it she who you have been WhatsApping?'

'What's apping?'

'Christ, Geoffrey, we need to get you an iPhone.'

'My phone handset is fine.'

It reminded me of boozy nights with Amy and other friends: the gossip, bickering, teasing. Did anything change? Through the continued mutterings of 'Here we go', 'Please God let her not be in her forties again', I could make out my grandad's low chuckle and I felt heartened.

'She's quite the gal.'

'Like you need another one. What happened to Patricia?' Arjun asked.

'And Blythe?' Geoffrey piped up.

'Over, over, and they couldn't hold a candle to her.'

'It's Teddy here who needs a woman – spare one for him,' Arjun said.

My pen hovered over the pad I was writing on.

'I certainly do not,' came Grandad's voice, aghast.

I tapped my pen on the lined pad as I continued to eavesdrop.

'Well, a chance to see what's out there, at least.'

'I'm fine.'

'Teddy, you told me that last night you spent the evening rearranging the cutlery drawer.'

'You did say that,' Geoffrey agreed.

'It was a mess,' Grandad protested.

'I used a spoon to dribble honey on Blyt—'

'Howard, we don't need to know. We never need to know.'

'Please don't let him finish that sentence.'

Arjun wasn't giving up. 'I'm serious though, Teddy. You probably need something to take your mind off things—'

Howard excitedly chipped in. 'I'm telling you, Teddy, it's a buyers' market. We're completely outnumbered – it's probably three to one in our favour.'

I stifled a giggle, clamping a hand over my mouth. He really was appalling.

'So, if there are such rich pickings, how come you are settling down with this one of a kind?' Grandad had always been able to take on Howard, who, for all his bluster, loved my grandad like a brother.

There were more chuckles, the clink of glasses and I had clean forgotten the work laid out in front of me. It was enough for tonight anyway, I tried to convince myself as I packed my things away.

'Last week I was asked out three times,' Howard went on. 'Three times. By three separate women.'

'I wish I could say the same about men,' Arjun mumbled sadly.

'You'd think now that being homosexual is more fashionable you'd be inundated, my friend,' Howard said.

I paused, impressed with Howard's new-found sensitivity.

'But you are a lost cause, as we have learnt,' he went on, despite heckles from the other three. I'm pretty sure someone punched him in the arm as he made an *oof* sound before continuing, 'Stop that. Teddy here, however, is new on the scene: he is fresh meat, if you will.'

I got up, their voices louder as I stepped into the hallway. As I appeared in the doorway of the living room, all four men turned to look at me. The table was littered with cards, bowls of pretzels, bottles and four almost-empty glasses.

'What were you saying then, Howard? About Grandad?'

Howard's eyes rounded in panic, worried perhaps he was offending me. 'Oh, it was nothing. Well, I just thought, maybe it would be good for your grandad to look for some female company. He rearranged cutlery last night, Lottie.'

'Stop it!' Grandad protested, aiming a pretzel at Howard's chest.

'Do you think Howard's right?' I blurted, looking at Arjun and Geoffrey.

'Not you, Lottie,' Grandad sighed, a small smile as he drained his drink. 'Honestly, I'm fine.'

'Well, I . . . ' Arjun squirmed in his chair, clearly unsure as to the right answer.

'No, of course—' Geoffrey was immediately interrupted.

'Howard's always right,' Howard boomed.

'Shut up, Howard,' chorused Arjun and Geoffrey.

Grandad laughed.

'No, I mean, maybe Howard is a *little* right,' I continued. 'Dating might be good for you, Grandad, a chance to meet someone new, a distraction from . . . things.'

'I don't need distractions,' Grandad said, the expression on his face indulgent but not budging.

'No, no of course you don't,' I said, immediately realising the absurdity of what I had even suggested.

Howard, however, had no such awareness. 'But it would be great fun. There are so many ways to meet women now,' he went on. 'There's Facebook and Happen, Tinder and Match-dot-com.'

'No, no, I couldn't,' Grandad said, shaking his head slowly.

'Of course you can,' Howard scoffed.

'I suppose there couldn't be any real harm in making new connections, other friends,' Arjun joined in, readjusting his tortoiseshell glasses.

'Special friends,' Howard added, practically winking.

'You don't understand. Geoffrey understands, don't you, Geoffrey?' Grandad turned to look at his friend, the light shining on Geoffrey's head as he shifted in his seat. He wasn't keen on the spotlight; that was more Howard's forte. I hadn't known Geoffrey's wife – she had been a seamstress, had died years ago – but I knew they had been childhood sweethearts and he had never remarried.

'I do. When you've been married as long as we both were, and to your best friend' – I felt a lump form in my throat as Geoffrey stumbled over these words – 'well, you just . . . lose interest,' he said, palms up in appeal.

I bit my lip.

Grandad was nodding. 'There'll never be another one like her.'

I had definitely been wrong to even think Howard might have a point. I had just wanted Grandad to have some excitement, to remember life wasn't over just because Grandma was no longer here. Or was there a secret part of me that didn't want to feel *I* had to watch him all the time? I swallowed down the feeling that I might have wanted Howard to be right for all the wrong reasons.

Howard had the good grace not to snort too loudly after Geoffrey's words. 'Cora was a fine woman, Teddy, and we're not saying you will meet another one like her, but . . . you might meet a younger one at the very least.'

The howls started up again and I started laughing too at Grandad's horrified face before we were interrupted by the sound of the doorbell.

'Mail-order bride?' Howard laughed. 'That was quick. Tell them he'll be along just as soon as he begs me to borrow a blue pill.'

'Howard!'

'That is horrifying.'

'Straight red card.'

Rolling my eyes, pleased to hear the others berating him, I moved out into the hallway, seeing a tall silhouette beyond the wavy glass of the front door. Checking the latch was on I tentatively pulled it open, then fumbled to open it when I saw Luke standing on the doorstep. He had flushed cheeks and a beanie hat pulled down low, an unseasonably cold wind making him rub his hands together.

'Hey,' I said, opening the door wide, then feeling a wave of panic. 'What are you doing here? Is everything OK? Has the flat burnt down?'

Luke put his hands on my shoulders. 'Woah, breathe, Lottie, breathe. All is well. I just wanted to see you.'

I took a step back, one hand on my chest. 'Oh, oh, that's good. Come in.'

'Ask her if she can cook.' Howard's voice floated down the hallway to us.

Luke turned to me, his eyebrow raised in a question.

'Don't ask,' I said, pushing him along the corridor and into the living room.

'I wouldn't dream of it,' he grinned, pulling off his hat.

'Ah, Luke!' Grandad's face broke into a grin as he stood up. There was a lot of handshaking and hellos. Luke knew the golfing lads almost as well as I did. I could tell from their admiring glances that they were pleased to see him.

'Want to join us, Luke? This gin has got camomile flowers in it!' Arjun said, waving a bottle at him.

Luke wrinkled his nose. 'How disgusting.' He turned

to me. 'I was actually here to see you. I thought we could grab a drink?'

'A romantic evening planned, eh, Luke? Well, Lottie has certainly dressed for the occasion,' Howard said, looking at my threadbare slippers and baggy jumper.

'Hey!' I reached out and threw another pretzel at him.

'Assault!' Howard cried, as the other men hushed him.

'She's just going for relaxed chic,' Luke chipped in. 'It's a regular look,' he added.

Although I knew he was teasing me I couldn't help feeling a little offended. I dressed up. Sometimes. I suppose I was often dressed up for work or work-related functions and the moment I was back in the flat I was straight into leggings and large tops. And anyway I didn't have to dress to impress him. If he didn't like me as I was then he could damn well—

'You all right there, Lottie? You don't look so well,' Arjun asked, staring at my clenched fists and pursed lips.

Luke turned, concern etched on his features. 'Are you not feeling well?'

'I'm fine,' I mumbled. 'I'll go and change,' I added, trying to disguise the emotion in my voice.

'No need,' Luke said. I bit down an abrupt reply. I could feel the familiar stirrings of an argument move within me and if it hadn't been for our audience . . .

'And where are you fine young people headed?' Geoffrey asked.

Luke shrugged. 'I was, er, thinking of the pub on the corner,' he said, a note of apology in his voice.

Arjun and Geoffrey exchanged a look.

Howard didn't even pretend to hold back. 'God, it's not like in our day where we had to court these ladies, woo them,' he said, somewhat wistfully. 'You had to turn up with flowers' – pointedly looking at Luke's empty hands – 'and take them out for fine dining, treat them well.'

Grandad was chuckling into his glass, shaking his head from side to side. 'Leave him alone, Howard.'

I looked at Luke's crestfallen face, pushing the negative thoughts away as I saw that he seemed genuinely flummoxed. 'Howard – it's not like that any more,' I said, tucking my arm into Luke's. 'It's simpler. We own a flat together, for a start. I am way past being wooed.'

'A lady should always be wooed,' Howard said dramatically. Arjun and Geoffrey inclined their heads a fraction.

'I'll leave wooing to the professionals.' Luke laughed, putting his arm over my shoulders and squeezing me towards him.

'Leave them alone, Howard,' Grandad called, standing up and moving around the table to clap a hand on Luke's shoulder. 'Luke always treats my Lottie well.'

'The old ways are still the best ways,' Howard said, returning to his seat and picking up his cards. He flipped over the Queen of Hearts and grinned, holding it aloft. 'If you get Teddy here on the modern dating scene, the least you two could do is try dating in the old-fashioned way.'

Arjun nodded. 'Absolutely. Who doesn't want to be wooed?'

'Courting,' Geoffrey added in a soft voice. 'How romantic.'

Grandad turned to Howard. 'What do you mean?'

'Well, if you're going to consider putting yourself out there, the least you can ask in return is for your granddaughter to try our ways,' Howard said, raising his glass.

There was a pause. I was distracted, about to move into the hallway for my coat. 'So if I agree to this dating idea' – Grandad gestured to the desktop computer in the corner of the room – 'this modern stuff . . . Lottie and Luke would have to try dating our way, the old-fashioned way?'

He turned and looked straight at me, an expression I hadn't seen before making his eyes sparkle.

I stopped thinking about getting my coat. 'Grandad . . . ' I gave him a perplexed expression.

'If you agree, Lottie, I'll do it.'

'No, don't worry, it was all a bit of a joke. You were right. Howard was being silly.' What was Grandad saying? Did he want an excuse to get back out and meet people? What did he want me to agree to in return?

'Um, what's going on?' Luke interjected.

'I think,' I said slowly, unable to believe the one-eighty Grandad had done in a few short minutes, 'if Grandad agrees to test the water on the modern dating scene, we'd have to . . . '

Howard twisted in his chair to look at us both. 'You,' he said, a delighted smile splitting his face, 'would have to court each other the old-fashioned way.'

Luke's mouth gaped. I imagine he wished we had both left for the pub already.

'We could help,' Geoffrey said, half to himself.

'I could teach them how to waltz,' Arjun added, pushing his glasses up his nose and looking eager.

Howard joined in. 'They could join a boules club.'

'Or go tandem bike riding,' Grandad added.

'Yes, yes, exactly that,' Howard said, slapping his cards down, gin rummy forgotten. 'You would both have to try something different, an old-fashioned date, every time Teddy here tries something new. Is it a deal?'

I put both hands up in the air. 'No, we're not going to spend our days hanging out in social clubs so you can all have a good laugh at our expense.'

'It wouldn't be like that,' Howard insisted.

Luke was laughing now.

'It would be fun,' Arjun chipped in.

'But Grandad didn't even want to, did you?' I said, turning to him, his expression alight: energised. He ignored me. Frowning, I looked at Geoffrey, normally the most sensible member of the group. 'You don't really think this is a good idea?'

He wavered, not saying anything as Howard went over to the upright piano and started shouting things. 'Music halls, a night at the opera ... ballroom dancing, none of this twerking ... '

'They could try ... '

'Oh how about ... '

'Do you remember when ... '

The piano notes filled the living room and I couldn't hear

the specifics. Only Grandma had played the piano, I realised. I shot another look at Grandad to see if he had noticed, expecting his shoulders to sag at the sound: a reminder of her. But he hadn't even registered it. He was too busy scribbling ideas down on to the piece of paper they were using to score with, Arjun pointing over his shoulder to add something else to the list. I hadn't seen Grandad with this much energy in weeks. He seemed to be fired up again with his old passion.

'Any other ideas? Is Bingo romantic?'

'Not if you lose.'

'The lighting can be very harsh in those halls.'

'Honestly, we really don't have the time,' I tried to cut in at the same moment as Luke stepped forward, both hands out to silence them all.

There was a general hush, Howard's hands hovering over the keys.

'I'm not sure what's going on,' Luke said slowly, the four men tilting their faces towards us, 'but of course we'd think about it if it would help, wouldn't we, Lottie?'

'Well . . . I don't know . . . really, it's . . . '

'Oh a horse and carriage, *great* idea!' Grandad slapped Geoffrey's arm, beaming at him.

None of them heard me.

Chapter 8

Love is messy

IRIS, 91

What had just happened? We were ushered out of the house already armed with a list of ideas, leaving Grandad working on his profile for internet dating. As I was putting on my coat I could hear Howard and Arjun rating photos of him they were scrolling through.

'This one says, "Ladies, I'm available, single and ready to mingle . . ."'

'That was from that line-dancing evening, Howard.'

'This one is a bit edgier, older Cary Grant, although it would help if you purchased a motorcycle.'

'This one is grim.'

'God, it is. It says, "I know I look like I am in renal failure but let's hope it's just the lighting."'

'Sexy.'

'I like this one. It's very Distinguished Judge meets Friendly Policeman.'

'Cora took that one.'

'It's good: like you could handcuff the ladies any time.'

'Howard, isn't it time you left?'

Luke was chuckling as we walked down the street to the pub on the corner. I hugged my arms around myself, the wind biting at me. The glowing windows looked particularly enticing as we approached. Luke hesitated as we reached the double doors, the muted sounds of laugher, clinking glass and chatter coming from inside. 'You don't mind if we just go to the pub, do you? We could go to a nicer place if you—'

I interrupted him with a hand on his arm. 'Don't be silly. This is perfect.'

He looked relieved, smiling as he opened the door. 'After you,' he said with a small bow.

I stepped inside.

'I be a'wooing,' he added, following me.

He insisted on buying our drinks and I perched on a bar stool at a high round table, enjoying being back in the warmth, still not yet ready to remove my coat. I could see Luke chatting with another guy at the bar. He had the ability to strike up conversation with perfect strangers and would often return with titbits he'd learnt. Tonight was no exception.

'Do you know that guy was the amateur UK junior darts

champion?' He seemed to be an easy person to share things with. I was always amazed by what he could glean from two minutes of chat.

'So,' Luke said, once we had made vague attempts to discuss our working day ('OK', 'Fine'), 'that seemed to get out of hand fast.'

'It was the gin.'

'Well, it was flavoured with camomile flowers,' Luke said, laughing and holding out his hand. 'Let's have a look at that list, then.'

Scooping the list out of my coat pocket I handed it over, Grandad's barely legible slanted handwriting filling the sheet.

'Look all you like,' I said, 'but we're not doing it, all right?'

'Fine, fine,' he said, smoothing out the piece of paper. Luke scanned the scribbles, his mouth twitching as he read. 'What's a ceil-i-dah?'

Frowning I peered at the word, 'A ceilidh,' I laughed, 'It's Scottish dancing.'

'Christ,' Luke said in alarm, looking up at me, eyes wide. 'Dancing.'

'Quite,' I took a sip of my wine.

'What's a day of conchology?'

'A conch? Er . . . Something to do with shells . . . ?'

'Bell ringing!' He guffawed. 'Not sure that was ever a romantic day out.'

'Geoffrey added it. I think they need bell ringers in the church – might have been motivated by that thought.

Anyway, we don't have to do any of this stuff, it was just a crazy idea. They'll be over it after the next bottle of gin. I mean, who has time to attend dancing lessons with work and everything else? And I'm sure they just got fired up and have now moved on to another hot topic, like how to release equity from their home.'

Luke had grown still.

'Luke . . . ?' I prompted.

He circled the top of his pint glass with a finger. 'Well, they did seem very keen on the idea. And did you see your Grandad? He hasn't looked like that in months.'

I opened and closed my mouth, knowing I couldn't argue as I had thought the same thing. Grandad had been transformed for a moment, his words fast, spilling into each other. His laugh louder, longer.

Luke returned to the list. 'And some of these don't exactly look time-consuming. Actually, they look like they could be fun. Although admittedly I can't read a lot of them. Jesus, your grandad has bad handwriting.' He was squinting at the last one. 'Does that say Genital?'

I snatched the sheet back, reading 'General Knowledge Quiz Night'. 'General.'

'That's a relief.'

It had been good to see Grandad fired up again, bent over that stupid piece of paper as the others had egged him on. Luke had suggested some modern dating methods (Grandad had thought speed dating involved running and his bemused chuckle had lifted my heart). I had forgotten his laugh, gravelly and drawn out. Selfishly, as well, I knew that if he was busy focusing on this project I wouldn't have to spend so much time worrying he was on his own or trekking across to check on him. I tried to dismiss that thought the moment it arose – but the last few weeks had been exhausting and maybe it would be nice to feel freer. I glanced at the list.

'It might be good for him, you know,' Luke said, folding the sheet in half again. 'Something to do, a pet project.' He raised one eyebrow at me.

I paused, finished the last of my wine. 'No, we really can't. I mean, a jigsaw-puzzle evening, Luke? Seriously.'

'OK. Fair enough, you're right.' Was there a hint of disappointment in his voice or did I imagine it?

I desperately tried to stifle a yawn.

'Come on,' he said, finishing his drink and sliding off his bar stool, 'let's get you back.'

He flung an arm around my shoulders as we pushed our way out of the pub and back into the street.

'Thanks for coming over tonight.' I looked at the silhouette of his profile in the lamplight.

He stopped on the street. 'Lottie, I miss you.'

'Me too. These last few weeks have been a bit mad.'

We walked in silence for a while back to Grandad's, both lost in contemplation.

'We don't have to do lots of all-singing, all-dancing dates,' I said as I reached for his hand. 'It's fine just to have evenings like this. We should do them more.'

He circled his thumb over mine. 'We should,' he agreed. 'Absolutely.'

Darling Cora,

I never watched Bake Off with you but working my way through your recipe books is bringing some small joy into the lonelier days. Today I am trying to make banana muffins. All the ingredients are sitting in a Pyrex bowl waiting but I have been scuppered by the lack of a muffin tray. A muffin tray is different to a cupcake tray, the book tells me.

I remember you made me take a box of kitchen items up to the attic a year or so ago and I am hoping I will unearth it there. It was a heavy box. We'd had quite a disagreement about whether you really needed three glass juicers and you'd finally allowed me to put one up in the attic. Maybe it should go to the charity shop, I had suggested, but you had looked at me in that withering way you had, asking me that what would happen if the other two broke? Armageddon? I had blurted – which had led to two hours of frosty silence on your part.

It was this thought that lifted my mouth into a bittersweet smile as I pulled on the loft hatch handle and jimmied the ladder down.

I heard the front door open and close just as I was halfway inside the dark space, my feet still on the top rung.

'Grandad?'

'Up here,' I called, patting my way towards the dusty light switch, fingers brushing up against cobwebs.

I could hear Lottie moving up the stairs and tried to twist around to poke my head back through the hole.

She was already lurching forward, one hand on the ladder, a worried expression on her face as she stared up at me. 'Christ, Grandad, get down, don't fall. I can get up there. What do you need? You shouldn't be—'

'It's all right, it's all right. I need a muffin tray. It's very important,' I found myself saying, stepping into the attic. It was boiling in the narrow space. I dipped my head so as not to hit it on a beam.

'Not breaking a leg is important,' Lottie chastised, following me up the ladder with a tut. She stood next to me, her heels kicked off below, her stockinged feet making marks in the dust. 'What did you say you need?' she asked, glancing around at the myriad of boxes, bags, suitcases, broken lamps and more.

'Muffin tray.'

Lottie frowned. 'What does it look like?'

'A tray that can fit muffins in.'

'Right,' Lottie said, stepping forward and staring down at a nearby box labelled 'Hats'. 'Probably not it,' she said astutely.

'There's a box of kitchen stuff somewhere,' I said, taking in the numerous items we had dumped here over the years, things we couldn't bear to be parted with or things we didn't know what to do with any more. Amazing how it built up.

'Here,' Lottie said from behind me, opening up a box

filled with redundant saucepans, cheese graters and the blessed muffin tray.

'Excellent.' I took it from her with a smile, excited to start on the banana muffins.

She was about to walk back across to the ladder when she paused by another box, labelled 'Photos'. Sinking to her knees she bent over and looked inside, pulling out a stack of albums: burgundy, navy blue, a couple of photographs escaping the pages.

'Oh look,' she said, opening up the first one and seeing the date in the corner, 'it's Dad and you.' She grinned at the picture of Simon and me, a photo taken on a family holiday to Croyde when Simon must have been about five or six. Her face fell a fraction as she traced it with a finger.

'He'll be over again before we know it,' I said in a faux-cheerful voice, not fooling either of us. Simon was a workaholic, stuck to his desk in Singapore: annual visits weren't always guaranteed.

'Absolutely,' Lottie said, going along with the lie. She turned to the next album quickly, less keen to look at photographs of her father.

'God, these are from 1964,' she said, pulling out a photograph of a group round a long dining table. 'Grandad, snazzy shirt,' she said, holding up the photo of me dressed in a lurid purple and orange swirled shirt I had loved.

'That was in the flat I owned before we were married,' I said.

'Ah, look at Grandma. God, she looks amazing. Who's that sitting next to her?'

Glancing at it I felt the old envy rise to the surface. 'Trevor,' I sniffed. 'First boyfriend of your grandmother. She insisted they stay friends.'

'Jealous much?' Lottie giggled, studying the photo. 'He's quite devil-may-care, isn't he? With all that facial hair.'

'Hiding a weak chin,' I mumbled.

Lottie laughed and nudged me and we both stared at the picture of your younger self. I had always been jealous of anyone who had known you before I did. Now, though, I could just take in your long neck, your hair cut into a dramatic bob, your wide mouth open in a laugh, the light in your eyes. You were beautiful, Cora, through and through. I hope I told you that enough; I'm sure I didn't.

In the photograph we were all playing cards. Remembering those nights, long dinner parties with someone on the upright piano and others playing estimation whist, reminded me of the good times we had had when courting. 'Your grandmother was a whiz at card games.'

Lottie stared at the picture for a while.

I know in the last year you'd been more and more worried about her, and her staying this week has brought home to me how thinly stretched she is. She doesn't stop. She's almost manic in her approach. It reminds me of Simon in those days as a trader, desperate to get on, to work at the expense of everything else. I remember that day when he told us he would be emigrating to run the branch in Singapore and I could almost hear your heart breaking.

He'd gone, and of course we wanted desperately for him to be happy, and work really did seem to drive him, but knowing this meant our future was expensive long-distance phone calls on an unreliable line and bi-annual visits was devastating. In recent years there was Skype, of course, but it was still half a world away. It seemed a comfort at least to know that his decision did seem right, that he was truly happy in that world.

Lottie, though, she seems less certain, more torn in two. I remember the early days of her and Luke, her telling us about the lazy walks they'd go on, their constant visits to yurts in Wales, cabins in Dorset, spa hotels in Cornwall – they were always roaming and relaxed together. Now, though, work seems to have swallowed her up. I want Lottie to have the same fun we had, the same evenings with Luke, with their friends.

Lottie's mobile rings and she glances at it before stuffing it guiltily back in her pocket. 'It's Amy,' she mutters with a blush.

'So,' I said, my thoughts making up my mind. 'We need to plan your first evening together with Luke, something suitable for a young courting couple.' I tried to inject a lightness to my voice.

Lottie looked up, placing the photo back in the album. 'Oh, oh no, Luke and I are fine, happy with how things are, no need to do anything drastic, it was a crazy idea.'

Realising she wasn't going to go along with the scheme made me pause. I looked back at your face in the photograph, still hoping for another moment, another hour, another day in your company. She shut the album cover. 'You must!' I found myself saying. 'It wouldn't be fair to me. Howard has already chosen my profile picture for Tinder.'

I hadn't dreamed of actually going along with the ridiculous idea but now Lottie didn't seem keen either I felt a desperate desire to see it through. She needed to do this. She and Luke needed this time to remember what was important.

'But surely you don't really want to date or anything yet?'

'Oh I do!'

Her forehead creased in a frown. 'It's OK to say you're not OK, Grandad.'

I tried to sound enthusiastic. 'I just thought it might be a good way to take my mind off things!' (Sorry, Cora, I'm so sorry.) 'Not so much the women but more the chance to get out there, do different things, meet new people.' I felt like I was rambling now and came to a halt.

Lottie looked as surprised as I felt. 'But—'

'But fair is fair,' I interjected, removing the spotlight from myself, 'and I only want to do it if you and Luke agree to try things the old-fashioned way. That will give us all something to plan and help out with too.'

Lottie scuffed her stockinged foot on the floor, making

marks in the dust. 'I'm not sure, Grandad. There's so much going on, I don't really have the time to—'

'Nonsense. It won't take up lots of time.' I was sounding positively forceful but I realised this was my way to help. I might not have your skills in conversation, Cora, but I could do something practical.

'Well, I suppose, if you really want me to.'

'I do. I think it will be a fun thing for the both of us.'

'Luke didn't seem completely against the idea,' she admitted. 'All right,' she said, standing up, 'if you're sure . . .'

'I'm sure!' I almost banged my head on the beam as I stood.

'OK then!'

'Excellent!' I exhaled in a short, relieved burst. 'Excellent.'

With that agreed I ushered her back down the ladder, knowing I needed to get something before I followed her. I reached round behind me and rummaged through the kitchen box, extracting the glass juicer and holding it carefully against my chest as I made my way back downstairs.

Teddy

Chapter 9

Love is a commitment you need
to work at like any other

SIDNEY, 84

It didn't take long for Grandad and his friends to put plans in place. The first night back in our flat, Luke and I were met with a flashing light on our answerphone.

'Lottie, Luke,' Grandad began, voices cutting across him so that we could barely hear what he was saying.

'Are you trying their mobiles?'

'Did we write down Ludo? I have always really enjoyed Ludo.'

'No one else likes Ludo, though, Geoffrey.'

'Ssh, I can't hear myself leaving this message. Luke, Lottie,' Grandad repeated a little louder, 'so pleased you've agreed, can't wait to get started. We've been planning things a little more.'

'Where's the tonic?'

'Ssh, I'm leaving them a message. Oh, I needed to ask whether you both think I should join Grindr too. Howard seems to think it's another dating website. But enough of that for when I next see you, which is soon because we've got your first date all lined up. It's next Tuesday, in fact. Hope you can make it, I'll send the address. Should be a good one to kick off.'

'Is there a dress code?'

'He can send that in the message, can't he?'

'There won't be a dress code.'

'Does this gin really have cubebs in it? I can't taste them . . . what is a cubeb?'

An abrupt sound of a dialtone followed and I looked at Luke, whose mouth had fallen open a fraction, and then we both burst out laughing.

'What have we agreed to?' he whispered.

'I have no idea,' I said.

The following Tuesday came around far too quickly.

'We're late,' I said, tugging on the skirt of my teal green tea dress. I hadn't worn it in years. It had once been a firm favourite. I had pulled it off a hanger at the back of the wardrobe, realising I hadn't made an effort to dress up at all for an age. Moving past the sea of black and grey work suits to a row of forgotten colours and shapes, I reached for a dusty pink coat to wear over it.

'Teddy will understand,' Luke said, infuriatingly unfazed.

'I hate being late,' I huffed as we let ourselves out of the flat.

'Which is weird for someone who is always late.'

'Haha.'

Luke shrugged. 'You look pretty,' he said. 'So it's worth being five minutes late. What is a whistle drive anyway?'

'A whist drive,' I said.

'What's a whist?'

'Oh my God, Luke, you're an idiot,' I said, buying myself time because I didn't know the answer either. 'It's cards, isn't it?' Not wanting him to ask more I sped up, the train station just up ahead.

'Sorry, card shark, I'm more of a poker man.'

'Luke, you're shit at poker.'

He stopped walking, stared down at his feet. 'I know,' he said in a quiet voice, 'but I *want* to be a poker man.'

'Well, maybe we can work on that after tonight.'

'Maybe I'll become a whistle expert.'

'*Whist.*'

'Whatever.'

The train was on time and we arrived in the main hall to see lots of round tables scattered around the room, four chairs at each, people milling between them. I craned my neck to see Grandad, Howard, Geoffrey or Arjun, but came up blank. On a large wooden easel by the doorway an A3 sheet of paper denoted our groups for the evening and there were also laminated name badges on a table on the other side.

'Christ,' Luke whispered, 'it's very organised, isn't it. No escaping if you find out you can't whistle.'

I stared at him, mouth twitching as he grinned at me. 'Also, we are seriously bringing down the average age of the room.'

He was right: everywhere we turned there seemed to be white hair, walking sticks and bifocal lenses.

'I suppose that's to be expected,' I whispered.

'Funny idea of high romance.'

We had been put on a table with two women called Margaret and Paula.

'Stranger Danger!' Luke sing-songed pinning his name badge on his jumper.

'Ssh,' I elbowed him.

He looked good tonight, dressed in cream chinos and a maroon chequered shirt I hadn't seen him in before.

'Is that new?' I asked, pointing at the shirt.

'I bought it for our first old-person-style date,' he said proudly puffing out his chest. 'Gonna be taking this courting you seriously.'

I felt a glow in my stomach.

'Lottie, Luke – you made it.' I jumped a little at Howard's too-loud voice, turning to see him standing next to us dressed in red corduroy trousers and a blue and white striped shirt. 'Nothing like our biannual whist drive to fan those flames,' Howard said with a sarcastic eye-roll. 'Teddy's idea of your first date has a lot to be said for.'

'I think it's a good idea,' Arjun said, looking equally smart next to him. 'Hello, Lottie, hello, Luke. So, are you feeling lucky?'

Luke cracked his knuckles. 'Luck will have nothing to do with it, Arjun.' Even though he hadn't played the game before, Luke seemed irritatingly confident that he could win. Annoyingly, he probably would. He was horribly good at most things. My eyes narrowed as I stared at him, hoping the next time he ordered six Chicken McNuggets they only put in five.

'We'll see, we'll see,' Howard said, already looking over our shoulders at the gathering people. 'Christ, the whole place has come out for the evening.'

'Lottie, you OK?' Luke asked me. 'You're in one of your dazes again. Who are you wishing bad things on?'

I had the decency to flush. 'No one. Let's find our table.'

Arjun dived behind me as I went to move away.

'Argh, wait, shield me,' he whispered. 'That's Cindy. She always corners me to talk about politics in Asia and I haven't the heart to tell her I was born in Lincoln. She treats me like the Voice of the Common Indian and I find myself discussing caste issues and making up facts about the economy.'

A woman nearby with a sharp grey bowl haircut was scouting the vicinity. Her eyes lit up as she clocked someone in the opposite direction.

'I'd never even heard of the two main parties and I had to google them when I got home last time,' Arjun was saying.

'She's moving away,' I said out of the corner of my mouth.

'Right,' he whispered. 'I'm making a run for it.'

Giggling, I watched Arjun slink away along the wall, just missing Grandad and Geoffrey, who appeared next to me.

'You're here, excellent,' Grandad said, hugging me.

'And you're on a good table,' Geoffrey added.

Grandad nodded. 'That Margaret is a gem. And Paula is . . . ' He tailed away as if he'd forgotten what he was saying.

'Paula is . . . ' Luke prompted.

'Well!' Grandad clapped his hands together. 'It should be a great evening. You two better find your table. I'm playing with Geoffrey tonight so we are bound to lose.'

'Hey,' Geoffrey said, 'I heard that.'

'Did you turn your hearing aid on?' Grandad looked surprised.

Geoffrey folded his arms. 'Do not divert things. I am good at whist,' he said, bottom lip sticking out.

'You're satisfactory.'

'Good.'

'Fair.'

Geoffrey glowered and Luke clearly thought it was a good time to move on. Placing a gentle hand on my back he moved me through the clusters of people. Near the small stage at the other end of the hall Howard was perched chatting to a glamorous-looking woman in a silver grey dress.

One of the ladies was already sat at our table, iron grey hair pinned back with two hair clips just above her ears and a shy smile as we took our seats.

'I'm Luke. You must be one of the opposition,' he said, deliberately narrowing his eyes at her with a laugh. I felt immediately grateful for Luke and his ability to make strangers feel comfortable.

'I am,' the woman said. 'Margaret.' She pointed to the

name on her chest before fiddling with a silver necklace at her throat.

'I'm Lottie,' I said, reaching across to shake her hand.

'So, are you a bit of a whist expert?' Luke asked, pulling out his chair.

'Oh, no, I don't know about that. I do enjoy it but there is so much luck involved in the cards, you see.' Her voice was soft and she couldn't quite maintain eye contact with either of us. She reminded me of a fragile bird that might fly away at the first fright.

'Well, Lottie and I will no doubt be completely out of our dep—'

A loud voice interrupted him. 'If you're partnering each other, you need to sit opposite each other . . . although' – a large woman with a cloud of hair-sprayed, dyed blonde hair looked down at Luke – 'I don't mind you partnering me.' She lifted a thickly pencilled eyebrow at Luke.

I swallowed a laugh at Luke's terrified expression. He opened his mouth, then shut it again.

'All right, Mags,' the hair-sprayed woman continued, pulling out an e-cigarette from a shiny scarlet handbag.

'Hi, Paula,' the other woman whispered.

'Soooo, you're Luke and Lottie.' Paula pulled out her chair. 'Hadn't heard of you. No wonder, you're about eighty years too young for this place.' She took a long suck on her e-cigarette, hot pink lipstick puckered round the end.

'I'm Teddy's granddaughter, Lottie,' I said, unused to seeing Luke so completely lost for words.

Everyone had settled at their tables and there was a low hubbub of noise, the gentle shuffle of cards, coughing, laughter as people started to play. Paula had made us all get up and swap seats so I was now sitting opposite Luke, feeling him nudging me with a foot as we made eye contact.

Paula leaned forward conspiratorially, her breasts resting on the table. 'Want to make this all a little more interesting, if you know what I mean.' She wagged her eyebrows. 'A little bid whist?'

'Oh I'm not sure, Paula—' Margaret started to say before Paula gave her a look full of daggers and she fell silent.

Luke came to her rescue. 'We don't know any whist, I'm afraid, not even regular whist,' he said. 'We're whist virgins, so to speak. Never whisted before ever. I don't even drive,' he added.

Paula sat back in her chair and raised her e-cigarette to her lips again. 'You what now?'

'Come on, Paula, let's just play,' Margaret said, fiddling with the necklace again.

Paula leaned forward again. 'Oh, come on, you lot. How about we make this worth our while? Dennis banned it a while back but he's such a stick-in-the-mud. You only live once – am I right, Liam?' She turned to Luke, eyes rounded.

'It's Luke, actually.'

'Nah, you look more like a Liam,' she said with a wave of her e-cigarette, 'like that One Direction one who used to be with Cheryl. You should change it.'

'Change my name?'

'Why not?' Paula took a drag, narrowing her eyes as if she was blowing out real smoke. 'Luke's a bit . . . a bit androgynous. I had a husband called Lester – that was the same problem. He played a ukulele.' She circled a long nail around the rim of her glass. 'That's not even a proper guitar.'

'Right, well, I'll, um, I'll think about it.'

'So you're Teddy's granddaughter, are you?' Paula said, turning back to me as if we'd never been interrupted. 'That Teddy, he's a gent.'

I smiled, about to agree, when Paula continued.

'. . . and he's still got a good body. I always see him doing his lengths when I'm in my aqua aerobics and I try to time my sauna session for when he gets out.'

'That's, well, that's good to know,' I said, grateful to see wine on the table and reaching for a glass.

Margaret had picked up the cards. 'I'll deal,' she said, shuffling the pack like an expert. 'We can explain the rules as we go along.' She doled out thirteen cards to each of us.

I sagged with relief, my grandad's swimmer's body safely tucked away in a place in my brain to which I would never venture.

'Fine,' Paula said, sitting back. 'I suppose they're learners so we'll have to humour them.'

'Thanks,' Luke said, picking up his cards. 'So, how do you play?'

Margaret began explaining the rules, Paula interrupting when she didn't think Margaret was being clear enough (which turned out to be most sentences), and we started to play.

The first round went well, mostly because Paula won and the wine was flowing. I was getting the gist of the game. Luke was talking to Paula and Mags, and had somehow managed to tell them about the deal we had made with Grandad.

'So I'm now courting Lottie the old-fashioned way,' he said proudly.

'And you've persuaded Teddy to date again,' Paula said, her eager eyes swivelling over to Grandad's table. There he sat, innocently. Should I send up a flare warning?

'That sounds very romantic,' Margaret said, smiling sweetly at me, two dimples appearing in her cheeks.

'You need to get yourself a new man, Mags. First husband,' she said, barely lowering her voice, 'overbearing, dominated Mags here, didn't he?'

Margaret nodded slowly, a blush building. 'He was quite forthright on occasion.'

'Oh, don't look now, Mags, but it's Howard, he is such a dish. Hi, Howard,' Paula cooed, almost spilling her white wine spritzer in an enthusiastic wave.

Howard saluted her from his chair. He seemed to have about three wine glasses lined up in front of him and no cards. Paula made her excuses and headed his way. Luke went to fetch more wine.

'Sorry' – I turned to my right – 'is it Mags or Margaret?' I asked, liking this softly spoken woman with the kind eyes and not wanting to offend her by using the wrong name.

'It's Margaret. I always wanted to be Maggie actually,' she added in a quiet rush, 'but my parents wouldn't let me and then I suppose it felt a little silly, changing it. Stephen, my husband, told me Margaret suited me. I was never sure what he meant by that.' She trailed away, the flush creeping up from the bottom of her neck as she darted her eyes away.

I wanted to reach across and grab her hand but instead I just said, 'I don't think it's ever too late. If you want to be Maggie, you be Maggie.'

She sighed, adjusting one of the clips in her hair. 'Young women today are amazing,' she said. 'You're so confident. You know what you want and you don't mind saying it. Most of us never really spoke our minds. Feminism wasn't for everyone and it's a bit late to start now.'

'I hadn't looked at it like that. Sometimes I just feel completely exhausted wanting it all. You know: the job, the relationship, kids someday, hobbies, friends, family. Then I feel guilty because lots of women didn't get to do all of this. Imagine the frustration, all that talent that we will just never know about.'

We had failed to notice Paula had returned. 'Talent. I know. I was just saying they keep dying on us. They're quite literally a dying breed. There is no talent, Lottie. None. Well, your grandad and a couple of others but . . . '

'So, how do you two know each other?' Luke asked, returning with drinks and oblivious to the steer in conversation.

'Paula and I play golf together. She's very good,' Margaret

said, nodding earnestly at Paula, who shrugged and drained the rest of her glass.

'I am very good.'

'Oh, my grandad plays golf. I'm sure he'd love a game.'

'Well, the thing is, bar one morning a week the course here is men only so we have to get a minibus to the course a few miles away,' Margaret explained.

I thought I'd misheard her. 'Er, one morning – is that really true? Are they aware it's 2020?'

'It's not 2020 in Maplelands Club,' Paula sniffed, looking around for Luke, who had gone to talk to Geoffrey.

'No matter,' Margaret said with a small wave of her hand. 'What do you both do?'

I wanted to find out a little more but instead I took another sip of my drink. 'I'm a barrister, and Luke's a graphic designer.'

'But what do you do for fun?' Margaret asked, her amber eyes focused on me.

I paused, wine glass halfway to my lips. 'Fun?'

She gave me an encouraging smile and nodded.

'Um, we, we live together. That can be fun.'

Her smile was fading slightly.

'And we sometimes go for a drink. Out, you know,' I continued, knowing this all sounded pretty sad, even to me.

Jeez, this woman who must have been about fifty years older than me had more of a buzzing social scene than I did. We go out for drinks. Edgy, Lottie, really edgy and cool.

'Oh, sometimes we go to the cinema.' I said it way

too enthusiastically. Margaret was just giving me pitying nods now.

Maybe Grandad had been right to get us to go along to these things. Luke was standing at the bar laughing with Geoffrey and Grandad and I felt my heart swell for him. When we had first started dating we had been out loads. We had gone bowling, we had gone to museum exhibitions, art shows, the theatre, comedy nights; we'd gone on day trips at weekends, punting in Oxford, surfing in North Devon. We'd even gone to Amsterdam on the Eurostar just to cycle and eat our way round the city. I remember clutching his arm as we had rolled, giggling, out of the Soho Theatre bar, a stand-up night that had gone horribly wrong when the audience turned on the poor comedian. We had planned these mini-breaks and days away, taking the train, relishing just being in each other's company.

When had we stopped planning the adventures? Or had I stopped? Hadn't Luke suggested we hire some bikes, cycle along the Thames only the other week? When had we last really spent any quality time together? Our conversations now revolved around the recycling (yes, the food recycling is gross but it makes the main bin so much less gross that it's totally worth doing, and you really do feel you are doing a bit of good), the money we are saving for a deposit on a house that we are never going to be able to afford, discussions about whether you can really raise children on a houseboat (Luke thinks it would be slippery and 'an accident waiting to happen'), facts about the Tube that day (usual theme: it's disgusting – we both want to kill ourselves), how we should see that film/exhibition/show but then turn to Netflix for the eighteenth episode of a box set neither of us can remember.

Margaret was still sitting beside me, politely waiting for my weird daydream to end. Was it my turn to speak?

'So, yeah, we have loads of fun.'

I looked over at Grandad, roaring with laughter at something Geoffrey was saying. Arjun and Howard had joined them too and I watched him, his friends surrounding him, Luke slapping him on the back.

'Loads.'

I was quiet on the journey back, mulling things over still, and distracted by the fact I needed to go over what I was doing the next day. The evening hadn't been a complete waste of time but I probably wouldn't be joining the next biannual whist meet.

It had been good to meet Margaret and we had swapped email addresses. I wanted to send her some links to websites and podcasts by inspiring women I thought she'd like. Subject heading: It's never too late for feminism.

Grandad had been a bit flustered as we were leaving. 'This wasn't really your crowd, was it? We shouldn't have started it like that. Howard did warn me. Keep the faith, Lottie,' he said, and the passion in his voice made me laugh and nod.

Luke seemed to have enjoyed himself but then he could slip easily into most settings. If there was a vague excuse to be competitive and drink at the same time he was pretty content.

'All right?' he said, watching me change into my pyjamas and then wearily stack papers and folders in a pile to take through to the living room.

'Fine.'

'It wasn't exactly the most romantic evening,' he said, easing the papers out of my hands and moving through to the living room with them.

'It was fine, not bad,' I said, like a 3-star Trip Advisor reviewer.

'It made me think, though,' he said, placing the folders and papers on the table. 'We should be doing more stuff together, shouldn't we? That was the best part of the night, being slightly bored at times but being slightly bored and able to share that with you.'

'So whistling not your thing?' I said, trying not to look twitchy at the amount of paper I needed to look at tonight.

'No, but I like this new project of your grandad's. Let's give it another go.'

I pulled out the chair ready to take a seat and start work. 'I'll ask him what's next.'

Luke dipped down and kissed my shoulder. 'Do. And don't work too late,' he said, with no real feeling, knowing full well he would be asleep long before I made it back to our bed.

I watched him leave the room with a small, sad smile. He was right. We did need to spend more time together. Otherwise what was the point of being together at all?

Darling Cora,

Are you cross that I have agreed to date women in return for ensuring Luke and Lottie do more things together? I've been imagining that look you can give me, that arch of your eyebrow that could always put the fear of God into me. Those times were few but memorable: after I told you it would be extravagant to double-glaze all the windows in the house; when I was so unwell on New Year's Eve I vomited in your window box, and when I sat you down and told you I wanted to retrain as a zookeeper. You know what you mean to me and it isn't about me meeting someone else, I couldn't meet someone else, there is no one else but I want to play along, I want to show willing so that Lottie continues to play along too. But I am aware I haven't really asked your permission. You won't start haunting me horribly or send down your mother to do it for you?

The scheme has been launched and Lottie and Luke were present and correct at the whist drive in the hall. You would have loved seeing them there surrounded by blue rinses and our friends. I'm not completely convinced it was the triumphant success I hoped it would be but when they left they seemed comfortable and happy, Luke giving me a discreet thumbs-up and Lottie grinning up at him. I do believe one of them let slip our little arrangement, as worryingly Paula sidled over to me at the end of the night and although she said she was just returning her glass to the table I wasn't completely sure she wasn't trying to grab my buttock. It was rather alarming.

Geoffrey was suitably hopeless and we lost, of course we did. Arjun seemed quieter than normal perhaps, a little less energy this evening. Perhaps he is coming down with something? He was cross with me for not taking the D3 tablets he foisted on us a year ago now. The bottle hadn't been opened. I know he misses you and I enjoy sharing stories about you with him. Howard is, of course, the same: brash and ever-present. He has been telling me all the gory details from his own dating life – that man really is reprehensible.

I've got an absurd list of ideas to try and you would boggle at what people have to do these days to meet somebody. And there are so many ways it can go awry! Have you heard of breadcrumbing? I won't go into it, it is too horrifying. Oh, Cora, I wish you were here to laugh and cuff me round the ear. How I miss being endlessly teased by you, how I miss sharing this space and all the stories with you. How I miss you.

Teddy

Chapter 10

Love is the seed from which happiness grows

SOPHIE, 86

Grandad had texted me an address in Wimbledon and a start time for our next mysterious event a few days later. I left chambers feeling nervy, anticipation swirling in my stomach. I wondered if Luke was feeling the same way. I imagined a candlelit restaurant, discreet waiters, the kind of place that gives you an impossibly small but completely delicious *amuse-bouche* on a large white dinner plate.

Or perhaps we were due to see a movie together, a silent film or something from back in the day? Curled up in an old-fashioned cinema, hands sneaking into each other's. Feeling the flutter of excitement as I pondered the options made me realise Luke and I rarely made plans to do anything together. We would go for an impromptu dinner or some drinks in a pub but we didn't schedule in evenings like this. I smoothed my skirt and applied a fresh coat of pale pink lipstick on the Tube, feeling pleased that for once I wasn't late.

I hadn't reckoned on Luke being late. He was almost as assiduous as Amy about punctuality, so it was with some surprise that I turned up at Wimbledon tube station to be greeted by a grovelling text message telling me he would meet me at the venue. My stomach grumbled as I walked past numerous restaurants, mouth-watering smells emerging every time the doors were opened. Following the line on my map I failed to notice the rain until I felt the drops trickling down my neck and under my jacket, and by then it was a downpour. Sheltering under a bus stop, hair frizzing, feeling damp and borderline starving, I felt my good mood quickly evaporate.

The venue turned out to be a room at the very top of a vegan café. Moving down the corridor past signs for henna tattoos, meditation retreats, cupping and more, I patted at my hair as I climbed up the stairs, images of the candlelit dinner fading in my mind. Peeking through the square of glass in the door I was heartened to see Grandad, Howard and Geoffrey all huddled in one corner by a trestle table filled with glasses and jugs of squash. I wondered where Arjun was. I wasn't used to seeing them as a threesome. Also Geoffrey looked pale and nervous, fiddling with the buttons on his coat, eyes flicking left to right as Howard and Grandad seemed immersed in conversation.

Frowning, I pushed open the door and headed their way before being intercepted by a lady with a blonde beehive, dressed in a turquoise tunic and wearing bright orange lipstick.

In a thick Eastern European accent she asked, 'You are new to class?'

Class? Images of vintage cinemas, shared popcorn or *amuse-bouche* melted in front of me.

I looked closely at the other tables lining the walls, now taking in the tubes of paint, the jam jars filled with paintbrushes, the wooden boards, boxes of charcoal and stacks of blank paper.

'Art,' I said aloud, thoughts of dinner now well and truly drained away. My stomach grumbled. If it was a still life it would be in danger of getting eaten.

'You have very good aura, creative soul,' the lady said, her nostrils flaring as if she was trying to suck my aura into her.

'Er, thank you.'

'Are you beginner or more advanced?'

'Oh, well, I did Art GCSE.' I shrugged, distracted by Howard who was crossing behind her. 'But I only got a C. I did a picture of a windmill, though. I thought it was quite good.'

'What is windmill?'

'Oh you know, a—' I started doing wild hand movements, the Beehive lady's eyes widening in alarm.

'I do not know it. You get pencil and sit in circle.'

'Right, okey doke, thanks so much.' I seem to have been transformed into a female Hugh Grant. I was relieved to see Grandad and his friends heading my way.

The Blonde Beehive nodded and moved off.

'So you've met Aleksandra,' Teddy said, indicating her back. 'Cora used to love her classes. She is very good at charcoals. We thought you and Luke might enjoy the experience, something to do together, something to talk about ... '

I looked at the strip lights overhead, the table of squash and plastic cups, then back at the three old men staring at me expectantly, and wondered how romantic this could be.

'And just pretend we're not here, we'll be quiet as mice,' Howard said in his booming voice.

I put my hands on my hips. 'I won't hold my breath.'

'What? We can do subtle,' Howard whispered.

'You're about as subtle as a red suit at a funeral,' Grandad told him.

'Where's Arjun?' I asked, looking around the room.

Geoffrey blushed red and Grandad and Howard started laughing. My face moved into a frown.

'He's, he's on his way,' Howard said, clapping me so hard on the back I stumbled forward.

Grandad was smirking at something and I narrowed my eyes at them and looked around the room. What was so funny? Then I was distracted as a tall, good-looking man blustering his apologies to the lady with the beehive appeared in the doorway: Luke had arrived.

She was clutching his upper arms as she spoke to him and I could see him gesturing to me with a nod of his head. She released him and he made his way over, the ghost of a smile on his face.

'Hey,' I said as he kissed me.

'Hey. That lady just told me I had a creative soul.' Luke puffed out his chest and I opened my mouth before snapping it shut again. I didn't want to deflate this happy man.

'So, an art class,' Luke said to Grandad, who shook his hand in greeting.

'You both go and get some materials and find a place to sit,' he said.

Luke was full of energy, jacket shrugged off, eyes firmly on the table with all the art materials. 'This is a great idea. I wonder what we're drawing? Maybe each other.' Luke turned to waggle both eyebrows at me.

'You're a geek,' I said, grinning as he leant in for a second kiss.

Howard gave me a thumbs-up as he moved away and I tried not to feel too self-conscious. People were settling in the large circle, easels in front of them, fixing paper to their wooden boards with masking tape. I turned back to Luke to suggest we got going and started at the new expression on his face. His eyes were bulging, and a rare blush was creeping up his neck and into his cheeks.

'What is it?' I frowned.

Luke's eyes started darting around the room as if they couldn't decide where to rest before choosing the floor as he mumbled, 'There's anakedarjun.'

'A snake?' I squealed, hand on my chest, ready to leap into his arms.

'No, anakedarjun,' he hissed and I waited, panting as the words sank in before turning slowly on the spot.

Ah.

A naked man.

A very naked old man.

A very naked old smiling man.

A very naked old smiling man who was waving at us.

Arjun.

'Christ,' I murmured, waving back uncertainly, unable to stop looking at Arjun's penis. I turned to Luke. 'That *is* Arjun and ... that's his cock.'

Luke's mouth twitched and I saw tears fill his eyes as he pressed his lips together.

In the corner, Howard, Geoffrey and Grandad were practically bursting with suppressed laughter, hands clutching their sides as they stared at us and back at Arjun.

'What is going on?' I said out of the corner of my mouth.

'I think this is Life Art,' Luke hazarded a guess. 'Or we really need to take Arjun to see somebody.'

Beehive Blonde Aleksandra started clapping in the middle of the circle. 'Welcome to today's session and we ready for great, great time,' she said, indicating Arjun. 'Arjun today model and we going to work on shadows. I come round and show you how, as am very good artist.'

Trying desperately hard to hold it together and act nonchalant, we collected up an easel, board, paper and charcoal box and moved to join the group.

Every now and again my eyes would flick to Geoffrey, who looked like he wished his narrow wooden chair would be swallowed by the floor; Howard, who was doing a terrible job of pretending he wasn't perpetually pissing himself, and my grandad, who seemed relaxed with the whole situation and kept nodding at me encouragingly.

The next hour was spent furiously charcoaling, trying to draw Arjun without actually looking at him, sort of like the sun on a hot day.

Aleksandra would appear behind us at intervals murmuring encouragements. 'Ah very good around the groin region, you might want to make bigger the pubic hair.' But there were moments when I forgot who Arjun was, and instead enjoyed shading the muscles in the legs and trying to make the sketch on the piece of paper resemble the person in front of me. Mostly, though, I loved watching Luke, fiercely competitive and creative, shading and sketching with precision. When he held up his pencil horizontally, tongue clamped between his teeth, I started to laugh.

'Whatcha doing?'

His tongue disappeared. 'I'm just working out the proportions.'

Satisfied, he returned to the page, and when I looked down I gasped. His picture was wonderful.

'I didn't know you could draw.'

'Lottie, I'm a graphic designer.'

'Well, yes, but . . . this is *really* artistic, you've totally captured the expression on his face, and he is all in proportion. My Arjun looks like a star in the next Hobbit franchise.' I pointed to the stubby legs on my paper and then focused back on Luke's. He looked bashful as I continued, 'Honestly, that is brilliant, you should do more of this.'

Finally the hour and a half was up and Arjun was given a towel to wrap around himself as we all packed our materials away.

Grandad headed over, a tentative look on his face. 'Have you enjoyed yourselves?'

Luke was flushed with pleasure as the men gathered round to compliment his art skills. Trying to detract from himself he encouraged them all to show us their sketches.

Geoffrey hadn't brought his glasses. 'A sort of relief really,' he said cheerfully, holding up his picture, which looked like a Ken doll.

'Where's his . . . you know?' Luke said.

Geoffrey shrugged. 'Couldn't see it.'

Howard had drawn a penguin. It was pretty good. He'd found the time to sketch a dramatic backdrop of ice and mountains too.

'Why the penguin, Howard? Is that a surrealist take on the evening?'

Howard shook his head. 'No, no, it's just I can only really draw penguins so I gave up on Arjun early on. He was that penguin,' he said, pointing to a small penguin near an iceberg.

Packing up to leave I rolled my picture into a tube container that Luke had been given by Aleksandra, who was now gushing and discussing chiaroscuro with him, her pencilled eyes animated as she touched him on the arm.

'A talent, a talent,' she cooed as she passed me, stopping

to simply nod at my Hobbit-Arjun. 'It will come,' she said briskly.

I rolled my eyes at Luke, who seemed to have grown two inches taller in the last couple of hours. He threw an arm around my shoulders and kissed the top of my hair.

'Shall we head off? Thanks, Teddy, for organising it.'

Grandad gave me a hug. 'Well done, Lottie darling. You survived.'

I laughed. 'Just about, although a little warning might have been nice.'

'Well, I hope you enjoyed it. We thought you should do more together. These days it's all rushed TV dinners and Netflix and Chill.'

My eyes practically popped out of my skull. 'Grandad, do you know what Netflix . . . actually, don't answer that.'

'We were thinking of things you and Luke could share, do together. Grandma brought me along once. It was water-colours. We painted the Seine.'

'That might have been better, Grandad,' I said, imagining sketching the Eiffel Tower rather than Arjun's appendage.

'All I remember from that class is sitting beside her creating something, and her laughing at my terrible attempts. And Arjun is always keen to get us to come along to one of these classes so we thought, why not?'

'I can think of one good reason.'

'Oh, Arjun loves to get naked. He is always stripping down in the golfing changing rooms. We've become very used to it.'

Another insight into my grandad's life.

'And this way he can supplement his income: his pension is pathetic.'

We finally managed to escape and I enjoyed the feel of Luke's hand in mine as we walked down the street, the lights reflected on the wet pavement, cars and buses moving by, other couples and groups out for dinner, chat from restaurants, live music coming from the inside of a nearby bar, the smell of onions and petrol clashing in the air.

'I'm not in the mood to go home quite yet,' Luke said, squeezing my hand, the other holding a bag with our pictures rolled up. 'Let me treat you to dinner.'

My stomach rumbled, coupled with a momentary panic about the work mounting up, the things I had to do. Then I thought of our evening together. Grandad had been right, it had been nice to share it with Luke. I pushed all other thoughts away as I leaned in towards him. 'That sounds perfect.'

Chapter 11

Love is thinking you know someone
well and them still surprising you

PEG, 88

I slid the shower doors open.

'Sooooo, what's the surprise?'

'Oh my God, Lottie.' A naked Luke looked out at me, the shower steaming up the mirror as he pushed back his slick hair. 'For the eighteenth time, you'll have to wait and see.'

Water was sprayed in my face before I giggled and turned away. I felt giddy with it. The whole day stretching ahead, Luke being all mysterious. Recently I had started to crave these days: our times together. We had been on a wonderful treasure hunt in Hyde Park, an evening at the ballet, a champagne-fuelled picnic that had ended in the pub when it started to rain. This morning he had woken me up early despite it being a Saturday and told me to get ready for a surprise. I had been badgering him about it every minute since.

'What should I wear?'

'Actually your grandad told me to give you something. Hold on.'

I waited in my matching lemon yellow bra and pants as Luke moved across to our shared wardrobe and pulled out a plastic clothes cover.

'Here you go. Shoes are at your discretion. Also I like your pants.' He slapped me on the bottom and I felt the sudden urge to kiss him.

Instead I unzipped the cover and pulled out a mustard yellow tea dress, pale pink roses printed on the fabric, one of the dresses I had commented on that day at Grandad's when we had been clearing out Grandma's clothes.

'Oh, he kept on to it,' I said, holding it up.

'That's a pretty dress.' Luke looked up from the chest of drawers.

'It was Grandma's.' I felt a lump in my throat as I carefully pulled the dress down over my head, wiggling into the sleeves. It fitted perfectly: the waist cinched in a flattering away, the skirt skimmed my hips, the right mid-thigh length.

'Could you?' I indicated the back of the dress, twelve carefully sewn buttons leading to a V-neck back.

'You look *hot*,' Luke confirmed, coming over to button up the dress and staring at me in the mirror, his arms circling my waist for a second as he dropped a kiss on my shoulder.

I felt a warmth flood through me as I looked at our reflection. 'So ... what's the surprise?'

Luke pushed me gently away, 'Nice try. You thought I'd be all blinded by your beauty and reveal all but I'm too clever for you, Lottie Campbell. I am wise to your games ... and also I need to get dressed too now.'

He turned and stepped into his trousers, before buttoning up a pale blue cotton shirt, rolling the sleeves up to his elbows. I sat at the dressing table applying blusher and eyeshadow, enjoying blending the pinks and browns to complement the dress. It had been ages since I had taken time to do my face and I was enjoying it. With a last flick of mascara I stared back at myself, my cheeks flushed, the shadows under my eyes gone, my hair newly washed, fringe combed.

There was a horn going outside, on and off, over and over, shattering my preening. Luke had disappeared into the living room. Moments later he called my name.

'Your surprise is here!'

I raced over to join Luke at the window and stared out into the street where I saw Howard in a convertible, tooting repeatedly on his horn.

'Howard? Howard is my surprise?'

'Yes,' Luke said, turning to me with a solemn expression. 'I thought our relationship wasn't really going anywhere and you would be happier with Howard, more a man of the world ... *Of course* not Howard, you weirdo.' He turned back to the window and jabbed the glass. 'The car – the amazing vintage sports car that Howard stores in his garage for most of the year and he has loaned us for the day. Lottie Campbell, we are heading to the countryside.'

His face was animated, his grin wide as he grabbed my hand and pulled me towards the door, Howard still leaning on the horn outside.

'But you don't know how to drive,' I stuttered, scooping up my handbag.

'But you do,' Luke said, bundling me out of the door. 'Do you have everything you need? Sunglasses, mobile and maybe one of those neck-tie things ladies wear in convertibles? Like Audrey Hepburn in *Roman Holiday*?'

'You know if I wear a necktie I won't magically turn into Audrey Hepburn.'

'Look, the necktie would be a start,' he said, laughing as I pushed him. 'Seriously, you look amazing. Now let's *gooooo*.'

Buoyed by his enthusiasm I followed him out of the flat and down the stairs into the street. It was early and the pavement was almost deserted, the weak morning sunlight just lighting the roofs of the houses, the sky above us as pale blue as the shirt Luke was wearing.

Howard handed the keys to me, walking around the car to point out some of the features. 'When you start her up she might chunter a little but that's totally normal, and don't press too hard on the clutch. She's a sensitive beast and you don't need to pump her as if she were a common or garden Astra. And when you change gear try not to force things, be smooth, and remember—'

'Actually, Howard, I thought I'd let Luke drive,' I said, one hand circling Luke's waist.

Howard's chin quivered. 'But he doesn't have a licence!'

'So what better way for him to learn!'

Howard was pulling on his tie, a panicked look back at Grandad, who had appeared in his car to take Howard back. 'Oh, well, maybe, perhaps I wouldn't, well, you know, she's probably, um—'

'Joke! Ha, your face,' I said. 'Don't worry, Howard. Luke is a complete imbecile, I wouldn't let him near the wheel.'

'Oh!' Howard let out a bark of laughter. 'Christ, you had me there. Very good, very good.'

'I can't even be trusted with a bicycle,' Luke said cheerily, running round to throw himself into the passenger seat. 'I once chipped my tooth falling off a scooter.'

Grandad had started beeping his car. 'Well, I must go but Luke tells me you'll return her later, and of course I trust you,' Howard said in a deeply untrusting voice. 'So, enjoy the day.' He put a hand on the side panel of the bonnet. 'Go slow, no need for excessive speed, take in the weather and—'

More beeping from Grandad.

'Best be off then,' Howard said, one finger still making contact with the car until he heaved himself away.

'Road trip,' Luke said, pointing both hands forward.

'Great.' I got into the car, readjusting the driving mirror and tightening the knot in my neck tie. Looking sideways at Luke I placed the key in the ignition. 'So, Thelma – where to?'

Luke had booked us a pub lunch on the river in a small village in Hertfordshire. The drive was wonderful. We took the A roads and felt the sun streaming above us, the wind lifting our hair, swirling around us in the car as the radio played and we sang along unashamedly. It seemed for that journey as though nothing else in the world existed, just two people heading through the countryside, trees meeting in speckled canopies over our heads. We couldn't really talk, could only hear the roar of the wind in our ears and feel the warmth of the sun on our skin.

As we turned into the small pub car park and switched off the engine, we sat in silence for a second, noises heightened: the cheeping from the trees, the distant bleating of lambs in a field, the chatter of insects in the verge.

'It's lovely,' I said, staring up at the thatched public house, an enormous pub garden stretched along one side with a view over the hills, most of the picnic tables free.

'Only the best for you, your majesty,' Luke announced, stepping out of the passenger seat and coming round to open the driver's door.

I took his hand, letting him pull me into a hug, both hands round my waist, my head resting against his chest. 'Thank you for finding it, and arranging the car: it's already a brilliant surprise.'

We ordered drinks, two gin and tonics in honour of the absent Gin o'Clock Club, and headed out into the pub garden with two menus. The garden sloped down towards the narrow road, hedgerows high on either side casting shadows, a few houses and a wood beyond. The sun was warm on my back and I breathed in the scent of freshly mown grass. We ordered our food, sharing a wooden platter filled with different meats, a wicker basket of fresh bread, small bowls of olives dripping in oil. By the end of it all I was licking my fingers, soaking up the last of the oil with the final piece of bread. Luke was smiling at me indulgently.

'What?' I said through the final mouthful.

'You're a delight,' he said, squeezing my knee. 'And also you have some kind of herb in your teeth.'

He stood up, holding out his hand for me. 'Walk?'

'What's in it for me?'

'Er . . . my company?'

I paused, tilting my head to feel the sun on my face. 'Hmm.'

'Blackberries?'

I stood up immediately, Luke crossing a hand over his heart. 'That hurts.'

'A girl's gotta have pudding.'

'Full disclosure,' he said, 'I'm not absolutely sure it's the right time but we can have fun looking!'

Twenty minutes later, with not a blackberry bush in sight, we found ourselves meandering through the village, heading for the shade of the wood behind. The day had heated up and the sun was slicing lines across the road ahead, highlighting cheerful window boxes crammed with bright pink, red and purple flowers, wooden doorways, thatched roofs, and bouncing off the glass of casement windows. Someone was mowing their lawn, the familiar hum of the motor reminding me of afternoons at Grandad's watching him move slowly up and down the grass, the strips neat and lush.

A sudden movement caught my eye and I turned my head to see something streak across the road. The movement was jerky and unfamiliar, a squawk making me startle. Luke raised an eyebrow. 'Did you just see a chicken? A chicken that crossed the road?'

I nodded. 'I did.'

Then there was a gentle cluck and more movement and two more chickens appeared, following in the wake of the first one.

'What's going on? Is this a country thing? Who owns these chickens?'

'They're free range,' Luke said, shrugging and laughing.

I gave him my most scathing look.

The three chickens had congregated in the shade of the house opposite. One ginger chicken pecked at the dusty pavement and two others, both small and white like balls of cotton wool with beaks, strutted back and forward as if on a chicken catwalk.

Luke lingered. 'Do you think we should help them?'

I looked at him. 'Help them how? Offer them directions? Give them a lift back to London?'

'Not sure,' Luke said, biting his lip.

A red-faced old lady, cardigan on inside out, appeared in an alley opposite, bent over a walking stick. She pointed the stick at the chickens. 'Bastards,' she hollered.

Luke and I both jumped.

She shook her stick at us. 'Catch them then!' The chickens, having heard the profanity, had set off in different directions.

Luke and I responded to the order as if she were our headmistress, immediately chasing after the chickens, which only made them run faster, their scrawny legs furiously pedalling them away from our clutches.

'Jesus,' I said, leaning over and clutching my side, feeling beads of sweat meet on my brow, 'chickens are fast.'

Luke had backed one of the cotton-wool ones into a corner and it was trying to squeeze itself behind a large stone pot full of carnations.

He dived forward, there was a flapping noise, and he emerged, hair askew, cotton-wool chicken clamped under one arm.

More confident now, he approached the ginger one, who decided to play ball and sank low on her knees as if waiting for Luke to simply scoop her up, which he did.

'You've got two chickens,' I said, watching him manage to keep a handle on both.

Luke motioned with his head at the last cotton-wool one. 'Just get round behind it and head it back over the road towards the woman.'

'Bravo, bravo,' the old lady was saying as Luke approached her with the fugitives. 'It's the second gate on the right. If you could just pop them there, I'll be along.'

The last chicken, sensing her friends were no longer

roaming free, clearly decided she wanted to return home too. With little effort from me she trotted down the alley behind Luke, streaking into the gate before he closed it on all of them.

I caught up with the woman. 'You can both come inside now,' she said, her tone imperious so there was little hope of us refusing.

We ambled through the lady's garden. Stones sunk into the grass made a path to her back door.

'Come inside, inside. I always have a whiskey after four o'clock. You're in time.'

She disappeared into her kitchen and Luke raised an eyebrow at me. 'Is this how we die?' he whispered.

'Ssh!' I swallowed a giggle. He shrugged and followed her inside, ducking his head as he did so.

Her galley kitchen was long and narrow and the old lady was placing tumblers on a tray.

'In there,' she said, indicating the dining room through an arch.

I nodded, feeling the whole day had taken on quite a surreal turn. The low-ceilinged room, one wall covered with a large dresser, every other wall covered in ornamental plates of horsey scenes, smelt of cigarette smoke. I pulled out a wooden chair, its cushioned seat faded pink, the pattern long since worn away. Luke winked at me as he sat down opposite. I could tell he was enjoying the strange twist, beaming at the woman as she appeared in the doorway clutching her tray, refusing his help as he hopped back up to his feet.

'Pff,' she said, placing it down, the brown liquid sloshing. 'Whiskey.' She pushed the glass across to me.

My hand hovered for a second, aware I was driving back but keen not to appear rude I picked up the tumbler. 'Thanks,' I said taking the tiniest sip, wincing as the liquid burnt my throat.

Luke accepted his glass. 'You're my kind of woman.'

She shot him a look. Clearly rescuing her chickens was one thing but this over-familiarity quite another.

She sat at the head of the table and methodically sipped at her glass. Then, when she finished, after furnishing us with a few choice details (silky hens, her name was Peggy, the ginger chicken was so old she should be dead, neighbours hate the noise, they haven't attracted rats in years, those rumours are false) we were evicted as swiftly as we had been invited inside.

She waved us off at the back door and we made our way down the stone path, careful to close the gate. The three chickens gave us baleful glances as we passed. Then, turning the corner back down the alley, we collapsed in giggles on the side wall.

'Very weird,' Luke said, rubbing his eyes. 'Pub?'

I nodded, 'Definitely.'

Returning to the pub we found the same table as before, freshly wiped down as we placed our drinks on it. We watched the birds overhead, Luke beside me, one hand on my thigh, the blue sky streaked with aeroplane trails. Someone was barbecuing somewhere nearby, determined to make the most of the summer, the charcoal smell wafting our way.

'I could stay here for ever,' I said.

'That's good' – I could feel his mouth move into a grin in my hair – 'because I booked us a room.'

I leaned back, staring at him incredulously. 'Seriously?'

'Come and look.' He stood up and gestured with his hand and we walked back across the pub garden and into the car park. Luke opened the boot. 'Ta da!' He revealed a suitcase inside. 'I even remembered to pack your washbag with the scary unicorn on it.'

'Luke Winters, how did you know I'd agree to spend the night with you?'

'You look the easy type,' he said, shrugging his shoulders and making me snort unattractively. 'So now you can join me in a bottle of wine and some dinner.'

'Definitely.' I grinned. 'Although it seems a shame to go inside,' I said, the temperature just starting to drop as I wrapped my arms around myself.

'I thought of that too,' Luke said, pulling out two blankets he had stored in the boot.

'What else have you got in there?' I asked with a laugh, on tiptoes.

Luke closed the boot, turned to me, deadpanned: 'Just the body of my first girlfriend. Sooooooo, wine!'

'I feel someone might have had enough to drink already,' I giggled, tucking my arm into his and returning to the table we had sat at earlier, enjoying being wrapped in a thick blanket as the sun set and the tea lights and lanterns were lit all around us.

We stayed out for hours eating and drinking, Luke scooting behind me when the temperature dipped, wrapping us both in the blanket so we could stay outside a little longer. With his arms around me we talked about nothing, stifling yawns, taking occasional sips of our drinks. The bar had long since closed and all we had to do was head back to our bedroom.

'How did you find out about this place?' I said, leaning back into his body, enjoying the smell of him, faint hint of aftershave and fresh air.

I felt a stiffening around me as Luke rested his head on my shoulder. 'My mum and I stopped off here once,' he said, 'on the way back from one of her friend's houses.'

Luke didn't speak about his parents a lot. I knew they had been a close family, travelling together when Luke was a teen, camping in Wales and France, trips to Scotland, a road trip through Europe. Photo albums were cluttered with pictures from these places: Luke as a toothy child, then a gangly, awkward teen, always in the middle of his parents, their arms casually around his waist or shoulders: unselfconscious and content.

When I first met him he had been reeling from the sudden death of his father from a heart attack, and then cruelly, a year into our relationship, his mother had been diagnosed with cancer. She died less than six weeks later. Sometimes it was easy to assume his grief had faded with time but then

I would catch him sometimes staring out at something, not focusing, and recognise the expression: that he was somewhere in the past when they had both been there with him.

I didn't say anything, simply twisted a little and wrapped my arms around his neck, resting my forehead against his. I could feel his breath on my face and he brushed my lips with his.

'Let's go upstairs now,' he said, his meaning clear.

Whispered giggles as we navigated our way up the crooked wooden staircase, Luke narrowly missing cracking his head on a beam. We made it to our room, an upholstered armchair in the corner, a patterned rug, the glow of the bedside lamp and the bed immaculate, crisp white sheets and a small round mint left on each pillow. We left the small window open, the silhouette of the fields and treeline beyond, the sky spattered with a thousand stars, the moonlight streaking our bed. Luke tucked me into his arms and as we lay there together I felt his chest rise and fall beneath me. Everything slow and easy. It felt as if we were somewhere other-worldy for the night, and my eyes drooped.

We barely spoke over breakfast the next morning, the poached eggs runny and delicious, the bacon crispy. Enjoying the silence we meandered down the footpaths through the woods and fields, holding hands, listening to the chatter of insects, the dappled pathways smelling earthy and rich, gradually turning back, past streams where we played half-hearted games of Pooh sticks before knowing we had to head home.

Sliding into the driving seat, I glanced back at the old stone cottage, the weathered sign outside, the garden of the pub, empty now. I was glad to be wearing my sunglasses, feeling a sudden lump in my throat. Biting my lip I tied my hair back in a ponytail, blinked and placed the key in the ignition. Silly to feel emotional.

We'd been gone twenty-four hours but the time had seemed to stretch on and on as if I'd returned from a spa break or a week in the sun. I felt refreshed and energetic as I moved the car back through the lanes, sneaking glances at Luke leaning back in his seat, sunglasses on. Arriving back into London, carefully returning the car to Howard, petrol tank full by way of thanks.

'Did you have a fabulous time?' Howard asked as I handed him the keys.

I looked back at Luke, who was busying himself with our bags, his hair ruffled, his whole demeanour relaxed, and felt a wide grin crack my face open. 'The best,' I said. 'Just the best.'

Darling Cora,

I am pleased to report Lottie and Luke seem to have returned refreshed and reinvigorated from a wonderful weekend away together. They drove to the countryside in Howard's soft top so although they had a lovely time, I had a whole weekend of Howard fretting over the continued well-being of his precious car. It was, of course, returned without a scratch on it: that man really does love that vehicle more than any human being.

I'm pleased with the progress we've made with Lottie and Luke: this scheme has been rather successful thus far. Arjun had informed us that he would be doing a few weeks' work as a life model and we couldn't resist heading over to see him 'in action', so to speak. Luke in particular really seemed to enjoy the night and it was fabulous to see them leave together laughing. Then we sent them on a treasure hunt of Hyde Park – Geoffrey drew an illustrated map for them, must have taken the man days. They went on a picnic. Howard put three bottles of champagne into the basket and even then didn't think it would be enough.

I have laughed over this summer more than I thought possible: it's a joy to see them brought closer with each date. Arjun seems a little more himself at the moment so perhaps I was wrong to assume he might be battling some bug or have something on his mind. He claims he does all these extra-curricular things to supplement his pension but we all know it's to fund the golf trips and the bottles of vitamins. Oh, and Howard benefitted from the Life Art evening as Cindy saw his completed penguins picture and wants to commission him (she says penguins are 'majestic creatures' and collects lots of porcelain ones, so many that Howard described sitting in her front room as 'rather intimidating: eyes everywhere').

Despite all of these things I have had a few low days recently. I try not to be too melancholy but there are times when I just want to be stubborn, stay in my pyjamas and mourn you. Geoffrey has been very understanding, quietly coming over to sit with me. He brings crosswords and makes tea and doesn't say a great deal. I'm grateful to him for noticing. He knows grief, of course. It makes me a little ashamed I haven't asked more about his wife in the past, always assuming it would be too painful or awkward – what a coward I am. He obviously loved her in the same way. We have been so lucky, although you both leave these hideous holes behind.

Still, today I woke and dressed and was able to forget. As you know, I have had to dip my toes into the world of modern dating in a vain attempt to show Lottie I am making an effort to 'get out there'. She says I am way behind on my side of the bargain and I suppose she is right. I imagine she thinks all my loneliness can be fixed over dinners with a good woman but of course I am not lonely for company, just lonely for you, my darling.

All the same, you'll be irritated to learn that I have been swapping messages with a woman on Tinder and I actually think you'd rather like her (don't scoff). She plays golf, although was coy about her handicap, regularly attends the theatre (Twelfth Night is her favourite Shakespeare and I am sure you enjoyed that one too, with the man in the yellow socks, or was that The Tempest?) and she told me that she used to play the clarinet in an orchestra and you always did like woodwind. After a string of back and forward we arranged to meet and today was the big day! My first Tinder date!

I booked a table in a nearby Nando's establishment

because I was informed by the internet that it is a popular venue for the young and I wanted to do this right: date like the youth. Although I did take her a copy of Twelfth Night, which I'm not entirely sure is the done thing nowadays – but it would be wrong to turn up empty-handed, surely? I have to admit to feeling rather nervous as I sat nursing a half pint of beer, staring at the door. I had forgotten all the dreadful angst in those early days of not knowing someone. It's appalling. And even though I knew it wasn't a real date, all those memories of waiting in establishments wondering if they'll appear came flooding back as if it were fifty years ago and I was still that tongue-tied young man. Thank goodness you saved me from a lifetime of that, my love.

The time ticked by and the waiters started to loiter a little and – there is no other way to tell you this, Cora – she simply didn't show up. And when I messaged her she didn't reply, she just left my message in the ether. Lottie had shown me when the blue ticks appear someone has read the message, so she just didn't think it worth an answer. I didn't really know what to do so I read a chapter of Twelfth Night to buy a little more time and left a tip for the two half pints of beer.

Howard says I've been ghosted. I had to look up the term online as our edition of the Oxford English Dictionary is from 1991. It means that this woman ended our personal relationship suddenly, and without explanation, withdrawing all communication. 'It happens,' Howard told me, but then he laughed. He said he does it to women but has never been ghosted himself. What am I meant to think, Cora? That she turned up at the Nando's, took one look at me and left? I had made a real effort. I was wearing the checked shirt that you always said made me look very like Robert Redford and the jacket that you once told me seemed perfectly tailored to my shape. It rather stings.

The boiler is leaking again tonight and I've put that disgusting blue glass bowl underneath it and I laugh because you always hoped it would break. That bloody bowl has outlived you. Now it's the most precious thing, letting me recall your laughing voice as you complained about its ugly pattern.

I am going to bed now, and how I wish you were here about to lie down next to me.

Teddy x

Chapter 12

Love is finding a woman who makes
you want to switch off the sport
on the television and engage

GORDON, 83

I had finished for the day, leaving chambers early. For once the brief I was working on seemed manageable and I had time the next day to work on it as I wasn't due in court. The sky was blue, the sun disappearing briefly behind another high-rise building as I moved down the streets, a light breeze lifting my hair. The pavements were barely populated and I found myself browsing in bookshops, picking up titles and feeling a sliver of hope that I might have time to read them, remembering weekends in the past curled up on a rug in the park, head resting on Luke's stomach as we both got lost in a book. The weekend away with him had reminded me that there were other things in my life besides work, and that I had forgotten that in the last year or so.

Thinking about him made me smile and I glanced at my watch. I could head to his office in Pimlico and see if he was free to leave. We could head to the South Bank, sit watching the boats idle along the Thames, listen to the buskers and street entertainers, stay out and eat as the sun set over the water. We had spent so many evenings like that in the past and I felt the urge to relive one. He had arranged our weekend away – this could be a small way to do something spontaneous too. It wasn't old-fashioned but gin would be involved.

Stepping into the subway I headed for the Tube. Normally the stifling air, the bodies pressed near me, the squeal of the wheels on the tracks would set my teeth on edge, sweat breaking out on my hairline as I cursed someone nearby and waited for the ordeal to be over. Today, though, I simply stood near the doors, opened the book I had just bought and lost myself in the words.

Pimlico was looking as lovely as ever, soaring Regency homes glowing creamy pink in the late afternoon sunshine, dog walkers milling through the lush green squares as I ambled towards Luke's office building.

Mike, Luke's boss, was just leaving as I arrived. 'Lottie, so good to see you, you look well. Here to see Luke?'

'Yes, if that's OK?'

He waved a hand. 'Of course it is. He could do with taking a break; he works too hard. Going to celebrate his new role?'

I plastered a smile on my face and nodded, feeling a

stinging shame start somewhere in my stomach. What new role? Was it a promotion? What was going on? 'Yes, it's great,' I said, hoping I wouldn't have to keep up the charade for too long.

I bit my lip as I stepped inside the building. Why hadn't Luke told me? I barely noticed the security guard who signed me in, my hand wavering over the visitors' book, not sure now whether I should head up to see Luke or not. Would he want to see me? What else was going on in his life that he didn't share? Did he think I wouldn't care? Scrawling my name and the time of arrival in a daze I drifted towards the lift.

As it pinged open I stood for a second, still unsure, wishing now I had just headed home, my earlier idea of a stroll along the South Bank fading. Then something urged me inside and I automatically pressed the button for Luke's floor. In no time the lift door slid back and I saw the open-plan office in front of me, people busy at desks or computers, large whiteboards plastered with drawings and sheets of paper along many of the walls, the odd framed picture or poster. I recognised one of the ad campaigns Luke had worked on – he'd been nominated for an award for it. He'd been so proud.

What new role?

Glancing across at his desk I noticed two heads bent over a large A3 sheet. Luke was talking animatedly, tapping a pen at various points on the page. I could make out a storyboard, his face lit with passion as he described his vision. The other was nodding quickly, her red hair smooth, the overhead lights reflecting off it every time her head bobbed up and down. Storm. A light laugh filled the air and I froze near the desk as she reached out a hand and placed it on his upper arm.

I hoped next time Storm went for a manicure the nail varnish on one of her thumbs chipped within thirty seconds.

Luke hadn't noticed me there. I could turn and leave. It was just as I had that thought that he looked up.

'Lottie,' he said, his face breaking into an easy smile as he stood up. Then the expression changed, his forehead creasing. 'Is everything OK? Is Teddy all right?'

'Oh, yes, no, everything's fine,' I said, feeling like an idiot as I licked my lips, sensing people staring up at me. 'I got out a little earlier than expected. I was thinking we could head somewhere, if you fancied it, but' – I found my voice hardening, aware of Storm standing so close to him – 'you're obviously busy and I didn't—'

I hoped the next time Storm paid with her Boots reward card she was a few pence short for what she needed and had to put one of the items back.

'No, I'm not.' Luke waved a hand. 'We should head to the South Bank. Perfect. I was showing Storm the mock-up I've just finished. Come and look,' he said, walking towards me and holding out his hand, pulling me towards his desk.

Only I noticed Storm's eyes dart to our hands, her mouth move into a thin line as she wavered at the desk, clearly not wanting to leave just yet. I wondered briefly if Luke had told Storm about the new role.

Luke watched my face as he talked me through the

storyboard, one hand on my lower back, tapping at the paper with his other hand. His voice was infused with energy as he pointed out the details and I found myself forgetting everything else, forgetting even Storm being there as I enjoyed listening to him gush. I'd forgotten how much he really loved his work.

'Isn't it just awesome?' Storm said, flicking her hair behind her. 'Luke is insane on Photoshop. Insane.'

I nodded, barely glancing at her, taking in the stunning final image, gratified to see Luke standing expectantly, waiting for me to say something.

'So,' he said, running a hand through his hair, his nerves making me melt a little, 'what do you think?'

I loved that he really cared what I thought. Me, with not one creative bone in my body. I loved that Storm was listening to this.

'I think,' I said, leaning up to kiss him long and hard, 'it's going to be brilliant.'

He pulled me into his side. 'Thank you.'

I hoped tonight he might share some of his news with me, I wanted to celebrate his successes at work. I thought back to the casual way in which Mike had mentioned a new role. I must show more interest.

'Well, thanks sooooo much for showing it to me,' Storm said to Luke, pushing herself off the edge of the desk. 'I can't wait to see the final draft. Deffo.'

'Thanks, Storm,' Luke said, already turning to pack up the things on his desk.

Storm hesitated a moment, perhaps wondering if there'd be more. I felt a small glimmer of triumph as Luke looked up at me. 'Right, where do you want to go? Southbank Centre?' he said, adjusting his bag on his shoulder. 'Sundowners there while we make a plan, see what's on?'

He was still talking to me as we moved past Storm towards the lift, as she called out, 'Well, bye then.'

As Luke waved distractedly behind him, asking me about my day, about my case. As I made him laugh.

The lift doors shut, her face still staring over at us, eyebrows drawn together in a small frown.

I met her eyes. Haha. Storm: 0. Lottie: 1.

The river was choppy and steel grey, as we walked hand in hand over Lambeth Bridge, the sun disappearing momentarily in the clouds. I loved the Thames, pleasure boats and working boats moving through the water, the London Eye glinting ahead of us, the intricate architecture of the Houses of Parliament opposite. I always felt that we were at the heart of everything. So many people clustered together, walking, in cars, on phones, street performers, shoppers, sitting outside restaurants, heading to the theatre. Luke clearly felt the same, enjoying the meandering pace of our walk, stopping to run his hands along the vinyl records and books under Hungerford Bridge. After a short while we found ourselves heading up the steps to the Southbank Centre, able to find a table on the terrace looking across the river, the pedestrians moving below.

'Perfect,' Luke said, taking both our bags and dumping them on the spare seat.

'My treat,' I said, leaping away so he didn't have time to argue.

I returned with two glasses clinking with ice and lime.

Luke was sitting at the table looking out over the water, his phone nowhere in sight, just staring and looking relaxed. I needed to take a leaf out of his book. I was always too busy tapping on my phone or flicking through the paper or a brief to really sit still and be in the moment. Luke had always moved at a more languid pace and I could see now that this was one of the things that had drawn me to him.

'Gin?'

'Of course,' I said, passing one to him. 'It's got thyme in it!'

'All right then.'

'So,' I said, after a moment, 'is everything good? At work, I mean . . .'

Luke frowned at me. 'Yes, Lottie.'

'Great,' I said in a faux bright voice.

This would surely be the perfect moment for him to tell me about his new role. He must be proud if Mike had promoted him. I picked up my glass, spilling a little liquid down my chin, my eyes wide, expectant: I was ready for the big reveal.

'Any big case coming up?' Luke asked.

'No, so, youooooo,' I said, placing the glass back on the table so I could lean forward. 'Good, good, as in something, anything, different happening, with work?'

Luke's eyebrows drew together. He rubbed one hand along his chin. 'Not especially. Well, the campaign I showed you earlier, that should take up some time, and Mike's pleased with the progress, he's wanted to work with them for ages.'

'Really,' I said in a slightly too-loud voice, 'so he must be so happy, happy enough to, you know . . . reward you.'

Luke started to look increasingly confused, 'Are you all right, Lottie?'

My shoulders drooped, this wasn't getting me anywhere. Clearly I was being too cryptic. 'Yes,' I muttered. 'Just thought you might tell me about your new role.'

'What, you mean becoming a senior designer?'

'Are you? That's *fabulous*.' A couple passing both jumped at my exuberance.

Luke, however, simply continued to look confused. 'Yes, you remember, I told you last week.'

'You didn't—' Then I saw his face. 'You did. You . . . did! You just didn't stress the . . . the importance . . . of the new role.' I was floundering and Luke could sense it.

'You didn't remember, did you?'

I wanted to lie. I wanted to say of course I remembered. I wanted to not be that shit girlfriend, but as I looked at his open face, his trusting eyes, I couldn't do it. Shaking my head miserably from side to side I stared at the water rings on the surface of the table.

'Hey,' Luke said, 'that's OK, Lottie, it's no big deal, not exactly the Nobel Prize or anything. It's not like I've made art director . . . yet.'

I shook my head more fervently now, looking back at him. 'No, it *is* important and I'm sorry, God, I obviously wasn't paying any attention when you told me. It *is* great, and I *am* proud of you. I know you want to get on in the company and they clearly adore you—'

Luke raised one hand, his cheeks flushed, a row of teeth sparkling as he smiled at me. 'Enough, enough, it's fine, honestly, Lottie, it's fine.'

I reached across and took his hand, cold from the glass. 'It's not fine. And I really am proud. And I'm sorry I'm only saying this now.'

Luke's expression was priceless, a sort of happy, embarrassed, self-conscious grimace at me, a swipe through his hair. 'My round, I think.'

'No, absolutely not, you stay sitting here, I'm getting them,' I said, standing up.

Luke laughed at my enthusiasm. 'You really don't have to.'

'I have to be a bit less shit, don't I? Let me at least wait on you hand and foot tonight.'

Luke shrugged and settled back in his chair, both hands up in surrender as I headed back to the bar, unable to resist turning back to look at him, a grin on my face. He returned my smile and I felt happiness flood through me, suddenly aware that it had been a long time since I had prioritised Luke and grateful that I had noticed now and could fix things.

Chapter 13

Love is . . . rather nice

ERNEST, 91

Luke had offered to come with me but I'd said no. It was great to feel so close to him again. I hadn't realised how much I had missed his company recently, just bustling from work to Grandad to home with barely any time to stop and relax. Today, though, I wanted to go alone, to do this just with Grandad.

I felt nervous as I tied my hair into a loose plait and smoothed at the cream dress I had chosen to wear. Luke moved behind me, circling me in his arms and resting his chin on the top of my head. Our eyes met in the mirror and I swallowed down the lump that was building in my throat.

'I better go,' I said, leaning back into him for a moment before pulling away.

He kissed me goodbye. 'Call me if you need me, I'll come straight over. I'm not doing anything much.'

I knew he had arranged to see Adam, his best friend, for a catch-up, knew how much he was looking forward to it.

'Thank you.' The lump was back.

Grandad had dressed up too, his grey hair combed, wearing the yellow cashmere jumper Grandma had always loved on him and a pair of chinos.

'You look beautiful, Lottie,' he said, kissing me on the cheek.

It would be just us today. Dad had tried to get a flight over for the funeral but hadn't managed to get out of a conference he was speaking at. Mum and Dad had both been over a few months before Grandma died, a tearful visit reminiscing about family holidays, favourite anecdotes, teasing: reminding her how much she was loved. It had felt like their goodbye at the time. So today it was me and Grandad, still something neither of us were used to. Grandma had always been at the centre of our small family. It felt as if we needed to channel her strength today.

'I made tea and we can toast muffins. I know you like them.'

His voice sounded bright and I wanted to give him another hug for it. I knew how hard he would be finding today.

I moved into the kitchen and a breath caught in my throat as I saw it. The urn was on the dresser: Grandma. I couldn't tear my eyes away from it and for a moment we both stood in silence, feeling the occasion weighing on us. It had a deep blue finish and the kitchen lights were reflected in its polished surface.

We had discussed what we were going to do. I thought Grandad would suggest scattering the ashes at sea – Grandma had loved visiting beaches, being near the ocean. I had wondered if there was a special spot I'd never known about that she had loved, a romantic bay, a bench that overlooked some spectacular sea view.

Grandad had been sure from the start, nervous, I think, to see my reaction. The moment he suggested the spot I knew it was the right thing to do. We wanted to wait for the right day, and her birthday in September seemed the perfect opportunity.

Grandma had always loved the garden. Even when her illness had forced her off her knees to rest, she had lain on a padded sun-lounger, directing us both as we weeded and watered under her watchful gaze.

'That's not a weed: don't pull on that.'

I would grumble, bemoaning the dirt under my fingernails, the ache in my lower back, but I loved seeing her face as she rested on the lounger, her breathing more shallow but her eyes peaceful as she took in the coloured beds, her careful creations.

'I said prune, not decimate.'

We struggled to eat the muffins, toasted and buttered to perfection, but the dough sticking in our throats. We were both aware of the urn in the same room with us, waiting. I almost burnt my tongue on my tea and now was simply waiting for Grandad to announce it was time.

He played with his paper towel, shredding the paper slowly, lost in another place for a moment.

This did seem more final in many ways than her funeral. This would be her last resting place.

'Are you all right?' I reached across and took his hand in mine, feeling the reassuring weight as he squeezed me back.

'I'm so glad we are doing this together,' he said, looking over at me. 'I don't say it enough, Lottie, but I love you, we both did, we were both so proud of what you achieved.'

I couldn't stop the tears that spilled down my cheeks now. 'I love you too, and I loved Grandma, so much. She was amazing.'

'She was.' Grandad laughed. 'She reminded me of that fact on many an occasion.'

I laughed, wiping at my face. 'Come on then, let's say a final goodbye.'

We moved out of the kitchen and on to the patio, the garden lush, laid out before us: borders filled with colourful plants, a wrought-iron bench set back in a small alcove where Grandma had loved to sit. A small apple tree nearby had dropped most of its load. Grandad had clearly been busy pruning and tidying, and in the middle of the lawn stood a beautiful rose bush, ready to be planted.

Grandad was carrying the blue urn towards a spot on the side of her bench. He had already dug a neat circle in the soil and he rested the urn down next to it. He patted the earth. I felt more tears threaten as I moved to hold his hand. His skin felt dry, soil clinging to the palms.

Gently Grandad poured the ashes into the hole, like a pile of pale grey sand, stark against the soil. Then, taking a trowel he removed the rose bush from its pot, roots trailing as he transferred it across, pieces of soil clinging stubbornly to the thin tendrils. As he held it straight I carefully returned the soil, gradually covering every trace of Grandma's ashes. Tears dripped from my nose, making dark spots in the soil. We spent an age ensuring it was packed down before Grandad went to fetch a watering can, dampening the patch and giving it a last pat.

When it was finished we both stood silently looking at the bush that we knew Grandma would have loved, feeling that she was back in her rightful place in her garden where she was always so happy.

'Well,' Grandad said, his voice choking, 'I think we better have a drink.'

'Absolutely.'

I felt lighter moving inside. Grandad left the urn just inside the back door. We could see the rose bush from the table in the kitchen and once we had poured ourselves a glass of cold white wine we both instinctively moved back outside to sit on the patio. Birds swept past overhead, light clouds skittered across a cornflower blue sky and the breeze lifted the leaves of the trees as we stared out at the garden again.

The peace was interrupted by the doorbell. Grandad looked quizzically across at me as if I had some clue as to who was there.

‘I’ll get it,’ I said, not wanting him to get up. He seemed comfortable sitting on the padded wicker furniture, sipping at his glass of wine, closing his eyes to feel the sun on his skin.

The doorbell went again as I was walking down the corridor, shadows moving in the glass panel beyond, more than one person on the doorstep. I frowned, sliding the lock across before opening the door. I’d read the papers; I represented people who preyed on the elderly. Maybe they had been watching, knew Grandad lived alone, were hoping to try their luck on a vulnerable old man. It was perhaps a little unusual to ring the doorbell but surely once they had access they could force their way in and run amok. I felt outrage building inside me as I prepared to face them, my hand shaking as I opened the door to peer through the thin crack. Three faces stared back at me.

I fumbled with the lock. ‘You!’

‘Us!’ Arjun, Geoffrey and Howard all exclaimed as they pushed their way into the house. ‘Knew it was today. Thought you’d both need cheering up.’

They were all holding carrier bags clinking with bottles. The rustle of jackets, perfunctory kisses on the cheek as they moved past me in the corridor. There was no polite request, no ‘Is he all right?’ ‘Can he face us?’ ‘We’ll only stay for five minutes’, they just bustled past, knowing to come on inside and inject some life and energy into the day. And hearing my grandad’s faux annoyed voice calling from the garden I grinned, knowing they had done absolutely the right thing.

'Thank you,' I whispered.

Arjun gave my shoulder a squeeze. 'Geoffrey's idea, and of course we'd be here. We all loved Cora. So if we miss her, I can't imagine what you both feel.'

Oh, the tears were coming again. I didn't respond, just swallowed, nodded and followed him through the kitchen.

They were all crowding around the patio table, pulling up chairs, producing drinks from bags, their voices filling the space. Plastic bowls were being filled with peanuts and crisps.

'Bit early for Gin o'Clock but it's a special occasion,' Howard said, twisting a bottle and reading from the label. 'This one is Spanish, flavoured with toasted almonds. Can't be any worse than that revolting one Geoffrey produced last week.'

'That cost me £36.'

'You were robbed, my man.'

'The garden looks wonderful. She would love that rose bush,' Geoffrey said quietly to Grandad. I watched them shake hands, clutching each other with both.

'It's almost big enough for croquet out here,' Howard was saying.

Arjun was sitting on a wicker chair, quieter than usual. I wondered if he was simply thinking about Grandma. He looked a little stooped in the shoulders. Grandad was glancing across at him too, a small frown creasing the skin between his eyebrows before his expression cleared.

They stayed for hours, telling stories about Grandma,

making me laugh. Sometimes the picture aligned with the woman I had known and sometimes things still managed to surprise me.

'What happened to that duck-egg blue moped?'

'Do you remember when she threatened to get a tattoo?'

'Terrified of emus. Never seen a woman so scared. Cheered up that boring outing to London Zoo no end.'

'Did she ever write another children's book, Teddy? Do you remember the one she said was so bad she threw it on the fire.'

'Oh my God, I had no idea,' I said, wiping at my eyes as they continued to regale me.

Grandad looked relaxed and happy and I stared round at this group of men, a group I had often dismissed simply as his 'golfing friends', Grandma and I rolling our eyes at each other as he sloped off out with them again. Now I really saw the connection between them, the easy jokes, the ability to be completely truthful, how they just knew what to do and say.

I wondered for a second if my friends would know to appear when I needed them. I thought of Amy. We had been so close as school friends and then flatmates, always sharing every detail of our lives, giggling, bickering, supporting each other. I had been there for the big moments in her life: celebrating with her when she had finished her PGCE, got her first job in a school, met Will, her now fiancé, been made head of department, then deputy head. I felt the urge to reach out to her, tapping a text to her on my phone, pushing the guilt away at seeing the three previous messages from her, all unanswered. I typed, *Love you, Ames.*

Then there was Luke, my other best friend. Here in this garden I suddenly saw our relationship clearly. He had known what to do this morning. He had known to offer to come, backed off when I wanted to be alone, made me feel loved but not stifled. I remembered our first holiday together, to Majorca. A woman had stopped to tell me that after I had fallen asleep on a lilo in the swimming pool, my boyfriend had spent an entire hour doggy paddling round me, stopping me from hitting the sides or other people. I think I fell in love with him on that day.

I felt a surge of emotion, knowing that in recent weeks, months, I hadn't invested the same time and energy into us as a couple as I had once done. I used to leave him notes, buy him little gifts for no reason, attempt new recipes with ingredients he loved, made thoughtful anniversary gifts, printed off photos of holidays together to frame on our walls. Now sometimes it was all I could do to get home, persuade him to order a late takeaway and fall asleep next to him. When had I stopped doing those things? When had I stopped investing energy in our relationship?

Grandad didn't need me. I stood up, phone in my hand.

'I'm going home,' I said, knowing exactly where I wanted to be.

Grandad smiled and nodded at me. 'Send him our love,' he said.

I moved around the table, kissing him on the head. 'Love

you, Grandad,' I whispered, seeing his eyes water again as I stood back to say goodbye to the rest.

I heard their laughter all the way through the house and out into the street.

I headed back home, knowing Luke would still be out with Adam in the pub, planning to spend some time cleaning and scrubbing our flat, making the place shine. I bought fresh flowers from the florist on the corner of the road, enjoying the scent, which brought the morning with Grandad back to me. A little piece of garden in our flat. When I pushed inside, however, I was greeted with a pristine place. Luke had beaten me to it. Every surface tidied, wiped down and polished; all the washing-up stacked up to dry on the side, the living room hoovered, a smell of beeswax wafting through the flat, the curtain billowing from a half-open window. His way of showing he had been thinking about me that day.

I arranged the flowers in the vase in the centre of the table and stared round at our spotless flat, realising how often I had taken this kind of gesture for granted. I couldn't remember the last time I had looked under the sink for cleaning things, the last time I had unearthed the hoover from its cupboard. The sight filled me with fresh determination. I took down one of Luke's favourite recipe books, searching for something truly mouth-watering to make.

Going out shopping I managed to find everything I needed, enjoying the sun warm on my skin as I made my way back to our flat, past the park opposite where people lay out on rugs, children cycled past, parents watched toddlers on unsteady legs. Everyone looked relaxed and happy in over-sized sunglasses, fading tans: squeezing the last drop out of summer.

A few hours later I was finished, a satisfying smell filling the flat. I had texted Luke summoning him home and, as I heard the front door, felt a little skip in my chest at the thought of seeing him.

'Lottie?'

'Hold on,' I called, pulling the warmed plates from the oven and spooning out the boeuf bourguignon I had made. It did look incredible, the meat succulent and tender, the sauce rich and thick.

'What have I done to deserve all this?' Luke laughed, taking in the rare sight of me in an apron that shouted *Barbecue King*, next to the laid table, wine glasses already full, the flowers in the centre, two candles lit and flickering either side.

'How was today?' he asked, pulling me to him, concern pulling his eyebrows together as he looked me in the eye.

I put my arms around him. He was warm, as if he was filled with sunshine, and he smelt of freshly cut grass and beer.

'It was perfect,' I said, resting my head against his chest for a moment.

'So,' Luke said, pulling back, 'talk me through this feast, what have you made?'

With a flourish and a giggle I presented him with his plate, watching his eyes widen as he took in the sight.

We spent the evening eating, talking and working our way through a bottle of expensive red wine that someone had given us when we moved into the flat. I felt happy and loved as I closed my eyes that night, Luke already asleep beside me.

Lying in late the next day couldn't be part of my plan. Moving through to the kitchen I caught sight of my brief-case and, as I nibbled half-heartedly on a croissant, all the calm and good thoughts from the previous day seemed to evaporate. Taking Luke a coffee I pulled back the curtains, the sun shining brightly. I felt jealous of the people moving past in the street below, imagining their Sunday: a barbecue in the garden, a game of football in the park, reading under the shade of a tree.

Luke was up and itching to get outside and do something. He could be like a small child, so much energy. I watched him attempt to hide the disappointment when I told him I would have to work all day; the smile he forced, not want-ing to destroy our recent fragile peace, as he reached for his phone and dialled one of his friends. Luke seemed to have a steady supply of friends and I was always impressed that he remembered their birthdays, important interviews and more. Last year we had so many wedding invitations we spent practically every weekend in a church, registry office or marquee. I listened to him laughing as he made a plan and stared wistfully out of the window at the sliver of blue sky I could see above the rooftops of the houses opposite.

'I'm proud of you,' he said, kissing me on the top of the

head as I jabbed at the laptop, trying not to take out my frustration on him. Luke had always been impressed by my job, asking me in awe to show him the wig I wore in court, attending a trial to watch me in action from the public gallery. I had never been so nervous as that day, aware of him somewhere above me watching every hand gesture, inflection, fact that came from my lips, watching my manner with the jury. What had he thought?

'I just couldn't believe it was you,' he had said afterwards, babbling in the café we had gone to, dissecting the case, wondering what the jury would do. His enthusiasm had reminded me that I did love what I did, I had worked for years to get myself there and found the thrill of debate, the formal atmosphere of the court, the drama that unfolded on a day-to-day basis exciting. It felt important.

But then on days like this, with Luke heading out of the door and the sun straining at the windows, and the pile of papers in front of me, the endless contradictory statements to work through, I suddenly felt it was the least important thing in the world.

'Bye,' I whispered sadly as he turned to go, not wanting to ruin his day, a small niggle at my ambitious plans to take on more work, to prove to everyone that I could make silk in record time. That *was* what I wanted ... wasn't it?

Darling Cora,

It was your birthday today. You would have been 78. Today was the day we finally laid you to rest in your beloved place: your garden. So after hours dithering over the perfect rose bush, returning to the garden centre with Geoffrey to get his opinion too, I knew the decision was made.

Lottie came over to join me. She wouldn't have missed it for anything. It was a still day: as if you were there sitting beside us in the dappled sunshine, holding both our hands on the bench as we thought of you. Some days I feel a weight on my chest and know there is nothing I can do to ease it but today I felt lighter as we moved back inside the house, lighter as our friends appeared too, sharing in the celebration of your life, telling Lottie stories she had never heard: you were so special, my love.

I try not to be angry, try not to rail that we still had years ahead of us. I try to live like you did, here in the present with joy, but it can be hard. As I lie here now I am thinking of you and all the other birthdays we celebrated together. I hope I gave you the best life, the most jam-packed life. Did we have enough adventures? Did we laugh enough? Sometimes I want to go back in time and be more present, notice more. But I can do that now in honour of you. And I hope I can teach Lottie to do the same.

I love you, my darling.

Teddy x

Chapter 14

Love is like my dishwasher:
comes with no guarantee

CYNTHIA, 79

A man in a balaclava stood at my door and for a second my life flashed before my eyes. Before I could scream or summon help he had rolled the material up over his face. I raised a hand to my chest, waiting for my heartbeat to slow.

'Is this an appropriate outfit for ice-skating?' Grandad was on my doorstep, looking to be wearing his entire wardrobe. The green cords he only ever gardened in had been tucked inside ski socks rolled up to his knees, his face was partially obscured by tartan fabric and he was wearing about eight jumpers and tops, different coloured collars all sticking up.

'You're going . . . ice-skating?'

He gestured with ski gloves. 'Howard has invited along

some of the female golfers. We're going to an ice disco. Part of this being-young-and-hip thing. A sort of group date. You should be pleased.'

'Oh,' I said, trying to arrange my face into an encouraging expression, 'I am pleased. Do you want to come up before you go? I have wine.'

Grandad pushed inside. 'Just a quick one. Can't get tiddly before I hit the disco. Are you alone? Do you want to come tonight?' he asked, moving up the stairs to our flat.

'Well, I really have, um, work, I could be . . . you know, maybe I . . . ' In truth I had finished my brief and was currently watching *Friends* reruns on Netflix. An open bottle of white wine stood as evidence on the coffee table in front of the big screen.

'Where's Luke?' Grandad asked, looking around the living room as if Luke might emerge from behind the other sofa.

'He went to an opening of some gallery to do with Pop Art or something – I'm not sure. Not my thing.'

'So, you're free. Do come. It will be much more fun with you there.'

Grandad was animated, a little nervous perhaps, although the perspiration could easily have been due to overheating. All the same, I felt an urge to go with him, to show him in this small way that I was here for him. I nodded.

'All right then,' I said. 'But I haven't ice-skated since I was about eight years old.'

'I have never ice-skated. It was Howard's idea. He thinks it's the kind of night that young people would go to and we are trying to embrace dating like the young, so . . . ' He shrugged. 'It's an improvement on his last plan – making us all join Tinder together.'

I managed to catch most of the wine I was drinking in my hand. 'You've joined Tinder.'

'Oh yes.' Grandad motioned to an imaginary mobile. 'I know how to swipe left, swipe right. My DMs are open,' he announced with a twinkle. 'But' – he dropped his head – 'no one writes to them.'

I was too shocked to commiserate.

'Actually I went to Nando's and . . . so,' he coughed, decidedly fidgety all of a sudden, 'how cold is it likely to be?'

'In Nando's?' I frowned.

'No, never mind about that.' His eyes darted away from me. 'I meant on the ice.'

'Well, I'm not sure you need all eighteen jumpers,' I said, standing up and stretching. 'Give me five minutes.' I went off to find some layers.

'A lot of it is padding if I fall,' Grandad called through to me as I rummaged in my cupboard. 'The ice can be a tricky beast,' he said, as if he had some idea.

Moments later I was sitting in a minibus driven by Dennis from the club, squeezed between Margaret and Arjun as we pulled away from our flat. They had detoured to pick us up, sliding the door back with a cheer as we bundled out of the flat: the Michelin Man and his granddaughter. The bus was full, a couple of people I didn't recognise but most I did, excited chatter filling the air.

'Glad you're coming,' Arjun said as I settled in my seat.

Margaret immediately offered me a Polo for the journey. 'And thank you for the links to those websites and podcasts. I am now a regular listener of *The Guilty Feminist* and have been discussing Third Wave Feminism with Arjun here, who is also going to subscribe.'

'Girl power,' Arjun said, solemnly punching the air.

I already felt glad I was there.

'I was in one of the first UK groups as an Ice Capade when I was younger,' I could hear Paula telling Geoffrey, who was pressed flat against the window in the front row as she leant towards him. 'I was extremely good. I used to wear very tight leotards.' She licked her lips. 'I hope I can remember some of the moves . . . '

'I imagine it's like getting back on a horse,' Geoffrey squeaked and I stifled a giggle.

We pulled up in a car park on an industrial estate, a large cinema and TGI Fridays opposite the warehouse-style rink. Dennis slid the door back, helping everyone down. As I watched the slow progress of our group, some already complaining about lower back problems, tricky hips, I sent up a quick prayer that we would be back on the minibus later with all limbs intact.

Teenagers in red peaked caps stood, slack-jawed, watching our huddle arrive. Taking out my phone I snapped the image of nine people in their seventies and eighties changing into ice-skating boots on wooden benches, the boy in the booth behind them still looking shell-shocked. Grandad had swapped his leather brogues for ice-skating boots. 'Such fun. Does he shine our shoes for us while we skate in these?' I sent the photo to Luke, knowing it was bound to make him smile.

'Are you coming on the ice, Lottie?' Margaret asked, her hair now hidden under an oversized hot pink bobble hat with a cat stitched into the front.

'I suppose so,' I said, laughing as 'Gangnam Style' started up on the speakers, neon lights flashing down on the ice. Everywhere we looked there were groups of children or teens racing around the ice, holding hands, wobbling unsteadily along the sides or skidding to a halt. The air smelt of hot dogs and old shoes and I was glad for the layers I had on.

I was enjoying the mindless activity, getting into the flow of things as I moved across the ice, grinning at Geoffrey as he clung, green-faced, to the side. Grandad was making slow but steady progress, his face set in a determined line, his balaclava now rolled up on top of his head. Margaret, was popping Polos like they were speed and following a few paces behind. Arjun was in his element, gliding seamlessly in a sweeping circle, giving me a double thumbs-up as he passed before narrowly avoiding a kissing couple holding hands.

Howard was drinking a bright blue Slush Puppie and talking to Paula, still stretching, on one of the benches on the side. He kept eyeing the ice warily, slurping on his straw.

I came to a stop next to Margaret, who was wobbling uncertainly. 'How are you finding it?' I asked her.

Her cheeks were flushed pink, her eyes bright.

'I'm hopeless. But it's wonderful to be out all together like this, and doing something so different, too. Apparently this is all down to you and your charming boyfriend.'

'Well, in a roundabout sort of way I suppose,' I said.

'How are you getting on with finding things to do for your challenge? I've had a few ideas,' she added quickly.

'Like what?' I asked, intrigued by her eager expression.

'Well, I enjoy the ballroom dancing lessons we have in the hall. I always think younger people should get involved, it's really made for them. Some of the dances are impossible, you wish you had more flexibility and energy. The Lindy Hop is beyond me. But you're young, you'll have the energy, and so many are great fun too.' She added, 'You can really connect when you're dancing, it's so intimate, having to read each other's body language, anticipate the moves . . . '

I screwed up my nose.

'Or board games,' she said, sensing my reticence. 'A simple evening sitting round a table together playing something as a group. It can be an excellent way to spend time.'

'That could work,' I mused.

'Oh, I'm so pleased,' she said, her face turning almost as pink as her hat.

'Do you want to hold my hand, we might be more confident together?' I offered her my gloved hand and she took it and we set off round the ice at a steady pace.

'I'm doing it, I'm doing it,' Margaret cried out as she started to grow in confidence. Grandad lifted a hand as we both passed and we nearly crashed trying to return it.

'Your grandad is a nice man,' Margaret said.

'You should spend more time together. This group seems really friendly,' I said.

'There are lots of different things going on at the club but we don't often come together in smaller groups like this. The men seem very close, it's lovely to see.' Margaret smiled as Geoffrey and Grandad were spotted in the distance, holding each other up on the ice.

'That's the golf, I think,' I said. 'Grandma always called herself a golf widow. It's such a shame you don't get to play with them too.'

'Oh, the men-only tradition goes back years,' Margaret said reverentially. 'There was enormous panic when they gave us a half day.'

'So?' I snorted. 'It's wrong. You should do something about it.' I was distracted then by a boy with ginger hair and a terrified expression bearing down on us. Margaret, who had grown thoughtful by my side, was saying, 'Do you know, Lottie, maybe I will.' I twisted to protect her, shouting, 'Watch ouuuuuu—' before the boy swept between us and we all tumbled down together.

Margaret survived, leaving in tentative steps. Just before setting off again I called over to Howard, who turned away from Paula and stepped gingerly towards me. I couldn't help staring at his mouth, tongue and lips, which were now entirely Slush Puppie blue, as if an inkpot had exploded inside him.

'You getting on soon, Howard?'

'Oh, I'm not sure I'm cut out to be on ice.' He leaned closer to me, lowering his voice. 'I'm more at ease on dry land.'

'Wasn't this your idea?'

'Yes, but I didn't think anyone would actually go for it. It was a joke. I should have shut up once I'd got them all on Tinder. That's the problem with being a natural leader.'

'Come on, Howard,' Paula said, beckoning him with a long scarlet talon, her other hand holding something grey and furry, 'you can put your hands in my muff if you like.'

Howard's mouth fell open, a large, stained navy blue maw, as I exploded into giggles beside him.

'Good God,' he whispered to me as he reached to take her hand and stepped on to the ice.

Darling Cora,

I had a text message from the daughter of the Nando's lady who ghosted me: it transpires she died! Which is obviously very sad, but also, terribly, a small relief. I just didn't want to think she had seen me sitting in Nando's and run a mile.

That's terrible, isn't it? The poor woman.

Although I am a trifle cross with myself because in a fit of paranoia I gifted the jacket and Robert Redford checked shirt to the charity shop, assuming they had had a bearing on my rejection. Maybe I could purchase them back?

Certainly the world of modern dating is extremely eye-opening. Howard is now threatening to take us all speed dating but Geoffrey has point-blank refused and he can be stubborn when he wants to be. Instead we came up with a few alternatives – the most fun part of this ridiculous scheme has been spending more time with the boys and getting to know others from Maplelands club better.

A few nights ago we all went to a youth roller disco on ice! Lottie came too and she and Margaret spent some time together. She's a nice lady, Margaret, and I'm glad Lottie has someone she can talk to, woman to woman so to speak: I know she misses you terribly. It has been wonderful to catch glimpses of the old, relaxed Lottie again: I think we're getting her back, Cora.

The biggest surprise of the evening was Arjun, who proved to be a secret ice-skating marvel. At one point he was skating backwards talking to Paula, his legs moving in a figure of eight like a graceful, elderly cast member warming up for Strictly. I do believe Paula was a little put out (she lost her muff trying to keep up). Skating on ice is probably not going to prove to be a new hobby for me, however. Geoffrey and I were both pretty hopeless, although we were fortunate enough to fall down only twice. He did teach me all the moves to the 'Macarena', which he says is a popular youth dance, so the evening wasn't completely wasted.

All these activities seem to have put even more of a rocket up Howard and he came over last night to get me on to an 'app' called 'Happn'. We discovered half the club, including Arjun, were on it too. It is done by location so now Howard wants to create a fake profile and arrange to meet up with Arjun. I have obviously vetoed such an idea unless Arjun does something that annoys me, in which case I will give Howard the green light. And you always said I wasn't mature!

Although I have zero interest in really meeting anyone on these 'online platforms', I am enjoying the japes and doing something other than moping about remembering how much I love you and the cruel fact that you are no longer here. I laugh more now and I am grateful to have friends who haven't given up on me. I never really knew how lucky I was until now: they are a tonic.

I love you, Cora, it will always be more fun with you by my side but I am trying, every day, to live my life and enjoy these moments while I have them.

Teddy x

Chapter 15

Love is like a flower: it needs
tending to for it to grow

TERRY, 84

It was the weekend of Amy's hen do. We'd spent approximately 15 weeks and 783 emails finding the date that suited everyone. Shift work, childcare, weddings, other hen dos had to be navigated around. Amy's sister, Natalie – the other bridesmaid and the biggest control freak I'd ever met – had stepped in when I'd proved useless. And now it was here. I had been in charge of bringing the novelty balloons and penis straws, which Luke had discovered and been using to drink his nightly water with that week.

'That's gross,' I said, pointing to him as he slurped.

He looked up, grinning at me. 'You brought them into our lives.'

'But I . . . you . . . '

He continued to slurp loudly.

I gave up and walked out of the room, listening to his low chuckle.

We were meeting at Natalie's house, which had an open-plan living room and kitchen spilling out on to a small terrace and narrow strip of grass. Natalie and I had kissed cheeks and then spun into a frenzy of activity, preparing things before Amy arrived, laying out glasses and finger food.

I had blown up one of the large penis balloons and thought it would be funny to greet Amy at the door with it. The doorbell rang and without thinking I ran down the corridor to open it, thrusting it out towards her. 'Haaaaappy hen dooooo,' I squealed.

'Muuuuummmmyyyyy,' came a cry. And rather than Amy, a woman in a beige three-quarter-length coat and a sour expression stood wide-eyed, staring at my offering. A tiny person streaked past me, pounding down the corridor as I stood, erect penis balloon in hand.

Oh God.

Natalie, eyes boggled, standing in the kitchen doorway, scooped up the toddler, who immediately hid his face in her shoulder. I started stuttering at the unimpressed woman on the doorstep to whom I had proffered the penis balloon.

'Thanks, Maureen,' Natalie called. 'Lottie, meet my mother-in-law, Maureen.'

'Hi,' I swallowed, offering the hand that wasn't holding the penis balloon. Maureen didn't take it.

Maureen left with a pursed lip and a muttered goodbye. I cringed against the door as I closed it behind me.

Natalie grimaced. 'Sorry, Lottie, I should have warned you. My au pair is ill so Tom is with us today. Maureen could only take him for an hour but don't worry, he'll be napping soon,' she said in a hurry.

I was frantically trying to hide the large inflatable penis behind my back as Tom kept staring at it bobbing around above me. 'Oh, oh right, that's great. Hi, Tom. How, how old is he now?' I asked, pretty sure Natalie had been pregnant the last time I saw her.

'Tom's just turned two, haven't you, darling? Two. Say hello to Lottie.'

Silence from the toddler person.

I returned to the large kitchen, the carpet now filled once more with crayons, plastic cars, bowls of uneaten goop and stray spoons. I swear the toddler had done catastrophic damage in less time than it took me to open the door.

'Balloon,' Tom piped up as I tried to secure the large cock to the back of a chair.

Natalie bit her lip. 'Yes, darling, it's a . . . it's a . . .'

'*Balloon*.' Tom confirmed as if his mother was a blind moron.

Fortunately at that moment the doorbell went and Tom turned to launch himself back into his mother's arms.

'Sorry, he gets a bit overwhelmed when people arrive,' Natalie said, scooping him up again and heading to the door. 'Breaks the routine.'

'Right, well I'll unpack the rest of the things here,' I said, realising almost everything in the two large carrier bags I had brought along were either penis-shaped or covered in pictures of penises.

Clearing a space in the living area, I then positioned chairs in a large circle in preparation for everyone's arrival. Hearing Amy in the corridor I looked up just as she appeared, stony-faced, in the doorway.

Natalie was following behind her, Tom tugging on her top saying, 'Play with balloon. Play with balloon now,' as she kept talking to Amy's back.

'. . . honestly he naps for ages, you won't notice, oh and Ems and Polly can't make it. And maybe Char because she was meant to be getting a lift from Polly.'

Amy's face had turned thunderous as she looked across at me.

'Hey.' I gave her a sympathetic smile and half-hearted wave.

'Sorry, why can't they come?' Amy said, turning to her sister.

Natalie ticked the reasons off her list. 'Ems: suspected chicken pox, her child not her; Polly got her dates confused and is meant to be at her boyfriend's family get-together in Swansea, and Char, well, Char can't drive and is worried about public transport.'

'Right,' Amy said, rubbing her eyes.

'Drink?' I sing-songed, realising this hen do was heading downhill and fast.

'What about public transport?'

'*Balloon now.*'

'No ... I ... not sure, is she frightened of buses or something? Maybe, darling, it's not a balloon for playing really ... '

'Mojito?' I lurched over to the counter.

'Oh,' Natalie said, 'that jug is the non-alcoholic one actually. We've got a couple of pregnant people coming, and Katy is still breast-feeding—'

The doorbell interrupted the rest of the sentence. Tom was now scaling the chair the penis was attached to and I was frantically pouring tequila into a shot glass.

'Come on, Ames, let's get this down you.'

Amy slouched over to me in the kitchen. 'God, Lottie, is this going to be the worst?'

'Of course not!' I said, smile plastered on as two women with enormous bumps pushed into the room and Tom released the penis from its mooring so it floated up to the ceiling to rest on its side.

Minutes later more guests arrived and Amy looked a little cheered, helped along by three tequila shots. A couple of her colleagues from the school appeared: a brunette head of PE with the kind of toned upper arms I'd only ever seen on professional tennis players, and an earnest-looking head of Teaching and Learning pushing tortoiseshell glasses up her nose. Then university friends and school friends joined us and the room was suddenly full with people clutching glasses, introducing themselves, Tom weaving between their legs on a continuous hunt for his mother.

After an hour the clock hands seemed to be dragging. It was only four o'clock as we sat in a small circle, Tom's episode of *Peppa Pig* filling the long gaps in conversation. I was sitting next to Amy's sister-in-law who didn't know anyone and was borderline obsessed with long-haired cats. After five minutes I'd had my fill.

The group was fading into intermittent coughs and silence. I was aware I should stop serving tequila for a little while as Amy's right eye was already wandering.

'This is a good episode actually,' Natalie said, around the group. 'It's about Peppa's fish being bored. They take her on the bus and . . .'

Stony stares met her story and I found my bottom clenching as she continued. Amy looked bereft, shoulders slumped, both hands cupping her watered-down mojito, her hot pink satin *Bride to Be* sash lacklustre.

I clapped my hands together. 'Sooooo, when is company arriving . . .' I waggled my eyebrows suggestively.

Natalie started shaking her head at me, making cutting motions on her neck. 'I'm sorry, I know we planned . . . I just couldn't have a S-T-R-I-P-P-E-R here, not with' – she gestured towards Tom – 'I'm sorry, Amy I cancelled him this morning. I made carrot batons and homemade hummus everyone!' She thrust the plate out in front of her.

No one reached to get one. Amy didn't even raise a smile.

'How about we do the Mr and Mrs Quiz?' I suggested in a hearty voice, eyes flicking nervously round the circle. I had already forgotten everyone's names.

Natalie looked worriedly across at Tom. 'We could, I mean, I don't like to turn off the television once he's settled in front of it, and we need it to attach the laptop to, but we could . . .'

'We could just play it on the laptop,' I suggested brightly, determined to move this party along and desperate to see Amy's face light up.

I fussed over the keys of the laptop, turning up the volume on the small screen to maximum. The whole circle of women gathered around the small coffee table to watch. Transpires maximum really wasn't very loud, Peppa's voice sailing above it all, and we spent twenty minutes straining to make out Will's answers in between his barks of laughter.

' . . . Amy . . . lucky . . . we used to . . . haha . . .'

Natalie, distracted now because Tom had started to roam the room, was attempting to translate. 'Oh, that bit was so cute, he said . . . he said . . . *Don't climb on the table* . . . he said, *Tom, I am warning you*, he said how much he was looking forward to spending his – *Tom, I am being serious, Mummy does not want you to do that* . . . life with you. His life. Or the rest of his life. I forget the exact wording, we filmed it a while ago. It was heart-warming. If you could hear it properly I really think you might be welling up.'

The video ended and there was an uncomfortable pause. The long-haired-cat sister-in-law got up to go to the loo and the silence was so complete that we could all hear her pee in the downstairs toilet. Oh God. Amy looked on the verge of tears, her willy straw drooping in her empty drink.

Two of the pregnant girls had started to swap stories of thicker mucus and sore breasts. Tom was currently attempting to drink from the cups left lying around, non-alcoholic mojito liberally poured down his front before Natalie leapt on him to wrestle them away. Then full-blown screaming, rolling on the floor, before he could be placated with another 'snack' (he'd also sensibly refused the carrot batons and was stuffing his face with Jaffa Cakes).

I had to rescue this day.

We still had money in the pot, a saving from not using the stripper, and with a quiet word to Natalie in the kitchen, Tom straining on her hip while intermittently head-butting her shoulder, she looked resigned as I outlined a new plan. Notably, hot-footing it out of there and heading earlier than we had planned to the bars and pubs of central London. Natalie would join us once her husband got home.

'Right,' I said, clapping my hands together, twisting my body to the rather sad-looking circle of women.

Amy looked hopefully up at me.

'Drink up, ladies, we're heading into town.'

We lost a couple of people on the way. Katy needed to head back to feed her baby, cat-obsessed sister-in-law couldn't face the last-minute change of plan and was muttering about *Outlander*, but the rest of the group were herded out of the door and into the taxis I had ordered. Stepping into the last cab I felt sheer relief as the house disappeared from view in the rear window and Amy reached across from the leather seat opposite me to squeeze my hand.

The rest of the night was a blur of happy, smiling memories. I took responsibility for the group, ushering them into the nearest pub from the Tube station, ordering a round of tequila shots and then fabricating absurd made-up dares to make everyone behave badly or drink more.

Within twenty minutes the head of PE had flashed a table of football players and the earnest head of Teaching and Learning was swapping her number with the goalkeeper. Amy watched in amazement, clamping a hand over her mouth.

That seemed to set the tone and it wasn't long before one of the pregnant friends was dancing provocatively on a low velvet stool, penis straw clamped between her teeth, and another girl from Amy's university days, with the whitest teeth, lay down on the bar while the football players did shots off her stomach. The barman started yelling at her, and us as we whooped and cheered, and we were ejected at that point by a giant of a bouncer who also ended up swapping numbers with the head of Teaching and Learning.

Moving on to another bar packed with pinstriped men drinking and nodding along to terrible house music, we immediately forced most of them to join us on the dance floor. I remember grinning across at Amy as we pulled out some of the old moves, moving my hips and shaking out my hair as if it was five years earlier and we were in a nightclub before collapsing back at our shared flat.

It became hazy after that but I remembered directing everyone down the stairs of a dimly lit karaoke bar, straight into a booth where I forced people to sing every song on the *Grease 2* soundtrack. We moved swiftly on to ballads, all believing ourselves to be as good as any *X Factor* winner. We were awesome.

I remembered choosing 'Nobody Does It Better' and dragging Amy into the centre of the room.

'Be the Barbra to my Carly,' I had crooned at her. I remember her grin, so wide it forced my mouth into one too, as we clutched our microphones and sang like it was nobody's business.

I remember smuggling an inflatable plastic guitar, a blue Afro wig and a long blonde curled wig with a hot pink rhinestone cowboy hat attached to it under my coat as we weaved back into the street to head home.

I remember the taxi ride back, the tickle on my face as Amy, now wearing the electric blue Afro, pulled me towards her to give me a hug. 'Thank you for tonight, thank you. You're back.'

I was too drunk and exhausted to really notice the last words, just filled with a woozy warm glow that my best friend was happy and that I had helped make that happen.

Chapter 16

Love is knowing something will
be made better simply because
you are sharing it with me

SHEENA, 81

Hangovers really shouldn't last this long. It was Monday morning and I was outside the court hoping I could stay on the hard wooden bench all morning.

Sunday had been spent in a fog of misery, Luke bringing me Lucozade Sport and painkillers at various intervals. I had practically snapped his head off when he had slid a hand across my bare stomach that morning.

'Are you trying to have sex with me?' I mumbled into my pillow.

'Oh, well, I cou—' His voice was low and drawn-out.

'Cos are you kidding me?' I interrupted him, feeling the damp patch where I'd dribbled into my pillow. 'Na-uh. I need . . . '

I passed out before finishing the sentence.

I woke two hours later, a glass of water and two white paracetamol tablets placed on the bedside table, the flat looking clean, the living room hoovered, the surfaces in the kitchen wiped down. He'd left a note next to the kettle.

'Out for a couple of hours on a secret mission!' The jaunty smiley face next to it blurred in and out. I could feel the energy leaping off the page. Why had I drunk so much? Why wasn't I feeling in a buoyant mood drawing emojis on notes and flitting round the flat on my day off with energy and the desire to do things? Instead I closed the curtains, slumped down on the sofa, picked up the remote and trawled endlessly through Netflix, bemoaning the fact there was simply nothing on television before picking up where I'd left off in my last *Friends* rerun marathon. Then I trawled social media and read a beauty article about the fact that noses never stop growing in your lifetime, and spent the next half an hour looking at my nose from every angle in my camera phone. It boggled my mind. I was convinced my nose had already grown in those thirty minutes and I was doomed soon to be all nose.

Covering my nose I stared across the room to the desk in the corner, the half-finished statement for the plea and directions hearing I had the next day waiting for me. I had met with the client last week and was trying to structure her rambling answers into some kind of a concise document.

The key went in the lock and I felt a small swell of relief for the excuse to resist work.

'Hey,' Luke called as he closed the door behind him.

He was holding a small bunch of bright red tulips tied together with a piece of twine and held them out a little self-consciously. 'I bought you these,' he said.

Still in my dressing gown, hand over my nose, hair mussed up, eyeliner smudged beneath my lower lashes, I probably didn't look like a worthy recipient of flowers. I took them from him.

'Thank you,' I said, feeling a little shy. 'I'll get the vase.'

Returning with the flowers I kissed Luke on the top of the head. 'Thank you, they're lovely,' I said. 'In celebration I thought I might get dressed! Also, did you know that noses never stop growing? As in, they keep getting bigger until you die.'

'Er, I did not know that.'

'It's OK for you, you have a neat nose. What am I going to do? This could get serious.'

Luke's face twitched. 'I think you'll be all right, your nose is lovely, on the small side even . . . '

I covered it again. Was he slagging off my nose? Saying it was too small?

'You're worried I think your nose is too small, aren't you?'

I nodded.

'Go and get changed, crazy person.' He pointed at the bedroom, flopping down in the space I had left on the sofa.

In all the flower/nose excitement I failed to ask him where he had spent the morning. His squash racket hadn't moved from the rack by the door and he hadn't been out running.

Luke rested his head back on the sofa. 'So, tell me about last night,' he said, when it was clear I wasn't going anywhere. He pulled me into a hug as I sat back down.

I had told him about Amy's hen do, memories patchy and blurred, and we had laughed and eventually I had got dressed and Luke had made me food and let me finish my work. And then we'd gone to bed ridiculously early.

So I should have felt a lot better by now. Instead I wanted to weep as I was called through to the court, my scalp itchy and hot under my wig as I adjusted it outside the heavy oak double doors, nausea at the clash of beeswax polish and mothballs.

The hearing didn't take long and I was soon back in the corridor, slumped on a bench and psyching myself up for the public transport ahead. A familiar voice called my name and I sat up quickly, smoothing at my hair.

'Lottie, hey.' A figure took a seat beside me.

It was Toby, an absurdly slick and good-looking solicitor who often sent me work. He was clean-shaven and smelt of lemons, skin radiant, exuding health. Angling myself away from him I nodded a quiet hello, mouth clamped tight in case I still smelt of drink.

'I'm glad I bumped into you. I was with my boss and Alan only yesterday at a drinks party and your name came up.'

Alan was my head of chambers so immediately I started an internal panic. Why had my name cropped up? What had they discussed? I mentally scanned the last few cases he'd sent me for problems, still none the wiser. The same creeping feeling I got when I saw a policeman, as if suddenly I would remember the terrible murder I'd committed, stole over me as I continued to wrack my brains for something to confess. Toby was smiling, though, even rows of white teeth good enough for any Colgate advert.

'Don't look so worried. He was gushing about you, determined that you'll be the youngest silk they've ever had, etc, etc. Full of all the wonders you've pulled off . . . '

I felt myself swell with the praise, wriggling upright. 'Oh, well, I'm sure—' I bumbled a response, grateful when Toby cut me off.

'Actually, I've got a case for you. The client has just fired someone on it. He allegedly rammed his ex-wife with the family car but he claims he didn't know it was in Drive mode. Want it?'

'Always.' I grimaced at the bare details. 'Everyone deserves a defence,' I stated as a mantra.

'Quite.' Toby nodded earnestly. 'And perhaps one day we could go for lunch? Always good to get out of the office.'

Something in his look, his eyes darkening, his lowered voice, made me bite my lip. 'Lunch would be . . . ' Lunch would be what, Lottie? For a start there was a code of conduct to adhere to, ensuring barristers weren't seen to bribe solicitors to send them work. And Toby and I weren't friends, so what was this? And Toby was absurdly good-looking, so there was that too.

I hadn't spoken in what felt like an age. 'Great,' I finished.

Toby thrust his card at me. 'My mobile is on that one. I think you've only got the office line.'

I pocketed it with what I hoped was a normal smile. My skin felt taut across my face. Maybe this was normal and I had just been with Luke too long so I didn't know the signs. He didn't seem to be reacting in the same way.

'Well, give me a call when you're around,' he said cheerfully, getting up and straightening his jacket.

'I will,' I said, looking up at him, trying not to stare too long. His face was so symmetrical.

'I'll get that brief over to you then.'

'Great,' I said again as if I only knew this one word.

'Great,' he repeated, his voice slightly mocking, a smile lifting the side of his mouth.

As he walked away I shook off the exchange, holding the card between two fingers. Then, as if making up my mind, I tapped his mobile number into my mobile. It couldn't hurt to have it. I thought back to what he had said about Alan. I knew Alan liked me but it was gratifying to hear that he really thought I could become a QC in my thirties.

That thought triggered something in me, the knowledge that I needed to concentrate, to seize this opportunity. Recently I had lost focus and, although things had been great fun, I shouldn't be neglecting my career. I had worked too hard to let things slip now. And my life was fine now that Grandad was happier, Luke and I were back on track and I had even proved to be a decent friend to Amy this weekend. I needed to ensure I wasn't slacking off any more, no more days hungover from having fun. I knew I could do more, needed to be seen to be working the hardest if I was going to make my goal. If that meant a few things had to be sidelined, then so be it.

Chapter 17

Love is why I kept marrying them

PAUL, 79

'So, what have you planned for us tonight?' Luke grinned as Grandad let us both in, wearing a striped apron. 'Cupcake making? Pancake tossing?'

'No, no, nothing like that,' Grandad said, drawing me into a hug. 'It's good to see you both, come through, come through.'

I could make out noises from the living room and we walked in to see furniture pushed to the edges of the room, the dining table pulled out and a cluster of people sitting or milling around. Arjun and Geoffrey looked to be deep in conversation next to the reading lamp, Howard was lifting his shirt up and seemed to be showing Paula something on his lower back, and Margaret was sitting quietly on the armchair, sipping a drink.

'Hello, Lottie,' she said. 'The gin's infused with a rare tea, apparently.'

Laughing, I moved across to her. Grandad had placed some flowers in a vase on the mantelpiece and the room was filled with the sweet scent.

He returned with two more glasses on a tray that he placed down on the table, carefully avoiding the familiar board game in the middle, the rows of coloured money round the four edges, and the counters and cards in neat piles.

Monopoly.

'Seriously, Grandad?' I couldn't help but look pretty underwhelmed.

He ignored my expression as he removed his apron and threw it over the arm of the sofa. 'It was Margaret's idea, actually. She said you thought it would be fun.'

Luke was already cracking his knuckles and calling, 'I want to be the racing car, I want to be the racing car.'

'We thought we'd play in teams,' Grandad explained. 'Four teams of two people. Luke and you can play together.'

'I'm going to go with Paula here. You seem like an ambitious sort,' Howard said, turning to her.

She simpered and smacked her glossy pink lips. 'I always saw myself as a property mogul.'

Geoffrey and Arjun both looked up at the same moment.

'I'll play with Geoffrey here,' Arjun said, mostly, I suspected, so neither of them needed to move. They dived straight back into their conversation. Arjun was trying to persuade Geoffrey out on his next foreign golf tour. 'You'll love it, the course in Portugal is fantastic, the views, the landscape, the excellent wine. And if we share a twin room we can save £40 . . . '

I watched Grandad walk over to the armchair, holding out his hand to Margaret. 'That leaves you and me, Margaret. I hope that's OK with you.'

She blushed and nodded, staring into her glass. 'I'm not the luckiest at board games but I can try.' Then, allowing Grandad to help her up, she moved over to the table.

'No luck involved in Monopoly,' Howard boomed, pulling out a chair for Paula and steering her into it. 'Killer instinct. Killer instinct and a thirst for capitalism.'

'Christ,' Geoffrey muttered at Arjun.

Paula looked like she was in heaven, staring at Howard with a delighted smile. 'I do like a man who's good with money.' She poured herself some more gin.

We settled at the table and it took precisely ten seconds for the first row about the rules to break out. It transpired Howard was aiming to hoard one of each set of properties, Arjun would only sell anything for 'a million dollars', Luke seemed intent on only collecting the train stations – 'Honestly, Lottie, it's a good tactic' – and Grandad spent most of his time in jail refusing to pay his way out.

'When you land on Free Parking, you collect money from the middle.'

'What money?'

'The money from all the fines.'

'The money from the fines doesn't go into the middle. It goes into the bank.'

'Who even pays the fines anyway?'

'Howard, you have to, that's the whole point.'

'Are you stealing from the bank, Arjun?'

'I'm getting change.'

'Change for what? The hundred you stole?'

'Is it four houses then a hotel or three houses then a hotel?'

'Why won't you sell me Park Lane? You're just being a miser.'

'You can't sell Old Gloucester Road for a million dollars, Arjun, it doesn't work like that.'

'Will someone please land on my hotel.'

'Will there be a spa experience?'

'Why are you buying the utilities, Luke? No one wants the utilities. They are like the losers of Monopoly.'

'Arjun, seriously, put that money back.'

'Oh my God, am I going to die before this game is finished?'

'Right,' Grandad said, tapping his glass, hushing the raised voices around him. 'I'm not sure this is the bonding experience we were hoping to introduce our young people to, Margaret,' he said, turning to her. 'What else did you bring?'

'They're my daughter's games. They didn't have a massive selection so I just brought them all.' She motioned to a carrier bag and Paula got up to peer inside.

'What is Hungry Hippos?'

'Is that Scrabble?' Geoffrey was craning his neck.

'We're not playing Scrabble, Geoffrey, unless you really do have a death wish.'

'Oooooh,' Paula said, drawing a box out of the selection. 'Let's play this,' she said, holding it up to us all.

It took me a few seconds to recognise the polka dots on the front. Oh God. Twister.

'Is it a game about tornadoes?' Arjun asked. Nobody responded. Grandad and Margaret were engrossed in conversation and Howard was checking his teeth in the back of a teaspoon.

'It will be fun,' Paula said, clapping her hands together. 'Come on, Howard, be a sport.'

He looked up. 'Of course, of course – excellent.'

'You're only saying that because you were losing at Monopoly,' Geoffrey called out.

'What twists in the game?' Arjun asked, still keen to hear more about this new option.

Luke was laughing into his gin, the liquid bubbling.

Somehow we found ourselves gathering around the mat, four of us sitting on sofas and chairs as Grandad, Margaret, Arjun and Geoffrey took their turn to play.

'Are you sure you're all right?' I called as I span the wheel for Grandad.

'Just about,' he said, his voice strained, his legs straddling two polka dots in an uncomfortable-looking starfish. Howard was directing salted popcorn at his feet as Paula took photos of them on her mobile.

'Right hand to yellow spot, Margaret,' Luke called out,

tears forming in his eyes as he stared at the group crammed on to the mat in front of him, a look thrown to me as if to ask quite how this had happened. I couldn't help shrug and grin at him.

'Oh my,' Margaret said, looking positively petrified as she reached down and placed her palm on the yellow spot, bottom in the air. 'Not very ladylike,' she called, her voice muffled.

'Do hurry,' Geoffrey called. 'I'm really not sure my left foot can stay on the blue spot if Arjun here continues to take an hour to place his hand on green.'

'It's harder than it looks,' Arjun complained, staring across Geoffrey at the green.

'Are you all right, Margaret?'

'Thank you, Teddy.'

'Paula, show me that one.'

'Don't photograph my bottom!' Margaret cried.

'Arjun, man, for God's sake, we have lives to lead, hurry up.'

Luke had by now fully lost it, tears leaking out of the sides of his eyes and setting me off too.

'I can't possibly reach red,' Grandad called, as Arjun launched himself over Geoffrey to connect with the green spot.

'Got it,' he mumbled from somewhere below them all.

Then with a collective shout the whole pack collapsed and we had four sprawling pensioners on the floor of the living room.

'Is everyone all right?' Grandad called from somewhere underneath the pile.

'That's my breast,' Margaret squealed.

'This looks excellent,' Howard said, clapping his hands together. 'When's our turn?' he asked from the sofa, eyes gleaming.

As the group gingerly stood to dust themselves off and stretch, Arjun remained on the floor, one hand on his hip, a pained expression on his face.

Luke immediately stopped laughing and bent down next to him. 'All OK, Arjun?' he asked, concern filling his voice.

'Just a spot of bother with my hip,' Arjun said, wincing as he spoke.

He was holding his hip, his knuckles strained white as he clenched, his face draining of colour.

'Oh dear, oh dear,' Margaret said, wringing her hands.

'Box does say 8 to 80. Isn't Arjun 79?' Howard joked. 'Twister need to update their packaging.'

'Do shut up, Howard.'

'Arjun, can you get up?'

'Has anyone got any ice?'

'Should we phone an ambulance?'

'Are we going to get to play now?'

'*Howard*.'

'I'll get some peas.'

'Oh dear, oh dear.'

It seemed Arjun wasn't going anywhere and the decision

was made to phone an ambulance, Grandad running a hand through his hair.

'Lottie, why don't you drive your grandad and I'll go with Arjun in the ambulance?' Luke said, taking control as we were all just uselessly wafting about.

'Right, good idea, OK. Grandad, do you need to fetch anything?'

'What can we bring for you, Arjun?' Luke asked.

Arjun was gritting his teeth and I felt a real flash of worry, racing back to the kitchen to fetch frozen peas.

'Here,' I said, handing them to Luke. 'It might help.'

'Thanks.' He met my eye and smiled. I felt a little calmer as I crouched down next to him on the mat.

'Did we win?' Arjun gasped between breaths.

I laughed at that and rested my hand on his shoulder. 'Not long now, Arjun, we'll get you to the hospital. They have amazing pain medication.'

'And nurses,' Howard said from the mantelpiece where he was leaning towards Paula, plucking something off her shoulder. 'Fluff,' he said, as she giggled and slapped his chest.

Well, at least Twister was bringing some people together, I thought.

The paramedics appeared and they stretchered Arjun out of the house, promising him some relief once in the ambulance. Grandad appeared at the bottom of the stairs, clutching a leather holdall and handing it to Luke. 'I popped in a spare set of pyjamas, a toothbrush, a book on the Boer War, things like that.'

'Great,' Luke said, taking it from him. 'The Boer War, eh?'

Grandad shrugged. 'I panicked.'

'He'll be all right,' Luke said softly, pulling Grandad into a quick hug. I felt my heart ache at the sight, gratified to see my Grandad's shoulders ease up, the lines on his face a little less deep as he clung to Luke.

'We'll follow you,' I called to the paramedics as Luke turned to kiss me on the lips. 'Come on, Grandad.'

Grandad grabbed his coat and hat and followed me outside. Geoffrey called from the living room, 'We'll get things sorted in here.' Margaret already wearing the apron and moving through to the kitchen with a tray of glasses to wash up. I felt a swell of pleasure that Grandad had such good friends, a momentary flicker of guilt wondering if I could call myself one: I must phone Amy and check all was OK with her after her hen.

'You let us know how he is,' Geoffrey called.

I nodded my head and focused on getting Grandad in the car and to the hospital, reminding myself not to be so self-obsessed just when Grandad needed me.

The blue lights reflected on the surface of my car, ghostly flashes lighting up the street, curtains pulled back in nearby houses, the silhouettes of people in their living rooms looking out on the dramatic scene. It all looked horribly real, and I thought then of Grandad summoning an ambulance many months before for Grandma. It must be bringing back all those memories. I opened the passenger door for him and made sure he was settled inside, crouching down quickly to hold his hand. 'It will be all right.' He nodded slowly.

We sat in silence in my car waiting for the ambulance to leave. Arjun had been rolled into the back of it, already connected to what looked like a drip. I felt a lump form in my throat as I saw Luke next to him in the small space, speaking reassuring words as the ambulance doors shut on them.

I started the engine. 'Let's go.' I could hear the false cheer in my voice. This wasn't how tonight was meant to turn out. I glanced across at Grandad's pale face beside me. This wasn't how it was meant to turn out at all.

Darling Cora,

I loathe hospitals. The sounds of them; the incessant buzz of noise that doesn't rest even at night: beeps, wheels turning, low voices, coughing. The unsettling feeling that the next drama is only seconds away at any given moment. Then there's the cloying smell: cabbage, tea, sweat and urine, overlaid by a pervasive bleach that makes the orderlies' hands red. The looks from strangers, everyone wondering who is in for what reason, visitor or patient, the strained glances as they wait to be seen, wait for news they don't want to hear, the feeling they would rather be anywhere else than in the hospital.

Arjun seemed impossibly small in the grey metal bed, propped up on flat white cushions, a blanket tucked up under his chin.

We had waited a while for his hip to be X-rayed and

I'd offered to stay the night. You can pay for a room in the hospital. It's normally used for first-time fathers, I think, but it was late and one was spare and I think they felt sorry for me. That can happen a lot now. I gave them my most pathetic, widowed look: it has to be good for something.

Despite the place I was glad to be there with Arjun the next morning. There was muttering: they wanted the radiologist to see him, and the radiologist then requested a consultation with the oncologist. We shared a look then, we both know what that department meant. I felt bile rise up in my throat and swallowed it down. The oncologist was a young woman with large brown eyes and a soft voice.

The moment she looked at the X-ray her mouth moved into a thin line and I recognised the expression from all the appointments we had attended together. It wasn't going to be good news.

'There does seem to be a shadow.' She indicated an area on the X ray that to my eye looked like a grey cloud in the shape of a tulip. She kept talking. Arjun was doing his pretend nod, the one he did when you used to talk him through the plot of Poldark. His eyes had misted over as she spoke, using big words and promising further tests.

I felt a stone lodge in my stomach and throat, a dead weight as I watched her leave. Arjun met my eye and gave me a weak smile, shoulders lifting in a small shrug.

'I had wondered, recently—'

Cutting him off I stood. 'It's good they've caught it

now,' I blurted, already feeling awkward and wrong-footed. You would have known what to say, Cora, you would have made him feel comforted. Instead I found myself standing up, offering to get him a coffee he didn't want and wouldn't drink. I miss you so much at times like this. Why, Arjun? He's so utterly full of life. Why does this dreadful illness go after the best of people?

I left the room and went into the corridor, walked across to the coffee machine and then walked straight past it and out of the electric double doors, as if I was just going to keep walking and not have to go back there and be brave for him. I stood on the concrete slabs just outside the hospital, a man younger than me in a gown clutching his drip for support as he inhaled a cigarette, two women not much older than Lottie sitting on the low brick wall in earnest conversation. All these stories, all these lives. I looked at the people passing in the street beyond holding carrier bags, talking on mobiles, the cars and buses inching past in the early morning traffic. I wanted everything to stop. Stop still so I could think.

My mobile beeped. Luke had called and left a message, checking on Arjun, such a thoughtful boy. What would I say to him? Nothing had been confirmed and yet it felt everything had changed. I forget how much loss Luke has seen already, and yet he has this incredibly joyful air about him – perhaps that is part of the reason why.

I know I need to head back into the hospital, back to Arjun. He'll need me, hopeless as I am. I know it might not all be doom and gloom and a grim prognosis, but the optimism I used to have about these things has extinguished since you.

I love you, Cora. I miss you and I love you and I wish you were here so I could hold you and stroke your hair and you could give me the strength to be the kind of friend I need to be.

Teddy x

Chapter 18

Love is not always found
where you were looking

SAMUEL, 77

'Remember we have an evening of parlour games tonight,' Luke called as I pounded down the stairs for the third day of a trial that was sucking all the energy from me. A complicated case with a never-ending stream of witnesses, none of whom seemed to have witnessed the same event, all watched under the hawk-like eyes of family members in the public gallery, every tut and huff echoing round the court.

Parlour games. Inwardly groaning, I fiddled with the collar of my jacket. It was possibly the last thing I would feel like after today. It had been a gruelling couple of weeks and I hadn't seen Grandad since the drama of the Monopoly evening. I knew Arjun had stayed in hospital overnight but was home now, one leg propped up on his sofa. Grandad and I had barely spoken. I felt guilty as I remembered another missed call from him last night when I was working late in chambers.

'Great,' I called back, not absolutely sure Luke could hear me as I had already shut our front door and was heading down the street.

The Tube was rammed and sweaty, the sound of a thousand people sighing, chewing and tapping on phones. It set my teeth on edge as I unfolded the *Metro*. The front cover was a picture of misery and a scandal in Westminster that everyone in chambers had been talking about yesterday. Something about a politician and an escort and a pumpkin or a courgette, I wasn't absolutely sure. I didn't have my usual curiosity to find out. Today everyone annoyed me. Particularly that guy over there who had pushed his oversized suitcase into me as he wheeled it in. I hoped the next time he went to a bowling alley they didn't have any of the right weight balls and he spends a miserable evening straining his wrist trying to play with the ones that are too heavy.

My morning in court came to an unexpected close when the trial cracked because my client suddenly decided to plead guilty to the charges against him in the hope of receiving a reduced sentence. It transpires he had rammed his car into his ex-wife to try and break her legs deliberately, and not because the car had been accidentally shifted to Drive.

I should have been happy. I was free and it wasn't even midday, and yet all the work we had done, all the earnest pleadings of the client, left a bitter taste. I left the court feeling flustered and fed up, the judge prickly about the wasted day.

Leaving the courthouse I discovered one missed call from an unlisted number and six missed calls from Amy. My pulse started to race as I fumbled to press on her name. Six missed calls. What had happened? Was she OK? She wasn't one for a dramatic gesture. I hadn't seen or spoken to her since the night of her hen do and I felt a new surge of guilt for how much time had already passed. We used to speak regularly on the phone, daily sometimes, but over the last few months when I went to return her calls I often realised it was too late, that she'd be in bed for a new school day, and sent an apologetic text instead. My palms were slippery as I gripped the phone. The last missed call had been less than half an hour before.

'Lottie.'

'Oh thank God.' I was so relieved it was her voice, having imagined a paramedic or a doctor in a hospital desperately trying to get through to a friend. 'Amy, what's wrong, what's happened?' I turned away from the traffic under the awning of a shop so I could hear her properly.

'It's the brooch,' she said.

I thought I'd misheard, the worry and panic subsiding as I tried to understand what had happened.

'Are you working in central London today?' she asked.

'I was just in court but I'm heading back to chambers.'

Amy took a breath. 'Right, is there any way – you know I wouldn't ask if it wasn't important, but I have to run the inset here on Assessment for Learning and I can't get out of it and the woman in the shop is threatening that if I don't pick up the brooch after 3 p.m. today but before 5, I can't pick it up at all . . . '

Words were running into other words and I was distracted by someone moving past me into the shop, a toddler bucking and crying in a pram at the same time as text messages were making the line momentarily freeze.

'I can't believe she's sprung it on me this last-minute, it's ridiculous. I should have used someone else.'

'Right, sorry, Amy, you need me to do what?'

A motorbike roared past in the street, the smell of diesel in the air, the sound fading into the distance.

'Do you remember – my mother gave me that brooch that Grandma wore at her wedding and it's this tradition within our family, and I went to have it repaired with this antique dealer, and she is suddenly going to visit family for weeks on end that she failed to tell me about and is just shutting her shop so if I don't get it today then it'll be too late. I can send you the address on an email.'

I caught sight of my reflection in the shop window, two deep lines in between my eyebrows as I tried to follow Amy. 'That's fine,' I said, widening my eyes so that the lines became a little shallower.

'Can you really? Oh, that would be lifesaving . . . '

Were those lines new? I wondered, moving my face again and staring intently at my reflection.

'Thank you so much, Lottie.'

'Of course,' I said, frowning again as I noticed another call on the line. 'Amy, I have to go, there's a call waiting . . . '

'That's fine, I'll email now, thanks again, I need to go anyway, inset starts in ten minutes, God I hate teaching teachers things . . . '

'Oh, poor you,' I said, biting my lip as the other call continued to distort her voice.

The toddler in the pram emerged from the shop clutching a rice cake in his fist. I smiled distractedly at the mother as she set off down the pavement. The other call ended.

'Right, thanks so much, bye.'

Amy had hung up and I frowned at the other missed call. It must be one of the clerks in chambers – they always called me on an unlisted number.

The text message was from Toby, the solicitor who had given me the brief. *Heard how today ended, c'est la vie. Drink sometime soon?* My finger hovered over the Reply button but I felt an unease nudge at me, something about him making me think I could be walking a fine line. Was this purely professional?

An email popped up, the address from Amy, which I opened and scanned. Another email followed, a clerk in chambers wanting me to check in immediately, the tone bolshie, commenting on the recent missed call. I felt the usual frisson of panic and immediately phoned them back.

'Lottie,' the clerk dived in, no time for pleasantries, 'can you get over to Slough for a last-minute appearance this afternoon?'

'Today?' I asked pointlessly, my nose wrinkled. Although last-minute appearances weren't unheard of, this seemed to be cutting things fine. 'What is it?' I asked, assuming it would be something straightforward, a request for an adjournment or similar.

'It's a new case. The client has fired George Thorpe on the first day of the damn trial and Alan recommended you take it on.'

George Thorpe was one of the other barristers in our chambers, quite an abrasive character when butting up against the wrong person. People described him as 'old school' when they were being polite, other things when they weren't.

'It would mean a lot to Alan, shore up the damage done.'

My brain was full. This could be a tricky, prolonged case, stressful and complicated. I had heard George discussing aspects of it last week, a GBH with a number of witnesses. I was being thrown in at the last moment, felt the swirl of worry at the lack of preparation. Then I thought of Alan, a man in charge of my career and possible promotion. The excitement when I heard he thought I had it in me to become the youngest silk in chambers had spurred me on to work harder than ever in the last year or so. He would be so pleased. And if I did step in now the judge might be impressed too and give me a reference when the time came to apply to become a QC.

I agreed without more thought, the clerk sighing with relieved satisfaction.

'We'll courier the papers over to you now, and contact the court letting them know you're on your way so they can move things around. You can get the train there from Paddington.'

'Great,' I said, already heading off to hail a taxi to Paddington. As I walked I noticed another unread text, this time from Luke, sent an hour earlier. Striding purposefully towards the kerb looking out for a black cab, I glanced at the message.

2 words, first word 7, second 5. Tonight. Love you x x

Frowning, it took me a second to realise it was a reminder of the parlour games later that evening. It felt silly next to all the other messages and calls. I'd call him, let him know I might be a little later than I said.

Then I paused in the street, a strange moment where I felt as if I'd forgotten something important. I checked my bag for my wallet, checked the time on my mobile. Shrugging off the feeling I pressed Luke's name, still scanning the road for an approaching cab as I waited for him to answer.

'Hey,' I said launching straight into the call. 'Where are you?' I asked, hearing voices in the background.

'I'm with Geoffrey and Arjun,' he said, sounding distracted. A girlish giggle, high and loud.

'Who's that?'

'What?'

Why did I feel Luke could hear me perfectly well? 'Who was—'

'Luke,' a voice called, interrupting my question. A woman. Something familiar in her tone.

I frowned into the phone. 'What are you guys doing?' I asked.

Luke sounded distracted as he burbled a response. 'Um, we're not doing much, I just thought I would see how Arjun was getting on.'

Why did he sound so strange? Stilted and guilty. It made me bristle a response. 'All right for some. Work going well then?'

'Yes, fine,' he said, clearly not picking up on my tone.

I hoped the next time he went to the Tube the screen announced the next train was eight minutes away.

'Well, I was just letting you know I've been asked to take on a case at the last minute. I might be a bit late tonight.' Luke was saying something to someone else, his distracted tone making me bristle more, a cab heading towards me in the distance. 'So that's it, I have to go, the taxi's here . . .'

'Right, sorry, OK, see you lat—'

The taxi pulled over next to me as I jabbed at the call. Job done. I needed to head to the train station. As I stepped inside the cab I suddenly realised where I had heard that girlish voice before: Storm. But how? Why would she be with Luke if he was visiting Arjun? It made no sense but I didn't have time now to unpick it.

The afternoon was a blur: meeting with the client, reading up on the case, trying to get a handle on the statements

I'd read. The judge, a middle-aged woman with tortoise-shell glasses, had thanked me for stepping in and although things had been up in the air I felt heroic on leaving the courthouse a few hours later. The moment I headed back to London on the train I wanted to rest my head against the seat and fall asleep. I knew I should cancel the night ahead, I had so much to do. The thought spurred me on to drag my eyes over the documents in front of me.

Paddington was just getting busy as I grabbed the escalator, passing adverts for West End shows I would never have the time to see, books I would never read. I froze as the escalator went to spew me out on to the bustling floor, people jostling around me, some pushing past, bags and briefcases pressed to their chests. I froze to the spot. Oh my God. That was the niggle in the back of my mind today: Amy. The brooch.

I stared back up at the escalator, at the stream of people. Did I have time to head back outside, get to the shop? What time had Amy said? Maybe I could make it, if I raced back up, ordered a taxi from there, prayed the rush-hour traffic was less than normal? I checked my watch, feeling a sinking sensation, knocked off balance by someone tutting as they passed me. It was five thirty. The shop would be closed. I had forgotten. I couldn't move from where I stood, chewing my lip as if I could will time to move backwards. I thought of Amy's words, her desperation, the ultimatum. And this wasn't something I could replace.

Someone else tutted as they skirted me.

I started to be pulled along by the crowd, moving in a daze as I ran through any options I had left. I wanted mobile reception. Maybe the woman would agree to a later time, perhaps she had been exaggerating and could open it tomorrow? How early was her flight? I could try. It wasn't over yet.

I felt desperate as I headed to Grandad's. Amy never really asked for anything. She was absurdly capable and efficient. She was always the one turning up with a lasagne because she knew I would burn whatever I offered, the one who booked tickets for things when I expressed an interest in wanting to go. She would arrange the holiday details, flights, hotels and make everything ridiculously easy for me, needing only to transfer her half the cash with a click of my mobile.

She juggled the problems of kids and parents; she had been like a mother to me when my own mother was on the other side of the world. She had never let me down. I felt acid churn in my stomach, knowing at some point I was going to have to dial her number, tell her that I had forgotten, that I had completely failed to come through for the one thing she had asked me to do.

'Parlour games,' Luke chorused as I stood on the doorstep of Grandad's place.

He was holding a glass in one hand, looking casual, relaxed and happy. It made me feel even more taut.

'Charades are beginning. Thank God you got here when you did – you might have missed it.'

I could barely raise a half-smile.

'I've got you a gin and tonic. The gin's got black pepper in it but don't worry, it's nicer than it sounds, and we're just running through the rules for the eighteenth time with Howard ... he is struggling with the not-speaking element of the game.'

I should have told Luke there and then about the day I'd had. Luke would understand, he knew what Amy meant to me. But I couldn't, the shame building within me: what would he think?

'Come on. Arjun's up, two words, it's a film. I'm frightened it's going to be *Free Willy*, he has form.'

In that second I wanted to turn and head straight home. Luke's mood was so completely at odds with mine. Why couldn't I shake off this irritated gloom and give him the smile he wanted? I could still ring the shop tomorrow, it wasn't completely hopeless. I should just explain my unsettled mood and—

'Is that Lottie?' I could hear Grandad's voice from the living room as I wearily stepped inside the house.

'*Tall! Big! Very big!*' Howard's voice was booming out.

'Stop guessing for a second, Lottie's here,' Geoffrey was saying.

'*Very, very big!*'

'*Howard!*' everyone shouted.

I couldn't face heading into the living room. The energy and high spirits was too much. I looked down the corridor to the door of the kitchen, imagining for a second pushing it open, stepping inside to spill all my troubles on to the sympathetic shoulder of my grandma. She had always known how to bring me round, listening with her pale blue eyes trained on my face, moving in for a sympathetic cuddle before a few stern words, rallying and inspiring to put things into perspective. A photo of her taken on her sixty-fifth birthday stared down at me from the wall of the corridor, a laughing shot of her clutching a full glass of Pimm's next to the barbecue in the garden, smoke haloed around her, Grandad looking on in admiration.

She wasn't here any more and the pain hit me all over again, as it did sometimes at the strangest moments, taking my breath away. She simply didn't exist. She wasn't in the kitchen fixing up a drink, grumbling about the men not knowing a coaster if it hit them in the face, singing, badly, along to the radio that she always had turned up too loud.

'Lottie!' Howard called. 'Arjun's pausing his frankly disastrous performance for you. Two words. A film, apparently, although I'm not convinced.'

I took a breath, stepping into the living room to see Arjun, his back to the group, hands hovering over his flies as if he was genuinely planning to drop his trousers. He then turned back to the group as if he'd forgotten something, cupping one hand behind his ear. Everyone was frowning at him in confusion, staring at the hand lingering at his crotch. I wanted to loosen up, accepting the drink from Luke with a quiet, 'Thanks.'

'Glad you're here,' Luke said, squeezing my shoulder.

'None of that, Luke. Lottie can be on our team,' Howard said, beckoning me to sit next to him. 'Sit on the pouffe here. It's two words, a film apparently. I think the first word is something to do with something being tall or big.'

'What's he doing with his ear?' Geoffrey muttered to Grandad.

'*Ear!*' Howard shouted. '*Hearing aid! Face!*' As if all the words might add up to the right answer.

'Hearing difficulties,' Teddy threw in, sounding as confused as I felt.

'*EAR!*' Howard screeched, perhaps assuming it was missed the first time.

Come on, Lottie, say something: it's not all about you.

'I think he's trying to say it *sounds like*,' Luke said slowly. Arjun gave him a grateful nod.

'No nodding!' Howard barked, clearly determined to follow all the rules now that he had learnt them.

Arjun turned back around again and stared pleadingly at the group, both hands back over his crotch, reaching for his zip. He wiggled his bottom at everyone.

'Sounds like . . . bottom?' Luke hazarded a guess as Arjun turned away from them.

'*Cotton!*' Howard shouted.

'That in no way sounds like bottom,' Geoffrey stated.

'*Mottom!*'

'And that's not a word, is it?' Geoffrey added.

'*Flotsam!*'

'Wiggle!' Grandad barked suddenly. 'Very Tall Wiggle. Arjun, are you sure it's a film we know?'

Arjun had undone the buckle on his belt and was starting to fiddle with the top button, all the time wiggling his bottom and staring round at them.

'Bloody impossible,' Howard huffed, throwing himself back in his armchair, arms folded as Arjun continued to move from side to side, one hand undoing his fly. He pulled down his trousers to reveal a conker brown bottom. It was weird that this wasn't the first time I had seen it. It was fast becoming a habit.

'*High Noon*! *High Noon*!' Grandad had sprung to his feet.

Arjun turned to Grandad, grinning. 'Exactly.' At the same time that the rest of the room shielded their eyes.

'*Arjun!*' Geoffrey shouted. 'You can pull them back up now.'

'Christ,' Howard said.

'Oops, sorry, *High Noon*, I *knew* you'd get there in the end,' Arjun said, fiddling with his zip again.

Luke was clutching his sides in mirth.

I wanted to take part but found I was always thirty seconds behind. I noticed that Grandad was distracted too, a strange sad smile on his face, before the noise of everyone else prompted him to join in. I tried too, my smile fixed, too bright, feeling that I was outside the group looking in. I took another sip of my drink, hoping to blend into the background of the evening, surround myself with the noise and the fun before slinking back to our flat and bed and the worries circling inside me. Then a sentence made me freeze in my tracks.

'Lottie, your turn, show us how it's done,' Geoffrey said, giving me a gentle nudge.

I slopped gin over the side of the glass. 'Oh no, I'm really not r—'

'Yes, come on, Lottie, we're in desperate need of a win,' Howard said, removing the glass from my hands.

'No, honestly, I'm—'

'Lottie, Lottie,' Luke had started chanting, clapping his hands twice in between saying my name. He was pissed, eyes squinting as he grinned at me. I felt disproportionately furious with him, hoping then and there that the next time he went online to buy something he wanted they only stocked it in every size that wasn't his.

The others had joined in the chant. Even Grandad was now clapping and saying my name. The living room was alive with it and I stood up wearily, not reacting to the great cheer that followed.

'She's up.'

'Give her space.'

'Remember it's a book or a film or a television show,' Howard stressed, topping up his own glass, 'but don't make it something we won't know, something only young people know, like *Love Island*. Or *Tattoo Fixers*.'

Geoffrey looked across at him. 'What are they?'

Howard clapped his hands together, making me jump. 'See! Old fogeys don't know what these things are. It's only because I'm such a culture vulture that I stay up on what's hot and what's not.'

Luke was clutching his sides again. Arjun seemed quiet next door to him, one hand on his chest as he lowered himself into an armchair. His turn seemed to have wiped him out.

'Come on, Lottie.'

Dragging my eyes away from Arjun I stood on the rug in front of the electric fire trying to summon an original thought. Book. Film. TV Show. It was like I had never heard of these phenomena. I swallowed, my mouth dry. I was devoid of all thoughts. Only Amy.

I closed my eyes briefly and then opened them again.

'Is it a film?' Howard called out loudly.

'Let the girl start, Howard,' Grandad said quietly.

Time ticked on and I felt the whole room staring at me, waiting for me to move, to come alive.

'Is it a book?' Geoffrey asked in a kindly voice, prompting me to begin.

I nodded. 'It's sort of both—'

'She's talking,' pointed out Arjun in an accusatory tone. 'You told me we couldn't do that,' he said, turning in his chair to glare at Luke.

'You can't.' Luke laughed, swigging at his drink.

'Cheat!' Arjun said with a low rumble.

My mouth snapped shut and I felt strangely exposed, sweat dampening my palms.

It was horrific. I went through torturous motions, desperately trying to make Howard and Geoffrey understand what I was getting at. How hard was it to act out *Pride and Prejudice*, which I soon realised was a book, film *and* TV series? I tried to add TV series halfway through but they just kept shouting '*Square*' at me. I felt sweat bead in my hairline and it was only after a ridiculous amount of time that Luke quietly came to the rescue, whispering the correct answer across to Geoffrey.

'Hey, that's not fair,' shouted Arjun, suddenly absurdly competitive after his *High Noon* success.

Grandad had got up to get more drinks and I was simply glad to be moving away from the rug and all the eyes following me, back to the pouffe, taking a grateful gulp of gin, the tonic flat and the ice melted. I had to get out of there. I needed to look over the brief for the next day in court. I needed to think about how to fix things for Amy.

My phone vibrated in my pocket as Luke got up to have the next go. I looked down at the screen, feeling a renewed wave of sickness swell up inside me.

It was from Amy. *Thanks sooooo much for today. You're a total lifesaver.*

'Film, film . . . '

'Four words.'

'First word.'

'Film.'

'We've already said that, Teddy. Keep up.'

Oh God, what was I going to do? I hated myself. I hoped for all the bad things I normally wished on others to happen to me. I should step on every upturned plug. I should lose all my teeth bar one and that one should be the tooth that gets the toothache. I was a shit friend, a shit person.

Luke was gesturing behind him, the others calling out answers. They were arguing over his use of two fingers to denote the word 'to'.

'I thought we couldn't do that.'

'It's just a preposition, don't sweat it.'

'It's vital. It's a quarter of the whole thing.'

The answer was clearly *Back To The Future* but it took Luke's team about fifteen minutes to get there, by which time I had collapsed into an even deeper gloom, the gin long gone, shoulders drooping, my body slumped on my pouffe.

Luke, returning to his seat, stopped by me, noticing my expression. Placing a hand on my knee he leant down. 'Everything all right? Worried you're losing?'

'God, Luke, don't be so obnoxious,' I snapped, shoving his hand away, redirecting all the anger I felt at myself and firing it at him like bullets.

He stepped back quickly as if I really had shot him, mouth pursed, eyes dark. The room fell silent, just the quiet tick of the carriage clock, the odd muffled cough. There was shuffling in the room as Howard, Geoffrey and Arjun's eyes flitted, never resting, Arjun inspecting his nails as if there was something under one, Geoffrey scuffing at the carpet and Howard blinking at the ceiling lights, window and mantelpiece, eyebrows twitching.

Only my grandfather was looking at me, the expression on his face making me feel even worse. His eyes sad, his mouth turned down: a look of utter disappointment.

'I've got to go: work,' I explained, standing up quickly and stumbling towards the door, not even bothering to apologise as I opened it, feeling hot, shamed tears filling my throat.

Luke didn't follow me out as I moved down the corridor, fishing my coat off the hook, thrusting my phone in my bag.

Grandad emerged in the corridor, the room still hushed behind him, aware his voice was carrying.

'That wasn't like you,' he said, moving towards me.

I stayed turned away from him facing the rack of coats, feeling the same anger, tiredness and confusion swirl in me. 'I'm tired,' I snapped, clutching my bag to me. 'I just need to get back and work.'

'Not everything can be about work, you know,' he said.

'God, Grandad, I don't need a lecture from you now, all right?'

'I'm not, that's . . . ' He tailed away.

'I'm heading home.'

Grandad didn't reply, just watched as I opened the front door. Rain had created a misty sheen on the pavements and the streetlamps glowed orange. I stepped outside.

He didn't call me back.

Darling Cora,

Oh dear. Since the rather awkward end to our charades evening Luke has been a bit down. Lottie rather took things out on him, the poor boy, and he left that night dreadfully quiet and sad. He hasn't said anything since, of course, but normally he bounds in, a ball of energy, launching immediately into a forensic breakdown of Liverpool's latest game, keeping me updated as to what he's been working on and, when he thinks I'm not looking, quietly getting on with scrubbing coffee cups I've left around the place, wiping down the table, sweeping the kitchen floor.

This week, though, he's been lacklustre. I've been prompting conversation when it seems he has disappeared into his own thoughts, when his smile seems slow to come and a little too wide, not reaching his eyes. I know if it was you you'd simply ask him, bustle him to the table, foist on to him the largest chocolate cake slice you could cut and look him in the eye directly. I can't do that, of course, and I'm frightened, too, that the reason for his mood is all down to Lottie *– and I know really that's none of my business, not that it would have stopped you.*

So I thought I would take him fishing. A lake seemed like a good place for two men to chat, the only snag being that, as you know, I can't fish. But how hard could it be, I thought? Geoffrey had the equipment we needed, he's talked me through how to put on the bait and cast off, and he'd given me some fishing lingo so that Luke *wouldn't suspect I was an amateur. It should have been fine, I thought. Geoffrey rarely returned having caught anything anyway, so I just hoped for a similar outcome.*

I picked him up reasonably early, unsurprised to hear

that Lottie had already left the house to work on a brief in the library. I hadn't realised how many weekends she spent preparing for the week ahead. I so admire her work ethic, but I can see why it would be a strain. Luke was quiet as he sat staring out of the passenger seat next to me. I was a little uncomfortable in my fishing outfit. Geoffrey told me to wear sand or khaki and had lent me a rather ugly floppy hat. Luke was simply dressed in jeans, boots and a sweatshirt and I felt about one hundred and five.

I tried to look confident as we pulled up into the car park, relieved as Luke took the rods and bag from me. I'd already forgotten how to extend the rod but fortunately Luke worked it out without me having to admit the fact. I had borrowed a couple of low folding canvas chairs and realised as I sank into mine that I would probably never be able to get out of it again. Proud to have remembered my Thermos of tea, I offered Luke the larger of the plastic cups.

Things seem to be going remarkably well. We had got the bait on, we had propped up the rods and the lake stretched out before us, its surface largely uninterrupted, the odd ripple caused by a landing insect. The lake was edged with trees that cast dark shadows in the water on the other side and above us the clouds were lifting, turning the water of the lake even bluer. I was beginning to see what Geoffrey saw in the activity, my head resting back against the canvas, warm tea in my hands and the promise of a whole day of calm.

I was just gearing up to ask Luke one of my questions. I had a few planned in the hope that they would lead us to a suitably deep conversation. The opening question was to be a simple 'How have you been?', followed by a second question, 'You've seemed a little quiet recently, has anything changed?'

'So, Luke, how have you b—'

Before I could finish there was a disturbance in the water and I could see my rod vibrating a little.

'Christ.'

I jerked forward, grabbing the end of the rod in time and giving Luke a rather too panicked glance. I hadn't really covered with Geoffrey what to do in the event of actually catching a fish, and I was fast descending into a full-blown panic attack.

'Oh God.'

Luke looked across at me. 'All OK?'

'Oh, oh yes, fine,' I said, attempting to bluster my way through but really struggling just to get myself out of the chair. I had seen enough films to realise that I probably needed to start winding the line in but whatever was on the end of it was making it hard work. My hands, arthritic at the best of times, couldn't get to grips with the damn thing.

'Can I help?' Luke was hovering above me, a concerned look on his face. I suppose it was fair enough – I was currently twisted half in and half out of the chair, clinging to the rod with an expression on my face that did not exude confidence.

'Er, if you could' – I tried to remember a few of the lines Geoffrey had taught me – 'bring in the tackle, wind in the reel, you know, land the fish, that would be excellent.'

Luke took the rod from my hands and, as if he had been doing this all his life, wound in the line with apparent ease. Emerging from the water was a silvery flash of fish and I realised with renewed horror that I would have to put this thing out of its misery. I had not thought this fishing trip through. I still couldn't even get out of the chair but the wriggling fish was almost upon us and, as the senior member of our party, I would surely be expected to dispatch it. I've never been of farming stock, purchasing all my meat and fish from the deli counters of Waitrose, and I had a distinct memory of fainting as a teenager when forced to dissect a frog. I was staring at the end of the line, dread building inside me.

Geoffrey had run me through the items in the fishing bag, which included a small wooden mallet. Was this the instrument of death I was expected to wield? It would really help if I could get out of the chair.

Why hadn't I taken Luke to a bar like a normal man? We could be sitting at a table, two beers in front of us, the light strains of some popular music being piped around us. Or a football match, we could have talked in the car on the way there. Curse Geoffrey, he definitely didn't prepare me well enough. Who doesn't talk through what you're meant to do with a fish when you catch a fish when you're going fishing? I really must get out of this chair.

Luke, who by now had done literally everything, was holding the wriggling silver muscle on the grass and awaiting further instructions.

'I'm just getting the mallet!' I called, tipping forward and nearly breaking both my wrists as I tumbled headfirst onto the ground.

With shaking hands I tore through the bag, emerging with the item, which immediately seemed heavier in my grip.

'Right then.' I approached the fish with about as much enthusiasm as I had approached Paula on the dance floor of the recent 1970s themed disco night. 'Best do it.'

Why had I had the bad luck to actually catch a fish? Once I'd hit it, what then? I hadn't exactly bought the wherewithal to start smoking fish.

'I'll hold on to it, you hit it,' Luke called, energy in his voice as he watched me with no short amount of respect. Oh God, he expected it. I must get a hold of myself and put the poor thing out of its misery. It seemed to be staring at me out of its one wild eye. Beseeching.

I brought the mallet down on its head, missing it by an inch, smacking the grass with the blow and relieved to have narrowly avoided Luke's other hand.

'Er, should I?' he offered.

Nodding pathetically we swapped places and Luke in one swift, humane swipe had done the deed.

I felt impossibly relieved, sinking back on to my ankles and hearing the crackling of bones. My hat was set at a jaunty angle in all the excitement. I felt I had run a marathon in the last ten minutes. Now, however, staring down at the catch, I felt a swell of satisfaction.

'How extraordinary,' I said, admiring the subtly shifting rainbow of colours on its scales.

Luke offered a hand and we both sat back in the chairs, staring again across the water. What had I been meaning to ask him? It all seemed rather distant and confused now.

'I can't believe you caught one, that was amazing.' He seemed more enthused now than in all the times I'd seen him recently. I realised I had missed his energy, coming to rely on his visits, looking forward to them. You had always had that same spirit, that same desire to live in the present. I think it's what you so liked about him and what you felt Lottie really needed in her life.

'So,' I said, the lake in front of us calm once more, a couple of dog walkers passing on the other side, 'is everything all right?'

'Yes.'

'Good.'

I bit my lip, knowing this wouldn't really cut the mustard. There's no way you'd let him off this easily. But I didn't want to ruin this mood, this post-triumphant daze we were both in.

'I just thought . . . ' I cleared my throat, determinedly staring straight ahead. God, why was this emotional stuff so difficult? Since you died I have realised how much of this I had left to you. When we spoke to Geoffrey about

his wife, it was always you probing with the trickier questions. I would leave the room to make more tea, veer off into comments about the weather or Geoffrey's recent concert trip.

'I thought, maybe, you've seemed a little, that is . . . oh look, a hummingbird. Oh no, no it's not, it's a duck. More common, ducks.'

'Are you all right, Teddy?' Luke was looking at me, his face etched with concern.

'Me. I'm excellent, thank you! Excellent.'

'Well, that's good. Thanks for bringing me fishing. I've never done it before. I get it, though. It's nice, peaceful.'

I thought then of his father, who might have introduced him to fishing. So easy to forget sometimes that Luke didn't have as many people in his life as he might have liked.

'What I really, well, I thought . . . ' I really had to get the words out, this was getting ridiculous, soon he would assume I was having some kind of stroke. 'I hoped you haven't been too down about anything recently. You've not been quite the same,' I said in a rush, staring at the duck as if I was addressing it. It did turn to look in my direction, as if it was glad I recognised he had been a little low too.

There was a momentary silence and I was half tempted to glance across at him. I heard him sigh and the sound was a small, sad sound.

'Perhaps a little. Sometimes . . . '

He tailed away and I held my breath, waiting for more.

'I worry, about Lottie and me,' he admitted, 'that we have changed. That we want different things now.'

It was my turn to fall silent.

'Things seemed to have got so much better recently, old Lottie was back, all these outings we went on together, the dates, but . . .'

He tailed away again and I scuffed my toe into the grass, desperately wanting to say the right thing.

'She can be' – I scuffed at the grass again, not wanting to be disloyal or critical – 'I think she can forget sometimes what makes her truly happy. She is so incredibly clever and ambitious and talented but I want her to be sure that she is living the life she really wants. I suppose that was why the old-fashioned courting idea so appealed. A way to get her to focus on something else for a while, on your relationship. I thought it was working . . .'

Luke settled back, looking out across the water glumly, 'I thought so too.'

We both sat like that for a while.

A small bird dipped into view, hovering for a second before skimming the surface of the water and leaving as quickly as it arrived. It seemed to have woken Luke from his thoughts.

'Thanks, Tedd— Oh my God,' he said, sitting up with a jerk, twisting in his chair, 'I think something's biting.'

I stared at the mallet, my stomach turning over, 'Oh . . . great,' I said, watching him turn the reel. 'That's excellent.'

The things I do, Cora, honestly. I'll have nightmares for weeks . . .

Teddy x

Chapter 19

Love is . . . enough

MAX, 80

I should have been desperate to see Amy. I needed my best friend, needed to spill out my worries about things at the moment. Ask her about work and stress and Luke and listen to her advice. Instead, though, I was dreading seeing her. Somehow I still hadn't told her about the brooch. Every time we'd texted or spoken I had distracted her with excited, wedding-related squealing: 'Soooon', 'Future Mrrrrsssss', 'NOT LONG NOOOOOOOW', cutting her off like a bridesmaid on speed. She didn't seem to suspect and I felt worse as we worked each other up into a fever of hysterical excitement. Maybe I could get her so excited she wouldn't remember at all? Brooch amnesia?

Even on the way to meet her, the supposed handing-over

of the beautiful antique family heirloom brooch, I didn't have a plan. Like I somehow thought the brooch might magically appear in my hand, as if I was suddenly a character in Harry Potter and could just summon it from the air. I closed my eyes and muttered, hoping when I opened them to see it lying on the chewing-gum-spattered pavement, twinkling. 'Hello, Lottie,' it would sparkle, 'you haven't screwed up completely: here I am to save the day.'

I had also spent way too many hours trawling Etsy believing I might be able to somehow pass off any old antique brooch as *the* antique brooch, taking it along with me and then practising my best surprised face, 'What do you mean, this isn't the one? This is what the woman gave me. I am disgusted, appalled, nay, horrified' (pause for dramatic hand to chest). I knew that lie would be busted the moment ever-efficient Amy tracked down the poor woman back from visiting her family to bawl her out. And she could always tell when I was lying anyway. Like the time I told her I hadn't snogged Garry Peel outside the men's loos of a nightclub, or when I told her I'd never eaten foie gras. She just knew.

I stood outside the glossy John Lewis store, breathing slowly in and out. Stay calm, Lottie. Stay calm. You are here to help Amy choose her wedding presents. This is exciting. Just keep talking to her about presents, constantly distract her with sandwich-makers and crystal jugs in different shapes. Ask her a lot of questions about the thread count she wants in a summer duvet. Maybe she won't ask. Maybe she won't remember. Maybe by the end of today she'll still like you.

I felt too hot in my jeans and cotton shirt as I pushed my way inside, weaving round prams, people clutching bags of shopping, others pausing to browse the make-up counters. I headed to the lift, feeling my palms dampen with every step. My bag was hideously, horribly empty. I regretted not buying something from Etsy. Anything seemed better than producing nothing.

Amy was, of course, already in situ, looking relaxed and lovely in an orange shift dress which made her dark skin look even smoother and more gorgeous. Her hair was glossy under the lights and she gave me an enormous grin as the lift doors opened, holding up a small white plastic item. 'It's for bleeping stuff. I can't believe Will didn't want to do this with me,' she said, stepping across to give me an enormous hug and then stepping back to bleep me.

I swallowed, all ready to break down in confession. I was a terrible person, I would do anything I could to fix it, I really was desperately sorry, I was still leaving messages for the woman in the shop in an attempt to salvage things . . .

Before I could say anything, however, a glowing, impossibly skinny woman with a strawberry-blonde ponytail descended on me, her straight white teeth flashing as she welcomed me to the store. 'You must be Amy's partner— Oh, I'm sorry' – she held up a manicured hand – 'my colleague is calling me back, hold on.'

The shop assistant moved away so I had time to turn to Amy, a perplexed look on my face, other thoughts fading.

Amy shifted her weight from one foot to another. 'Oh, I was a bit embarrassed that Will didn't want to come, so I panicked and said you were my partner ... just go along with it, all right?'

The lady was returning and I hastily nodded before tucking my arm into Amy's and resting my head on her shoulder. 'I am.'

'You are ...?' The lady tipped her head to one side in question.

'Amy's partner,' I announced in a loud voice, following it up with a strange giggle I had got from somewhere. 'She's wonderful. I'm so lucky,' I gushed. 'I never thought I would find someone who would just *get* me, you know ... '

I could just hear Amy whispering, 'Too much,' as I stroked her forearm with one finger.

I trailed off.

'I'm ... glad,' the lady said slowly, straightening her skirt. 'As I've told Amy, the process is pretty simple. We can edit anything you like at the end so don't worry too much, just enjoy our selections. And I will be nearby if you need any assistance.'

'Thanks again,' Amy said, smiling and clearly wanting to get on and start shopping. 'We're going to head to Homeware.'

'Something for the bedroom,' I chirruped, the weird giggle back.

'Er ... fabulous,' she nodded, moving to a safe distance.

'Do you do that stroky-arm thing with Luke?' Amy asked.

'Why, you like it?' I asked, resting my head on her shoulder again for show.

'It tickles. Right, come on, life partner, let's furnish our marital home ...'

Half an hour later and we were just having too much fun for me to go and ruin things. In fact, as the minutes passed it really did seem possible that Amy just wouldn't ask. Any time we had a lull in conversation I would direct her attention to another candlestick, coaster set or teapot.

We had already zapped a stunning set of dinner plates, a cake stand, a set of magenta napkins, pepper and salt pots, place mats, table runners and more. Now Amy was hesitating over a ceramic pestle and mortar.

'What do you even do with it? Which bit is the pestle and which is the mortar?'

Amy's forehead wrinkled at my question. 'Well, you grind stuff in it.'

'What stuff?'

'Small stuff that needs to be made smaller ...' Amy sounded unsure.

I picked it up and turned it over in my hands.

'My grandma had one,' Amy said, 'Although I think she might have just kept small change in it.'

Grandmother.

That prompted her. I felt my grip on the ceramic tighten, my knuckles whitening.

'Oh, that reminds me . . . ' she began.

I felt my stomach drop, my throat dry up. I licked my lips, turning away. 'Maybe a pestle and mortar would be worth getti—'

'Did you bring her brooch?'

I thought I might drop the pestle and mortar.

'Maybe you should get a KitchenAid. I've always wanted a KitchenAid,' I said, my voice suddenly an octave higher, faster too.

'Lottie?'

I placed the pestle and mortar back on the shelf in front of me with shaking hands. 'Mary Berry uses one, doesn't she, I think, I mean, if she doesn't I imagine she would want one . . . '

'Have you got the brooch?'

I really couldn't avoid it. I closed my eyes, ready to turn around.

The shop assistant reappeared. 'Are you both all right? Finding everything you need?'

Amy ignored her. 'Lottie . . . ' Her voice was low, a warning. I felt tears prick the back of my eyes. Oh God.

'More time needed?' she asked, oblivious to what she had walked in on.

I turned to face Amy, palms up, appealing already. 'I'm so, so, sorry, I . . . '

The shop assistant was still standing next to us, her stuck-on smile faltering as she started to sense the tension.

'Did you just leave it at home?' Amy asked.

Maybe I should have leapt on that chance to escape the

inevitable but my face couldn't hide it. I felt it crumpling, slowly shaking my head side to side. 'I . . . I'm so sorry. I went back, I called, I . . . '

The shop assistant attempted to make her exit. 'Well, I see you have things in hand so I'll just . . . ' She cupped a hand to her neck as Amy took a step towards me.

'You didn't even get it,' Amy whispered, her whole face draining of colour, her free hand curling into a tight fist.

'I . . . I meant to, I . . . ' What could I say? I knew there was nothing that could give me a good reason. This wasn't court, I couldn't argue my way out of it.

'I can't believe it.' She raked two hands through her hair, her voice loud in the high-ceilinged room, seeming to bounce off every shiny surface. 'You knew, Lottie, you *knew* it had to be that day.'

She was pacing up and down. The shop assistant stifled a cough into a hand. 'I could have rung someone else. If I'd known I could have . . . God, why did I even . . . '

The lady brought her hands together, her voice bright and hopeful. 'I'll be over here then, I'll just . . . ' She seemed to hover in between us, really not sure of the etiquette, or maybe concerned Amy might start throwing pestles and mortars at me.

' . . . trust you? What was I thinking? Recently you've been so caught up in yourself you don't have time to think about anyone else. I'm amazed you found the time to squeeze me in today.'

The words hurt, fired at me in a sarcastic rush as Amy revved up, in her stride now. I felt the tears on my face freeze, heard the accusations levelled at me, felt unable to do anything but stand there, hating the shop assistant for not leaving, noticing two of her colleagues staring from over at the till.

'Do you even care? I told you that brooch was special. My mother and my grandmother wore it on their wedding days . . . '

Amy's words started to break up, choked by tears. I hadn't seen Amy cry in years, she was always impossibly stoic. I felt nausea swirl in my stomach, feeling any fight I might have had leak out of me. She was right. I had completely messed up. I hadn't thought about her.

'If you want any further assistance . . . ' The assistant looked on the verge of tears herself, stepping backwards, palms up as if we were two quite dangerous animals and she shouldn't show her back to us. She melted away, heading to the till and the other two women staring at us. They all started whispering.

Amy had grown quiet, the plastic white bleeper held limply by her side.

I took a breath. 'I'm going to try everything I can to get it back before the wedding,' I said in a quiet voice, tinged with my desperation. God, why had I messed up? I was causing Amy this pain so close to her wedding. Amy, who had always been such a loyal, steadfast friend to me: sending me flowers when I broke my wrist, paying my rent one month when I'd spent all my money on the deposit for a new flat, inviting Luke and me away to her parents' Majorca holiday home, treating me like a sister.

'Don't bother,' Amy said slowly, all the anger seeped out of her. She couldn't meet my eye. 'Don't bother to do anything else. I don't want you to.'

'But the woman ... maybe she'll be back soon, maybe I could—'

'Lottie, I don't want you to do anything.'

'But I think—'

'I don't want you to be my bridesmaid.'

I heard the words seconds too late, feeling all the breath leave my body as she said them. She met my eye now, a steely determination I had seen in her before, knowing she had made up her mind. She had looked the same when she told me she was going to be a teacher, when she said she was going to run the London Marathon. When Amy committed to something she did it, she was amazing. She was my amazing best friend. I felt a terrible ache deep inside me.

'I ... ' Now my eyes were full of tears. I couldn't help it, aware still of the hush in the shop, the shop assistant and her colleagues half-heartedly pretending to stack shelves, wipe down surfaces, neaten stock, all the time snatching glances across at us, wondering what had befallen our happy party of two.

'Just go,' Amy said, folding her arms, no more emotion in her voice, her face set, her voice brisk. She looked every inch the no-nonsense deputy headmistress.

I nodded, not trusting myself to open my mouth and speak, stumbling away from her in the direction of the lift, almost sending a row of egg cups reeling as I blinked tears out of my eyes. 'I'm so, so sorry,' I whispered, feeling a terrible blackness inside me, a hole. I had done this, I deserved this.

I jabbed at the lift, hating the wait, aware of Amy watching behind me, other shoppers staring, wondering what had happened. A flushed-face couple in the middle of a joke appeared as the doors opened, the woman's face changing as she took in the tears spilling down my cheeks, my hunched shoulders.

'Are you—'

I stepped in past her, not wanting to talk, just stabbing the buttons to get away from the place. The couple moved away and the last thing I saw as the doors closed on me was Amy's face, cheeks glistening, mouth set in a line, watching me leave.

Darling Cora,

I think that fishing trip might have done the trick. Luke accosted me a couple of days after it with a plan and I have just returned from helping him with it.

I had been pruning the garden, fairly sure you would be chastising me for letting weeds grow. I've never been completely convinced which ones are weeds, sometimes they seem rather pretty. Luke approached me looking uncharacteristically nervous, his normal relaxed demeanour ruffled, a hand through his hair, his eyes darting around the plants.

'It is looking very good,' he finally said.

I sat up. God, my body ached. I see now why you were so keen on purchasing that heated roller massager for your back. My knees sounded like something was popping in there as I stood. I knew he wasn't here to talk about our garden. For an enchanting moment I wondered if he might be here to ask for our permission. For Lottie. I know you always wanted him and her to stay together. A 'keeper' you had called him. It had been when he brought you those dark chocolate ginger nut biscuits a week or so after you'd made a comment about loving them. You were putty for him after that. That and his 'lovely hands', which I still can't quite seem to see are different to anyone else's hands, and I swear sometimes he catches me looking. He certainly has very neatly clipped nails.

I never asked what you thought of my hands. I hope you liked them.

He dithered about the subject for an age, following me inside in silence, pacing the kitchen before finally sitting down. In fact, our tea had almost gone cold. He had been twitching in his chair in the kitchen, tapping on the placemat, and I was about to make my excuses and get back out to the garden.

'Do you think you could help me with something?' He blurted it out, spilling the last of his tea on the Formica table and then leaping up to wipe at the puddle.

'Calm down!' I laughed and threw a cloth at him. 'Of course. What do you want?'

'I was thinking, after our fishing, about what I could

do. And well . . . I've been seeing a bit of Arjun lately, helping him with something, secret, just work really, so I thought I could ask him for a favour too and he was keen but, of course, with his hip like it is . . .'

What secret project was Luke working on with Arjun? Why would his hip stop him? I was desperately trying to keep up, Cora, unused to seeing Luke so flustered.

'Well, the long and short of it is Arjun told me that you and Cora could dance. That is, you were, are' – he corrected himself quickly – 'quite a good dancer. Arjun wants to help too but he's out of action so he told me to ask you.'

I frowned, trying to unravel what he was asking. I wasn't sure there was a question as yet.

'You see, I was telling him I'd like to do something a little special. I know we've both been doing the odd thing, dating the old-fashioned way, but I wanted to really show I could make an effort. So I thought, what could I do? I could learn a dance. Women love a man who can dance, I know, I see it at weddings all the time. I'm the man over by the bar making my way through the circle of Brie and the wedding cake and hoping Lottie is too distracted to want to dance, but really I know she would. And I've never felt equipped, left-footed, like a giraffe on roller-skates.'

He finally paused for breath and honestly, Cora, I almost roared with laughter. The poor man looked like he might melt into a puddle of red-faced embarrassment in our kitchen right then and there. You would have made him feel a lot better, you would have gushed and enthused over his idea. As it was I bumbled through it, his own embarrassment making me more awkward.

'I could help,' I offered.

His shoulders sagged with relief but the crimson didn't leave his cheeks. 'That's great. I wanted to learn something straightforward, something I could lead Lottie through. Arjun mentioned a waltz or a cha-cha. I wasn't sure. They all sound like different brands of whiskey.'

He was about to rattle away again so I interrupted him. 'A paso doble might be a good option,' I said tentatively.

He leapt on it. 'A paso doble, right, yes, that sounds ideal. Well, when could we make a start, so to speak? Arjun mentioned that the smaller of the two function rooms in the main building of the club is often empty and it has a very polished floor.'

I could feel my face pulling into a frown. Arjun had clearly enjoyed setting this up, knowing I would be out of my depth – although it was nice to hear Arjun had something else to focus on too. 'Yes, a polished floor is, um, very important. Vital in fact,' I said solemnly.

'Great. Well, I could maybe make it over on one of the days I work from home, or I can do a lot of evenings after work.'

'Won't Lottie notice you're missing?'

Luke paused then, something different shifting in his expression, 'She works late a lot,' he said, not wanting to offer more.

I nodded, hoping again that Lottie was all right. I hated the thought that her job took every ounce of her time and energy. This was a great idea of Luke's, and I knew Lottie, a romantic at heart, like you, my darling, would love the gesture. Do you remember you both went completely cuckoo after that cinema trip to La La Land*? And then you both made me sit through that Ryan chap on the DVD. So much swooning and sighing from you both I'd had to put in earplugs.*

I picked up my phone to Arjun when Luke had left.

TEXT: Luke just asked me to teach him to dance.

*ARJUN: *Crying laughing emojis**

Well, this evening was our first lesson. Luke arrived on time, looking even more nervous. I almost expected him to make his excuses and leave. Arjun appeared clutching a CD and a portable ghetto blaster, you know the type, although Luke then did something on his phone and the same song came through on his speakers. Phones really can do everything now. It's terrifying.

I stood in the middle of the polished floor (!) and attempted to show Luke the steps. I had to lead him, my dry hands in his (they were surprisingly soft, I am sort of coming round to what you see in them), absolutely not making eye contact.

Arjun was shouting instructions from his chair, leg stuck out in front of him, getting more and more frustrated with us both and clearly wanting to leap up and intervene. You always said Arjun felt music in his bones.

I hadn't seen him so energised in days and I was grateful to Luke for that too. No one knows what is happening with Arjun and he has sworn me to secrecy. Now his thinning face was animated, his voice strong as he issued more commands.

Luke took a while to get going, fumbling initially, bewildered by Arjun's shouted instructions to 'Stay out of your heels!' and 'No lazy toes!'

'What does he mean when he keeps saying "Spaghetti Arms"?' he whispered to me.

'I think he thinks he's Patrick Swayze in Dirty Dancing.*'*

'I haven't seen Dirty Dancing,*' Luke said, eyes rounded with panic.*

I just shrugged uselessly. (You had made me watch it a second time, do you remember? After I had fallen asleep during the first.)

By the end of this evening, though, he seemed to look more relaxed, had learnt the first few steps and could lead me confidently across the floor. We exchanged a victorious look at the end – I had forgotten not to make eye contact – and we ended up laughing and clapping each other on the back. He's a lovely boy. I left in such a good mood I even forgot to ask Arjun what his secret project was all about. We all seem to be involved in subterfuge nowadays.

Oh, Cora, I miss you on evenings like these. Dancing in that room, even with Luke treading on my toes and swearing under his breath, reminded me of evenings with you. We did love to dance. You made me feel much more strong and capable, and I used to love holding you gently, watching you turn, your hair and skirts swirling. I hope wherever you are, you are dancing.

I love you, my darling.

Teddy x

Chapter 20

Love is not wanting to hurt her
because that would hurt you more

HARRY, 82

After leaving Amy I was at a total loss. Wiping at my face, biting my lip as another passer-by muttered something under their breath at me, I pressed myself up against a window display, taking my mobile out of my bag. I wanted to talk to someone, hear a friendly voice. The dull ache had spread and I felt utterly wretched.

My finger hovered automatically over Luke's name. We'd been stepping round each other in the flat, barely talking since the night of charades. In fact, recently he'd been out more and more. Normally I would return to find him in the flat, evidence that he'd been there all evening (three beer bottles, saucepans soaking, empty pizza boxes) but I had often returned to an empty flat or he would appear moments later refusing to be drawn on where he'd been.

'Work,' he'd say.

Dark thoughts nudged at me briefly but I trusted Luke and I couldn't say anything much. I was out all hours too. I pressed his name decisively: he would understand. He knew how much Amy meant to me. I heard the ringtone and already felt hope swell inside me.

'Hello, Luke Winters' phone.'

I frowned at the airy female voice, realising I had pressed his work number and not his mobile. In the next split second I realised I was on the line with Storm. Why was she always nearby or answering his phone? Did she have aspirations to work on a reception desk? Was she just loitering there being all sexy and red-headed in the hope I would phone and she could rub my nose in it?

'Um, hello ... Luke Winters' phone. Can I help?'

'Hi, Storm, isn't it? It's Lottie,' I said, knowing I had ice in my voice, not pausing for a reply. 'Could I speak to Luke please. It's important,' I added. Yeah, Storm, important.

'Oh hey, Lottie,' she said, as if we were Best Friends Forever. 'He's just popped to the loo actually, oh no, hold on, he's heading back this way. Luuuuuke!' I could hear a giggle and a sentence and Luke's reply. 'Here he is,' she sing-songed so that I made a face at the phone. I could feel my knuckles tightening on my mobile.

'Lottie,' Luke said. 'Is everything all right? Are you OK?' I felt a swell of relief at the worry in his voice, and also the fact that Storm was probably close enough to hear it too. Ha, Storm. Then I heard a giggle again and I hoped that the next time she went to her wardrobe to look for her favourite heels they weren't there, or that she could only locate the left one. 'Lottie? Are you OK?' Luke repeated, interrupting my latest Storm curse.

I couldn't keep the recent hurt from my voice. 'I just . . . ' It felt strange and selfish now to launch into my story about Amy. 'I just thought I'd call, see how your day is going—'

'Look, I'm really sorry but we're quite busy this end, can we speak later?'

The use of 'we' made me clench my jaw. 'Sure,' I said through gritted teeth. 'Wouldn't want to get in the way.'

Luke paused a moment. I could almost see him turning inwards as his voice dropped a tone. 'Everything all right, Lottie?'

'Bad day,' I mumbled. 'I was going to head to ChoccyDee.'

'Well, that might cheer you up, you love that place,' Luke said quickly and loudly, clearly wanting to leave the call.

'Oh yes,' I snapped, losing my patience, the phone call not going as I'd intended, 'a cup of hot chocolate should definitely compensate for the potential loss of my best friend.'

Nothing on the end of the line. I thought I might have lost connection. Then a weary sigh. 'I didn't mean . . . look, I am sorry, Lottie. I'll talk to you later, OK? I've got to go—'

'I understand,' I interrupted dramatically. 'You are obviously far too busy. I just wanted to hear your voice, more fool me,' I said, firing the words down the phone.

Luke lowered his voice. 'Hey, I get that you've had a bad day' – I felt the tears start up again; why did I have to be such a Super Bitch? – 'but, look, I can't help you from here and I don't want to fall out with you, OK?'

I should have agreed. He was right. I was always barking at him; he was the first person to feel the full force of any bad mood of mine. I felt chastened as I stood there. Then a stupid woman's voice and a little laugh distracted me. 'Well, you must get back to Storm and all the important work,' and with a quick swipe at my phone I hung up on him.

Glowering at passers-by I set off down the road, elbows sharp today, just wanting to get out of there, sit down, order a large hot chocolate and lose myself in a Pity Party for One. Storm with her stupid thundery name and her stupid red hair. Luke with his 'I'm too busy'.

Then I had another idea and pulled out my phone, sending a casual text. I just wanted to be somewhere to forget, be with someone I could talk work with, who didn't know my friends, who didn't have opinions about my recent behaviour, who, I admitted begrudgingly, made me feel better about myself. Startled at the returning beep I swallowed as he named a nearby restaurant and time.

I moved down the high street, through a narrow cobbled alley leading towards a sunlit square. London was a maze of tiny areas like this that you could walk past and never stumble on if you didn't know they were there. People were sitting on low stone walls in their coats, chatting. The air smelt of garlic and I felt a momentary thrill for being somewhere so anonymous.

Loitering nervously by the menu out front, time ticking on, I felt a creeping panic that I shouldn't be there, that I should be heading back to find Amy, fixing things with her, speaking to Luke, but I knew this was easier: I was in a square of Autumn sunshine, about to enjoy a glass of wine with someone who wouldn't judge me for an hour. And it was work, helpful for work, I was convincing myself as I felt a hand on my shoulder and turned to see a tailored grey suit, Ralph Lauren sunglasses and straight white teeth.

'You found it.' Toby kissed me on both cheeks and I felt myself flush. Had he always been this tall? This good-looking? I remember Amy once saying that everyone looked better in sunglasses and realised that must be it.

I also realised I hadn't responded. 'I did!' I said, a little too loudly.

Toby had commandeered a passing waiter and guided me to a small table in the corner, the waiter frantically clearing and wiping at the surface before we sat down. Toby seemed to have that impact on people. He had requested the wine menu and pulled out a chair for me.

'I'm glad you got in touch. I was about to send some work your way. A new case.'

I knew I should have asked about it – we always talked about work. Toby had sent me numerous cases and I had always been flattered that he asked for me, the clerks smirking sometimes as they handed it over. I didn't want to talk about the case, though, not in this quiet haven, wine soon on its way and an urgent desire to remove myself from everything that reminded me of my normal life.

Without much thought I launched into new territory. 'Did you watch the BBC documentary on last night about sea life? I never knew hermit crabs weren't, you know, hermits. They really like company!'

If Toby was surprised he hid it well, maybe a fractional lift of one neatly clipped eyebrow but that was it. Did he think I had summoned him here to discuss the social life of crustaceans? Did he wonder why I had texted at all? I was wondering myself as I sat there, trying to think of something else to say. (How does one follow up facts about hermit crabs?)

The waiter returned and Toby ordered a bottle of Chablis and I nodded my appreciation. I knew nothing about wine. For a moment I was distracted by the memory of Luke and I on a wine-tasting event my grandparents had bought us as a Christmas present a few years ago, lots of swilling and spitting. Luke had pretended to be quite the connoisseur, but had messed up his French accent so badly and forgot to spit out most of his wine that by the end he was just a burbling wreck in a taxi muddling the words for Sancerre and Sauvignon and slipping lower and lower down the seat.

The waiter reappeared, bottle in his hand, label covered by a crisp white napkin, waiting as Toby swilled it expertly around his mouth before swallowing and motioning for him to fill my glass, the sharp coolness a relief. I closed my eyes and sat back in the chair. 'That's wonderful.'

'It's a 2014 bottle and I find the fact it is unoaked compared to other white wines in the Burgundy region appealing.'

I nodded rather than reveal my stupidity and hoped he wouldn't think I had anything to add. I just stopped myself saying, 'Tastes fruity' and took another sip. I was starting to feel a little nervous. It was all very well bumping into Toby outside court: normally I was high from an appearance, buzzing from the adrenalin of it, dressed in my professional best, on familiar turf. It suddenly seemed more intimate, to be here by design and not luck. He had removed his sunglasses and his eyes crinkled as he lifted his own glass to his lips.

I found myself stuttering over simple sentences, wrong-footed and red-faced. Was it getting hotter?

'London is warm for this time of year.' I cringed inside. I was choosing to discuss weather. And not even in an interesting or unique way. I was like a two-year-old who had just learnt some words. *London warm. Woman silly. Man bored.*

'Global warming, I suppose,' I rattled on. 'Probably bad for hermit crabs.'

Fortunately Toby rescued me from my own terrible chat. 'Did you hear about Clive Henbridge?'

I sat forward in my chair. Clive was a notoriously excellent barrister in a rival chambers, brutal but sharp-witted and charming. He had always been friendly, but I had been glad not to come up against him. The last time I had seen him he was leaving court after reducing his opposition to actual tears after he had used an obscure law from 1854 to prove precedent and got his client off all charges. Clive was known to be an absolutely ruthless opponent. If I ever made silk I would have to go up against the likes of him and I felt wobbly just thinking about the prospect. 'What about him?'

'Apparently he broke down in court the other day. Lost his cool with Judge Reynolds.'

'Really?' It didn't sound like the Clive I recognised. I felt a small moment of interest and then a larger sense that it was information I perhaps shouldn't know. I wondered who else was discussing it.

'Rumour is his wife found out he's been out for one too many dinners with one of the clerks from his chambers and she left him.'

'Well, I suppose we can't know all the facts,' I said, trying to be tactful, and then attempting to change the subject: 'Are you off on holiday anywhere soon?'

Toby wasn't to be deterred so easily, however. 'Someone said he was crying in the robing room. Can you imagine their surprise? He is always such a cool customer.'

'No, ha.' I sipped my wine and tried to look neutral. It felt wrong to be gossiping like this.

Toby read my silence. 'Ever the barrister, waiting for the evidence.' When he smiled I could see sharp incisors, like a sexy vampire.

He had kept my glass topped up and I had drunk to fill silences, or when listening to him, barely noticing him reaching across with the bottle. We were on safer ground when we discussed work but I realised that beyond that we were struggling. Although I hadn't yet needed to mention more sea life, I was worried that I would need something else in my arsenal. My head was swimming a little, woolly with drink, as I thought about making my excuses and leaving.

'Well, thank you for this, I think I better get back, a lot to read through for tomorrow,' I lied.

Toby stared at me over his glass, then, as if deciding something, signalled to a nearby waiter that he wanted to pay the bill by making a wiggly hand gesture in the air.

I leant to take out my purse from my bag and he stilled me with a hand on my arm. 'I'll get this.'

I swallowed, squeaking a thank you and clutching my handbag to me as I sat in my chair.

We walked together towards an alley that led back to the high street. Toby paused as we moved into the shadow of it, stilled my arm once again.

'Well, thank you,' I gibbered, my eyes flashing across and past him, fixing somewhere to his right. I thought I recognised a face in the square, a glimpse of Luke's best friend Adam, and found myself shrinking back against the wall. Had he seen me?

Toby took a step forward, joining me in the shade. I blinked at the closeness, feeling a rush of panic as I wondered if he was going to try to kiss me. He bent down, a hand on my shoulder as he went to say goodbye, kissing me on the cheek. I turned my face so that our cheeks clashed awkwardly, misjudging the space.

'Any time,' he said, his voice low, his eyes focused on me.

'Good, great, excellent,' I said, feeling ridiculous. Why was I jeopardising a professional relationship in this way? Why had I rung him in the first place?

As I walked away I felt him watching me, a gnawing sense of unease building in me, as if I had started something and I wasn't even sure what.

Oh Cora.

Tonight was the big night we had been working towards with Luke. He had really started to improve after his fourth dance session. Arjun had stopped yelling quite so hard, and I had completely forgotten to be embarrassed and positively enjoyed being swept around the floor by this new, confident gentleman. And you really are right about his hands. I do understand now. Never too dry, never moist: they gripped me with assuredness and I thought, here's a man any woman would be lucky to dance with.

He was lighter on his feet, relaxed and passionate. He had a determined glint in his eye, and we had toasted our session at Arjun's apartment, cheering and getting very tiddly on a bottle of gin – this one had treacle in it! I'm fairly sure Arjun shouldn't be drinking with his medication but there was no stopping him that evening. He had taken Luke's progress as a personal aim and it has been wonderful to see him so cheered by things. I have been so worried about him; so frightened. And I hate keeping secrets.

We were set to make the great unveiling tonight. Margaret had been persuaded to shift things around a little and the band that normally only ever come on the third Thursday of the month had agreed to do an extra session in the hall that Friday night. Luke had told Lottie that he had signed her up for a beginner's lesson and she had agreed to come along. Then he would wow her with his new moves. How excited we all felt when the week passed and Friday crept up.

I bought Luke a buttonhole and handed it over with a gruff 'Good luck'. He had hugged me then, a brief, quick, one-armed hug, and I was reminded that he was someone who needed family around him. The thought made me rather emotional and I wished I had held him a little longer. Honestly, Cora, I am a changed man. It is like you dying has forced me to take over where you left off. The other day I was crying over a car insurance advert and when Geoffrey appeared to take me to golf I had to pretend I had chilli in my eye.

We had arrived early, Arjun issuing a last-minute pep talk, forcing Luke to sit opposite him as he walked him through the steps. He made the poor lad so nervous that he poured the first part of his beer down his newly washed shirt. Still, the band arrived and other couples from the club appeared. Paula was there in something feathery and startling in lime green and Margaret looked lovely in a pale pink dress that fell flatteringly below her knees. I believe you would have loved it and I told her so and then I had tears in my eyes and I had to pretend I had still got chilli on my hands when Geoffrey asked what was the matter. How did you ever get anything done with all these emotions? It is quite exhausting.

The first songs started and Luke was looking over at the clock, his newly polished shoes tapping in time to the waltz the band were playing. We had discussed things with them beforehand so they knew to hold off until Lottie arrived. Luke was clutching his mobile in his hand, the screen blank as the time ticked on. I got him another beer and we sat and watched the couples dance past us. I could tell he wasn't really concentrating, just glancing at the door and then his phone before fixing a smile on his face for my benefit.

A whole hour passed, Cora: it was excruciating. The band took a break and Luke looked rumpled and sad, his eyes dulling as Arjun and I both crowded round him trying to ask him pointless questions about work that he fielded in monosyllables.

Where was our granddaughter?

The band returned and Luke's face was stricken and I felt a new crack form in my heart for him. All those evenings we had spent. Now the buttonhole was wilting and his face was pale, his voice lacklustre. He seemed defeated as the clock ticked on and on. It was completely dark outside now, street lamps glowing, headlights moving past every now and again, a spattering of stars outside.

She finally arrived, dressed in a trouser suit, her hair scraped back in a bun, pale, although she was always pale now, too thin, her eyes scanning the room. The muscles in her neck were tense and her arms rigid as she hugged me, barely touching me. I could feel the nervous energy, smell the day's dirt of London on her.

Luke had approached, still looking dashing in his suit, holding out a hand for her. She hadn't realised the importance of the moment, of course. Practically the whole room had paused to watch him, the band readying to play the song they had rehearsed, Arjun tapping his crutch on the stage as their prompt. But then, oh, Cora, Lottie shook her head. 'I really need a drink, Luke, OK?' But Arjun had given the band their cue and they had begun and I watched Luke's eyes widen as he recognised the opening bars of the music, his hand still hovering in the space between him and Lottie.

She stayed for a drink and then she made her excuses, kissing me on the cheek, Luke looking forlornly at me as he muttered something about an early start, a lot of work. Oh, Cora, I could have wept for him.

Teddy x

Chapter 21

Love is . . . overrated

EVA, 76

Luke was very quiet but not in a normal way – lots of heavy sighing and wistful looks out of the car window. I didn't really understand his problem. He'd been moaning about going to the ballroom dancing evening for a couple of days now and I had released him early. A bit of me thought he'd be more grateful. Another sigh. I found myself gritting my teeth. I couldn't be bothered to ask him why he was sulking. I just wanted to get home, have a quick shower and get into clean pyjamas and our bed.

'Why didn't you call?' he asked, twisting in his seat to look at me.

I kept my eyes on the road ahead. 'I was rushing and then I had no signal.'

'And we didn't need to leave so early,' he said in a rush.

'Your grandad will think we were rude. The band were brought in especially.'

Why was Luke suddenly Mr Concerned when it came to my grandad? 'He seemed fine with it,' I said, realising I hadn't really seen Grandad, too intent on dragging Luke away. 'And the band are always on there. They all love it.'

The room had been filled with couples dressed up and enjoying being spun around the floor. I had seen Margaret in a fetching pink number being steered across the dance floor by Geoffrey, and Howard and Paula, her scarlet talons bright red against his jacket as she clutched him. 'We didn't need to stay, they had enough people.'

He sighed again. I wanted to open the passenger door and tip him out. Sometimes I just need Luke to say whatever is on his mind. It was infuriating trying to work out whether he was cross or just struggling with his sinuses.

'Are you going to be like this all the way home?' I asked, an edge creeping into my voice.

A beat.

'Like what?'

'All this.' I did an impression of heavy sighing, tipping my head from side to side as I did so.

'I'm not being like that.'

'You are. You're steaming up the windows with it.'

I could see him clutching something in his hand, a single rose head, shredding the petals into his lap one by one. 'I just wanted a pleasant evening with my girlfriend. Is that so hard for you to understand?'

'Why didn't you say? I could have stayed a bit longer,' I said, conveniently forgetting my mood upon arrival. I had practically downed the warm single vodka and Coke Luke had ordered for me, before complaining the music was giving me a headache and everyone was ancient and could we please just go home it had been a really long day. I hadn't really waited for much of a response from him.

'You didn't give me a chance,' he protested, the rose now petal-less in his hand. 'You never do.'

We had pulled up outside our flat and I switched the engine off.

'What's that supposed to mean?' I asked, turning to face him, a streetlamp opposite making an orange halo behind him, his face largely in shadow.

'You didn't even think what I wanted tonight, did you? You'd just made up your mind.'

'That's hardly fair and you weren't exactly being Fred Astaire.'

'I was waiting to dance with you,' he exploded.

Luke rarely raised his voice and for a second I was dumbfounded into silence. Still, the barrister in me, the woman who had raced around all day worrying about trials and friends and making silk, soon lost her cool.

'Why didn't you say something then? I'm not a mind reader. I can't be expected to know what you're thinking every second of the day.'

'News to me that you ever want to know what I'm thinking—'

'That's not fai—'

'God forbid it might not be what you want and we always have to do what you want.'

'That's not true.'

'Name me one time I get to set the agenda. It's always "I'm tired".' He said the last bit in a high whiny voice that made my eyes narrow.

'I don't sound like that.'

He kept going in the whine: 'I need to go, I need my sleep, I've got to work . . . '

'I do have to work . . . hard.'

Luke raised both his hands in the air in exasperation. 'I know you bloody do but other people work hard too. You haven't got a monopoly on working hard—'

A man walking his dog paused by our car, clearly bemused as to where the screeching was coming from.

'—and some people' – Luke was really in his stride now – 'some people actually work hard and don't bloody go on and on about it, boring the rest of us with it and ruining our own days.'

I reached for the car handle, anger surging through me as I opened it and stepped outside, ignoring the still evening calm, the people tucked up in bed behind darkened windows. Slamming the car door I moved across to our flat, reaching for the keys in my bag. Bloody Luke. So I ruin his day, do I, daring to talk about my life? Well, I hope the next time he goes to talk to someone about his work, they pretend to listen but are really just thinking about what they are going to make for dinner.

I was inside and up to our flat, bleeping the car locked and hoping Luke 'I breathe through my nostrils too loudly' had shut the door already. I didn't even care to check. I didn't deserve any of this. I was tired, I was dirty, I just wanted to go to sleep.

Luke didn't carry on arguments so I was surprised when he appeared in the doorway of our bedroom still looking mad, a sort of angry James Bond in his sharp suit. I noticed then the newly polished shoes, the tie I didn't recognise. He had made an effort to dress up for the evening. Guilt fuelled my anger.

'Have you finished telling me how shit I am and what a ball ache it is going out with me? Can I have my shower now?'

'You'll do whatever you like,' Luke said, some of the anger leaving his voice, now looking a little sad. 'Go ahead.'

Somehow this made me crosser. 'I just don't get what the big deal is. What have I done to deserve this?'

Luke didn't answer, just turned his back and headed into the kitchen.

I followed him. 'You can't just say all this stuff to me and walk away, Luke.'

I could see his back tense, knuckles gripping the kitchen sink.

'Why do you always get to be the nice guy? Why am I always cast in the role of villainous bitch?'

He wouldn't turn around.

'You always make me feel like I'm letting you down but I'm just tired, I'm stressed, I can't be bloody perfect.'

When his voice came it was pitifully small, I barely caught the words, 'I thought things were . . . tonight was . . . '

'What, Luke?'

He snapped: 'It doesn't matter. Clearly I was wrong.'

Confusion, tiredness, stress, guilt were all fuelling me now and I felt ugly and red as I hurled more insults his way. 'It's not like you're perfect,' I said.

He sighed. 'I know, Lottie, I'm not pretending to be, I just miss—'

'Miss what?'

'You.'

My chest heaved up and down as he moved past me out of the kitchen. 'I'll sleep on the sofa and then, well . . . ' He looked back at me. Did I imagine the watery eyes? My heart was still racing, my body pulsing with adrenalin. 'Then we can decide what to do.'

That last line scared me into silence. I stood, only my own breathing loud in my ears, realising I had backed myself into this corner, still feeling every muscle tense. 'If that's what you want,' I said huffily, wondering for the first time if I had gone too far.

Luke moved through to our bedroom and fetched his pillow and simply said, 'None of this is what I want, Lottie. None of it.'

Darling Cora,

After the disastrous ballroom dancing evening, Arjun and I were drowning our sorrows in his living room. It was there that he confirmed the latest prognosis, and, Cora, it is not good. He has declined their treatment, wanting to tackle things with diet and exercise. He was told even with the treatment he would have a couple of years at most.

And did I comfort him at this announcement? Did I ask how I could help? I did not. I panicked, of course, and immediately changed the subject. Although I think he was grateful.

And so we play golf, laugh at Howard's terrible jokes, tease Geoffrey every time he sends the ball into a hedge, bunker or water hazard (the man literally can't find green) and Arjun is the same. Perhaps I notice tiny changes: a slower pace on the fairways, steadying himself when he picks the ball out of the hole, a slightly delayed laugh at times as if he was only just returning to the conversation. I wonder if Geoffrey can see it too. I want to ask. It's so strange carrying around such a big secret. I would have wanted to tell you.

Arjun finally did confide in me on another matter. It seems he has been meeting Luke on a regular basis, working on a secret project. I'm not allowed to speak about it, Cora, to anyone – not that there is anyone to tell any more. Something about copyright. He sounded very solemn so I promised immediately.

All the dates and outings we'd been arranging for Lottie, Luke and the other members of Maplelands club had triggered a thought in him. He just didn't know how to execute it.

Enter Luke!

Arjun approached him not long after the fateful night he broke his hip, sidling up to him in the clubhouse and dragging him off to a darkened corner to talk. He then spent much of the rest of the night swapping secret looks and winking at him, so much so that he believed Howard thought he had developed a crush.

This week Arjun's boiler needs repairing so they have arranged the latest meeting at our house, a new centre of covert operations. This morning I opened the door to find Luke and a pretty redhead standing on the step swapping a joke. Arjun arrived moments later and they all gathered round the kitchen table with lots of bits of paper and coloured pens. It looked very official. I was chief tea bringer and I think performed my duties rather well. No one was short of tea (or biscuits) at any point. There were a rocky few seconds at the start when the redhead asked for green tea and I didn't know what that was, but fortunately you came to the rescue as I produced something from a yellow box in our kitchen that you must have bought for just such an occasion as this. You were always very prepared.

The redhead seemed very animated. She put me in mind a little of a young Paula, and certainly seemed very enthusiastic about both Arjun's idea and Luke's plans for it, touching him on the arm with excitement when he came up with a new thought. I hadn't seen Arjun so cheered in days, and I was so grateful to Luke for doing all this for him. Apparently he has been working on it for a while. He assured me it really was an exciting project and was happily designing potential logos and titles with the different coloured pens as Arjun explained more. The redhead seemed to know a great deal about the technical side and I was soon lost in a sea of complicated tech jargon, so I simply did what I knew best – offered to fetch more tea.

Luke was quiet again, smiling long after the moment had passed, his eyes often drifting to some other place. I hadn't found time to talk to him about the disastrous ballroom dancing evening but I could see something had broken a little in him. I think he was glad to have something else to focus on.

It was all very cloak and dagger and I was reminded in serious tones by Arjun that to speak of it might lead to future problems, a hostile takeover by another company, so I swore once again not to breathe a word.

They've just left and the house is empty once more. I'm still not used to being on my own in this way, knowing that for the rest of the afternoon and evening I might not see another soul or speak to another human being. Perhaps Arjun's project will change that for others in the same boat. I always took it for granted that you would be there to listen to my ramblings, to humour me, to fill the house with noise. I miss hearing your chatter, I miss being confused about the members of your book club, I miss you getting cross with me because I can't remember the names of the people in your book club despite the fact that you've told me their names a hundred times. I miss your thoughts and your insights. I just miss you.

Teddy x

Chapter 22

Love is in the little things

MAX, 86

Work, everyday life, phone calls and meetings were draining. Every moment of the next few days was spent going over and over in my head how our row had escalated so far out of control. I desperately wanted to pick up the phone to Amy and tell her but knew I couldn't. I was the last person she wanted to hear from. Why was I making such a complete and utter cock-up of everything?

Alan, my head of chambers, had approached me about applying for silk in a year's time. I watched his mouth opening and closing but my brain could barely process the words. What had seemed my ultimate goal a few months ago, my ultimate route to being happy, successful and sorted, suddenly seemed trivial, and that thought frightened me.

Luke had stayed at Adam's house the night before, a

brief text told me, no kisses on the end. I didn't really deserve kisses. I thought fleetingly of returning the message with a whole string of them, some heart emojis and an amusing yet moving gif that would soften him up, but knew I needed to see him to fix this one. I cringed as I ran through some of the things I'd said, my voice cold as I'd levelled horrible comments at him. He had been brilliant these last few months, patient and caring, and I had been taking advantage of his good nature. That was going to change.

After meeting with a new client to go over their defence (in a nutshell: yes the CCTV is correct – he did break his nose but only because the other guy was definitely going to punch him) I set off for Pimlico, glad of a cloudy but still afternoon and hoping to be able to persuade Luke to walk with me somewhere. That morning I had worn my red polka dot shirt and pencil skirt combo that I knew he loved, with high heels that had made my feet ache all day. Applying red lipstick on a juddering Tube using a compact hand mirror had almost undone me but finally I was there, feeling positive, feeling ready to fix what I'd broken.

Heading out of Pimlico station I wound my way down a side street, a shortcut to Luke's office. Stomach leaping, almost there, I passed by a chain coffee shop on the other side of the road. What I saw in the window caused me to dive for cover next to a large black bin in a graffitied doorway. Barely noticing the smell, I trained my attention on the two people sitting on stools in the large picture window. There was no doubting it. Luke was in earnest conversation with a petite, glossy redhead: Storm.

I scanned the scene for more of his colleagues. Perhaps it was a work meeting? Perhaps they were on some team-building exercise where they had to drink lattes and stack caramel shortbreads? Perhaps ... At that moment Storm flung her head back, her smooth creamy neck (enticingly small, definitely small enough for two hands to close around it) on show as she laughed at something Luke said. He in turn looked delighted with the reaction, gesturing passionately with two hands as he always did when he was excited about something.

I felt my stomach disappear. I wanted to slump against the wall behind me. Unable to drag my eyes away I watched them for a while. They seemed positively buzzing with energy. A little piece of my heart broke away and I tasted bile in my mouth. Oh God, the smell of the dustbin was suddenly filling my nostrils and the whole scene was swimming before me. I had to get out of there. I lurched away on stupid, painful heels. The humiliation would be enormous. I couldn't let Luke see me spying on them. A small voice inside me was protesting that this wasn't something Luke would do, but I couldn't shake the image of them. Even from this distance I could read his body language, leaning forward, the urgency as he spoke, the light in his eyes. It was familiar because it was how he used to talk to me.

My throat thickened as I retraced my steps to the Tube, clutching a set of iron railings for a moment, wanting to wish away what I had seen. It should have been fine, everyone had colleagues who were the opposite sex, I reminded myself. I trusted Luke: Luke who had held me close when I had found out Grandma had died, who'd bought me a silver keyring in the shape of a house when we'd signed our rental agreement together. Oh God, the flat, our entwined lives: it was all suddenly in jeopardy. My cosy world that I had been so sure of seemed to be dissolving around me as I stood next to the railings worrying about splitting assets, the soft grey suede sofa we had chosen together, the oak table and chairs – would we take two each? He had never liked the overhead yellow lamp but had let me buy it because I had loved it: would he fight for it now? Would I stay in the flat?

I knew I was racing on, knew I was getting out of control. I shook my head as if to fling off the madness. This was Luke, I reminded myself. I had to believe that this was a misunderstanding. This had to be innocent. I pulled out my mobile. I needed to find out. I could still turn around.

'Lottie,' he said and I could picture him now in the coffee shop mid-spiel, scooping up his mobile, a smile still on his lips from whatever story Storm was telling. Probably something about her five-a-side naked volleyball team or her part-time job as a contortionist. I hoped next time she straightened her hair a little bit of fringe burnt off.

'Are you all right?' He had forgotten to be frosty with me and for a second it was like any other phone call we had ever exchanged.

'I'm fine, I . . . ' What could I say? I'm in Pimlico and I was standing in a smelly doorway staring at you with your new girlfriend, and who is going to get the chairs if we split? You arsehole, you no-good lying piece of—

'Lottie, sorry, I can't take long.' His voice became more guarded.

'Right, well, I wondered ... I just ... hoped we could meet, to talk,' I said, the words stilted.

A fraction of a pause, someone dropped a spoon near him. Stupid, spoon-dropping Storm with her tiny hands that can't even hold cutlery right.

'I'm just busy working on something right now actually, Lottie. Is it OK if we catch up later?'

The lie threw me. Working? So supping a cappuccino and sharing a carrot cake qualified as work, did it? My grip on the phone tightened. I found I didn't have the words. I could hear the gurgle and steam from a coffee machine. Oh, so they do macchiatos in the office now, Luke, do they? *Do they?* Nothing came out of my mouth, though. My brain dried up. Even my usual curses had left me. A hole was opening beneath me: black and impossible.

'I'll be back tonight,' he said, a stiffness to his voice.

'Great,' I whispered, not knowing what else to say, ending the call with a muffled, 'Have to go.'

He would be back tonight, but then what?

Darling Cora,

I think I've got myself in a bit of a pickle. Lottie was here today. She arrived earlier in the afternoon, having got out of court unexpectedly. She turned up with the usual leather bag stuffed with paper and despite the mountain of paperwork seemed distracted. Even under the glamorous outfit, all dots and flame-red lips, she looked pale, eyes red-rimmed, and for a horrible moment I thought she was going to start crying. She fiddled with the collar of her shirt, clearly needing to talk. She was hesitant at first.

'Grandad?'

'Yes.'

'It doesn't matter. Nothing.'

She sat at the kitchen table and I loitered and tried to seem uninterested, pretending to rearrange the fruit bowl. There was one apple and two bananas in it so there was only so much rearranging one could do. I was about to move on to checking the cutlery drawer, as if somehow the cutlery might be missing, when she piped up again. 'Do you think, did you know . . .'

Lottie, who is normally so eloquent, able to turn a fine phrase since she was a young girl, seemed to be tying herself in knots to get something out. I remember listening to you two, conversation flowing freely, from my spot in the living room. I desperately tried to think of a way to make things easier for her. 'Anything on your mind?'

My direct approach seemed to do the trick. Lottie took a breath and began.

'I was wondering, in the early days with you and Grandma, whether you knew.'

She stopped then and I realised I would have to say

something but this was a little subtle for me and I wasn't absolutely sure what she was getting at. Christ, this is hard. I have attempted more emotional conversations in the last few months than I have done in twenty years. I do sometimes resent you for not training me harder in this area. 'What do you mean "knew"?'

'Did you know Grandma was right for you? That you were meant to be together?'

The question took my breath away. How to sum up what I thought about you? Did I tell her that I knew from that first evening we met? That when you looked at me at that summer barn dance with that candid expression, your skin flushed pink from the heat of the day, your eyes glittering, that I was sure I wanted to spend the rest of my life looking into that face?

'I desperately wanted her to be because I felt lost when I was with her,' I said slowly. 'Tongue-tied, hopeless, short of breath.'

Lottie looked a little taken aback. Certainly as I reviewed my words in my head I realised it was rather more Heathcliff than she perhaps thought I was capable of. She did break into a thin smile. 'You sound so romantic.' For a moment she seemed happier but then the same troubled expression crossed her face and she shuffled papers in front of her as if summoning up courage to go on. 'Did you trust her?'

I couldn't help answering immediately, without a second thought. 'Oh, absolutely. She was loyal, she was the finest caretaker of my heart I could imagine.' I never once doubted you. In fact, I remember early in our courtship overhearing your mother cast a doubt on my suitability, and the certainty with which you told her, 'Teddy is the best man and will make an excellent husband.' I'd overheard it. How my chest had puffed and I returned to the room with renewed swagger, unable to resist planting a kiss on your cheek, much to your mother's distress.

Lottie was quiet again, nodding to herself, and I knew this wasn't just idle curiosity, this wasn't about us. I might not be as adept at these conversations as you, but something must have rubbed off because even I'm not a complete idiot.

'Are you worried about Luke?' I couldn't keep the surprise from my voice. She had always been so sure about Luke, telling us in those early weeks that she'd found someone special. We were so excited for her, and it had been clear from early on that she was absolutely right.

She didn't answer and I felt the start of a small fear grip my heart. I always hated to see her unhappy.

'I think he's lying to me.'

I was surprised at this statement. Luke didn't seem like the furtive type. He was a straightforward fellow. You'd always said he had an open, friendly face and I knew what you meant.

'There's someone who works for him. She's young, pretty and, well, I think he was with her earlier.'

Did 'with her' mean anything more these days? I wasn't

at all sure of the latest lingo and started to panic. 'With her?' I needed clarification.

'Yes, with her, in a coffee shop by his office.'

Breath left my body as I realised 'with her' still just meant 'with her' in the normal way. Not like when Howard told me something was 'sick' and that meant it was good.

'And she often answers his phone, and she's around him a lot. I've seen her at his desk and she even told me once that she fancied him . . .'

The last bit came out in a one long gush and I frowned. It wasn't like Lottie to doubt him, and Luke wasn't the sort to stray.

'I'm sure it was nothing. Luke is always friendly, always nice to people. It's probably completely innocent. You should ask him.'

Lottie was quiet again, folding a paper napkin in her hands, then shredding it bit by bit. 'He sees her every day. And you always read about affairs happening in the workplace, don't you? And they work together.'

'That doesn't necessarily mean anything,' I protested, pulling up a chair opposite her.

'She's pretty. All red hair, big eyes and an amazing figure.'

I started to feel a creeping sense of dread. This sounded suspiciously like the girl Luke was working with on Arjun's secret project. Is that why they were meeting outside work? I wanted to say something but I had promised Arjun and you know how I loathe breaking a promise. You never really forgave me for not telling you that Geoffrey had bought that lemon drizzle cake for the fête competition from M&S. Lottie looked so sad, though. My eyes roved the room as she continued.

'I'm too scared to ask him. I've been such a grumpy cow recently, always sniping at him.'

I opened my mouth to protest but even I had seen Lottie snapping at him lately, rolling her eyes at the smallest thing, tired and impatient and taking it out on him. 'We all behave badly sometimes,' I compromised.

She looked at me weakly and nodded, aware that I hadn't exactly batted her statement away. Her eyes had started to swim then and I cursed you, Cora. Why weren't you here? I am sure this conversation would have gone a hundred times better. 'But Luke is a trustworthy man and I have every confidence that there is a simple explanation for what you've seen.'

Lottie swallowed once, twice, trying to compose herself. I covered her hand with mine. 'Have some faith in him.'

She pressed her lips together and nodded, slowly sweeping away the shredded napkin into one hand.

'Thanks, Grandad.'

I felt a warm glow at that, perhaps a glimpse into what it had been like for you, always on the end of the phone ready to listen or advise.

'Any time. I want you to be happy, Lottie.' I had more I wanted to say then, things I had been thinking recently, but

I knew this probably wasn't the time. She looked drained and I switched the subject to Tipping Point. *I had about 35 recorded!*

After a while I offered to order a Chinese and she glanced at the clock above me. 'Thanks but I better go.' She indicated the packed briefcase.

I knew not to push it, gave her a quick hug and she left me with my thoughts and half a portion of egg fried rice that I will eat for lunch tomorrow.

I love you, Cora.

Teddy x

Chapter 23

Love is like chicken pox: we
all catch it in the end

STANLEY, 82

I was late, dishevelled, head pounding, make-up long gone. I just wanted to be alone, to curl up under the duvet, close my eyes and try to forget the day. I had barely slept after getting back from Grandad's the night before, Luke already asleep (or pretending to be) beside me. The day in court had zapped any remaining energy. The work wasn't complicated but I had travelled to Winchester for a hearing, loitered outside the court to be heard and then headed back on delayed trains, trying to juggle the work I had lined up and focus rather than replay the images I had seen in that Pimlico café. He had lied. I knew that. Why had he lied?

And now I was off to another evening being wooed by

a boyfriend who I was fairly sure might dump me at any moment. What a joke! How could we get through the evening when we were barely on speaking terms?

Geoffrey's house was compact and impossibly tidy. Shoes lined the polished corridor, coats hung in a regimented line, a small side table was bare but for a glasses case and a pair of golf gloves.

Geoffrey welcomed me with a shy kiss on the cheek. 'It's good to see you, Lottie.'

'You too,' I croaked, not wanting to give away the fact that I had been trying not to weep on public transport for much of the afternoon.

He showed me into an equally neat living room, a large sofa pushed back against the wall, on which sat Grandad, Howard and Arjun. Against the opposite wall a mahogany table was covered in wine glasses, all filled with varying degrees of liquid. I could definitely do with the drink and headed straight for the table.

Reaching out a hand (I believe Geoffrey had somewhat over-catered, there must have been eight times the number of glasses that we needed), I was stopped in my tracks by all four of the men shouting, 'No!'

'What? What is it?' I cried, leaping backwards, one hand flying to my chest.

Geoffrey started forward. 'They're not for drinking. Let me get you something from the kitchen. Those are part of the evening's entertainment.'

I frowned, unsure. Were we going to play drinking games?

My mind boggled as I took a seat on a stiff-backed wooden chair, the older men now taking their seats. I felt a surge of relief to see their kindly faces and wondered guiltily if Luke might refuse to come.

Geoffrey returned with a glass, two ice cubes fast melting. 'It's flavoured with warmed coriander,' he said, handing it to me.

'Disgusting,' Howard said. 'I threw mine away, Lottie. Try the wine.'

'I'm all right,' I said, simply grateful to be sitting down with a drink.

'Any interesting cases?' Arjun asked, leaning forward a little and bringing his hands together in a steeple as he looked at me. It struck me then that he looked different, his cheeks a little hollower, his normally glossy dark hair flecked with more grey. I frowned, wondering if it was the lighting or just my imagination.

'Nothing too gripping. My guy broke another guy's nose but my guy says that it was self-defence and he's been stitched up because that guy fancies his wife. It got pretty ugly during questioning.'

'High drama.' Arjun lifted his eyebrows. Did I imagine him pausing to take a breath between those two words?

Just then the doorbell went and Geoffrey disappeared. I sat up in my chair, placing my glass on the floor to fiddle with my hair, straighten my top. I felt nerves flutter in my stomach. I could hear Luke's voice in the corridor, footsteps getting closer. Grandad looked across at me, an inscrutable expression on his face. I swallowed, picked up my glass again and tried to look as casual as I could in the world's most uncomfortable wooden chair when he appeared in the doorway.

He looked tired, his normally smooth face lined, bags under his eyes. He glanced across at me and then away. I felt my body droop, bit my lip to stop myself from reacting any more. I wouldn't have a meltdown in Geoffrey's living room. I remembered the words I had spat at him during our last row. Why did I always have to be so vicious to the one person who always supported me? I seemed to possess a self-destructive streak, tempting my relationship to implode. No wonder he was seeking solace in Red-Haired Cow Face.

'Hey,' he said, looking at me again, accepting another glass from Geoffrey and moving across the room to sit on the other side of the sofa next to Howard.

'I don't even want to smell it,' Howard said dramatically, staring at Luke's glass.

'Hey,' I replied a little too loudly, a little too bright. I felt my mouth ache with the false smile I had fixed on my face.

Geoffrey returned from the kitchen, fiddling with his collar as he cleared his throat. I wasn't used to seeing him in charge, normally so softly spoken and happy for others to take the limelight. Now, though, his voice was direct, louder as he stepped in front of the table filled with glasses, clutching some A4 papers in his hand. For a moment I wondered if he had prepared a speech.

'Well, we're all here now and I am excited to introduce

you to musical glasses, something extremely popular in the eighteenth century. I have spent the day carefully working out the correct levels of liquid needed in each glass—'

'Loser,' Howard heckled, earning a boo from the rest of the sofa.

Geoffrey flushed. '—and have printed off sheet music to be distributed amongst you.' He licked a finger and carefully peeled off the top sheet from the pile in his hands, handing it to me, before doing the same with the others.

There was some muttering as people took in the dots, lines, squiggles and numbers, and then some reaching for glasses cases and general rustling. I looked down at the music in front of me, numbers circled in a careful hand. It had obviously taken him an age. Geoffrey finished handing out the pieces of paper and stepped back to his spot in front of the table.

'I will be conducting each song, so just follow my directions. I thought we could start simply and go from there. I hope you find it a fulfilling and worthwhile way to spend your evening.'

I wanted to clap this speech, feeling grateful for the effort he had so obviously gone to. Luke, of course, didn't hold back, calling out, 'Sounds great,' so that Geoffrey turned an even deeper red.

'Well, yes, so let me arrange you in the room and direct you to your glasses.'

He gently guided me over to stand near the mantelpiece, placing five wine glasses on a tray on the seat of the wooden chair in front of me. Then he directed us all to stand in a loose semi-circle facing him, like a choir.

'Luke, if you could help me shift the sofa, then people can sit down if they want, but don't forget which tray of drinks is yours. I have numbered the glasses to coordinate with the sheet music. Glass One is Song One and so on. It should be very straightforward.'

'What's in them?' Howard asked, lifting one of his glasses off the tray.

'Just water,' Geoffrey said, before turning puce as Howard raised it closer to his lips. 'Don't drink it! I would have to re-measure your glass,' he cried in a loud voice, Howard almost spilling the glass in surprise.

'Calm down, man, I was just taking a closer look.'

'Ah,' Geoffrey said, clearing his throat again. 'Apologies, it's just things have to be very precise.'

Luke and he rearranged the furniture so that everyone could sit down and rest if standing got too much. Arjun was humming an obscure tune, Grandad was peering at him over his glasses and Howard kept picking up a glass to drink from, huffing, and finding the one with his wine in.

'Bloody confusing.'

'Should have stuck with the gin.' Grandad laughed.

Luke had barely glanced in my direction, actively setting himself up on the other side of the semi-circle. I sneaked a look across at him, his mouth turned down, his eyes duller. Had I done that to him? Or was it guilt? He seemed less buoyant than normal, his tone dull, sentences shorter.

'Right, let's see how this goes,' Geoffrey began, holding up both hands. 'The circled numbers correspond to the glass you need to play. I have ensured the glass will play the correct note.'

'How clever,' Arjun said.

'Did England win today, by the way?' Howard interrupted.

'Win what?' Grandad asked.

'The cricket.'

Geoffrey was staring at them. I had that uncomfortable feeling I used to get in the classroom as a teenager when the teacher was staring at a pupil who was completely oblivious.

'Who were they playing?'

'Pakistan.'

'When you have quite finished,' Geoffrey said in a stern voice.

'You're in trouble,' sing-songed Arjun, nudging Grandad.

Grandad looked up. 'Sorry, sorry, although Howard started it.'

'I just wanted to know the score, should have known he wouldn't know. What is the point of having the Sky package if you don't watch it?'

'I do watch it.'

'Pah.'

Geoffrey refused to be drawn into the row, asking everyone to hold up the glass that corresponded to the first number on their sheet. 'Then dip your finger into the water and run your finger round the rim until you need to change glass with another number.'

Dipping my finger into the glass I left it poised over the rim, staring at Geoffrey and awaiting my cue, not convinced anything would really happen. For a strange moment I imagined this was how a cult started. Would it be the Emperor's New Clothes and we would all have to pretend we had heard the music? Geoffrey didn't seem the usual cult leader type but you never knew what lurked beneath that quiet surface. The whole semi-circle seemed to be holding their breath now, even Howard had fallen completely silent and was ready for the next instruction.

Then we began, with a sound that built like a chorus of pan pipes in the small living room. It surprised me, my mouth turning up as I realised we were all making music together. Geoffrey was nodding, pointing at me now so that I bent to pick up the next glass before starting again. The tune changed as Geoffrey directed people to start their new note. There were a few huffs, Howard panicking over whether to come in or not, but you could hear the tune underneath, building if enough of us joined in at the same time.

Then halfway through the song Geoffrey was shaking his head at me as the wrong note emerged – I had picked up the wrong glass. Then another note jarred and I looked towards Howard, who was wiping his mouth.

'I thought it was my wine.'

Arjun had put his own glass down and had picked up another one. 'I liked the taste.'

Grandad was searching his table. 'I put one of the glasses down somewhere. I can't find Number 3.'

I felt a giggle build in my throat. Geoffrey was looking a little boot-faced as he called us to a halt.

'Is it with yours, Arjun?' Grandad asked, still searching.

'Not sure.'

'Tidy up your tables,' Geoffrey said, his voice rising. '*Stop* drinking from the glasses, Howard, and we will begin again in sixty seconds.'

We started the piece again but this time it was all going horribly wrong, the notes flat: clashing hideously so that Geoffrey shut his eyes, his conductor hands falling to his side.

'This wasn't Glass Two, I think it was Five.'

'Did you take my glass?'

'I haven't touched your table.'

'Well, one of them has gone.'

'Oh my God, will you stop drinking from them! You are ruining the sound,' Geoffrey burst out in a most out-of-character display of emotion.

Howard paused, glass to his lips. 'I forgot where I put my drink,' he said.

'It does look very like his wine,' Grandad said. 'Maybe you should have coloured them with dye?'

'I didn't think I would need to,' Geoffrey blasted. 'I didn't think I would be surrounded by so much idiocy.'

Grandad started stuttering, 'Well, this is my first time and there is a lot going on: paper, glasses, Arjun poking me in the ribs every two seconds—'

'I haven't poked you in the ribs.'

'You made me spill Glass Four!'

'Be quiet, both of you,' Geoffrey said. 'Only Luke and Lottie are behaving.' Luke looked a little happier at these words, mouth twitching, shaking his head slowly at the older men.

'I saw him nearly drink one,' Howard said disloyally.

Luke leaned over to pat Howard's knee. 'Nearly. But remember only Lottie and I are behaving.'

I felt a surge of camaraderie: had I been forgiven? I looked up at Luke, who didn't return my gaze, and felt my shoulders droop again.

The others continued to bicker over water levels, food dye and whether Geoffrey had made the letters on the sheet clear enough, as Luke sidled over to me. I licked my lips, trying to act nonchalantly as he stood in front of me.

'We probably need to talk at some point,' Luke said, a serious tone to his voice, one I wasn't used to hearing. It was the same tone he used when he had first discussed the new recycling system for our block of flats, the same tone he had used when telling me about mortgage rates.

'Yes.'

He sipped his drink and looked at me carefully. 'Things haven't been great—'

'We probably shouldn't talk right now,' I said, cutting him off, trying to keep my voice down so that no one could overhear what we were saying. I couldn't bear to have a public showdown.

Luke's eyes flashed as he opened and shut his mouth. I

rarely saw him anything other than cheery and relaxed. Now he was clutching his drink, a muscle going in his cheek.

'We can't keep on like this, with you snapping at me every time you want to lash out at something.'

That stung. I gritted my teeth, still trying to talk out of the side of my mouth. I could see Arjun and Grandad glance up at us, sticking a smile on my face in response.

'I don't lash— look . . . let's not do this now. We can talk later.' I could feel the room shift as the others had perhaps cottoned on to the fact Luke and I weren't in deep discussion about Glass Four in the second song.

'I'm going to stay at Adam's actually. He's got a spare room. I thought it might give us a bit of time and space.'

My hand froze over my glass, the fixed smile slipping from my face. 'Right.'

Luke turned to me, eyes serious. 'Not for ever, just, well . . . it's a chance for us to think.'

'Is this about Storm?' I blurted.

'What? No.' Luke swiped a hand through his hair.

'I saw you two looking pretty close,' I hissed.

Luke looked at me. 'There is nothing going on there, and you can talk, Adam said you were cosying up with some man near Oxford Street the other day.'

'That was work.'

Howard was openly staring at us, a soap opera in the room with him. The others had all made various excuses to leave the room, asking Geoffrey in too-loud voices where the loo was, then whether they could see his basement. I didn't even care, worried where this was heading. How could Luke possibly doubt my loyalty to him?

Luke sighed, turning to face me. 'Look, maybe a bit of time apart will give us a break. You need to work out what you want, Lottie. I want you, but this distracted, stressed version of yourself . . .'

Even Howard had left the room now. We were alone.

'Fine. Run away,' I said, waving a hand at him. 'You might as well go now.'

'I . . . Fine.' He threw up his hands.

And then, just like that, he headed to the door. I heard him making his excuses to Geoffrey and the front door opened and closed. He had left. I slumped in my chair.

There was a pause and then urgent whispering in the corridor. I could feel the shame steal over me, imagining the four old men discussing what to do. Finally Grandad appeared in the doorway, glancing back as if reluctant to enter.

'All OK, Lottie?'

He edged into the room and sat on one end of the sofa, clasping his hands together in his lap.

'I'm fine,' I said, undermining the words by hiccoughing a small cry.

There was a silence that stretched on and I was about to make my excuses and leave.

'Do you know why I was so keen to get you and Luke to do all this?' Grandad swept a hand around the room, abandoned wine glasses littered on every surface.

I sat on the other end of the sofa. 'You were missing Grandma,' I said, my voice wobbling.

He shook his head. 'No, it wasn't that. It was a way to make you happy.'

'Me?' Frowning, I looked at him in surprise.

He shrugged. 'I knew why I was sad, I'd lost her, but I had my friends, you, Luke, the knowledge that I had shared my life with the best person. I've come to know what's important. You were unhappy, taking it out on people. Grandma and I had talked about it, we thought perhaps you'd lost your way—'

'I haven't los—'

'—and you used to shrug off the stresses of your job, spend time doing things with people you liked. That seemed to have slowed down, almost stopped . . . '

Perhaps it was hearing that Grandma had agreed with him, that they had discussed me like this, but for some reason the sadness at hearing it all morphed into anger. Everything these days seemed to be so near the surface. Clenching my hands I spoke through a tight jaw. 'Well, I'm sorry I've become such a bitch. It's only my job, after all,' I scoffed, slightly proving his point.

Grandad flinched at the words. 'Look, Lottie, we understand, we do, but for a while there you have to admit things were better. You were happier when you spent more time enjoying things other than work, having some fun again.'

Looking down I blinked the hot tears away. I didn't want to admit that he might be right. I was fed up with always feeling like the person in the wrong. Wasn't I allowed to be stressed? Feel some pressure? 'Well, thanks for letting me know. I'm sorry I've been such a disappointment.'

'Lottie' – Grandad appealed to me, palms out – 'you're not a disappointment. It's just no one wants to see you like this.'

I didn't want to hear any of this. Defensiveness made me spit out the next sentence. 'I thought you might have a bit of sympathy, being that my oh-so-put-upon-boyfriend is cheating on me.'

'He's not cheating on you, Lottie. He's with her bec—' Grandad's lips pursed tightly.

Stung, I twisted my whole body towards him. 'What?'

Grandad's eyes widened.

'Oh my God,' I whispered. 'What do you know?'

His face drained of colour, his eyes slithered away. I knew guilt when I saw it. I had come across enough of it in court.

'I don't' – both palms up in an appeal – 'I . . . '

'Oh my God, you know what Luke has been doing!' I couldn't believe it. I felt my stomach sink. Was Grandad really holding something back from me? Was he choosing to be loyal to Luke over me?

'He brought her over because, well, I can't say, but it really isn't what you thin—'

'You've *met* her?' I felt nausea rise inside me. Luke had introduced her! This was all becoming too real. I had suspected something was going on but this was so much worse than I'd imagined.

'No, well, it's just, it's not what it ... Arjun could ...' Grandad was scraping his hands through his hair.

Did they all know? I felt everything swim inside my head. I was utterly alone. I stood up abruptly. 'Tell Geoffrey I've got a headache.'

'Lottie, wait.'

'I have to go.'

'Lottie.'

'No,' I said, voice wobbling as I looked down at his ashen face. 'I can't even ... I can't believe you ...' Knowing I was about to start crying I didn't carry on. Snatching my bag up, I swept out of the living room to the front door, aware Howard, Arjun and Geoffrey were all crowded into the kitchen trying to avoid listening to the exchange. Humiliation made me angrier and I slammed the door behind me.

Moving down the street I ignored another call from the house. Arjun had tried to follow me but I was walking too quickly. Grandad's guilty face, the knowledge that something was going on with Luke. The lies. The betrayal. Whatever Arjun wanted to say couldn't help me.

When I'd got some distance I removed my mobile, wanting a cab, a quick way to get back home. A name appeared on the screen and with a small swell of relief I realised the message was from Mum. That was what I needed. I wanted someone who loved me to tell me it was going to be OK. My parents' next visit was in a few weeks' time. I wished she was here right now. I clicked on the message. *Had to cancel flights. Your father got given tickets to the test match in India. We'll rearrange soon! Hope all well! Love to Luke!*

Standing stock still I read the message over and over, feeling everything crash around me again. I was returning to an empty flat, my boyfriend was probably cheating on me, my best friend wasn't speaking to me, my grieving grandad thought I was a cow and was keeping secrets from me, and now my parents had chosen to go on an international cricket tour rather than spend time with me.

I had never felt so alone.

Chapter 24

Love is like a good mystery book: you
never know what's coming next but you
know you must keep turning the page

AGNES, 88

The week passed in a fog of misery: barely present in court, dazed with clients as I tried to make sense of everything. What was Luke keeping from me? What did Grandad know?

The work wasn't acting as a distraction. What did I really love about the job? I'd always wanted to study law, enjoyed representing people, trying to help them articulate what they wanted to say in court. I knew I had lost sight of my original love of the law: a new case, a grateful client, the research involved. Instead I'd become caught up in the idea that I needed to work on anything that might advance my career and to hell with the consequences. I hadn't even thought about applying for silk and then suddenly I'd decided to be in a great rush to get there. Yet I didn't really know why I was doing it. I had seen the way my father had given so much up in his quest to get to the top of his industry and it made him happy. But did it make me happy?

My phone remained silent. Amy, Grandad, Luke – all absent. It only highlighted how messed up things were and a terrified ache in my stomach told me I might never get these things back. The anger was fading and the doubts were creeping in: would the two people who loved me most really be lying to me?

Saturday dawned and the buzzer to the flat went, hope lighting in me at the thought that Luke might be here.

'This is your fault,' Howard announced down the intercom. 'It's us, we need to come in,' he said.

Frowning, I pressed the button on the intercom, opening the flat door to see Howard halfway up the stairs already.

Grandad was a little slower, calling out behind him, 'You can't blame Lottie for this.'

I felt weary as I heard his words. What had I done now? Could I do anything right? And shouldn't I be angry with him? He was keeping something from me: I was sure.

I stepped aside as Howard and Grandad came into the flat, Grandad unable to disguise the surprise on his face at the state of the place. The curtains were half closed but even the semi-darkness couldn't hide the dirty plates, bowls and cups, the scattered papers, the flowers long dead in their vase and the crumpled duvet on the sofa. The air was stale and I fitted in perfectly: my hair tied back into a greasy ponytail, hands spattered with biro ink, wearing an old T-shirt of Luke's still streaked with mud stains from Glastonbury a couple of years ago.

Howard was talking to himself. I could feel my face pulled into a frown wondering just what it was that had got him so excited. He was pacing the rug in the living room. 'Figured you might be able to talk them down. They'll listen to you. They certainly aren't listening to us.'

Grandad had surreptitiously started to remove crockery to the kitchen. Unable to catch his eye, I felt my heart sink seeing the man I loved having to tend to me when after Grandma died that was what I vowed to do for him. Would he really be choosing to hurt me? Surely I needed to trust him?

'It's preposterous,' Howard continued. 'No respect for history, tradition . . . '

'What's going on? How can I help?' The focus gave me a much-needed shot of energy, something I simply hadn't been able to muster in the last few days. I wondered why Grandad wasn't asking where Luke was and then realised that he probably already knew.

'As if you don't know,' Howard huffed, his lower lip jutting in a pout.

'I honestly don't.'

'You'll have to see for yourself,' Howard said.

'Come on, Lottie, let's go,' Grandad said. Was he avoiding looking me in the eye? I felt confused, thoughts whirring. I didn't want to ask more in front of Howard but not knowing was torture.

Howard wouldn't let me change. 'No time, no time, it could all be much, much worse by now,' he was saying as I fumbled to put on my trainers.

He escorted me out and down into the street, straight into his car. I barely fit into the bucket seat in the back. Grandad got into the front passenger seat.

I tried to make light of it. 'Shouldn't you cuff me?' I said, but Howard just stared at me wordlessly in the driving mirror.

Briefly I pictured the last time I'd sat in that car, the roof rolled down: that slow magical weekend Luke had arranged.

I didn't dare make conversation, the car journey an excruciatingly silent affair interrupted only by Howard making the odd disgruntled snort. I realised we were heading to the club and was running through various scenarios in my mind. I couldn't remain quiet for any longer. 'Is everything OK, Grandad. Are Geoffrey and Arjun all right?'

Howard cut off his reply. 'They're fine. Well, they're probably not happy either because of this *travesty*, which I am sure is down to your influence.'

'That was not what Margaret said,' Grandad said gently.

Margaret? I frowned.

'*Pff.*' There followed a few more snorts and, as we turned into the familiar setting, I was relieved the journey was coming to an end.

There was no time to even whisper questions to Grandad, who I wasn't sure I was ready to talk to anyway, as Howard beckoned me out of the car.

We'd parked near the entrance to the golf club and I could hear a hubbub of noise somewhere ahead of me. 'Is there an event on?' I asked.

Howard scoffed. 'You could say. Come on, young lady.'

Howard turned and marched towards the clubhouse, the sound of voices louder as we approached. Confused, I could make out lots of people lying down on the ground, lots of people with grey hair. Everywhere elderly women were sitting or lying down in front of the entrance to the clubhouse. There were placards, too, with slogans I couldn't quite make out from this distance. Every now and again the voices would converge into some kind of chant and I would miss the words because Howard would start mumbling obscenities.

'Still bloody at it. There are more of them, Teddy. More.'

Grandad was completely quiet by my side. What was going on? How was this meeting of prostrate women my fault? And when would I get a chance to talk to Grandad?

Nearing the group I instantly recognised Paula brandishing a placard that read WE WILL NOT BE PUTT IN OUR PLACE and, more surprisingly, Margaret dressed in a hot pink long-sleeved top and sporty leggings with a fleece hairband, hands cupped around her mouth as she appeared to start up one of the chants.

'They won't let us in – it is a sin!'

It was catchy and I found a small smile building as I looked around the group. There must have been at least thirty women there. Some had obstructed the door by lying horizontally on the path, blocking the way in or out. A young guy in his twenties, dressed in the customary royal blue polo shirt of the club, was standing nervously in the doorway, wringing his hands and every now and again trying to clear the path of horizontal women.

'This is ridiculous. It must be stopped. Teddy, get her to say something.' Howard was gesturing at me.

Forgetting my own troubles for a minute, I looked at him in amazement. 'How am I meant to stop it? And what do they want anyway?' I asked, starting to realise I knew the answer.

Margaret spotted me, her face breaking into a wide smile, both hands waving enthusiastically.

'Christ, it's a coven. This is what it will be like, Teddy. There will be no escape. Women. Everywhere.'

Grandad had turned to fill me in. 'They want to be allowed to join the golf club. They're only allowed to play on a Wednesday morning at the moment and a lot of them are taking a taxi to a club a few miles away but they want the Men Only rule on the course broken.'

'And what do you think?' I held my breath, not sure I really wanted to hear the answer, but before I could I heard a roar from Howard.

'Arjun!'

Turning, I spotted Arjun walking past not ten feet away, both hands clutching a placard that said, OUR TREATMENT OF WOMEN IS WELL UNDER PAR.

He jumped and froze as Howard's cry hit him. Some of the women nearby looked around.

'Arjun, what are you doing?'

Arjun stayed rooted to the spot.

'Tell me you have confiscated that,' Howard asked in a warning voice.

Arjun looked momentarily terrified, as if he was considering throwing the placard at us and escaping in the other direction, but then he puffed out his chest and jutted his chin and met Howard's eye. 'I agree with them. They should join us. It's an archaic rule. It's a sin not to let them in. No longer shall we oppress them!' His voice wobbled on the last line and I couldn't help but grin as he bravely waved the placard around.

'You fight the patriarchy, Arjun,' I called out, nodding at him enthusiastically. He gave me a sisterly fist pump and went back to his placard and the latest chant.

Howard turned on me. 'I brought you here to end this madness, not encourage it. Margaret claims to have picked up this notion from you. Have. A. Word.'

'Me?' I said with surprise, glancing at Grandad, who I could have sworn was laughing into his hand. 'OK, I'll go and see what's going on.'

Feeling rather conspicuous as I moved through the gathering crowd, I stepped over the liver-spotted legs, some surprisingly tanned and toned, past flasks of tea, grey heads bent together and the odd golf club (possible weapon if the polo-shirt attendant got frisky?) and headed towards Margaret.

'Lottie, you came! How lovely. Did Teddy tell you to

come? How sweet of him. I did hope he might approve of what we're doing.' Margaret's cheeks were flushed, two pink spots, and her eyes sparkled. She looked to be burning with restless energy. I couldn't dim that gleam on her face.

'Did you organise all of this?' I asked, staring round at the women, some of whom were looking curiously over at her as if awaiting instruction. She bent down and picked up a loudhailer.

'What do we want?'

'Inclusion!' the crowd chanted.

'When do we want it?'

'Now!'

Then she put down the loudhailer and continued chatting to me. I didn't recognise this Margaret, this sharp-eyed, confident woman bossing people around. 'Phyllis, take that placard to Hetty. I think her F has fallen off and WOMEN'S GOL makes no sense. Paula, could you round up that group at the back? They've just arrived and they look lost.'

She picked up the loudhailer again. 'We want in, we want in.' The crowd took up the chant.

Arjun was front and centre joining in, grinning at me and giving a thumbs-up. I was glad to see him looking a little healthier, more colour in his cheeks, energy in his stride. I was being swept up in the atmosphere, the cries from the women, the bickering of the polo-shirt man who had been joined by a polo-shirt woman who was looking rather confused, all my other thoughts fading away.

Men were picking their way across the women lying down, manoeuvring their clubs over their bodies to get inside.

I returned to Howard, wondering just what I was going to say.

'Well,' he said breathlessly as I approached. 'Did you talk her down? Woman to woman?'

'Er . . . not exactly.'

Howard's eyes narrowed. 'What do you mean, not exactly?'

'Um.' I scuffed my toe along the ground. 'Um, I agreed to take over the loudhailer for her so she could go to the toilet.'

Howard was turning a funny shade of magenta and Grandad had definitely lost it now, patting him on the back and stifling a laugh with his other hand. 'Maybe it's for the best, old chap. Give the club some new energy. And we could use the green fees. Clubhouse looks rather dated.'

'Clubhouse will be turned into a pink hell on their watch, all china cats and tea pots,' Howard spluttered. 'They'll get rid of Sky Sports, they'll demand one of those fancy coffee machines. They'll want wine in those silver ice bins.'

'You've been saying for ages we should get a cappuccino maker,' Grandad protested.

'This was not how I wanted it,' Howard spat. 'And I'm not talking to Arjun ever again.'

Grandad opened his mouth and sensibly shut it again. We both knew we would get nowhere while Howard was in this mood. I bit my lip and stood there, listening to the chanting behind me and trying to look vaguely like I cared. I tried to sympathise: Howard was a man who didn't like change, knew where he stood. On the other hand the rule was archaic and ridiculous, and of course the women should be fighting to access the golf club they all live close to.

'Why don't we get off and get Lottie back to her flat, eh?' Grandad said, clapping a hand on Howard's shoulder.

'Fat lot of good she did us. Inciting things further,' he said, glaring at me as I realised Margaret was beckoning me over for her loo break.

Feeling strangely shy I turned to Grandad. 'Don't worry, I can make my own way back. I'd better . . . ' I nodded my head in Margaret's direction.

'Lottie, about the other night . . . it really isn't what you think.'

I nodded slowly, knowing there was more to say but realising this was enough for now. 'OK,' I said, a weak smile on my face.

'Lottie!'

The loudhailer called me. I cringed. 'I better go.'

Grandad tipped his head in acknowledgement. 'Right, well, Howard, that leaves you and me,' he said in a bright voice. 'How about we head home, put the kettle on and—'

'HEAR OUR CALL, GOLF IS FOR ALL. HEAR OUR CALL, GOLF IS FOR ALL.'

He had to raise his voice. 'I'm sure all this will die down soon enough.'

I crept away back towards the gaggle of women and Margaret. One elderly lady had hoisted herself up on to the low stone wall and was marching along it with her placard.

The polo-shirted workers were desperately pleading with her to get down and simultaneously asking the lying women to get up. I felt a burst of pride for Margaret doing what she thought she needed to do to be heard. Heading over to her, I took the loudhailer.

'Thanks, Lottie,' she said, almost crossing her legs she was so desperate to get to the toilet.

Grandad was leaving, a shy half-wave in my direction. Feeling marginally better I switched on the loudhailer and raised it to my lips. 'WE THOUGHT YOU LOVED BIRDIES. LET THE WOMEN IN.'

Darling Cora,

I saw Lottie today. Howard frog-marched her to the golf club to help stop the protest (a long story). I'd made things so much worse between us the other night and could barely look at her. She looked wan and pale and her flat was unkempt and as sad as her and Luke. How did I get myself into this position? She thinks I'm withholding all these terrible dark secrets from her, when really I am just trying to keep a promise to Arjun. I know I need to fix things but I don't seem to know how. And I couldn't find the right words today. What should I say? How do I make things right again? Why aren't you here to advise? You would know precisely what I should do.

I miss her, my darling, and of course I miss you too.

Teddy x

Chapter 25

Love is like a good pair of shoes – you search for the prettiest but the ones you need are the most comfortable

CELIA, 83

The morning had been a bit of a boost. As I headed home on the bus I couldn't help replay the scenes: more women had appeared, one of the polo-shirts had started handing round refreshments, the crowd had been joined by some of the male members of the club and the atmosphere had felt like a mini carnival. With a renewed gush Margaret had told me that she had secured a meeting with the general manager of the club. 'It's such a coup,' she cried, squeezing me before leaving to tell Paula the news.

Arjun had then sidled over to persuade me to give up the loudhailer. 'I've come up with a really good chant. Please, Lottie.' He held out his hand and I paused, secretly not wanting to relinquish the power. He looked so earnest, though, with his drooping placard and his flushed cheeks that I handed it over with a nod.

He took it and switched it on but then the crowd turned, assuming he was the enemy, there to shut them down, and began pelting him with balled-up socks/headbands until he began his new chant: 'I'M TEED OFF WITH HOW WE TREAT OUR WOMEN' and they all delightedly started screaming along with him.

'WE'RE TEED OFF . . .'

Ascending the stairs to the flat I felt my bright and breezy mood plummet. Opening the door into the stale, semi-dark space it hit rock bottom. I had envisaged telling Luke all about it, seeing his face crinkle as I described the scene. As I stared round at the cluttered flat I realised the silence would stay until he returned, if he ever returned. I didn't even move from the corridor but slid down the closed door, feeling drained and hopeless. I deserved this scene. I had driven him away. In the wall mirror opposite I took in my appearance: hair scraped back, no make-up, filthy clothes. Who would return to someone who couldn't even look after herself?

Resting my head against the wood I started as the buzzer went. Frowning, I dragged myself to my feet, finger lingering over the intercom. An irrational thought that it might be Luke made me press down. Maybe he'd lost his key? Maybe he thought this was more formal?

'Hello?' I couldn't keep the hope I felt out of that one word.

'Lottie, is that you?' A female voice, I realised with a flash of disappointment. I pressed the buzzer. 'It is, come up.'

Margaret appeared in the bottom of the stairwell and I watched her, still dressed in her fluorescent outfit, move carefully up the stairs, one hand on the banister.

'Margaret, what are you doing here? Shouldn't you be celebrating?' I tried to inject my voice with enthusiasm but my words sounded hollow, even to me.

'Hold on, let me catch my breath,' she said, three-quarters of the way up.

I waited as Margaret moved past me into the flat, her eyes scanning the debris. I felt hot shame creep up my neck and into my face.

'I, um, sorry, I've been working, it's not very . . . ' I tailed away. This wasn't exactly the flat of someone over-working, it was the flat of someone who had lost the will to function in a basic way. I appeared to have reached Amateur Hoarder status in a single week. There could be another species living under those pizza boxes – I couldn't be sure and the smell wasn't pretty.

There wasn't really a clean space to offer her and I fussed in the kitchen, hoping she was one of those people who didn't take milk in her tea because I was fairly sure the milk was now a toxic substance.

'Why don't we head out, love?' Margaret said, a gentle hand on my forearm.

I bit my lip, knowing she was right but feeling embarrassed all the same.

We made a strange pair as we walked past various shoppers in the weak afternoon sunshine. I steered us to a small café on the corner of the street.

The bell tinkled as we entered a room full of the aroma of fresh coffee with a counter crammed with cakes and pastries. Realising I had barely eaten in the last couple of days my mouth watered at the sight. A small round table was being wiped down as we arrived and I headed towards it. Margaret watched me closely as I ordered our cakes and coffees. I found myself threading my fingers together under the table, crossing and re-crossing my legs from the scrutiny.

'Can I say something, Lottie?' she said in her soft voice, her kind eyes trained on me.

I swallowed, 'Of course.'

The waitress brought over our cups and plates, taking her time to place everything on the table as I tried not to fret as to what Margaret was about to say.

'You don't seem yourself. I was a little worried about you this morning. You looked so drawn, tired, your clothes weren't you at all, dirty and shapeless . . . '

I wanted to be offended, to lift my chin and challenge her words or storm out of the place, flounce down the street huffing about meddling old women, but I couldn't. My hand shook as I went to lift the cup to my lips, coffee sloshing into the saucer. 'I . . . '

'And your flat . . . ' She tailed away, perhaps noticing the misery etched over my face.

Momentarily panicked, I felt tears build in my throat. I

took a decisive sip of coffee, scalding my tongue in the process. The pain distracted me from anything else.

Margaret was leaning towards me in her chair, 'What's happened, Lottie? Things seem to be getting on top of you.'

I stared at the top of the table, unable to meet her eye. Shoulders slumped forward, any attempt at false bravado fading.

'I've really messed everything up,' I said, my voice choked.

Margaret was quiet and I kept my eyes down, trying to put into words all the things I'd been thinking these past few days and weeks. 'I've been a rubbish friend, a rubbish granddaughter – I was a cow to Grandad – and I've been so' – one slow tear tracked down my cheeks as I admitted it – 'so horrible to Luke. He didn't deserve it and now he's probably gone for good, or with someone else, and I'm alone and I know I deserve it but' – I sped up, my worst fears spilling out between us – 'I'm scared I've screwed up the best thing I had going for me and I don't know how to do anything right.'

I was fairly sure people were watching now. The café seemed horribly silent and I wished we had stayed in my flat if I was going to have this breakdown. Tears dripped on to the table and Margaret pushed a paper napkin towards me.

'That's all right, here you go.'

Dabbing at my face I stared glumly into my lap.

'Do you want to know why we were all there this morning?'

This wasn't the response I had envisaged and I found myself looking up.

'Because I organised it. I thought enough is enough and I made posters and I went door-knocking and I asked those women to join me in our fight.'

I smiled weakly at her. 'It was brilliant.'

'Ssh,' she said chidingly. 'I asked those women to do it because I felt stronger, I was inspired by someone with courage and passion and belief in their convictions.'

I sniffed pathetically, glad to have the napkin.

'I thought, how can I change this unfair thing? What would *Lottie* do?'

As she finished the sentence I almost dropped the napkin, my mouth fell open.

'What would *I* do?' I repeated, unable to believe that anyone would feel inspired to behave like me. Surely she had seen me? I was an actual walking mess, a dustbin of a person right now, clothes I hadn't bothered to wash in days, grubby skin and hair, neglecting everyone in my life to the point that now I was utterly alone. Why would anyone think I had any answers at all?

'Well, not this you, this you is rather a diminished version,' Margaret went on, a teasing smile on her face, 'but, Lottie, when I met you I was blown away with your energy, your sense of justice. You are so impressive, trying to juggle so much in your life, trying to be a good granddaughter to Teddy – and don't think you haven't succeeded there, of course you have, he loves you, deeply – and your work, your beliefs. Lottie, if I had had half that passion when I was younger I can only imagine what I could have done. I held myself back for years, not realising I could just grab opportunities, that I was worthy of them . . . '

It was quite a speech and I could feel the tears building again. 'I think you're giving me a lot more credit than I deserve.'

Margaret waved cake on a fork around. 'Don't you dare put yourself down. You need to be kinder to yourself, Lottie. You are trying to take on the world and it's all got on top of you, but you can fix it.'

'I . . . '

'What is important to you?'

In that moment her simple question put so much into perspective. I hadn't always been the girl who placed ambition above everything else. I had allowed myself to become swept up in chasing impossible goals, working myself into the ground, competing with others and not even stopping to ask if I was competing for something I truly wanted. And on the way I had ridden roughshod over the people I had always loved, the people I needed in my life. Amy, Grandad, Luke . . .

'Now what do you need to do to stop yourself being miserable? How can you get things back on track?'

'I don't think I can, I don't think—'

'Hush,' she said. This new authoritative Margaret was quite a formidable figure. 'Of course you can, you are a confident young woman who knows her own mind. So . . . '

I couldn't help feel buoyed by her faith in me. I sipped the last of my coffee and placed the cup down on the saucer.

'I need to apologise to Grandad, properly. I need to make things up with Amy, and I really need . . . '

I couldn't bring myself to say it. What if it was too late? What if I couldn't get him back?

'Luke,' I said simply. 'I need Luke back.'

'Right,' Margaret said, stacking our plates and saucers and pushing them to one side. 'So let's work out exactly how.'

We left the café a little over half an hour later armed with a plan. I felt lighter, less hopeless after sharing my worries and making plans to fix things. I realised as we moved slowly down the pavement back to my flat that this was the kind of conversation I would have had with Grandma. She would have chided me and encouraged me at the same time. I felt incredibly lucky to have Margaret in my life, to have someone looking out for me still. I hadn't realised how much I had needed it.

'Thank you,' I said, squeezing her arm as we reached my flat. 'Do you want to come up?'

Margaret wrinkled her nose and laughed. 'Maybe once you've had a tidy,' she said. 'And a shower.'

I couldn't stop the small giggle escaping. 'Thanks, Margaret,' I said seriously, pulling her into a hug.

'Any time.'

Chapter 26

Love can be mistaken for mild food poisoning

LEN, 84

I spent the rest of the day tidying, scrubbing, hoovering, wiping and dusting until the flat gleamed. Then I headed to the shower and transformed myself under the hot water: exfoliating, cleansing, clipping nails, removing hair, tweezering. I emerged like a new woman, ready to tackle things. It felt good to be standing in a spotless flat, in clean clothes with glossy hair and some subtle make-up. I could do this.

I had thought long and hard about how to make things up with Amy. In the last few months I hadn't prioritised her at all and this was doubly insensitive because this was the time when she needed me and wanted me to share in her excitement as she planned her wedding. I couldn't get back all the times I'd missed her call or fobbed her off with another excuse in order to work late, but I could make a promise that I wouldn't miss anything more.

Amy wasn't answering her phone, to me at least, and I knew I shouldn't apologise on a text or voicemail anyway. I stopped phoning after sixteen unanswered calls, perhaps believing seventeen would make me seem a psycho. Spurred on by something Margaret had said, about the fact that Amy and I had roots that went back years, I felt a spark of excitement and rushed through to the living room to find my laptop. A thoughtful gesture might work? I spent the rest of the evening working on it and finally took myself to bed just after midnight when it was finished.

I wasn't in court the next day so was able to head out early, memory stick in handbag, and a renewed feeling of optimism. If Amy wouldn't answer her phone I knew exactly where she would be.

'Visitor for Miss Otaru,' I announced, thrown by the security measures at her London day school. Locked gates, intercoms and security booths: things were a little different from when I'd been at school.

The intercom crackled and after a pause a disembodied voice asked, 'Is she expecting you?'

I hated lying so instead bleated, 'I'm here on business,' in a panicked tone, as if that salient fact would gain me access. 'She will know what this is regarding,' I said in my most formal courtroom voice.

Unbelievably the buzzer sounded and I pushed open the heavy gate with two hands. Walking down a stone path, a blue Astro Turf pitch on one side, netball courts on the other, I headed for the main building. 'Reception' announced a jade green wooden board and I made my way towards it. I had barely stepped inside when the receptionist, a middle-aged woman with a close cropped hairstyle and magenta pink lipstick, stood up and headed my way, thrusting a laminated badge in my direction. 'Excellent. Welcome,' she said. I marvelled at the efficiency. This had been easy!

'Good morning. Where can one find Miss Otaru's office?' I asked in my politest voice.

'Oh, she can take you there once you're done, but the pupils are waiting in the hall for you now. Follow me.'

Still congratulating myself on gaining access I barely listened to what the receptionist had said as I followed her fast clacking walk down a corridor that smelt of bleach and was lined with various artworks by the children.

Sorry,' I said, almost tripping in my haste. 'Is she not in her office?'

'She'll be in the hall waiting.'

'Right,' I said distractedly.

'I imagine they'll all be very keen to hear what you have to say.'

'Will they?' I asked, confused now and wondering who 'they' were. I glanced down at my laminated badge and realised with a frown that my name wasn't Jacinda Brown. For the first time an uneasy feeling stole over me as the receptionist paused in front of two wooden double doors, panes of glass showing the backs of heads of what must have been hundreds of teenagers.

'Are you ready?' she smiled.

The uneasy feeling intensified and I felt my hands grow clammy as I asked, 'Ready for . . . ? Is Miss Otaru in there?'

'She'll be with the other teachers. They tend to sit on the stage.'

'Right,' I whispered.

Something definitely wasn't right but everything had moved so quickly and if it was true that Amy was inside she could surely sort this mess out. Oh God, I didn't want to make things worse. The whole point of coming here was to fix everything, not make her hate me more.

The receptionist was staring at me, her magenta pink lips puckered. 'Well, go on then. And lots of luck!' she added brightly.

Luck? Why would I need . . .

Holding open the double doors she beckoned for me to move inside. The million teenagers peered round, straining to see who was disrupting their morning. Up ahead on a stage lined with chairs sat various staff members. I frantically scanned the room for Amy's face. When I did land upon it, I could see even from this distance the total confusion that drew her eyebrows together. She rose from her chair and then sat back down again. We must have been more than 100 yards away from each other and all the million teenagers had started to whisper. Holy actual shit, what had I walked in on?

I wanted to turn and run back through the double doors,

thrust my laminated badge at the receptionist and clatter back down the path outside and into London where one million teenagers weren't looking at me.

A middle-aged woman with shoulder-length brown hair approached me. 'Jacinda, a pleasure, I'm Mrs McDonald, the head teacher here. I'll show you to the stage.'

To my horror I was being led down the side of the room of millions of teenagers towards the stage, where an empty lectern stood in the middle. Amy was watching me, her mouth opening and shutting. I gave her a grimace and a small smile, torn between abject fear and pleasure at seeing her.

'Does the technician need to help you set up?'

'I made a memory stick,' I whispered.

'Lovely. Well, Mike here can sort that out for you. We have the projector all ready.'

Mike had joined us. Mike was dressed entirely in black, which matched his black beard. The head teacher stood, waiting for me to hand over the memory stick.

Realising what was on it, I refused to hand it over to Mike. Mike gave up asking me for it and stomped back to a booth at the back of the room.

'Er, right, well, I'll introduce you now and we'll get started,' Mrs McDonald said, smiling warmly at me as if she wasn't sending me to my death.

'Could I just have a word with Miss Otaru?' I asked in a quiet undertone.

'Plenty of time to catch up in the staffroom afterwards,' Mrs McDonald said briskly. And with no further warning she steered me up on to the stage and we headed for the lectern, two million eyes following us.

Silence fell. 'Good morning, everyone. Thank you for your patience this morning. We are delighted to welcome Jacinda Brown from the Duke of Edinburgh scheme to talk us through some of the benefits of this excellent venture. Let's give Ms Brown a warm welcome to our assembly.' She stepped backwards and started clapping and it seemed the whole room shook with the noise as everyone else joined in.

The Duke of Edinburgh Award.

Right.

Oh God.

I hadn't been brought to see Amy, I had been brought to speak to the million people. About something I knew very little about. Vague memories of dried food in soggy campsites and afternoons in care homes swam in my head.

I stared at the empty lectern in front of me, willing notes to appear. Then I stared at the ceiling, willing for it to fall and crush us all. Or just all the millions of children and other adults. And not in a horrible fatal way, just enough to get me out of talking to them. I stared then at the audience, the crowds of faces, some chewing gum, some whispering, some glancing down and around, some glazed and staring into the distance. Gah.

A member of staff coughed loudly behind me and I felt the rustle of fidgeting people as the silence yawned on.

Right! Duke of Edinburgh! I could do this. I would get it over with quickly and then talk to Amy. And if I did it well, we would laugh about it and it could be really bonding for us. An icebreaker!

I swallowed, my mouth impossibly dry. Shouldn't they give their speakers water? Feedback for Mrs McDonald. Right. Think of it as a courtroom, these are your jurors. Smile! I felt my face move but from the reaction of the pupils in the front row I wasn't sure the smile shouted an easy confidence. Some of them flinched.

I cleared my throat. 'The Duke of Edinburgh Award, or D of E as I knew it. Ha!' The microphone squealed as I barked with false laughter. 'It's really, really good.'

The faces stared at me, someone's mobile buzzed.

'You can do things like expeditions and things where you go camping and walk and have to follow maps . . . and stuff.'

This wasn't going well. I could feel the staff squirming on either side of me. I made the mistake of glancing round at Mrs McDonald, who rearranged her perplexed face into one of polite encouragement.

'I actually went on one of these expeditions with A— with Miss Otaru here,' I said in a louder voice, one arm sweeping round theatrically to where Amy was sitting. She shifted in her seat as the faces all angled to stare at her. 'Yes, we went to Dartmoor and our rucksacks were very heavy.' Christ, what was I doing, preparing for French GCSE? 'It was fun. We carried rucksacks. We walked far.'

'Also,' I was getting desperate, could feel sweat beading my forehead, 'you can choose to do charity work and I worked in a care home helping the elderly. I met one gentleman who loved crosswords and I still remember him telling me, Lot— Jacinda, he would say, when a cryptic clue says *scrambled* it often means it's an anagram, so, you know, I got stuff out of it too. And *sport*!' I shouted at them. The microphone squealed again. 'I think, I know, you get credit for sport and things so it's really worthwhile.' I was really wracking my brains now. 'And you get a medal at the end ... which is nice.'

Oh God, Lottie, oh God. Shut up. I am pretty sure that boy in the second row is openly laughing at you. There is definite smirking.

What more could I say? Was that enough? Could I leave it there? They had the rough idea, surely?

A woman and the receptionist were peering through the glass windows in the double doors. Oh God, I think the real Jacinda Brown had shown up. She had brown hair secured back in a tight ponytail. She looked far more likely to be taking groups of teenagers up mountain ranges in Wales than I did. The receptionist looked very put out. Even from this distance I could see her narrowed eyes, magenta pink lips screwed up in displeasure. I needed to wrap this up and fast.

'So I think, as you have heard, there are just lots of benefits really to, um, doing the, um, D of E so I think, you know, you ... totally should.' I petered out and took a step back from the lectern to indicate my inspirational talk had come to an end.

The headmistress had got to her feet, a small frown

puckering her forehead before she found her composure. 'Well thank you for that presentation,' she said, 'I think we should all consider signing up for the course and let's give Ms Brown a hearty round of applause for coming to talk to us this morning.'

Oh God, the receptionist had opened the door and was moving down the side of the hall as all the clapping was happening. I looked nervously over at Amy, biting my lip. Her eyes were rounded in her head, startled, and I chose that moment to try to melt away into the back of the stage, tripping over the microphone lead on my way to safety.

I stayed back there, frozen, as I watched the pupils all stand up and make their way out, jostling, bumping, pulling out mobiles. Amy had got up from her chair and was making her way towards me, pausing as another teacher stopped her with a tap on her arm. Her eyes darted to me and back as she spoke quickly to him, nodding frantically.

'What the actual fuck are you doing?' Amy hissed as she approached, a smile plastered on her face as pupils padded past the bottom of the stage near us.

With both my palms up I took a step forward. 'Oh God, I'm sorry, I—'

One of the pupils had broken free from the pack and had ventured up the small set of stairs towards us, lingering as we spoke. We couldn't really ignore her.

'Are you all right, Cassie?' Amy turned and plastered a helpful smile on her face. Only I could recognise the wobble in her voice.

A serious-looking girl in a headband clutching a lever arch folder to her chest motioned to me. 'I wanted to ask her whether doing Gold D of E would contribute to my UCAS points.' The girl stood looking at me for an answer.

'Oh, I, um, I . . .' I licked my lips and tried to remember to blink as I rooted around for an answer.

'Do you know what, Cassie,' Amy said, 'I'll get all the information you need and let you know, all right?'

Cassie looked mildly put out, adjusted the lever arch folder and sloped away. ''K.'

'Thanks,' I breathed out, a small, nervous giggle escaping. This almost felt like the old days. Amy and I against the world. Except for the expression on her face, which didn't seem particularly friendly, rather frosty in fact.

'Seriously, Lottie, what just happened? What are you doing? Have you lost it?' Amy drew a hand through her hair before pulling me to one side.

'I'm sorry. I'm not sure how it happened. I came here to talk to you. You didn't answer your phone,' I started.

'This is so not a normal response to that,' Amy fumed. 'When people don't answer they don't want to talk to you, Lottie. You don't turn up to their place of work and pretend to work for the Duke of Edinburgh scheme and run assembly for seven hundred pupils.'

'Seven hundred? It felt like more,' I said weakly.

Amy didn't smile.

'The thing is, I desperately wanted to see you, to make up for everything. I've been so crap and useless and I know you love a PowerPoint. So I made you one about our friendship.' I scrambled in my bag and drew out the memory stick I had refused to hand over earlier to the bearded technician. It hovered in the space between us.

Amy stalked past me, into the space behind the thick stage curtains, the memory stick falling from my hand as I went to follow her.

'Amy?'

She turned, her face largely in shadow. There were dusty benches behind her, props dotted about: a plastic crown, a skull, two coat stands, a faded chaise longue. She began to speak, her mouth pursed tight. 'This is what's going to happen, Lottie. You are going to leave, quickly and quietly, no more talking to pupils about UCAS points or trying to set up a new circus skills hour as an after-school activity etc. I am going to fix this shitty mess that you've made, God knows how.' She raked a hand through her hair. 'And try to ensure my boss doesn't think the whole school needs to reassess our security procedures to stop fucking lunatics prancing into our school assemblies.'

She sounded mad: her voice was really low and I couldn't meet her eye as she talked. If this was the treatment her sixth formers got I felt my heart go out to them. Nothing was worse this. Nodding frantically I allowed her to lead me through a back corridor, down a small set of stairs and skirt the building so that I found myself back by the security gate that led to the reception. Amy opened the gate for me.

'Amy, honestly, I'm so sorry . . . I honestly don't—'

Amy held up a hand, shaking her head from side to side. 'Don't, Lottie, don't make this any worse. I haven't got time, I need to get back and fix this. Just go, please, just leave.'

Feeling tears sting my eyes for about the eighteenth time that week I backed off, stumbling back up the path and out into the busy London street. I rested my back against the wall of the school. God, what had I done, I thought, head in my hands as I replayed my visit. Why was I intent on hurting everyone closest to me? Shivering in the shade of the wall I thought back to her dead eyes, her cold voice. Amy didn't deserve this and I had just made a bad situation a hundred times worse. Hands drooping at my sides I sloped away, feeling desperately alone and knowing it was all my fault.

Darling Cora,

It has become a bit of a habit for Arjun and I to head to the pub on the corner after hospital visits. He has changed his mind about treatment and this latest appointment was finalising his course of chemotherapy. He was warned of the side effects and we both knew enough people who had suffered through the gruelling treatment to be depressed as we left the hospital car park.

'You'll have to tell the others now,' I said.

Arjun was peering gloomily into his half pint of ale. 'I know.' He picked up the glass and sipped at it. 'Even Howard might notice if all my hair falls out.'

I tried to laugh but only a thin smile was roused.

'I just wanted a few more days and weeks without

pity, or talking about the treatment, or hearing other uplifting stories about people who had battled cancer, as if it will all end well if only you are determined enough . . .'

It was the first time I had seen him angry, raging at the disease, and I gripped my own glass. I understood.

'Launching the app, that seems so much more important now: something to do, to focus on, something really positive.'

Nodding, I felt relief at the change of subject. We were on safer ground here. Selfishly I did not want to think too much about Arjun's prospects. I couldn't contemplate it really: it hurt. Am I a coward, Cora, for not saying more? You, of course, wouldn't have let him off the hook that easily, but then you would have made it better, not worse; comforting rather than awkward.

'Luke will be here soon,' Arjun said, wiping at the watermark on the table. 'And Storm emailed me with mock-ups of the new title page.'

'You know I don't know what mock-ups are?'

'Of course!' Arjun said brightly. 'But even you should be able to navigate the app. It's simple. It's straightforward. You type in your postcode and choose a radius and then bam!' His eyes were dancing now, his black hair gleaming under the pub lights as he twisted in his seat to look at the door. 'They should be here soon.'

As if he conjured them, Luke appeared, holding the door open for Storm, who was wearing an extraordinary skirt like an adult tutu and an oversized bow in her red hair. Now, I don't want to be mean, Cora, but really, how could Lottie be threatened by this human version of Minnie Mouse? I could feel my eyes narrowing as she placed a playful hand on his chest. Arjun didn't notice as he got up to greet them both: shaking hands, taking their drinks order.

Luke moved across to me, held out a hand. Close up I was shocked to see he looked even gaunter than last time, eye bags more pronounced, patches of stubble that he'd missed shaving. As I pulled out a stool for him, even his smile didn't reach his eyes in the same way. 'Sit yourself down,' I said, knowing this separation from Lottie was taking its toll. God, Cora, how I wanted to tell him everything I knew. Lottie and he were both miserable and hiding these meetings had only made things worse. Storm hopped up on the stool opposite. Suddenly everything she did seemed predatory.

'Right,' Arjun said, carrying two more drinks over to the table and settling himself on the stool once more. 'Thanks for coming and I'm so pleased we're so close to being finished!' He seemed buoyant and relaxed, our earlier conversation already forgotten: no longer worried about hospitals and treatments but doing what he was passionate about.

Luke opened up an A4 glossy file in front of him and pulled out various sheets of paper – highlighting features as he talked Arjun through what they had done.

Storm leant over, proffering her phone. I made sure her hand didn't brush against Luke, Cora, you'll be pleased to hear.

Plans were put in place and Arjun talked us through the first event he was planning, Storm explaining how they could use social media to help raise the profile of the app. Lots of words I didn't understand were being bandied around and I sat quietly sipping at my drink and watching Luke closely over the rim. He was quiet, answering questions but not quite there somehow, eyes glazing, periodically starting and then rejoining the conversation.

Finally it seemed Arjun was finished and everyone was saying goodbye. I was losing my window of opportunity. I needed a reason to linger with Luke. I couldn't exactly ask him to escort me to the toilet. But what?

'Luke,' I said, no real plan in place, 'can you possibly . . . if it's not too much bother, show me how to . . . how to . . .'

The whole group was staring at me.

'. . . how to work the cigarette machine!' I finished triumphantly.

Luke and Arjun frowned.

'You don't smoke, Teddy,' Luke reminded me.

'It's not for me,' I said. 'It's for' – I wasn't the best liar – 'someone else.' I knew it all sounded rather cryptic. Who was I supplying cigarettes to?

Luke shrugged. 'All right.'

Storm headed to the door. 'I'll wait for you here, Luke.' Her light voice tinkled. 'Bye, Ted, lovely to see you again.'

Ted. Hmmph. I tried to smile at her but found my mouth wouldn't move much. 'Goodbye,' I said stiffly.

Luke had walked across to the cigarette machine.

'So, Teddy,' he said, standing in front of it, 'you put your money in here, and you press the cigarettes you want, here.'

It was the least complicated machine you could imagine.

Luke was staring. I realised I might have to buy cigarettes. I took out a £2 coin.

Luke was waiting. 'All right?'

God, cigarettes are expensive. Tentatively I drew out a tenner from my wallet.

Then, placing a hand on his arm, I drew Luke to one side. 'Luke,' I said quickly before I could change my mind, 'just wanted to say I saw Lottie. And she told me she saw you with' – I indicated Storm by the door with my head – 'and it looked like I was hiding something. So I think I made her think, think the worst.' I waggled my eyebrows in an attempt to show him what I meant.

'Oh,' Luke said, dragging a hand through his hair. 'Oh, well, I imagine it did.'

'Sorry.' I hung my head.

'Teddy, don't apologise, it's just another thing that would have made things worse between us.'

Luke didn't deny anything was going on? Oh, Cora, should I have spoken up earlier? Had he been driven into Minnie Mouse's arms?

'We have some things we need to, um, work through,' Luke finished.

Feeling heat build in my neck I realised I was back in one of those conversations I was hopeless at. What was the right thing to say? I needed to defend my Lottie, but Luke had always been a good boy. I rubbed at my face. Fortunately Luke seemed to understand my dithering and changed the subject. 'You don't want to buy cigarettes, do you?'

'No,' I said miserably.

'I'm glad. I was wondering who the secret smoker was you were buying for.'

I scuffed the floor with my foot. 'Just needed to get you alone,' I admitted.

'Well, we'll pretend I didn't know how to work it.' Luke patted me on the shoulder and I looked up as he seemed to smile for the first time that day.

Feeling lighter I walked back across the pub with him to say goodbye.

Watching Luke leave I felt better for having said something. He gave me a last nod as Storm seemed to skip out of the door.

Turning back I watched Arjun sink into a nearby chair, all energy spent, catching his breath. It was clear the last hour of excitement had probably been all he could take. I felt my heart ache at the sight. 'Right, let's get you back home,' I said in a faux-jolly voice.

Arjun just nodded, unable to respond, and I felt a swirl

of sickness inside me and suddenly wished I was able to share my sadness with Lottie. I'd missed her visits and the easy atmosphere we had fostered between us. I realised as I guided Arjun outside that I needed her now more than ever.

As I always need you, my love.

Teddy x

Chapter 27

Love doesn't have to be perfect
but it does have to be true

ALBERT, 79

I knew I should get up, was slumped on the sofa, the curtains half closed, a streetlight opposite flickering distractedly. Making food seemed an effort and I had found a half-open bag of crisps, tomato in flavour, which I hated but Luke loved. Eating them was making me feel closer to him and only a little bit nauseous. Nothing appealed on the television and the volume was funny and I'd forgotten how to fix the speaker attached to the television, something I'd always made Luke do. Obviously it wasn't the only reason I missed him, but right now it was definitely top three. A stack of work on the table reminded me that I had a busy day ahead but I had lost all motivation and popped another crisp in my mouth.

The buzzer sounded and it was a moment before I realised it was for our flat. Something inside me skipped and I leapt off the sofa, frantically smoothing at my hair and wishing my breath didn't smell of tomato. Who would call round at nine o'clock apart from Luke? Although why would Luke use the buzzer when he had a key? Fumbling to press the intercom button I bit down the nerves.

'Helloooo.' Oh God I'd pitched it too cheery, immediately hoping the greeting wouldn't make him change his mind about coming home.

'Lottie, it's me.'

My heart sank at the female voice, no Luke at all, but then lifted again as I registered who was speaking.

'Come up.' I pressed the button to unlock the front door and tried not to feel too hopeful. Maybe I had left something at the school? Maybe she was coming to shout at me more? Maybe one of the teachers had complained? Maybe, oh God, the headmistress had fired her for her association with me? All these worries almost stopped me opening the flat door to Amy. She could be scary at the best of times but an angry, fired Amy was beyond even my imagination.

Her knock came, brisk and efficient. Swallowing, I edged towards the door, opening it in tiny, timid movements as if she were here to mug me.

She was standing in the hallway underneath the single lightbulb, still dressed in her work clothes.

'Hey.'

‘Hey.’ I gave her an awkward smile.

‘Can I come in?’

‘Of course,’ I stuttered, pulling the door open wider and standing back. No weapon visible. Good.

‘Thanks.’ She moved inside. ‘Is Luke in?’

‘No.’ I didn’t expand and she didn’t question it further.

‘That’s good. I was hoping we could talk.’

Nerves fluttered in my stomach at the statement and I followed her through to the living room, heading over to the curtains to close them, finally blocking out the blinking of the streetlight.

‘Tea, coffee, water, wine, I think I have some juice, it might be off . . . ’ I knew I was talking quickly but I couldn’t seem to stop listing beverages.

‘I’m all right.’

‘Right,’ I said. ‘Ginger ale? No, probably not. Me too. I’m great. Not parched.’

Wow, shut up, Lottie.

I wondered if I imagined Amy’s mouth twitching into a small smile. ‘I’m glad.’ She sat on the armchair next to the sofa, her dark hair black and gleaming against the light grey fabric. ‘So . . . ’

‘I really am so, so sorry about today,’ I began, moving around and almost tripping up in my haste to sit on the sofa next to her. ‘It was so stupid and if you’ve been fired I will go and see your headmistress and I’ll beg her, *beg* her to take you back because you shouldn’t be punished for having a total imbecile as a friend.’

'I don't think you should go in and see her,' Amy said in a flat voice.

Oh God, she *had* been fired. I had ruined everything. Not only had I ruined her wedding with the brooch no-show but now she was unemployed. With no salary she would probably struggle to pay her rent so soon she might be homeless and it was literally all my fault. I wished that the next time I went to eat something innocuous I had become suddenly allergic and came out in hives all over. I deserved that much at least.

'But I must, I need to try and fix things. I have no idea what I was thinking. I just was so desperate to prove to you that our friendship really does mean something to me and I know I've been crap and selfish and awful and hideous, and just when you need me to . . . just when you need me to be a best friend, I've been shit.' I could feel my whole face creased with anxiety as I looked at her. My amazing, talented friend about to lose her job because of my idiot move.

'Lottie, about today. I shouldn't have reacted like I did.'

'You had *every right* to react like you did. I mean, what I did was *full mental*,' I said, refusing to let her take any of the blame in this debacle.

'Look, shut up for a second, OK?'

I snapped my mouth closed.

'I haven't been fired,' she said, a small smile now on her lips.

'You haven't?' I felt my whole body loosen a little. Amy

still had her job, the job she loved. Then I tensed again. 'But I *implicated* you, I told all those pupils we had been on an expedition together. They knew I knew you.'

'Lottie, seriously, it's OK, I explained everything.'

Frowning I said, 'But how?'

'Look, I did say you were my friend but I said you were having a breakdown and were prone to strange episodes. They totally bought it. I think they just assumed that no sane person would do what you did. In fact, Mrs McDonald thanked me for my tact and swift handling of the situation.'

'Oh my God,' I said.

'Are you pissed off?' It was Amy's turn to look worried.

I shook my head from side to side. 'No, that is *brilliant.* Why didn't I think of saying that? You're right! Who in their right mind would do what I did?' I felt my whole body relax. Crisis averted. I would have hated to damage something Amy truly loved.

Amy grinned. 'Thank God, I was quite nervous about telling you. You seem remarkably OK with me telling people you're certifiable.'

I shrugged. 'Always happy to oblige.'

'Oh, although the receptionist is being sent on another course on Security so if you ever bump into her in the street, I'd do a runner.' She smiled at me and gave me one of her throaty laughs.

We fell into an amicable silence.

'I really am sorry, Amy.'

Amy reached across and took my hand. 'I know. And

honestly, when you started talking to the pupils about "maps and stuff", I actually died laughing inside.'

'Oh God,' I groaned, flashbacks coming thick and fast, all those faces.

'So, look, I brought this too.' Amy fished something out of her bag and held it up. It was the memory stick that had dropped on the floor between us. 'And I really want to watch it with you now. If that's OK?'

I nodded, taking it off her and slotting it into the television. 'Of course,' I said, feeling an enormous excitement and relief that maybe, just maybe, I had got my friend back. I sat back down next to Amy and grinned at her before pressing Play.

Images started up and music played and all the old photos I had dug out and scanned and put on the PowerPoint fired up. Videos from nights out, photos from school right up to those in our shared flat. There was even one of us sitting on a stone in Dartmoor, both weighed down by huge backpacks, hair tied back with matching bandanas, heads cocked together, grinning at the camera. 'D of E!' Amy squealed, snorting as she pointed at the screen.

It finished and there was a thick silence in the room as I got up to get the memory stick back.

Finally Amy looked across at me. 'Thank you, Lottie.'

She seemed to be on the verge of saying more and I mentally bit down on my tongue, not wanting to push things or start apologising over again. The silence extended and I found myself bursting with it. 'I am so sorry, Amy, about the brooch, but also I just haven't been there for you at all and that is not cool—'

She was shaking her head and holding her hand up and I tailed away as I realised I was being forgiven. 'Lottie, I know. And I love you for your mad apology and I'm so relieved. I've really missed you.'

Then suddenly we were reaching across and hugging each other and I felt tears swim in my eyes as I realised how much I'd missed her too.

'And obviously you still need to be my bridesmaid,' she said into my hair. 'I need you there to tell me it's going to be OK and drink champagne with me and sort my sister out.'

'Of course, of course.' It came out muffled and in a rush.

Wiping at my eyes I sat back. 'You need to catch me up on everything. Has your mum made any more demands on your seating plan and is your sister still threatening to dress Tom in knickerbockers?'

Amy rolled her eyes.

I held up a hand. 'Wait. I'll get wine first.'

'I thought you weren't parched?'

'Shut up.'

I'd just got to the kitchen when she asked the question, 'Won't Luke be back soon? Have you got time?'

Not really wanting to ruin the atmosphere or shift the focus back on to me, I mumbled something as I rootled in the fridge for a bottle of wine and then reached up to the cupboard for two glasses.

'Oh I'm, um, he, well . . . '

Amy was already giving me her X-ray look as I returned. 'What's happened?' she asked, sensing immediately something was up.

'Oh nothing, I want to hear about the wedding,' I gushed, unscrewing the bottle.

Amy wouldn't stop staring. 'Lottie?'

Sitting back down on the sofa I poured two glasses of wine, avoiding eye contact for as long as possible. As I handed her a glass it seemed she probably hadn't blinked for the last five minutes.

'Lottie? Where is he?'

'Nowhere.'

'What do you mean nowhere? You don't know?'

'No, I do know. It's really not important, fine actually. Sooooo, your wedding.'

'Lottie!' Amy squealed.

'He's just staying with a friend.' I tried to sound breezy, added a small shrug of the shoulders, which caused me to spill a bit of my wine. I leapt up to get a cloth.

Amy asked me more questions. 'Just for the night? So you two are OK?'

Returning, I realised she wasn't going to drop this any time soon. 'Well, he's been staying there for a little while.'

Amy sipped wine and seemed to be waiting for me to say more. If she wasn't a deputy headmistress she could easily be a detective. She'd be insane at making people talk: leaving them to fester in their own silence, her watchful eyes on them, soaking up their body language and getting to the heart of the matter in an instant. No one would stand a chance.

'We had a bit of a row, not major, well, quite major, I mean, he sort of moved out for a bit but, you know, nothing that can't be fixed.' My voice sounded strangled, around ten tones higher than normal. Oh God, could it be fixed? I'd said that so easily but felt a crushing weight as I realised I wasn't sure. Had I lost him? Of course, these thoughts made me well up and then it was easy for Amy, detective extraordinaire, to worm the rest of the story out of me. By the end of my confession I was dabbing at my eyes, pouring myself a second glass of wine and feeling as if my world was slowly coming to an end.

'I'm not sure when he'll come back and I don't dare phone him and find out. It's my fault. I need to give him time.' Amy scooted across the sofa.

'Oh, love, why didn't you say anything?' she said, looking upset herself.

I sniffed and wiped my eyes. 'Um, hello? Because I had managed to completely screw up our friendship as well. I have been on full self-destruct mode for months now. I totally deserve it, honestly, Amy. I just spent so much time moaning at the poor guy and taking out all my frustrations on him.'

Amy held my hand. 'But we all do that. I know Will has to put up with me biting his head off after a long day of some shitty teenager being shitty.'

'But not every day,' I said, refusing to be cheered.

'Luke gets it. He knows you love him. You guys are so strong. I don't know a better couple.'

This only tipped me over the edge more. We *had* been a great couple. Luke was my best friend, we had travelled together, lived together, laughed all the time. I wondered when that had ended, when had I started to take it all for granted?

'So,' Amy said, business voice on, 'how are you going to fix this?'

'What if I can't fix—'

Amy held up a hand. 'Of course you can,' she said in the voice that I knew to be her no-nonsense voice. I needed that voice. I needed someone to give me strength. 'Right, I think I have an idea. You have got some work to do, woman.'

I looked at her, hope flooding my face. 'I'll do anything,' I said.

Amy grinned at me, lifting up her wine and raising it at me. 'Excellent.'

Chapter 28

Love is your wife offering to do the drive home after a boozy lunch

ARNOLD, 81

Amy left just after midnight and for the first time in ages I fell into a deep, dreamless sleep and woke the next day feeling refreshed. Even the hangover didn't affect me as I stepped into the shower, feeling a renewed buzz. Relief that Amy had forgiven me coursed through me and I was now determined to fix other things in my life, to make things right again. I phoned Grandad.

He told me he would meet me there and I dressed quickly for the occasion, not absolutely sure of the right attire. Gym wear coupled with thick knee-length socks and a peaked cap seemed about right. I wasn't sure if there were rules at the driving range but I knew golf was one of those sports where you had to look a bit strange to play. I think I'd nailed that look nicely.

The moment I parked I realised my mistake as Grandad was waiting for me outside, his golf clubs propped up next to him, looking 100 per cent normal. He gave me a brief hug and didn't comment on the sock-hat-leggings combo, and I was grateful.

'So, thanks for meeting me here,' I said, feeling strangely nervous.

'Of course, you know I love the range.'

'I thought it was about time I learnt.'

Grandad couldn't disguise the glow as I said the words. I had never shown any interest in golf before.

'And now they're going to let women join . . . '

'Don't let Howard hear you. Right' – he rubbed his hands together – 'let's get you set up.'

I followed him inside and we paused at a big steel box where Grandad leant down to pick up a small wire basket. 'We stick it under here,' he said, popping the basket in a large hole and inserting pound coins into the slot machine. The thud and rattle made me jump and suddenly the basket was filling with a thousand golf balls. 'Right,' Grandad said, lifting the now-full basket and moving down a thin corridor. To our left people were standing on small squares of green artificial grass, striking balls off the square out into the field beyond. Numbers on distant markers announced the distance they'd travelled and every now and again the air was filled with the swish of a club and the loud tink when someone connected with their ball.

'We can take the two booths at the end,' he said, pouring

half of the balls into a separate basket. 'You take these and I'll lend you an iron.'

I knew enough about golf to understand this referred to one of his clubs. I couldn't identify which one but that was what this lesson was for.

'Why don't I show you the rough idea and you just have a crack at it?'

'Great,' I said, happy to be here, showing an interest and seeing Grandad's animated face. This had been a good idea. He clearly had no clue it was a guise to ensure I got things back on track with him.

Grandad showed me what a tee was, where to put the ball, how far back to stand and how to swing through. It looked reasonably straightforward and I felt pretty confident walking into my booth. How hard could it be?

This outing was my way of making amends. I knew this probably wasn't going to be an emotional make-up scene with lots of hugs and apologies like my session with Amy. I was glad for the thin plywood wall that separated our booths and the distraction of attempting to hit a tiny white ball with a really long stick to show him I was sorry.

'This is haaaaarrd,' I said after the fifth swipe, the ball stubbornly remaining on the small tee in front of me.

''Tis a bit,' Grandad said, popping his head over the partition. 'Do you need me to watch your swing?'

'Hmm, I think I'll just keep having a try, thanks,' I said, not wanting an audience to my humiliation.

He nodded and disappeared back to his side.

It seemed to take an agonisingly long time to get rid of the balls in my basket. At one point I made the whole range cry out as I hit a ball into the steel rutted roof above our heads, and later, when Grandad wasn't looking, I picked up three balls at a time and simply lobbed them into the field. Annoyingly, two of them travelled further than the majority of the balls I had hit with the club.

Grandad appeared behind me as I struck the last ball, actually managing to connect with it and send it zipping off at a 45-degree angle. 'At least it got into the air,' I said, turning with a small triumphant smile.

'Not bad for a first go, Lottie. It's a damn difficult thing to do. You just have to keep at it.'

I was under no illusions that this would be my only foray into golf. I was here simply to ensure that Grandad and I had cleared the air. I'd missed him.

'Time for a break?' I asked, handing him back the club.

'Absolutely.'

We headed into the clubhouse and I was grateful to see no familiar faces. Hushing Grandad as he tried to pay for our order I handed over my card and then moved to the table in the corner with two pints of beer.

'Well, this is an unexpected pleasure,' he said, raising his glass to me.

I could have left it there, I knew he would let me, but I suddenly realised I really did need to say something. Taking a breath I looked at him and in a small voice simply said, 'I'm sorry, Grandad, about before.'

He tried to wave me away but I wouldn't let him. Now that I had started it was important that I finished.

'No, I need to say it. The things you said before – well, you were right, and I was rude and stubborn and trying not to listen to you. I didn't want to hear it, and I'm sorry I said such unpleasant things when you were just trying to point out what I knew really. And I'm sorry I didn't trust you, about Luke. I know you wouldn't hide things from me.'

Grandad was casting around for somewhere to look and his self-conscious avoidance made me stop and giggle. 'OK, I've finished now, you can relax,' I said.

He took a sip of his beer. 'You don't need to apologise, Lottie. I love you and just want to see you happy.'

These were pretty big words from Grandad, I was fairly sure I had only heard him tell me he loved me three times before. (When he won £240 on a horse I picked for him on the Grand National in 1996; when I ended up in hospital after falling out of the wheelbarrow he'd been pushing me in, promising to tell Grandma he knew nothing, and when I'd solemnly offered to give him my 'life savings' when I'd overheard him talking to Grandma about money worries.) So, of course, as was my way in recent hours, I found the never-ending well of tears I'd barely known I had fill up once more.

Grandad looked stricken. I was fairly sure there was a stringent 'No Crying' policy in the clubhouse.

'Did you see they are banning children from sitting on Santa's lap in the mall? Has the world gone mad?' he said, obviously hoping to distract me from melting in a pool of saltwater in front of him.

I let him. 'Really?' I said, and he brought me back from the brink, one quick hand patting mine, and we were off talking about Santas and the sweet innocence of childhood.

Getting up to leave an hour later he folded me into a hug, smelling of toast and cedar wood. 'You take care, Lottie, you're a wonderful girl.'

I gave him a squeeze back, feeling lighter and loved. 'Thanks for teaching me how to play golf.'

'Any time. And you'll get better,' he said, giving me an uncertain pat. I couldn't help but laugh as we walked out to our cars.

Darling Cora,

We were standing in the car park and the reunion had gone well. How my heart had leapt this morning when Lottie had suggested we meet, and at the golf range no less! What a morning ahead, golf and Lottie, my cup overfloweth!

Desperate to get things back to normal I was early as I pulled into the car park. Lottie appeared looking rather strange. I honestly have never understood fashion, but it was good to see her looking more relaxed and happy as she stepped out of the car and greeted me.

The golf was hopeless, she really is dreadful, but it was wonderful to talk with her and make things right again.

And I almost managed it but moving out to the car I

realised I needed to be braver. Things were right with us but I was worried about her and Luke, about what she thought. I knew I had to break Arjun's promise.

Lottie was about to leave and I stopped her with a hand on her arm. 'You said earlier that I wouldn't keep things from you.'

Lottie's eyebrows lifted in surprise.

'Well, that wasn't completely true. I did keep things from you about Luke, things you should know.'

Oh, Cora, the look of betrayal. It was terrible. I thought I might start weeping at her reaction. She put an arm out on her car as if righting herself. 'What is it?' she whispered, face draining of colour.

Worrying her knees would buckle I knew I needed to say things quickly, get it over with. 'I did know Luke was spending time with Storm.'

She let out the smallest whimper and I almost thought my heart would break.

'No, it isn't what it sounds like. He has seen her because Arjun has recruited them to work on something with him. An app. They're working on the practical aspects of it.'

Lottie's face was a picture: confusion, relief, questions. 'Oh . . .'

It was clearly not what she had been expecting.

'An app?'

I nodded. 'It's given Arjun something to look forward to because, well, I know he'll tell everyone in his own time and I don't want to break another promise today.'

Lottie looked up at me sharply. Had she noticed the changes in Arjun too? Instinct told me she knew exactly what I was hinting at and I quickly continued. It wasn't my news to share.

'It's a good idea really. The app. It was actually inspired by our ridiculous challenge. Doing all those events and getting you and Luke doing a lot of new things gave Arjun the idea. It's an app that tells you about events in your area aimed at an older crowd, people wanting some company and some fun. We want to be active and social and so it is a place to advertise painting classes, dance lessons, trips to the theatre. He's running the first outing next week too, getting others to organise things and upload them. Luke thinks it could take off.'

'That does sound good,' Lottie said slowly, clearly struggling to keep pace with the conversation now that she realised there was no terrible, dark secret.

'It's a chance to forge new friendships, new relationships. A chance to intervene if someone is lonely. It's given Arjun a real boost at a time when he needs it.'

'Right,' Lottie said, her shoulders lowering, hands unclenching.

'So I wanted you to know. Luke has been instrumental and there is nothing going on with this Storm character. She can't hold a candle to you anyway,' I added.

Lottie couldn't help smile at that.

Oh, Cora, I felt so much lighter watching her getting

into the car after that, seeing her face clear of troubles as she waved at me before starting up the engine.

I hope I have helped. I hope they can see things right. Oh, Cora, how we love her.

And how I love you.

Teddy x

Chapter 29

Love is like throwing yourself out of an
aeroplane – giddy, reckless, amazing –
you just have to trust you'll land safely

MAISIE, 81

I had basically spent the last forty-eight hours apologising to people and I was exhausted. Grandad's reveal had made me feel so much lighter and I was excited about seeing Luke at Amy's wedding. It was worrying to hear about Arjun and I was so grateful Luke was helping him on such a wonderful, positive project.

Picking up the phone I called Luke to make plans. It hadn't been the big, tearful reunion I had in my head. It was a somewhat stilted conversation made worse by the fact he immediately launched into practicalities and I was distracted by trying to get a sesame seed out of my teeth.

'So, Amy's wedding – we'll travel separately because you're needed earlier.'

'OK.'

'I need to come and pick up my suit.'

'OK.'

'So I'll do that on the morning of it and then get on a train.'

Aware I had said 'OK' too much already I plumped for, 'Sure.'

'Right.'

'Right.'

'Well, I'll see you there then.'

'OK.' Gah. This was harder than it seemed. I should have said, 'I miss you', I should have said, 'Luke, I'm a prize idiot, you're awesome and I shouldn't have pushed you into leaving and Grandad told me what you've been doing, which I think is fantastic, and I know Storm is just a Little Mermaid Wannabe who you aren't sleeping with and I wuv you so baaaaaadddd', but I said nothing, just sat, scraping at my teeth and feeling tongue-tied.

'Sleep well.'

'You too,' I said miserably, waiting for him to hang up first.

Chinese takeaway abandoned, sesame seed from tooth removed, I swept around the whole flat ensuring it was spotless. Although I wasn't going to be in the flat when he returned at least I knew where he was going to be. In a careful round hand (so many emails and texts meant my handwriting still surprised me), I spent an age composing a letter for him. That had been Amy's idea. Her big plan. And she was always right. So with no excuses, no explanations, I just sat and wrote a simple letter outlining how sorry I was, how much I cared for him and how I missed him and hoped he could forgive me. It felt like the most weighty, important envelope in the world as I tasted its rank, salty edges and sealed it shut. Placing the small box that contained cufflinks I had engraved with his initials on the top of it I stood back. A small gesture for him to find.

Leaving the house early on the morning of Amy's wedding, her mum's car waiting for me in the street outside, I laid out his dry-cleaned suit and put the two items on the top. Nerves fluttered inside me as I stared back at my offering, and then I pushed through the door carrying bags and hangers with me as I clattered down the stairs to help my best friend get married.

Five hours later I was standing outside a church in a small village in West Sussex where Amy's parents had retired, wearing a blush pink chiffon maxi dress and trying to herd errant pageboys and flower girls into some kind of order. The guests had all filtered inside and we had arrived in a car just ahead of Amy and her father. Amy's sister Natalie was bent down negotiating with Tom, who had refused to give up his Spiderman figurine in favour of a basket of rose petals. A full-scale row was ensuing and it was eventually deemed acceptable that Spiderman would be making an appearance too.

Amy drew up in the car outside and as she appeared through the lychgate with her dad I couldn't wipe the big grin from my face. She looked spectacular, the lace overlaying the satin making her dark skin look even smoother,

her eyes glittering as she looked at the church ahead. The cream veil lifted in a passing breeze as if she was a Disney princess. The photographer was snapping from every angle. Even Tom had stopped scowling.

Moving down the aisle, clutching tiny hands on either side and trying not to scan the pews for Luke too obviously, I felt grateful to be there. Amy and I had shared champagne as the make-up artist had done her hair and make-up and everything had seemed comfortable and relaxed. She had laughed over the blue lace garter I had given her, insisting on wearing it underneath her dress. Now Pachelbel's *Canon in D* was playing and I was walking down the aisle, staring straight ahead, leading the rabble of children like a well-dressed Pied Piper.

Will looked grey as he waited for his bride and I tried to give him a reassuring smile before slinking into the pew opposite him. He turned, caught sight of her and his face relaxed, colour flooding back into his cheeks.

Smoothly stepping forward to take the bouquet from Amy, the strong scent of roses and sweet peas wafting round me, I saw him. He was standing at the end of the third pew back looking straight at me, his navy blue eyes trained on me as I bit my lip and tried to drag my eyes away and focus on the Order of Service in my other hand. I could feel the beats of my heart hammering through my chest and hoped he liked the way my hair was done, the dress. For the rest of the service I was aware of him, tantalisingly close but so far away, trying to detect his voice among the hymns and promises, eyes swivelling to him in the silent moments. Always his eyes flicked over to me too and I found myself glowing inside, desperate to see him, to feel his arms around me, to know things were going to be all right.

As he reached to smooth his hair I saw a flash of silver and knew, with a grin, that he was wearing the cufflinks I had left out for him. Reminding myself I shouldn't get too excited, he might just be being friendly, I tried to keep my gaze neutral and not stare back at him too much. The service seemed to go on for ever and I was considering leaping over pews one and two to get to him. I needed to know. I needed to know now. Amy had chosen hymns with lots of verses and I started to pray the organist would play double tempo, get that beat going, get us out of there. I almost forgot to hand over the bouquet at the end and tripped down the aisle after Amy, clutching Will's brother's arm, craning my neck over my shoulder to see that Luke was watching me leave.

Loitering by the doors, holding out a basket of confetti for people to take, I could see him slowly moving towards me, in the shadows of the church interior. He was talking to some girl with an enormous peacock-style fascinator and had yet to notice me in the doorway. I practised my surprised-to-see-you-smile, which felt strained as the minutes ticked by and an older couple in front of him had paused to tell the vicar the sermon had been good. Yes, yes, it had been excellent, well done, I'm sure he knows, let's keep this queue moving, people, some of us have lives to live and boyfriends to see. This was the moment. He emerged blinking into the sunshine and as he passed me he reached his hand into the basket.

'Luke, hi,' I said softly.

'Lottie.' His voice was loud as he spilled rose petals around my feet. 'God, sorry.'

The queue was still moving and a bald man behind Luke was leaning his grubby paw into my basket. Luke seemed to be swept away in a tide of bodies and that had been our big reunion. My body wilted with the anticlimax.

I couldn't fix it as the moment I was outside I had to become assistant to the photographer, ushering family members, flower girls and pageboys into the right place for some pictures outside the church. Every so often I caught Luke in a huddle of guests and almost tripped over the pageboy I was shepherding. He looked incredibly handsome in his tailored suit, neatly shaven, his eyes flashing as he turned to smile and caught my eye. Did he seem pleased to see me? Was that a smile of excitement? A pity smile for something he was going to do later? Dump me at a wedding? The tension was unbearable and I truly thought there couldn't be another photo taken. When I finally looked up, the guests had all moved down the road to the reception and I was left carrying a single bay tree, being bundled into one of the usher's cars.

The reception was held in a marquee on the edge of a lake and guests were milling in the sunshine, eating canapés and laughing as waiters topped up their glasses with champagne. Amy looked excited and radiant, greeting people with double kisses and generous hugs, leaning into her new husband Will looking every inch the happy bride. I felt tears well in my eye as I looked across at her.

'Lottie!' One of the ushers called out to me, I'd forgotten his name, he had a luxuriant ginger beard. 'I need your bay tree,' he said, and I walked across to deposit it in the marquee.

'Lottie, I . . . ' Luke had appeared behind me just as Luxuriant Ginger Beard was instructing me to talk to the band about their meal requirements and to triple-check they were on track for their first set. I could have tugged on those ginger hairs and yelled, 'Nooooo, let me talk to this ravishing man in the tailored suit with the sexy smile' but instead I nodded, desperate to ensure I was the best bridesmaid I could be: I needed to do that at the very least for my Amy.

'Sorry, Luke, I promise we'll catch up in a bit,' I said, stepping away.

Luke nodded, waving me away with a hand. 'Of course, go and sort them out. You look' – I froze as he spoke – 'amazing.'

'Thanks,' I mumbled, aware Luxuriant Ginger Beard was watching our exchange. I felt a blush move from my chest to my face.

After the band were sorted, Amy asked me to join her in the ladies' loos. 'A catch-up,' I giggled, enjoying the feel of her tucking her arm in mine as we sloped off.

'No, I am desperate for a pee and this dress is so complicated you are going to have to sort me out.'

'Ah,' I said, giggling as we stumbled up the Portaloo steps, a strong smell of lavender and bleach assaulting our nostrils.

We didn't really fit in the cubicle and various female guests joined in at one point, deciding on pulling at various ribbons and buttons. Finally Amy was released and redressed and I was dabbing at my face trying to tone down the flush, combing at my fringe. My hair was up in a loose chignon and my eyes were made up in soft pastel shades.

Amy gave me a quick hug, meeting my eyes in the mirror. 'You look stunning, Lottie, and thank you, you're being completely brilliant.'

I gave her a grin, reaching up to squeeze her wrist. 'I'm so happy for you, Amy. You're going to have the best night.'

'Have you seen the drummer?' one of Amy's guests called from the closed cubicle.

Amy frowned. 'Not yet.'

The guest emerged, an athletic woman in a hot pink fascinator who I recognised from the hen do as being head of PE. 'Well, let's just say Will should be relieved you already made vows to him. Fiiiiit.'

As we exited the loo, Amy veered away, determined to go and see 'her drummer'. I watched her great-aunt moving in an unsteady line beside the lake. 'Might go and rescue your relative,' I said, darting off to steer the woman back to the safety of the crowds and the canapés.

'You're a lovely girl,' the aunt said, patting me on the arm. 'Have you seen the band? There's a man holding two sticks who is devilishly attractive.'

Finally a dinner bell was rung by an enthusiastic pageboy and guests started moving into the marquee, the guitarist in the band strumming a gentle melody as everyone took their seats. Moving around the edge I felt a hand on my arm and, turning, sucked in my breath to see Luke standing in front of me. He drew me to one side and I let myself follow him, hoping there wasn't another job I needed to do or another relative in need of rescue.

'Finally,' he laughed. He seemed a little on edge, one hand straightening the collar of his shirt.

'God, I'm sorry, being a bridesmaid is effort,' I said, feeling myself desperate to lean into him, to feel close to him. I hadn't touched him, not properly, for weeks.

'Thank you for your letter.' He launched into it immediately. 'And the cufflinks, they're great, I was thinking—'

I bit my lip, not wanting to risk spoiling anything.

'—well, I was hoping we could talk about me moving back in.'

'Oh my God, yes, yes, yes please, I have hated you not being there,' I burst out. 'I've missed you so much. And I'm so bloody sorry for being such a cow. I'm going to work on that, on the not being a bitch to you, I promise.' My voice was loud and a couple at a nearby table had peered round to see where the profanities were coming from but I didn't care. I hadn't realised how much I'd missed him until he'd left. The flat just didn't seem right without him. I didn't care about what people thought or said, I just wanted him to come home.

He was grinning, relaxed again, no more fidgeting. 'Thank God for that. I've been getting a really bad back on Adam's sofa. And he just doesn't make sweet love like you do.'

I made a face and Luke burst out laughing.

'Right,' he said, taking both of my hands, 'let's go and have the best night.' Pulling me towards him he bent down and kissed me. I felt my stomach plummet.

We broke away and I wasn't able to answer for a moment, the relief so enormous. He was back, he was coming home, he still loved me, I hadn't stuffed up the best thing that had ever happened to me. 'Definitely,' I said, reaching to kiss him again.

He grinned and pressed me back to arm's length. 'Also, have you seen the drummer?'

I nodded.

'Yeah,' Luke said. 'You're not allowed to hang out with the band any more.'

Laughing, he moved inside the marquee with me, one arm around my waist. Amy, preparing to enter the marquee with Will further down, looked across at me, grinning as she saw us together. I couldn't stop the massive smile splitting my face.

'Love you,' she mouthed.

'Me too,' I mouthed back. Feeling Luke's hand on my back as he guided me to our table I thought my heart would burst. I would not mess this up a second time.

Chapter 30

Love is the absolute frickin' best

GEORGE, 87

Luke moving back in was a wonderful blur. It felt like the first few weeks of living together, spending evenings laughing and talking, making dinner on alternate nights and remembering all the things we loved about each other. I had stopped sniping, stopped bringing home the stress from my day, was careful not to let any frustration out on him.

Keeping a diary had helped; telling my head of chambers I wouldn't be applying for silk until I felt ready had also been pain-free. Swapping stupid WhatsApp messages with Amy and spending time with Grandad again had also made me feel so much better.

I loved being in on the great app secret too. Arjun and

Geoffrey had been working with Luke and his agency on LOOP – an app for the over-70s to combat loneliness. It contained local information on all events targeted to the older crowd. It mentioned dance classes, art lessons, charity walks and more. Groups were encouraged to add their own events to the app and Facebook group and it had really looked to be taking off already with bingo evenings, golf days, coffee mornings happening in different parts of London. Luke was really excited about the growth.

He had left that morning to add some finishing touches to the scheme and I had run to the window in mock-distress, palms flat on the glass as he walked down the street laughing back up at me. Glowing like an idiot I collapsed on the sofa smiling, a languid Saturday stretching ahead: no work – the new rule.

Moments later the buzzer went and I pressed the intercom button. Familiar voices on the stairs made me open the flat door to see Margaret and Paula struggling up clutching two large bags, Howard waving from the window of his car before speeding away.

'Oh, hi.'

They were grinning. 'Surprise.'

'We're here,' Paula stated as if I'd been expecting them. She strode straight past me, commenting on the décor as she arrived inside.

'Mint green . . . and I like the stripped-back floorboards . . . the light is good . . . we should set up in here.'

Margaret followed her, allowing me to take the bags she

was carrying from her. I frowned as I shut the door.

Both women were now fussing about in the living room, clearing a chair, setting the bags down on a table.

'OK, OK, what is going on?'

Margaret turned around. 'Well,' she announced, a gleeful smile on her face, 'we're here to give you a wonderful makeover.'

'We're going to make you into a vintage siren!' Paula said.

I stared down at my cotton harem pants and T-shirt.

'Yes, we have a lot of work to do,' Paula said, her glossy lips in a disapproving line.

'Right, take a seat, take a seat,' Margaret said, patting the back of the chair.

'But . . . what's the occasion?'

'Oh, that's all to come,' Paula cackled. 'All to come. Now come here, I'll heat the rollers.'

'Let me at least make you a tea or a coffee,' I protested, feeling strangely nervous.

'We'll do that, we'll do that, you just sit down,' Margaret said, sounding positively bossy. 'The flat looks great, Lottie,' she tinkled and I blushed, remembering the state of the place the last time she had dropped by.

'Thanks,' I said, feeling a rush of affection for the two women and a flicker of excitement to see what they had brought along.

Margaret guided me over to a chair she'd placed in the middle of the room. Paula was bending over, trousers straining at the seams as she plugged something into the socket. She had started to hum, 'Stop! In The Name Of Love.'

Margaret was now removing various bottles, brushes and pots from one of the bags on the table, as Paula moved towards me holding a paddle hairbrush.

'Right,' she said, lifting a chunk of my hair and letting it fall, 'let's see what we can do with this.'

'I haven't washed it yet,' I said, my own hand raised to the nape of my neck.

'That will work well, actually. Better for what we have planned to style hair a day or so after washing.'

I felt the flutter of nerves at the same moment that Margaret asked, 'What can I get you, Lottie? We've got champagne.'

'Champagne?' I said, eyes widening.

'It's early, but there is nothing nicer. Or I can make you a Bucks Fizz.'

Paula started brushing my hair. 'Top us up, Mags.'

Moments later I was holding a chilled glass of champagne as Paula detangled and fussed over my hair. Margaret was spending an age selecting just the right products. She had already chopped up two slices of cucumber and placed them over my eyes. 'It reduces bags – not that you have any,' she added quickly, 'but it should really help brighten your face.'

Paula was playing sixties numbers through her iPhone and I could feel my shoulders relaxing, the tension in my back easing as the two women fussed around me.

The next moment my feet were being lifted and dropped into a warm, bubbled footbath.

'Ooh,' I squealed, dislodging one of the cucumbers.

'Relax,' said Margaret as she placed a fresh one back over the eye. 'I've got a lovely nail polish that will look perfect on your toenails.'

'I dread to think what my toenails look like,' I murmured, wiggling my toes in the water, feeling the jet streams massage and pummel my skin. This was officially awesome.

One foot towel-dried and propped up on a cushion and Margaret set to work removing old polish and layering on the new colour – the softest pale pink, like the inside of a shell. Paula was placing heated rollers in my hair and I was sipping at champagne, listening to Motown classics and their conversation, which had flitted from the flower arrangements at Dorothy's funeral ('arranged by someone completely colour-blind, and she would never have wanted lilies, she was allergic'), to the new Pilates instructor who had started at the club ('he doesn't have a trustworthy face, I miss Kelvin'), to their friend's niece who was expecting twins ('she's as large as a house and she's only 18 weeks, we're going to buy her one of those bands for her stomach') to some strange behaviour among some of the men.

'I saw Arjun and Geoffrey looking very shady in the Four Bells, meeting a young girl with red hair.' I was too busy enjoying Margaret's foot massage, barely listening, to explain much.

Once my nails were done, the cucumbers removed and my hair curled into rollers, Paula swivelled me towards the natural light of the window.

'Right,' she said, eyes slanting as she roved over my face. I was suddenly conscious of my tired eyes and washed-out skin, wishing I had got more than six hours' sleep again last night. 'Let's start with some concealer to correct your skin colour and then we can put a foundation on top of that.'

'Sounds good,' I said, clearing my throat nervously as she continued to stare at me.

Margaret was topping up my champagne glass.

Paula spent an age carefully applying layer after layer, blowing on a powder brush, sweeping bronzer along my cheekbones, curling my eyelashes, applying the finest brown eyeliner and lastly drawing on lip liner and a bright scarlet lipstick.

'Press this,' she said, offering me a tissue for my mouth.

'Can I look?' I asked, feeling my stomach leaping, wanting to know what my face looked like.

'After Margaret's pinned your hair.'

Margaret approached with a cardboard strip of kirby grips, the paddle brush and a determined gleam in her eye.

'You're gorgeous,' she exclaimed, removing the rollers with gentle cool hands.

She twisted and pulled on strands of hair, winding them into curls and securing them in place. Fussing, she removed one or two before beginning the process again. Paula was sitting opposite me, champagne glass in hand, telling me about Arnold from her aqua aerobics class who had appeared in the ladies' changing room, blaming his dementia.

'I'm nearly done, Paula, time to get the dress.'

Dress?

My eyes rounded once more as Paula reached behind and unzipped a clothing bag. 'Close your eyes and no peeking.'

I stood up, following her instructions, stepping into a pool of material before I felt the dress move over my body, arms inside, buttons being fastened at the back. For a moment I was enfolded in a familiar scent of mint and then it passed just as quickly.

'You can open your eyes,' Paula said, as I felt both women move away.

I found them standing in front of me, heads tilted as they stared at me: silent.

'What?' I said, feeling a little paranoid, one hand to my hair.

'Turn around and see.' Margaret had carried through the full-length mirror that usually stood in our bedroom.

I had turned and blinked and exclaimed, 'I can't ... ' A hand went up to my mouth.

'Don't smudge the lipstick,' Paula called out, immediately forcing my hand down.

I couldn't believe the transformation. I looked like I had stepped off the set of an old black and white film. I was wearing the dress that had belonged to Grandma, the dress I had admired in the bedroom when we had cleared out her things. The dusky rose pink warmed my skin, and I moved slowly, careful not to snag any of the tiny beads sewn into the bodice. The floor-length chiffon skirt made me feel like a fairy queen but a really good one in a classy production *of A Midsummer Night's Dream.* It was overkill and I felt the buzz of excitement as to where we were headed.

Margaret had pinned my hair into a low side bun and I twisted left and right to glimpse rolled curls expertly secured, my long fringe framing my face. Paula's make-up made my pale blue eyes pop, the red lipstick making my teeth sparkle impossibly white. I grinned at them both staring at my reflection from behind me.

'I love the winged eyeliner,' I exclaimed, stepping towards the mirror. 'And my hair, and this lipstick is gorgeous, this colour is amazing.'

My skin looked luminous and smooth, no more tired eyes and broken veins. The woman in the mirror looked to have had a decent ten hours' sleep and a facial.

'Here,' Paula said, thrusting a pair of cream leather heels at me. 'This is to complete the look, and once you're ready, Howard will be outside to take you on to your next surprise.'

I put on the heels and paused to look up at both women, eyes rounded. They looked twitchy with excitement, Margaret breaking into smiles. 'You look perfect,' she said, clapping her hands together. 'Oh, this is just magical.'

Paula rolled her eyes. 'It is all getting rather Disney round here. I do hope Howard hurries up.'

They were packing up as a horn blasted and I rushed to

the window to see Howard in his car in the street below, grinning up at the flat window and waving, something lying on the seat in the back.

'He's here!' Margaret clapped. 'We'll let ourselves out, you go on, Lottie.' She was herding me towards the front door. 'You really don't need anything but here's a shawl – it's cold outside – a bag with a comb, a couple of items if you need to touch up your face, the lipstick, obviously, and a packet of tissues.'

I allowed her to thrust the shawl and small clutch bag into my hands, feeling confused and elated all at the same time. What was going on? Where was I headed?

I turned to thank the two women, feeling my heart swell at the sight of them. My eyes swam; I knew Grandma would have desperately wanted to be here.

'Don't you dare start weeping,' Paula said crossly, marching forward and forcing me to blink in surprise. 'You'll ruin our good work.' And with a gruff hug she pulled me towards her and then released me. 'Now get along,' she said, her voice coming out a little hoarse. I noticed Margaret looking over at her in surprise.

'Thank you for everything,' I said, hearing the horn outside go for the second time.

'Go,' Paula waved me away with a hand. 'We won't be a moment tidying up here, and then we're off into town.'

Darling Cora,

Tonight something wonderful will happen. And the

first person I want to talk about it all with is you. That will never change. I am always thinking of you, my darling, and I know how much you would want to be here with us all.

I love you.

Teddy x

Chapter 31

Love is . . . everything

CLEMENTINE, 86

'Where are we going?'

Resting my head back against the leather of Howard's car I felt a warm glow as I thought back to Margaret and Paula appearing in my flat laden with equipment to transform me. I knew Grandma would have loved to be there. She always nagged me to spend more time and care on myself; she adored clothes and dressing up and had been impossibly elegant. The lump that so often formed in my throat when I thought of her was lessened slightly by the fact her friends were still looking out for me.

'Excited?' Howard looked across at me.

I nodded, aware suddenly of my leaping stomach and dampening hands.

'We're almost there,' he said.

'Where?'

He had switched off again, unable to stop the smile forming on his face as he turned the radio up and shifted the car into a higher gear.

We drew up outside a house I didn't recognise, ivy climbing the walls, no lights on inside.

'Where are we?'

He didn't answer me. The day was darkening already, the evenings so much earlier now, lilac and dark blue strips like ribbons in the sky, the sun lost below the line of houses, a few stars visible overhead.

'Wait there,' Howard instructed as I reached down for the clutch bag.

I pulled the shawl a little tighter around me as Howard moved round to open my door.

'Luke asked me to give you this.'

I looked up sharply. Was Luke not here? I had assumed, but perhaps ... The house seemed still and silent. Howard was holding a long thin box and I took it silently, my hand shaking a little as I pulled at the bow wrapped round it. All this thought and effort ... it felt surreal to be in the middle of a real-life movie.

Tears pricked my eyes, making the contents blur. I took out a simple silver chain, a pendant in palest pink hanging from it: it would look amazing with the dress.

'Oh, it's wonderful,' I said, immediately reaching round to attach it. The clasp was tiny and I seemed to be all fingers knowing Howard was waiting.

'He's a good lad, your one. I don't normally go in for all this romance, that's more Arjun and your grandfather, but even I wouldn't mind being wooed by that Luke Winters. Man's got class.'

I grinned at Howard, feeling the clasp connect. He proffered his arm. 'You do look wonderful this evening, Lottie.' Then he paused, his voice lower. 'Right then, are you ready?'

I swallowed once and took a step forward: I was.

We stepped up a winding path, lanterns flickering on either side, to a gateway which led to a garden behind the building.

There was a pergola arch, climbing plants and small white flowers entwined around the wooden trellis, the strong smell of lavender from overflowing pots on either side. The arch acted as the perfect frame, a table beyond laid for two people, wine glasses glinting in the soft light, candles flickering on the table and more lanterns scattered on the ground. Luke was standing next to the table, dressed in a shirt I didn't recognise, a woollen brown dogtooth three-piece suit, a pink handkerchief peeking out of the pocket of the waistcoat, his face breaking into a smile as he stepped forward.

'Lottie, you look incredible,' he said, unable to hold back from laughing as he stepped around me. 'Like a Forties movie star. Your hair is brilliant.'

I felt myself grow hot with the scrutiny. 'Thanks,' I mumbled, feeling suddenly shy as he bent to kiss me.

He pulled out a chair for me and it was only as I took a seat that I realised I could hear music playing, the scratchy quality that could only come from an LP, the notes wafting round us at the table.

'This is lovely,' I said, taking in the polished silver, tea-light and single rose in a thin vase in the centre of the table.

Suddenly Geoffrey appeared through the arch dressed in full black tie: crisp ironed shirt, neat bow tie, cufflinks sparkling, his two remaining strands of hair combed backwards.

A hand flew to my mouth as a giggle escaped. He had flung a fresh white tea towel over his arm and dipped into a sort of bow when he reached our table.

'Sir, madam, welcome.'

Luke had sat down and was laughing at my expression.

'Can I take your wine order please? Would you like a refreshing New Zealand Sauvignon Blanc or a Rioja from South America?'

'Oh,' I said, shifting in my chair, 'I would like the refreshing Sauvignon Blanc please.'

'An excellent choice, madam.'

'Two,' Luke said, holding up two fingers, 'and step on it.'

Geoffrey did bow that time and backed away from our table. I looked over at Luke incredulously.

He shrugged. 'It was an offer I couldn't refuse.'

Geoffrey returned to pour the drinks, I realised the music had stopped and then, after some distant whispers and shuffling, he was joined by Arjun and Grandad, also in black tie, bar the tea towels. Howard had changed too and appeared in the archway straightening his bow tie as they all formed a semi-circle around our table.

I frowned. 'What is goi—'

Luke gave them a nod and Geoffrey started to conduct.

Then, in a hesitant a cappella, they began to sing. A barbershop quartet of a familiar-sounding song which had my mouth opening in amazed surprise. It was a wobbly rendition and I found myself clutching my sides as I focused on each face, screwed up in concentration, carefully watching Geoffrey's hand movements. The whole garden seemed filled with the sound and I wiped at my eyes, feeling an enormous warmth for this rabble of men all dressed up and singing for us.

I looked across at Luke and realised he was equally moved. I often forgot that he didn't have his own extended family, a group I had taken for granted, parents on the end of the phone, grandparents who had always been around. I felt incredibly grateful to Grandad and his friends for adopting him into their tribe. It was clear from their delighted expressions as we clapped and cheered their last note that they had done it for him, clapping him on the back as they all made a discreet exit, leaving Geoffrey to quietly produce a starter of mouth-watering pâté and toasted ciabatta.

I didn't feel like eating, still wanting just to soak up the evening, the touches Luke had clearly planned and, as I stared around me, realising yet again how lucky I was to be with someone so thoughtful.

Luke reached a hand across the table and I took it, feeling a frisson as he stroked my thumb with his own.

Forcing myself to concentrate on the food in front of me,

the pâté replaced with mouth-watering duck breasts and potatoes, I tried to stay calm, to ignore the pounding in my chest and simply enjoy the evening. Then, as the main plates were cleared, Luke took my hand once more.

He began to speak. 'Lottie, you must be wondering why I . . .'

Grandad and friends appeared eagerly in the archway and I glanced across at them, distracted for a moment. Luke did a double-take, an uncharacteristic blush flooding his face. 'You're a bit early,' Luke whispered at them. Grandad's eyes widened and he could be seen ushering the others backwards with frantic hand gestures.

I frowned. What was going on?

I could hear Howard grumbling in the background, Arjun or Geoffrey sshing him furiously and then a squeak.

'You stood on my foot.'

'Ssh.'

'Does Luke mean soon or should we wait a while?'

The trouble with people hard of hearing is they tend to talk loudly, and I glanced at Luke who was grimacing in the flickering candlelight, clearly hoping I couldn't hear their mutterings.

'Er . . . all OK?'

'I think they're just confused about *dessert timing*,' Luke said, loudly enough that the voices dimmed.

'Dessert?'

'What dessert?'

'Does he mean now?'

Luke cringed again and I could feel bubbles of laughter in my stomach, wondering just what was happening. It was clear they were messing up some master plan.

Luke coughed, stuttering as he reached for my hand once more. 'Lottie,' he began again, 'you must be wondering why I've brought you here.'

I felt the evening close in around me, just the feel of Luke's hand, his gaze on me.

'Lottie, you know we have been together now for seven years—'

'Almost eight years,' I corrected. Our anniversary was one month away.

'Stop being a barrister,' he said, the soft tone he was using not changing, which made me smile.

'Sorry.'

'That's OK,' he said in his new, I'm-a-zen-like-masseur voice.

'You quickly became my best friend. You were funny and intelligent and properly hot.'

I snorted inelegantly but Luke's face didn't change.

'You have always been supportive. When I wanted to change jobs, when I persuaded you to move in with me.'

I felt my toes squirm at the compliments.

'You were there.' He slowed down a little now, took a breath. 'You were there when my mother died and helped me through that time. I don't know what I would have done without you then. You just knew what to do and how to handle me . . . '

I felt tears build in my throat as he spoke, the whispers

in the background fading as I strained to hear every word he was saying. He was giving me too much credit. Who wouldn't have behaved like that after someone you loved had lost their mother? Their last remaining parent. I squeezed his hand.

'Don't be silly, Luke, of course . . . '

'Hey,' he said softly, 'I still haven't finished.'

I pressed my lips together.

He swallowed and looked down. 'You've always been the only girl who has made me want to be better, who has challenged me, made me snort-laugh, made me want to throw stuff, and you know, as I said, you're hhhhhot.' He coughed, his smile quickly fading. 'I know recently things haven't been easy for you, and I hope I've been there for you. Like you were there for me when life wasn't as, as easy' – he took a breath – 'as it might have been.'

I swallowed.

'Because I want to be there for you. For ever.'

Oh God. This is totally happening. There was urgent sshing behind me. I felt my whole body grow still, my breath suspended somewhere inside me. This. Was. Happening.

'I wanted to ask you something now.' And then Luke stopped. The speech ended with me practically leaning across the table horizontally.

'Yes,' I prompted.

Was this it? Oh God, was this not it? Luke had started to look a little panicky now, eyes wide, swivelling them over to the arch. Was he planning a speedy exit? Had it all got too intense? Had he changed his mind?

I was aware of voices through the archway, a face peering through the foliage.

'You're leaning on me.'

'Why don't we get chairs?'

'I didn't think he'd take that long.'

'Do we go now?'

'Has he finished his speech?'

'Did he say he'd bring us on or do we just go?'

'We should have had a code word.'

Four old men shuffled through the archway, glancing at each other nervously before lining up in a row next to our table. A few beats later and they were singing a cappella once more, hands timing the beats, voices shaking, concentrated faces serious and trained on Luke. Then with a final hand gesture Grandad produced a small box from his pocket and laid it in Luke's outstretched palm, before turning to usher them all back.

'Go, Howard.'

'Did you give it to him?'

'My hip.'

'Quicker.'

'Don't step on me.'

Luke was pretending not to be able to hear the harried whispers as they left the way they had come. I pretended not to notice they had all paused on the other side of the trellis: four eager faces peering through the gaps in the wood and foliage.

'So what I wanted to ask you, Lottie,' Luke was speaking loudly, trying to drown them out.

'Did you see the ring?'

Murmurs of 'lovely', 'big', 'cost a packet' made me start to giggle now, and Luke rolled his eyes back in his head.

'They were meant to make things more romantic. I have regrets,' he called, loud enough for them to hear.

'Hey.'

'We heard that.'

'That was your fault, Howard, you can't do anything quietly.'

I was openly laughing, trying to block out the bickering as Luke lifted the diamond ring from the small cushion in the box. Then he got up, moving to the side of the table and got down on one knee.

'Lottie Campbell,' he said, holding out the ring, 'will you please marry me?'

I stopped laughing as abruptly as I'd begun, feeling the world pause for a delicious second.

'Yes, yes, of course,' I said, taking the ring in utter amazement and then launching myself at Luke, who was struggling to his feet.

Cheers had broken out and faces were now appearing in the archway and I saw Grandad wipe a tear from his eye.

Then Luke and I were kissing and I could feel my whole body become lighter as he held me. Then I felt hands patting our backs and voices all around us as Geoffrey, Arjun, Howard and Grandad crowded around.

'It's quite a few carats,' Howard was saying, clearly impressed as he took a closer look.

'So happy for you,' choked Geoffrey, his eyes watering as he smiled at us.

'It was Howard making all the noise,' Arjun added quickly.

Grandad was completely silent, standing a little back from the group. Luke and I broke away and both went over to him. He smiled as we approached, his eyes brimming with tears.

It made me swallow, seeing Grandad so emotional.

'I got chilli in my eye,' Grandad said, swiping at his face. He stepped forward, taking both my hands in his. 'Cora would have loved to see you both do this.'

I nodded, knowing he was absolutely right and not trusting myself to speak. He let go of my hands as Luke placed an arm around my shoulders.

'I hope you are both as happy as we were,' Grandad said. Stepping forward, he hugged us.

'And,' he said, drawing back again, his hands on my upper arms, 'I know Cora would want me to say this—'

I held my breath, waiting for the wisdom, the heart-stopping moment of truth.

'You must hope and pray, Lottie, that if you do go on to have children together, that they inherit Luke's incredible hands,' he said solemnly, and then, with a smile, moved in for another hug.

A Letter from Rosie

Dear Lovely Reader,

Thank you so much for reading my book, I really hope you enjoyed it.

I was a bit worried about writing a note at the end asking you to do stuff, but – SILLY YOU – it worked a treat last time and I ended up having lots of lovely online conversations with so many wonderful readers.

As a mother of tiny people in a small village, I don't have the buzzing social life you might imagine. My top three thrills include: that pistachio ice cream they sell in Waitrose, when my husband cooks for me, and reading a lovely review.

Now, you can't help me with the first two – sending me ice cream is not logistically going to work and if I can't make my husband cook every night I am not sure pressure from you will do it either – however, you can totally help me out with the third.

If you read (and enjoyed) *The Gin O'Clock Club*, it would

be brilliant if you would spend a couple of minutes writing a sentence or two online, telling the world. This helps other people find and enjoy my book.

If you want to get in touch with me directly, I am over on Facebook and Instagram. Extra fun for you if you are a fan of: twins, pictures of rivers and/or trees and stories about what my four-year-old dreams about. I like to hear nice things, particularly cute stories about your own grandparents.

In all seriousness, THANK YOU for choosing *The Gin O'Clock Club* – it is always amazing to think that someone has chosen your book out of the thousands out there. And if you don't write a review, or message everyone in your contact list to read it too, that is OK – you have already made me very happy.

Love,
Rosie
x x x x

/RosieBBooks
rosiebbooks

Acknowledgements

I have plenty of people to thank but there is always someone I forget. Apologies if that person is you. I did have twins, like a year ago, so let's blame that.

To the team at Sphere/Little, Brown, thank you for publishing another of my books. To my editor Maddie West for wanting to work with me again and for loving Teddy and Lottie's story more than I could have imagined. Your enthusiasm for my writing is such a boost and I can't wait to hear more from you from the world of academia. To Lucy Malagoni for being on it after inheriting me. I shall throw in a juicy crime or two in the next one. To Hannah Wood for producing such a wonderful cover and discovering the gorgeous illustrations by Anna Woodbine. It was such a joy to see the way in which you collaborated to come up with something really fresh and thoughtful. To Thalia Proctor for keeping a handle on the many edits and for being so pleasant to deal with. To my publicist Francesca Banks and Gemma Shelley my marketeer. I'm hoping there is some serious gin in our promotional plan. To Andy Hine for saying lovely things about my writing and working hard to boost me abroad!

To my excessively hard-working agent Clare Wallace. We've been so busy this year we have barely had time for one of our sixteen-hour catch-up sessions. Let's change that in 2020. To her wonderful maternity-cover agent Tanera Simons, who has such an exciting career ahead of her. Darley Anderson is a fantastic agency and I definitely need to acknowledge the tireless behind-the-scenes efforts of the rights team, led by the delightful Mary Darby. Thank you Emma Winter, departed to pastures new, to Kristina Egan and Georgia Fuller. To Sheila David for trying to turn these books into films. This is the one! I know it! To Rosanna Bellingham for sending me the best emails.

Over the course of this novel I reached out to numerous friends for inspiration. Special thanks must go to the JCBC for their help in coming up with love quotes and excellent, and varied, ways to hex people. To Sara Benwell for stealing her lilo story. To Kat Brown for coming up with the ideal venue to fall out with your best friend (John Lewis!) To Jo Ouest for putting me in touch with her fabulous, and fascinating, grandmother Jill Bayly. To my barrister friends for their advice: Richard Campbell, Roxie Cooper and Lynsey Burns. To Aunt Elisabeth and my late Uncle Julian for stealing the anecdote about the list of jobs. To Isabelle Broom for something I didn't note at the time. To Kirsty Greenwood for always being on the end of a WhatsApp. For my Book

Camp crew – a brilliant bunch of writers – for making me laugh and saying nice things about my writing.

Thank you so much to the reviewers and bloggers who spend their precious time reading and reviewing books for needy authors like myself. It never fails to blow me away how dedicated you all are to spreading word of a book you love. So many of you promoted my last book, *The Hygge Holiday*, and I am sure it helped make it such a success. Thank you so much. It is often your messages, retweets and lovely reviews that pep me up when I am writing the next one. And to the plentiful readers who take time out of their day to get on Amazon and Goodreads and share their thoughts. You all help people to discover my books and I am so grateful.

To my parents for their encouragement and excitement for everything I do. Dave for the barrister advice and Basia for being a stone-cold legend. You are both the best.

To my husband Ben. I know it isn't always easy being married to a distracted writer; the endless deadlines and the scattered approach to our domestic life would have sent a lesser man over the edge. You bear it amazingly well and I hope I can learn a little from Lottie and maybe spend at least part of 2020 giving you *some* attention. To Barnaby, Lexi and Ness – I love you guys so much. I removed loads of the swear words in the proofread.

The perfect recipe for hygge: make a hot chocolate, draw the curtains, snuggle under a blanket and read your way to happiness!

It's autumn in Yulethorpe and everyone is gloomy. It's cold, drizzly and the skies are permagrey. The last shop on the high street – an adorable little toy shop – has just shut its doors. Everything is going wrong for Yulethorpe this autumn. Until Clara Kristensen arrives.

Clara is on holiday but she can see the potential in the pretty town, so she rolls up her sleeves and sets to work. Things are looking up until Joe comes to Yulethorpe to find out exactly what is going on with his mother's shop. Joe is Very Busy and Important in the City and very sure that Clara is up to no good. Surely no one would work this hard just for the fun of it?

Can a man who answers emails at 3 a. m. learn to appreciate the slower, happier, *hygge* things in life – naps, candles, good friends and maybe even falling in love?

*

'Feel-good fiction at its absolute finest' *Heat*

'The most gorgeous read' *Sun*

'What a wonderful book! Rosie Blake's best novel yet – I had such a gorgeous time reading this story that I couldn't put it down. It was genuinely funny, warm-hearted, and full of unforgettable characters. A pure heartwarming pleasure of a read' Kirsty Greenwood

'Light the scented candles and hunker down on the sofa with a hot choc . . . this funny, warm hug of a book is the ideal companion' *Fabulous*